Praise for John David Krygelski

"...this book was one of the n
read. It touched me and made ...
to believe that this is anyone's first book. Thank you for writing it."

"...this book is our lives; we are living it as we read it. Krygelski reached into my most inner thoughts and put them in words. *The Harvest* will have you questioning the very foundations of your beliefs." Philip Melton - Professor of Fine Arts

"I have been reading nearly all of my 60 years. This is the most profound book I have ever read. I can't believe that this is the first novel of Mr. Krygelski. Please write more. It is profound and I plan on re-reading it again, as well as ordering more for my family."

"*The Harvest* had me completely enthralled from beginning to end. I never wanted to put the book down, being one of the most interesting reads I have ever had the pleasure to experience. I have difficulty expressing in words how much I truly loved this book."

"This dense and carefully plotted story involves a thoughtful look at religion. Reese Johnson, a professor at the University of Arizona, is teaching 'Religion Under Assault' when he suddenly finds himself investigating a man who calls himself 'the Creator.' For hopefuls everywhere looking for a second chance to create a better world, this is an intriguing novel." - J. C. Martin - *Arizona Daily Star*.

"...congratulations on *The Harvest*...I appreciate the way you clarify some of my deepest beliefs. I think your book challenges the reader to look inward and think. Brilliant. I'm telling everyone I know to get *The Harvest*."

"...haunting characters and alarming events are interwoven with such artistry and precision they pop off the page, raising the hair on the back of one's neck...." James Gjurgevich - Attorney

TIME CURSOR

JOHN DAVID KRYGELSKI

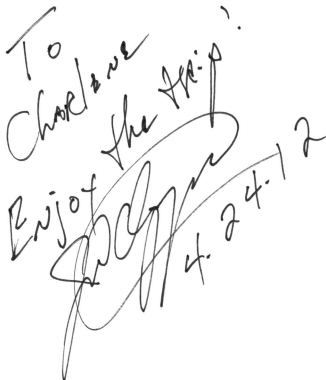

To Charlene
Enjoy the trip

4-24-12

STARSYS PUBLISHING COMPANY

Time Cursor

www.thetimecursor.com

Cover art - Michael Nolan.
Art Direction - Michael Nolan - *www.michaelnolanart.com*
Editor - Jean Nolan Krygelski

Published by Starsys Publishing Company
WWW.STARSYSPUBLISHING.COM
526 N Alvernon Way
Tucson, Arizona 85711

ISBN 10: 0982662297
ISBN 13: 9780982662298
Library of Congress Control Number: Pending

First Edition - November, 2010
Printed in the United States of America

Dedication

This book is dedicated to the one to whom I've dedicated my life – my loving wife, Jean. It is her guidance, support, dedication and love that makes everything I do possible and worthwhile.

Acknowledgments

I need to thank Michael Nolan. It was his vision, drive and intensity that created the final visual package you hold in your hands. And to Jean – the finest editor there could be – the only one I know who can polish a lump of granite until it shines like a diamond.

Prologue

John sat alone in Cal's office, simultaneously terrified and elated at the prospect of what he was about to do. Dwelling on the misery of his life, as it had played out for the past thirty years, was such a constant for him that the thought of having the opportunity to be proactive...to actually be given the gift of a second chance...made him feel an emotion he had long ago lost, the ability to conjure...to hope. And yet here he was, moments away from doing something that was truly far more than merely a second chance.

There was a soft tap, followed by the door swinging partially open. John saw Cal, with a sheepish expression on his face, peer in and say, "We're all set. Are you...ready?"

It was obvious to John that Cal was more than worried about what they were about to do; however, for John's sake, his best friend struggled to conceal his concern.

Standing from the chair, John stepped around Cal's desk. "As ready as I'll ever be, I guess."

Following Cal into the lab, he was once more filled with a sense of awe at the sight of the gleaming device which dominated the center of room. At rest on its specially designed platform stood the polished silver orb, its hatch swung into the open position, as if it were a living thing consciously waiting to receive its next passenger.

As they neared the open entrance to the machine, Cal turned to his friend, counseling him, "Now remember, make it quick and clean. In and out. And don't do anything else...anything that you don't absolutely need to do."

John nodded, listening to the admonition he had heard repeated like a mantra over the last several days as he had prepared for this trip. Trying hard to fight off the ever-present malaise that had become permanently embedded into his psyche, John tried to grin. Failing that, he simply stated, "I've got it, Cal. I really do."

Cal gestured toward the vacant platform adjacent to the sphere, and reminded him, "The backup is in place, just in case."

John nodded again.

"Now you know...."

"Cal," John began, interrupting his friend, "we've gone over it all a thousand times. Don't worry. Okay? Everything will be fine. I won't be there any longer than is absolutely necessary, and I won't talk to anyone else. I promise."

Cal looked deeply into the eyes of the man who had long been like a brother to him. This trip, he knew, was fraught with so many potential dangers that his mind could not even imagine them all.

Taking a deep breath, he let it out slowly. "Okay. Just don't tell him anything about...well, anything. Too much can happen if you do."

John tried a grin, which expressed itself feebly on his face, and promised, "I won't. Scout's honor."

Unable to think of anything to say that he hadn't said to John almost countless times before, Cal put his hand on John's shoulder and said, "Have a safe trip."

John turned to Cal and embraced him. "I know you're not crazy about doing this. I just wanted to say *thanks*."

Cal returned the hug. "Just be careful."

Stepping back, John turned and stepped into the hatch. Looking back at Cal, he said, "I'll see you in a few seconds."

– I –

I hate this kind of place, John Augur thought to himself, looking around the room at the frenetic drunks, all trying hard to have a good time. The voices were too loud. The laughter, too forced. And all of it was ricocheting off the hard floor, walls and ceiling, which were deliberately designed to amplify rather than dampen sound. If it were up to him, he would never find himself spending a Saturday night, or any other time for that matter, in an environment specifically designed to pander to the inebriated and the mentally challenged.

"Enjoyin' yourself?"

John swiveled on his bar stool to see that Kurt, his best friend of twelve years, had sidled up next to him, squeezing between him and the overdressed, gray-haired businessman who had been parked on the adjacent stool for the past two hours.

"Oh, yeah!" John answered sarcastically. His eyes took in Kurt's partially untucked shirt, tousled hair and mildly glassy eyes. "I'm surprised that you can still stand."

"Heh…heh…heh. I'm fine."

"Yeah, you look fine," John responded, reaching out and tapping the front of Kurt's shirt, "especially that guacamole. It's a nice accessory to your ensemble."

The act of looking down at his shirt caused Kurt to lose track of the orientation of his hand, and he dribbled vodka tonic onto his sleeve. "Damn.

That stuff is so hard to get off."

"Entropy," John declared.

The businessman left and Kurt slid onto the now vacant stool, sloshing the rest of his drink onto John's blue jeans in the process.

"Entropy, huh?" Kurt murmured with a slur. His face shifting into an expression of a student reciting something for his professor, he continued, "The natural decline and decay of all systems... people, planets, stars, solar systems, galaxies, even the universe. What does entropy have to do with guacamole on my shirt?"

John chuckled. Even in Kurt's current state, his mind functioned at a level that John had always found both fascinating and entertaining. John saw in Kurt's eyes the probable explanation for the durability of their friendship. Most people, upon hearing even the slightest hint of philosophy or science, would glaze over, immediately slamming a frozen smile of mild fascination on their faces as they pretended to listen while, in reality, were mentally composing their next text message to someone. Instead, he could see Kurt fighting off the nearly overwhelming effects of the probable 2.0 blood alcohol level as it coursed through his brain, and rallying to participate in what John was saying.

"Simple, pal. You're falling apart."

"I am not!" Kurt emphatically replied, the *t* at the end of his sentence causing a small bit of tortilla chip to fly from his mouth and bounce off John's cheek.

Ignoring the corn artillery, John explained, "Normally, the process stretches over eons. In a star, hydrogen slowly goes through the fusion process, producing helium. The helium gradually turns into the next heavier element, and on it goes until, eventually, after having created the so-called heavy elements, the star either burns out or blows up. The specific process is different for each type of structure, but the point is that eventually everything dies.

"We usually don't get to live long enough to observe it happening in most things, except for, you know, bugs and animals. But, with you my friend, I get to see the entire procedure play out all in one evening."

Not sure if he had been complimented or insulted, Kurt lifted his empty glass in a mock toast and said, "You're welcome."

Laughing, John slid off his stool, put his hand on his friend's shoulder and told him, "I'm going outside for a while."

"Okay, dude. You're comin' back, right? I mean, this is your party."

"Yeah, I'll be back. Just need to get out of this racket for a while."

"Cool."

Taking a sip from his empty glass, Kurt finally noticed there wasn't anything in it and turned to get the bartender's attention as John walked away.

Stepping through the same doors once used by John Dillinger during his brief visit to Tucson, John walked out into the clear, cool evening. As with Dillinger's exit from the Hotel Congress, an ambush awaited John, although a far different type of ambuscade than the local police poised to take a fugitive into custody.

The Amtrak station across the street was open to accommodate the three-times-a-week departing passengers for the westbound *Sunset Limited*. Augur walked the mandatory twenty feet away from the entrance, lit a cigarette, and leaned against the steel railing built to satisfy liquor codes and keep the Club Congress drinkers corralled within the sidewalk lounge.

Taking a long, deep draw on his cigarette, John stared, unfocused, into the night, wondering about his life. "God, I hate change," he muttered.

"You really should quit smoking."

The voice came from behind John. Tensing immediately, expecting this to be another confrontation with a stranger on the subject, he turned to respond.

"You know, I'm standing more than...." The words stopped as his eyes focused on the stranger. At first, he wasn't sure why. It was just an average guy, probably in his fifties, standing about ten feet away. John noticed that the man's face was spread with a smile, instead of the sour, confrontational glare of the self-appointed smoking police he usually encountered. Then he realized that this must be an acquaintance. Although he couldn't quite place him, John recognized the features.

The stranger stood just over six feet tall with brown, thinning hair. He was a little above ideal weight, but not too bad. However, what really captured John's attention were the man's eyes. He couldn't shake the feeling that he'd looked into them many times before.

"Do I... excuse me, do I know you?"

"Better than you realize," answered the man as he slowly walked toward John, the smile remaining on his face.

"I'm sorry. Your face is really familiar... still, I just can't... I guess I've had a couple too many tonight."

His grin broadening, the stranger replied, "Nice try. Only problem is, you don't drink."

The man edged closer, and John was able to get a better look at his face.

As the details coalesced, an inexplicable chill shivered through his spine.

"Okay. I give up. Who the hell are you?"

Reaching out his right hand, the stranger introduced himself, "I'm Jack."

Hesitantly returning the handshake, John responded, "John."

"I know, believe me."

"What does that mean?" John's voice rose slightly, irritation showing in his inflection.

"You don't recognize me, do you?"

"No. Already told you that. Should I?"

Sighing softly, Jack replied, "I guess not. It just would have made this a little easier."

"Made what a little easier? Come on, this is my bachelor party, and I'm in no mood for some 'gamer' out here on the sidewalk."

"Well," Jack reached up and lightly scratched his chin. "That's why I'm here. Tonight, I mean."

"Why?"

"The bachelor party. I knew about this night. I knew this had to be the night."

"Look," barked John, making no attempt at this point to conceal his frustration with the stranger, "last chance. What do you want?"

The man stared at John for nearly a minute before answering. Then, appearing to have made a difficult decision, he took a deep breath and blurted out, "You need to cancel the wedding."

John, stunned, took a moment to reply. "What?"

Gaining a little confidence, Jack reiterated, "No wedding. No marriage. Not to Gail. Not tomorrow. Not ever."

There was no outburst. John just stared at the stranger silently. Neither spoke as the tension gradually built. Finally, John took a deep draw on his cigarette, flipped the butt into the gutter and said, "Have a good night, man." With that, he turned to walk away.

"Wait. Don't go!"

John continued to walk, nearing the double doors which would take him back into the lobby.

"PLEASE!" the stranger shouted, a note of desperation creeping into his voice.

Unmoved, John took another two steps when the man yelled, "I'M YOU! YOU CAN'T DO THIS... TO EITHER OF US."

Augur froze. As the stranger's words penetrated his consciousness, his mind recalled the feeling he first had when he looked into the man's eyes... how familiar they were.

Seeing that John had stopped, Jack approached him from behind and, in a softer voice, said, "What do you want me to do? Tell you secret stuff that only you... and I... know? You want me to talk about Mom and Dad?"

John remained immobile, standing three steps from the doors, his back to the stranger.

"Tell you what. Why don't I tell you about Kurt's guacamole stain and entropy? I wasn't in there, you know that. And even if I was, it was way too noisy for me to hear that."

Still without turning, John spoke slowly, "There's one thing. There's one thing I know that I've never told anyone. What was...?"

Nearly bursting to get it out, Jack answered, "Jimmy. It was Jimmy. You forged some paperwork where you both worked so that he'd be fired. You wanted him fired because we... I mean you two... were always scheduled to cover each other's shifts and couldn't ever hang out together. You... I... wanted to go on that road trip to Sedona and we wanted him to go. We messed with the tally sheet after he left one day, and the manager ...."

"All right, stop."

John turned around and stared into the man's eyes.

"No shit. It really is me in there?"

A crooked half-smile formed on Jack's face. "Yep. You're in here, all right."

His eyes never leaving Jack's, John took a deep breath and let it out slowly. "Man, I did not age well."

~ II ~

The *Sunset Limited* idled at the station. This was a crew-change stop on its route between New Orleans and Los Angeles. Instead of the elevated concrete structures found in most of the other stations on the route, Tucson only had a cheap, asphalt, grade-level "platform." The off-loading engineer and his men mingled with the incoming group while the service crew refilled the fuel and potable water tanks, and the local food service vendor restocked the dining and club cars.

Sitting together on a bench near the old Southern Pacific steam Mogul which was on display, Jack and John watched as the attendants for each of the coach and sleeper cars dragged overstuffed, black plastic trash bags onto the platform for the local Amtrak employees to collect. It was almost exactly midnight and some of the train passengers, for whom Tucson was the final stop, sleepily emerged from each of the cars, jostled by the passengers who were going on to Los Angeles and had waited less than patiently for a designated smoke stop.

Both men sat silently, mesmerized by the archaic, unhurried procedures. After a time, John broke the silence. "God, I love those things!"

Chuckling, Jack answered, "I know. That's why Kurt set up the party at Club Congress. He knew you'd want to come across the street to see the *Limited* when it got here."

"I guess he thought it was a sure way to keep me at the party at least until midnight."

Pulling his eyes away from the gleaming transport, John turned to glance at Jack and stated, "This is going to take a little getting used to."

Jack just nodded, and they both settled back to watch the timeworn routines.

Finally, John said, "Aren't you wondering why I haven't asked you anything?"

"No. You will when you're decided."

"Decided?"

Twisting around on the bench to face John, Jack explained, "You may be me, but not for another thirty years. I've had all that time to think about how I...we...are. We've never been the type to immediately start talking. We like to sit back and listen, let everyone else put their cards on the table. After we listen, after we think about it and figure out who's on which side and what their best arguments are, then we begin to speak. We don't *like* to look or sound foolish or stupid."

"You're right, although I hadn't really figured out the reasons."

"As I said, I've had the time, you haven't. Anyway, you'll ask me questions once you've thought through all of the possible angles, explanations and ramifications. Not till then. Let me know when you get there. I'll wait. But, remember one thing, this is one time you don't have to do that. You really don't need to worry about what *I* think of you."

John's response was a muted laughter. "That's true."

"Okay, go for it. Take the huge breath through your mouth, loudly exhale it through your nose, and ask away. By the way, about five years from now that particular conversational mannerism is going to result in you accidentally blowing a snot rocket right on the microphone while you're in court giving testimony."

John burst out laughing. "What was I...I mean, what will I be in court for?"

"It's nothing. We weren't the plaintiff or the defendant. Besides, I think we've got a lot more to talk about tonight than that story. Don't you?"

"Yeah, you're right."

Drawing a deep breath and blowing it loudly out of his nose, John said, "All right. What's the deal? Why are you here? How did you get here? How are you getting back?"

Jack pulled his right leg up onto the bench, turning completely sideways to face John. "I've already mentioned the first one."

"Gail?"

"Yes. Gail. That wedding has to definitely not happen."

"Why?"

"First of all, and don't bullshit me, do you really love her?"

That was a question John didn't expect. Pausing first, he answered, "Yeah. I mean, I think so."

"Come on. No, you don't. How many times have you thought about breaking up with her?"

"Well, three."

"I said, don't bullshit me. I didn't ask you how many times you've *tried* to break up, I said how many times have you *thought* about it?"

Looking down at his knees and chuckling, John answered, "Oh, I don't know. Maybe a thousand."

"There you go. Why are you going to marry her, then?"

"I'm committed. I mean, come on, the wedding's tomorrow. We're out, like, five hundred bucks for the dress. Another fifteen hundred for the reception. All the guests…they're already here. They've bought the presents …."

"Knock it off. None of that has anything to do with whether you *should* marry her. All it does have to do with is that you shouldn't have let it get this far."

"But I've told her. I committed."

"Don't care," Jack stated, matter-of-factly.

"Well, why not just do it? You know, six months…a year…then pull the plug on the thing."

"Cause you won't. From the minute you're in it, you will feel hooked, obligated, honor-bound. Then, stuff's gonna happen that will make you feel even more obligated. That six-month date gets pushed back in your mind over and over again, until almost thirty years have gone by."

This perspective had an unsettling effect on John. Sinking deeply into thought, he fell silent for several minutes. Jack occupied himself by watching the last of the boarding passengers file onto the train, as the crew climbed up into the engine cab.

Breaking the silence, John said, "But now I know – it can be different."

"*That* I don't know. Right now we're still dealing with my past, and I can tell you with certainty what happened. Just the fact that I'm here, and we're talking about this, has changed things… or will change things. It's like I have the 'cheat' for one scenario of a role-playing game. I've got that right, right? I mean, it's been a while."

Smiling, John replied, "Yep. Role-playing games are here now. Cheats are for sale on the Internet."

"Good. Anyway, I'm only bringing you the cheat for one path. I know how it plays out all the way into the future. But, change the path, even slightly, and everything could and probably will be different."

"This is weird."

"Tell me about it. How do you think I feel?"

Shaking his head, John said, "Okay, let's get off the whole wedding subject for a minute. How in the hell did you get here?"

"Well, you know what they say – it's not what you know, it's who. About eight years from now you meet a guy…Callen, a real 'quint'…."

"Quint?"

"Oh, sorry. That word hasn't been coined yet. Quint is what we call a…just a second…a geek. It comes from *quantum intelligence*."

"Quantum intelligence?"

"Whoa! We can't go there. Really. One of the rules. Just bear with me, all right? You meet Cal and just click. Instant friend. You know, like never happens with us. He is a major, big-time, over-the-top genius and he's into physics, but he's also an electrical engineer. It's a great combo because he dreams things up theoretically and then he builds them.

"You and he become tighter than tight. Hang out all the time. Go on trips together. Everything."

"Like the brother I never had?"

"Right. In fact, he's the main reason you're able to survive being married to Gail for as long as you do. He's your diversion. He's your go-to guy when you need to talk. In a lot of ways, I guess you could say he's your soul mate. He definitely is the one who keeps you going when you just want to pull the plug."

"What do you mean, pull the plug? Suicide?"

"Oh, yeah. You'll think about it more than once. Even give it a shot."

"I try to kill myself? No way."

"Yeah, way! That's how bad it sucks. Did suck. Uh…will suck. Anyway, Cal's the one who finds you. Takes you to the care cent…hospital, gets your stomach pumped, saves you. That's how I got *here*."

"What do you mean?"

"I told him he shouldn't have saved me. I told him I'd do it again." A misty, faraway look took over Jack's face. This part of the story was obviously more painful than his words revealed. "That's when he asked me if he could help me change things if I'd promise not to keep trying. I had no idea what he meant. At first I thought he was offering to help me kill Gail, which, at the moment, sounded pretty damn good."

"What happened?"

"After I felt better and the hospital took me off suicide watch, he took me to his lab. By that point in his life he had about a zillion patents on devices he'd invented, and had a huge research and development facility. We used to talk about... well, I thought... about everything that he was working on. But he had one little secret."

"A time machine?"

"A time machine. He told me that he could send me back. Back to a place and moment in time of my choosing. That I would have a shot at changing things. And then he'd bring me back, you know, to my regular time."

Jack could see his younger self analyzing the story slowly, carefully turning it over in his mind, examining every detail.

"What about the *Butterfly Effect*? Unintended consequences and all that. Just you being here could make some tiny little difference that could amplify as time goes forward. You could go back just after this chat and your whole world could be different."

"That was my original question, but Cal explained that my trip wouldn't be the first trip taken on his contraption. There have been several. They started out incredibly brief, very unobtrusive. Nothing changed."

"How could he know that? If something did change, *that* would be the new reality, the new history. He wouldn't have any way of knowing there had been a change."

"You're right. The people who stayed in their own time wouldn't know. If someone went back in time and killed Joseph Stalin before he came into power, then, probably at the moment the assassin was sent back, everyone on Earth would suddenly share a new history without the monster that killed millions. However, and here's the big difference, the assassin, the guy who went back and did it, when he returned to his regular time – would know. *His* history would include Stalin living and everything that had happened as a result of his rise to power. The traveler is apparently immune to the change."

John shook his head in amazement. "Wow. That is weird."

"So, how it works is, after each careful trip, after each slightly escalated interference with the past, the traveler returns to his or her time. If something has gotten too fouled up...if the unintended consequences are an issue, then an additional trip is immediately made. That new trip is back in time all right, but it's only for a few minutes, just to the point where the traveler arrives shortly before the previous trip that fouled things up. The bad trip, no pun intended, is stopped, the traveler is popped forward again to his normal time, and everything is cool. It's foolproof."

"Not really."

"What do you mean?"

"What if the traveler were to kill Stalin, or do whatever he was going to do, and that change resulted in the machine never being built in the future? There would be no way to bring the traveler back. There would be no way to undo the mistake. There would be no way that Cal, or anyone else in the future, would ever realize what had happened."

Jack smiled. "You're right. That's why all of the trips have been performed by Cal and only Cal. If he were to go back into the relatively recent past that had adequate technology, and if something were to change and he didn't get back to his time, he could build another machine. If he had to go back farther, he could send a spare machine there first. If something went wrong...he could climb in the machine, jump back just far enough to undo whatever he did and, presto, the world would be back on track." Grinning, Jack added, "At least that's the theory. Nothing like that has happened on any of the previous trips."

"That makes sense. So, he came back with you?"

"No."

"What? You're kidding, right?"

"No, I'm not. I can't fully explain why, but supposedly only one traveler can be out at a time, so to speak. The machine attaches some kind of a data thread to the traveler. Cal said the thread was similar to Hawking radiation, which is able to escape from black holes. Anyway, on this trip the data thread remains tethered to me through time and back to the machine. If there is more than one traveler, I guess the threads gets tangled."

"Okay, then. He sent back a machine for you to use."

Grinning, Jack answered, "Yes. The spare is stashed here in this time."

"And you know how to use it?"

"Uh-huh. Got a crash course before I left. It's all pre-set anyway. Basically, all I have to do is get in and hit a button, and *BING!* I'm back to one day before I arrived here this time – in enough time to leave myself a message which would prevent me from doing whatever I did to cause the problem."

John didn't respond, turning his gaze to the train. Two car attendants physically lifted an overweight passenger from the low, asphalt platform and struggled to put her onto the train. After having manhandled her up, the attendants followed her in and pulled the door closed. The conductor shouted, "All aboard," and looked in both directions along the platform for any stragglers. Seeing no one dashing to catch the train before it left, he waived an "all-clear" to the engineer, confirming the status with his radio. A mournful blast issued from the engine's air horns, followed by the loud hiss of compressed air as the engineer released the brakes. The train began to slowly roll out of the station, and the conductor swung into the last open door on the train with the blasé technique born of a thousand repetitions.

Both John and Jack watched as the multiple tons of metal gracefully pulled out of their view.

After the distraction, John continued with their discussion. "That's good, I guess it would work. I'm a little fuzzy on one thing. I always thought if we could time travel, we could never run into ourselves. I thought that was a bad thing, or impossible, or something."

"It was one of the so-called time paradoxes, but it turned out not to be the case. At first, because of that, Cal avoided going anywhere he might be. Later, when he had to undo something, there was no choice but to try it. He popped back a few minutes, met himself, told himself not to do whatever it was he came for, and left. Worked like a charm. They didn't both self-destruct or anything like that. And, obviously, here *we* are. So far, so good, huh?"

"DUDE, THERE YOU ARE!"

Both turned to see Kurt stagger from around the corner of the wrought-iron fence that surrounded the old steam engine behind them.

"It's not cool splitting from your own party, dude. Hey…who's th…?" Extending his head far forward on his neck with his jaw dropping to half-mast, and exerting every ounce of available effort, Kurt focused his eyes on Jack. "This…is…strange. You're like John but you're not, you know. I mean, you're like lots older and…," looking up at Jack's receding hairline, "other stuff."

John jumped to his feet and put his arm around Kurt's shoulders. "Kurt, this is my uncle. Uncle Jack."

Jack rose from the bench and extended his hand. John glanced over and noticed an intense mixture of what appeared to be joy and sadness on Jack's face.

"Good to meet you, Kurt."

John also noticed that his older self sounded different than before. There was a definite tremor in his tone now.

"Yeah. Good to meet you, too. Didja come into town for the party? I mean, guess you're an out-a-towner or I'd know ya."

Chuckling, Jack replied, "I did. Came from a long ways away."

"No shit. Where from?"

"Phoenix."

Kurt paused for a second, then realized his chain was being pulled. "Got it. Wow! Phoenix. What's it like there?" He finished the sentence with a mixture of a chortle and a gagging sound.

"Hot. Really hot!" Jack answered, not taking his eyes from Kurt.

Using the arm that was already situated on Kurt's shoulder, John gently steered him around until he was facing back the way he came. "Thanks for looking for me. I'm fine and I will be back, I promise. I just have a lot of catching up to do with my uncle."

"No prob'em, dude," Kurt slurred. "How long zit been since you seen him?"

"Oh...a really long time. I don't even remember when it was."

"Wow. Okay. Well, I'll head back now." With that, Kurt extended his right leg as if to take a step, but his body remained stationary. Thrown off balance, he fell against John, nearly taking them both down.

"Whoa, buddy," John cautioned. "I think maybe we get you to that room we rented for you."

"You think?"

"Yeah, I think." Glancing over his shoulder at Jack, he said, "I'll be right back."

"No. I'll go with you."

"You sure?"

"Absolutely. Come on, let's go."

Jack circled around and took Kurt's free arm. The two sober men walked toward the front of the station while Kurt semi-walked and semi-dangled between them, like a wooden puppet with no hands holding the strings.

Counting on Kurt's stupor creating the equivalent of his absence, John asked, "So what *is* it like?"

"What is what like?" Jack replied.

Not wanting to gamble too much on his friend's inability to listen or remember, John remained vague. "You know...where you're from."

Jack paused for a moment before answering. "Part of the deal of being allowed to come here was that I don't talk about those things. According to Cal, even the most apparently mundane facts are like a mine field as far as the possibility of changing things."

"I can understand that. I guess I don't mean specifics, like who the next Microsoft will be."

They rounded the end of the station, coming out between it and the rail museum. John noticed that Kurt's eyes were closed and his chin now rested on his upper chest.

"What's it like, you know, generally? Is it better?"

Laughing, Jack responded, "That depends on who you ask."

"What do you mean?"

"Well...most things are the same...haven't changed a bit. Some things *are* new. There are people who love the new, and there are some who hate it all and wish it was still like...," Jack glanced over at Kurt meaningfully, "you know, like here."

John nodded. "I know what you mean. It's like cell phones. Most people can't imagine living without them, but I hate them. They make me feel as if I'm tied to a leash. And I can't stand the way public places like restaurants are now because of them. Especially those Bluetooth earpiece sets. Just a few years ago, if you were standing on a sidewalk and a lone person walked past you waving his arms and shouting, you knew he was crazy. Now you're not sure if he's nuts or having a conference call with his financial advisors."

Jack chuckled. "You'll be glad to know that the whole cell phone thing works itself out fairly well."

"They're banned?"

"No. Let's just say the novelty wears off and they're relegated to a more...societally acceptable...function."

They slowly eased Kurt down the curb and started to cross Toole Avenue toward the Congress Hotel. It was well after midnight and traffic was nearly nonexistent.

"You still haven't told me. Are things better? At least in your opinion."

"I'm not sure. There are times...."

Jack was interrupted by the rumble of an eighteen-wheeler rounding the curve. The three of them had progressed to mid-street and stopped between the trolley tracks. The food service truck had ample room to navigate around them and, with a loud hiss of air brakes, slowed down to proceed past them on its route to the produce warehouses a couple of blocks to the north.

Waiting for the roar of the diesel to diminish so they could resume their conversation, they stood and watched the truck as the tractor pulled even with their position. At that moment, most likely prompted by the clamor, Kurt choose to tune in on his immediate reality. Opening his eyes, he was startled by the closeness of the rig, the brightness of its running lights, and the intensity of the rumble.

Lashing out, arms flailing, his first instinct was to get away from the lumbering behemoth in front of him. Caught unaware, John struggled to maintain his grip on his friend. As Jack stepped back to maintain his balance, the heel of his foot dropped into the groove of the trolley track behind him. Instead of supporting Kurt, he now clutched the besotted and flustered comrade to prevent his own spill. Predictably, Kurt did not cooperate and, feeling the tug on his arm, jerked away.

As Jack fell, he heard a sound previously masked by the racket of the semi, the whine of a motorcycle heading southbound on Toole and careering straight for him.

Suddenly, the entire street was bathed in a harsh light, but Jack had no time to focus on the anomaly as the motorcycle rider, waiting until the last possible moment, tried to avoid Jack by veering to the right. For a moment it seemed he would make it when his front tire, bearing the brunt of the rubber's demand for traction, hit a patch of sand that had been spread on the street earlier in the day to absorb oil from an afternoon fender-bender.

Losing its grip on the pavement, the bike instantaneously flipped out from beneath the rider, causing both to viciously slam into the sides of two cars parked along the street in front of the old hotel.

John watched helplessly as the motorcyclist bounced off the hood of the second car and flew a distance of some twenty feet, violently crashing atop the wrought-iron patio railing next to the sidewalk. Jack was already to his feet, and both he and John, again holding Kurt upright, rushed to the rider. Delivering Kurt safely to the curb, they hurried forward, John pulling his cell phone from his pocket and dialing 9-1-1.

"He's not moving," Jack said anxiously.

As John gave the details to the dispatcher, Jack touched his finger to the neck of the still figure, searching for the carotid.

"Tell them I'm not feeling a pulse."

John relayed the information and agreed to stay on the line until the police or paramedics arrived. Twisting the phone around so the mouthpiece was behind his head, he told Jack, "I'm not sure you should be here."

Jack turned toward him, a mixture of concern, anxiety and fear twisting his features. "You're right. They are going to want to see some ID, and a driver's license from thirty years in the future will not go over well."

They could both already hear the first siren cutting through the night. Looking toward the hotel entrance, Jack observed the bachelor-party-goers rushing outside to check out the accident.

"I'll go in. I'll just be in the lobby."

"No. Somebody might tell the cops you were out here. I don't think you should stay visible."

Pulling out his room key, he handed it to Jack. "Go up to my room. I'll see you there."

Jack agreed and started to leave when he paused to take one more look at the stranger still draped awkwardly on the top of the five-foot-high metal railing. Shaking his head, he took a step forward, then suddenly stopped.

"Jack, come on. Get going. They'll be here any minute."

"Just a second." The limp figure was hanging on the top of the fence, the dead man's mid-section at eye level. John watched as Jack, his curiosity piqued by something he had noticed, gently lifted the waistband of the rider's jacket, revealing the rest of a handmade belt with a name tooled into the leather. Jack suddenly gasped. John saw Jack's hand abruptly grip the wrought iron to steady himself. Concerned, he walked closer.

"What is it?"

"Oh, no! Oh, my God, no."

John repeated, "Jack, what's the matter?"

Not answering, Jack straightened and reached into the inert figure's back pants pocket, pulling out the wallet.

"Jack! Don't do that. The cops are only seconds away."

Ignoring his younger self, Jack flipped open the wallet and looked at the driver's license. As soon as his eyes lit upon the name, his fingers slackened, and the wallet dropped to the sidewalk. John hurriedly retrieved it and stuffed it back in the pocket. Then he saw Jack wobbling, and reached out with his free hand to steady him, his other hand still gripping the cell phone.

"What's the matter? Talk to me."

The siren was noticeably louder and they both heard a second wail joining the first. Jack appeared to be in shock, so John gently pushed him toward the doors, as the people from the bar crowded closer to the dead man on the railing.

Abruptly ending the call on his phone, John put both hands on Jack's back and pushed him through the crowd of gawkers. When they reached the doors and passed through into the lobby, John turned Jack around to face him. "Tell me. What's wrong?"

Jack, his eyes slowly rising up to meet John's, said, "I killed him. I can't believe it."

"It wasn't your fault. You tripped. He was speeding."

Looking down again, Jack violently shook his head. "You don't understand. I killed him. I killed *him*."

"*Him*? You know him. Who? Who is it?"

The shriek and sudden decline of the siren outside indicated that either the police or the paramedics had arrived. John knew he had to get Jack out of sight, but curiosity and a contagious sense of dread overwhelmed his reason.

In a soft voice, almost below John's hearing threshold, Jack muttered, "It's Callen Mitchell. Cal! I killed the one person who was going to build the machine that sent me here."

– III –

After asking one of his friends from the aborted bachelor party to take Kurt up to his room, John turned his attention to the police officers who had arrived to investigate the accident. Throughout the forty-five minutes that he was tied up with questions, his thoughts were filled with nothing except his and Jack's dilemma. Fortunately, the lateness of the night and the fact that he was the star of the bachelor party provided John with an excuse for the quality of his interactions with the investigating officer, interactions which could best be described as distracted.

The policeman who questioned him finally turned him loose. John struggled to maintain a normal pace as he entered the doors of the hotel. Unable to resist the urge after he reached the top of the stairs, he dashed down the hallway to his room. Since he had given Jack the only key, he knocked, and the door opened almost immediately.

Jack was a mess. His hair disheveled and clothes in disarray, he reminded John of a person who had suddenly awakened from a long sleep without having undressed for the night. Saying nothing, Jack turned away and walked to the bed. He dropped heavily onto the edge, and as he fell back, his hands gripped the sides of his head. He eloquently expressed his mood with a loud groan.

John crossed the room and sat in the lone, straight-back chair at the antique desk near the window. The drapes were open, and it was obvious, from the perspective offered, that Jack had watched the entire gruesome ordeal below, including the paramedics removing Callen Mitchell's body from the top stakes of the wrought-iron railing, zipping him into the black body bag and sliding him into the back of the ambulance atop a gurney.

"I've been thinking," John said softly. "You can go back. Just to when we crossed the street. You can stop us."

Still lying with his hands gripping the sides of his head, Jack muttered, "No, I can't do that."

"Why not? I thought that's what you said."

Letting out a long sigh, Jack responded, "It is, just not exactly that way."

"I don't understand."

Releasing the grip on his skull, Jack slowly sat up and rubbed his face. "I can go back. I just can't go back to that moment or there would be two of us."

"There already are two of us."

"No. I mean two of *me* – fifty-year-old Jack – me."

John just stared at him, clearly visualizing the process in his mind. "I guess there would be. Isn't that okay? I thought you said it wasn't a problem."

"It isn't in the sense we were talking about. There isn't any time prohibition against it or anything like that; there's just one small issue."

"What?"

"Where do *I* go after I tell the thirty-minute younger *me* not to cross the street?"

Realization began to spread across John's face. "Oh! Well, after you talk to us, can't you just go back to your own time?"

"Yeah, I suppose I could. The machine is set up to do that now. I'd have to recalibrate it for the short hop, which I do know how to do, and then recalibrate it again to go back to my own time." Jack paused and stared intently at John. "But what about the other me, the one that I left behind. He'd be here without the backup machine, which would be dangerous as hell. And, because Cal would be alive again, when the other me was ready to go, he could show up at the originally predetermined pickup spot at the right time and Cal would bring him...me...back."

The complexity of the situation finally sank in fully for John. "Then there'd be two of you there. In your future."

Slack-jawed, Jack stared back at John and slowly nodded.

Brightening, John suggested, "What about going back and telling yourself not to cross the street and then returning to a time just a few minutes after you left for *that* trip? Then, you would be coming back right after the other you left to go do what you had just done. God, this is hard to explain! I feel like I need a critical-path chart to diagram it. Anyway, then there wouldn't be two of you at the same time."

Shaking his head again, Jack explained, "I thought of that. If I went back and stopped my earlier self from crossing the street, then Cal wouldn't die, and I wouldn't even make that trip later in the night."

"But when you tell him...you...not to cross the street, you could also explain all that and tell him to make sure that he makes the trip anyway, even if it's no longer necessary."

"John, think about it. I'm not sure that would work. Jack number one and Jack number two would be going back to the moment when you and Jack number, uh, zero were about to cross the street – from two different future paths. I'm not certain that both 'traveling Jacks' wouldn't show up at that second."

"Then there would be three of you. Good grief, it could be like a feedback loop."

"Yeah. We keep trying to fix things and, instead, we keep making things worse until there are a hundred of me all crowded on the sidewalk in front of the train station. And the other thing is the thread I told you about. I'm not sure that the machine could keep track of both of us if there were two traveling Jacks at the same time."

"I thought that was okay?"

"It is okay if only one is the traveler. One traveler, one thread. If I screw up and accidentally create a situation where there are two traveling Jacks at the same moment, who knows what would happen?"

Staring out the window as the scene on the street slowly returned to normal, John said, "Didn't Cal think of this when he prepped you for this trip?"

"I don't know if he did or not. We talked about the trip for about a hundred hours, but I don't think he believed for a moment that I would do anything resulting in the machine never being built, much less the possibility of his death. So we didn't get into a lot of details in that direction. We just never imagined such a simple, quick little trip could ever get so convoluted."

Both fell into silence. The only sounds penetrating the somber atmosphere of the room were the occasional passing car and the ticking of an old-fashioned clock on the nightstand.

After several minutes, John excitedly broke the silence. "I've got it! You go back...just not to the time we were together. Go back farther, to a time before you had arrived for this trip. Do something to stop Cal before he comes down this street."

John expected any reaction other than the one he received. Locking eyes with Jack, John recognized for the first time since coming up to the room that Jack didn't only look grief-stricken at the death of his friend-to-be. There was something else — a frustration, even a touch of despair — lurking just behind the bleary and bloodshot eyes.

In a barely audible whisper, Jack revealed, "I already tried that."

"You what?"

"When I came up to the room, my mind was spinning. I thought through everything we just talked about, and the only thing I could think of was just *that*...go back and see Cal...talk to him...stop him before he came downtown tonight.

"The machine is not far from here, about a block. So I slipped out and used the machine to take me back twenty-four hours...Friday night."

"When did you arrive here tonight, on this trip?" John asked, trying to keep the picture clear in his mind.

"Just a few minutes before you came outside to take a break from the bachelor party."

"Okay."

Jack continued, "I knew that I had to be in and out before my arrival time for this trip, but I also figured I'd need enough time to find Cal and do something to change what happened tonight."

"Right. I think." John's brow furrowed as he struggled to visualize the timetable.

Seeing this, Jack said, "Let me take it sequentially. I left the hotel while you were talking to the police, and went to the machine. Got into the machine and traveled back twenty-four hours. I pre-set the machine to bring me back to tonight — to arrive at a time just after I left for tonight's trip — with a departure time which was just a couple of minutes before I was going to suddenly pop into existence on the first trip, 'Trip A.' The pre-set time was my absolute deadline. Whatever happened with Cal, I had to be on the machine and gone by then."

"God, this is confusing!"

"I know. So, after I programmed in the departure time, I left the machine and went to find Cal."

John, realizing his memories still contained the images and details of the accident, said, "Obviously, it didn't work."

Jack shook his head and said, "I tried. God, did I try."

"What happened?"

"Like I said, I had to find him. I didn't have any idea where he would be, where he lived, anything. The machine is capable not only of sending you through time, it can send you to any location you specify. But since I didn't know where he would be, I just tripped back to the alley near the hotel."

Jack paused, weariness forcing him to take a moment to marshal his thoughts. In a monotone, he continued, "I came to the hotel, checked in and used the lobby Internet to find him. Or tried to, anyway."

Curious, John interrupted, "What name did you use when you checked in?"

Jack smiled, "In homage to our sci-fi hero, Wells. Jack Wells."

A slight smile was the best John could muster. He motioned for Jack to continue.

"See, Cal's not the famous guy now that he becomes…or was supposed to become…later. Nothing came up on him. Nothing! I remembered that he went to the U of A. He told me stories about the dorm and about his roommate. It was the middle of last night, and there wasn't really anything I could do until morning, so I left a wake up call for six and went to sleep.

"This morning," Jack looked down at his watch and remembered that it was still on his 2040 time. Swinging his gaze to the room clock, he corrected, "Or rather yesterday morning, whatever, I got up, left you a note and caught a bus over to the campus."

"A note? You had this room?"

"Yeah. I had no idea how the trip would turn out and I wanted to make sure that, whatever happened, you wouldn't go through with the wedding. That was, after all, the original reason for coming here."

Jack slowly lifted his hand and pointed up. John saw, taped to the ceiling above the bed, a hotel stationery envelope with his name written in large print across the face.

"I wanted to leave it someplace where you'd see it but the cleaning staff wouldn't. I figured if I screwed up somehow and changed things so that you didn't meet me last night and had no memory of all this, you could, at least, read the message."

John got up and climbed on the bed. Stretching, he couldn't quite reach the envelope, so he started to bounce on the mattress, using it like a trampoline. With the box springs complaining noisily, by the fourth rebound his fingers grasped the edge of the paper, ripping the tape loose from the old plaster.

He climbed down from the mattress and returned to the chair by the desk, tearing open the envelope. Inside were approximately a dozen pages, filled with familiar handwriting.

"No reason to read it now. I'm here."

Folding the pages, John stuck them back in the envelope, and set it down on the desk. "This is so unnerving."

"Yeah, it is."

"No. I mean, you are the one who makes the trips. You get to keep everything that's happened in your head. I just realized that at any time, like when I was coming up to the room, I could have suddenly slipped back to the way it was – just walking to the room after the party ended, with absolutely no memory of you or anything."

"Reality is a little more tenuous than you thought, isn't it?"

"You're not kidding! You left me the note, sure. But since it didn't work, we... I mean you... are going to have to try something else. Depending on what that *something else* is, not only could I not see you again, it's possible or even probable that the last few hours would be undone and I never meet you. If that happened, this note, in all likelihood, would never have been written."

Jack agreed.

"And there's no way I can send myself anything... leave myself a note that I would be sure to get... nothing. I feel like a scrap of paper floating down a creek. Helpless."

"And we hate feeling helpless."

"Yeah, we do." Fighting back the rising sense of frustration, John asked, "So what happened? What went wrong?"

"It turned out to be a disaster. I caught a bus to the campus. It was still early, about seven, so I started hitting the dorms. Man, I was striking out. Nobody knew him. He hadn't really made a mark yet.

"I wasted hours looking. It was the middle of the afternoon and I didn't have a clue. I went to the Student Union building to grab a bite and heard some of the students talking about their Facebook accounts. I had completely forgotten about the whole social-networking thing."

"No Facebook thirty years from now?"

"No. Anyway, there were Internet terminals there that I could use, and I found him."

"How did you log in?"

"Went to Yahoo! Created an email account."

Chuckling, despite the reality of their situation, John asked, "What's your email address?"

"*TimeTraveler070@yahoo.com*," Jack answered, with a wry grin on his face.

"Why *070*?"

"*TimeTraveler* was taken, so I just combined our ages."

Grinning, John nodded as Jack continued. "So I found him on Facebook. Sent him an email telling him that I was a friend of a friend and needed to talk to him. They have everything at that place. I used the money Cal and I put together before the trip, you know, money that isn't dated five or thirty years from now, and I bought a disposable phone so I could put a phone number in the email.

"Some of the posts on his account also mentioned which dorm he lived in, so I headed there next. I didn't want to just sit around waiting for a phone call all day."

"Did you find him?"

"Not right away. Not for a while, actually. His roommate was there, and he told me he didn't know where Cal was. I tried to get Cal's cell phone number, but he wouldn't give it to me. I did talk the roommate into calling him, though. Cal didn't answer, so he left a voice message. He sent him a text message too, with my phone number.

"I guess Cal hasn't changed much… or, I mean… hadn't. He didn't answer the roommate's call. He didn't respond to the text message. He's always been that way. I could leave him a message saying I was in a ditch somewhere dying, and he wouldn't get back to me for two days."

"So what did you do?"

"I didn't know what else to do, so I just waited at the dorm the rest of the afternoon and into the night. God, I was going nuts. I was sure he wouldn't come back to his room before he headed downtown for his after-midnight ride. I even pestered the roommate to call him and text him two more times.

"It was getting near the time I arrived on the first trip, so I was cutting it close."

"Yeah."

"He showed up. I had worked myself into a frenzy and was pacing on the sidewalk in front of the dorm when I saw Cal walking toward me. At that point, I had about ten or fifteen minutes before I had to leave!

"I was wound up pretty tight to begin with and I knew that I didn't have the time to calmly sit Cal down and slowly explain things to him. So, instead of telling him the story I'd cooked up, I just blurted out that he couldn't get on his bike tonight, that he couldn't go downtown."

"What did he say?"

"What would you say? Some stranger in his fifties lying in wait for you in front of your dormitory late at night, the same guy who had been emailing you, having you called, having text messages sent to you, just suddenly telling you not to go downtown tonight? He flipped out. I always knew Cal had a temper, but at this age he was a hothead.

"He told me to screw myself and brushed past me to go inside. I grabbed him. I just wanted to explain, to try and make him understand that I wasn't just some crazy person. That's when he really lost it, jerked my hand off his arm and pushed me down.

"By the time I got up, he was inside the front doors. By then I only had a few minutes left so, instead of following him, I ran over to where he parked his bike. I planned on just disabling it so he couldn't ride it, at least soon enough to be able to come around that corner when we were crossing the street. Right as I got to the bike, Cal came back. He must have been watching me from the windows. He saw what I was doing.

"He came running straight at me, screaming that I better get away from his motorcycle. I tried to talk, to explain again, but he just punched me. I took a swing at him and clipped him pretty good on the jaw. That was it. He really blew up – pounded me with a couple of real smashers in the gut, climbed on the bike, took off burning rubber, and popped up on the back wheel.

"As I watched him speed away, I realized that he had been going back to his room for the night when I stopped him. If I hadn't gone back…if I hadn't even been there…if I hadn't made 'Trip B,' he wouldn't have been on his bike, driving downtown and speeding; he would have stayed in his dorm room. He was out riding because he was furious at me."

John stared at his alter ego in disbelief. "Are you telling me…? I don't understand. If you hadn't gone to see him, he wouldn't have gotten back on his bike and been killed. But you wouldn't have gone back if he hadn't died."

"I think so." The pain of his reality contorted Jack's face.

"I don't understand why you went to see him, anyway. When you explained all of this to me earlier tonight, you said that the plan, if something went wrong, was that you would go back to the day before you arrived and leave yourself a note so that when you arrived here on Trip A, you would just read the note, get back in the machine and leave."

Obviously disgusted with himself, Jack explained, "That was the plan. That was what Cal and I discussed. However, I had been successful in meeting with you and talking to you about the marriage, and I didn't want to undo that. So I thought I would just head Cal off before he got on his bike and that would be just as good."

Jack dropped his head down into his cupped hands and muttered, "God, was I wrong!"

"What's bothering me," John said, "is if you *had* to go back to play out your part of the sequence so that Cal would get angry and storm away on his bike, that must mean it's all preordained."

His face still buried in his hands, Jack didn't answer.

"Then there's nothing we can do, is there?"

"I don't know. It definitely seems that way. One thing is for sure. We're in way over our heads."

– IV –

After a fitful night's sleep, John Augur checked out of his room while Jack silently stood beside him. They walked to John's car without conversation. It was less than a two-minute drive to breakfast at Del Taco, and both continued their self-imposed silence until the egg and sausage burritos were eaten.

They topped off their large Diet Cokes and moved out to sit on the patio. Although this day in May promised to reach a high of ninety-five, the morning was still pleasantly cool.

Gazing at the traffic on Broadway, Jack sipped from his drink and said, "This *is* your wedding day. What are you going to do?"

A half-grin bending the lines of his face, John answered, "I'd actually forgotten about it this morning. Haven't given it a single thought."

"You're not going to do it, right?"

"After what you've been through, I'd feel like a total jerk if I did. But you never really explained why I shouldn't. I'd like to hear it."

"Fair enough."

Jack's mouth twisted in a grimace as he gathered together his recollections of what had been his life for the past thirty years. "Gail was...is...a classic narcissistic personality with a borderline personality disorder. Real whack job. At this point in her life she was able to keep it under control. Not too long after the beginning of the marriage, it started to show and just kept escalating.

"At first she seemed, you know, spoiled. That wasn't too bad. Within a year or two, spoiled became self-centered to an extreme. Everything, and I mean everything, had to be about her. It became so oppressive that I tried to leave her during our second year together."

Jack paused, his eyes adopting a distant and misty look.

"She tried to kill herself. At least, that's what I thought at the time. I eventually suspected that it was orchestrated just to get me back. It wasn't until many years later that she told a therapist it had been staged. But...it worked. I did come back. I stayed with her.

"Not only did I come back, we had two children together. At least I thought, or assumed, they were mine. I didn't learn they weren't until after she killed them both."

"WHAT?" John, stunned, stared at Jack, hoping he had misheard.

"Killed them. Both. Burned to death in a fire."

Jack, expecting a question or comment, paused – but John was too shocked to say anything – so he continued, "She even tried to make me feel like I was responsible for their deaths."

John recovered enough to ask, "How?"

"The arson investigator said the fire started in our spare bedroom, where I kept my train layout. He said it looked like one of the train transformers overheated and started the fire. I thought, hell, I was sure I had turned them all off. I had everything on a power strip and...anyway, after he told me that, I wasn't sure. For years, I thought *I* had been the cause of their deaths. You can imagine what that did to me."

John just nodded.

"I carried the guilt for that until just a few days ago...well, a few days ago, thirty years from now. That's when I found out she had done it."

"How did you find out?"

"Her psychiatrist told me."

"I thought...."

"Right. Me, too. They aren't supposed to break the patient confidentiality rule. I guess the exception is when they find out something that leads them to believe a major crime is about to be committed. Then they have an obligation to stop it.

"When she, the psychiatrist, figured out during one of their sessions that Gail was planning to kill again, she went to the police. Then she called me."

"Who was she going to murder?"

Matter-of-factly, Jack replied, "Me."

Staggered, again, by the story Jack was telling him, John said, "But why?"

"Well, the deal with narcissists, especially those with borderline personality disorder, is that the whole world, in their minds, is structured for their purposes and their desires. As long as I was someone she wanted as a husband, there was nothing she wouldn't do to keep me. Once she decided that I didn't fit in to the vision she had for her life anymore, I became as disposable as a used tissue."

"What changed? Why didn't you *fit in* anymore?"

"Another guy. There had been plenty of them, all through the marriage. Didn't find that out either, until I had the long talk with her shrink. It was because of some other man that she had killed the children."

"Why?"

"They were his, not mine. At that point in the marriage she was maintaining this dual life. She had her marriage to me, with all that came with it. And she had life number two with the other guy – Kevin. She needed both. She believed she was so special, so unique, that she deserved both lives. He wanted kids, so she had kids.

"Apparently, at some point, Kevin became unhappy with the arrangement. He didn't want to be the secret lover anymore. He didn't want his children growing up thinking I was their father. He started begging her to leave me and marry him. He was married also, and told Gail that he was going to leave his wife.

"The problem was…that was not her plan. It wasn't the way she had structured things, and she became furious that someone *else* would dare to try to dictate the terms of *her* life.

"The way the psychiatrist explained it, Gail's decision to kill Beth and John, Jr. was made by her as calmly as normal people would decide that it was time to trade in their cars. I guess that goes with the syndrome. In the minds of narcissists, everyone else is inferior and only exists at their whim. And once Gail had figured out how to do it in a way that would put the guilt, emotionally rather than legally, on me, she viewed the decision as a win/win choice. With both of the *wins* going to her, that is."

"This is unbelievable! Didn't this Kevin do something after his children died?"

"Like what? What could he do? The fire investigators ruled it an accident. She had minor injuries from burns and smoke inhalation. And his children were dead. I guess he talked to her when she was in the hospital, and she told him it was over between them. She played it that, with the grief from losing her children and the guilt I was suffering from, she didn't feel right about continuing to see him.

"Apparently, he fell into a bad depression, started drinking and never stopped. His wife left him shortly after that. His liver failed about twelve years ago, eighteen years from now."

Jack paused, the faraway look returning to his eyes. "He was just another casualty...incidental damage from Gail's romp through this life. He spent the majority of his life in love with and obsessed by her, and I'm sure that she never gave him another thought."

John was overwhelmed by this glimpse into his own future. All the pain and suffering. All the guilt and misery. If it had merely been a fortune-teller sharing with him this view of the years to come, he was certain that he would tell her to jump off a cliff as he stormed out of her parlor. But the peek that he was afforded at the pages ahead was being provided by, if not the author, at least a character from the latter chapters in the book of his life. Try as he might, John could not invoke the ofttimes helpful and soothing mechanism of denial.

Finally he spoke, his voice low and melancholy, "I'm sorry. This is so.... I'm just sorry."

"Yeah," Jack responded. "Me, too."

"I've been meaning to ask...how did you get her to go to a psychiatrist?"

"I didn't. It was her idea. Again, supposedly, that's fairly normal for people like Gail. They're certain that they are superior to everyone else, that we are all just bit players on the stage of their lives. Since, out of necessity, they are forced to do almost all of their stage direction secretly, manipulatively – they want their recognition. They want to be able to brag to someone about what they've done."

Another few minutes of silence passed between them until Jack added, "And that isn't all of it."

"What do you mean, that isn't all? Isn't it enough?"

"Oh, it's more than enough, believe me. Despite that, you still haven't heard, as what's-his-name used to say, the rest of the story."

John lit a cigarette, needing the nicotine to calm him, leaned back in the molded plastic chair and said, "Go ahead."

Jack's gaze was riveted on John's as if trying to communicate the next part without having to say it out loud. Several seconds ticked by before he spoke, his voice flat and so soft that John was barely able to hear him. "She killed our parents."

John gasped, finally shocked speechless.

In the same flat tone, Jack continued. "Not too long after we got married, Gail started to notice some friction developing between them and her. Even the slightest negative directed at her was intolerable. So she took off from work one day, went to their house and confronted them. According to the therapist, she expected them to deny it. She thought they would tell her that nothing was wrong and it was all in her head. They surprised her. I'm not clear about whether it was Mom or Dad who broke the ice, but I guess they told her that they both felt the marriage was a mistake and they didn't think she was good for their son."

John just listened, having no trouble visualizing his parents doing just that.

"They must have expected her to blow up at them. I'm sure they were surprised when she broke down into those fake tears. With plenty of drama, she told them how much she loved me and that all she wanted was to be the ideal wife and the perfect daughter-in-law.

"When that bitch of a psychiatrist told me all this later, she said that Gail bragged about how she manipulated them with her crying and thanked them both for being so honest, telling them how she knew it must have been hard for them to admit this to her. How she loved them both as much as she loved me. How she would spend every day of the rest of her life trying to earn their love. And the whole time, she was already planning her next move."

Finding his voice, John asked, "What did she do?"

"We had a key to their place. She went in the middle of the night and tampered with the furnace while they slept. The next day they were both found dead. In their bed. Carbon monoxide poisoning."

Tears pooled in Jack's eyes as he recalled the moment. "I was the one who found them. That horrible, rotten witch sent me there to check on them, knowing the whole time what I'd find. She told me that she had been trying to call them all morning and they didn't answer their phone. I told her that it was probably nothing, that they had likely gone shopping together or something. But she just *knew* something must be wrong and told me she wouldn't be able to relax until she knew they were okay."

"Good God."

Reliving the dreadful day, Jack continued, "When I first got there, I thought they were both just still asleep, but almost right away I knew there was something wrong. They were gray, not, you know, regular color. At the same time I started to feel dizzy…light-headed. I was already not thinking very clearly and thought there had been a gas leak, even though I couldn't smell anything, so I ran outside and called the fire department.

"As soon as I went out front and made the call, I guess I had enough oxygen back in my brain, and I knew I had to make sure...try *something*, in case they were still alive.

"I took a deep breath, held it, and ran back in. I left the door open and slammed up the living room windows, turned on the exhaust fans in the kitchen and hall bath. I ran back out and caught my breath and ran back in. Went straight to the bedroom and...I was going to carry them out one at a time, but I suddenly realized that I had to decide which one to take first. I guess I was fuzzier than I thought. It was stupid. I was just frozen. I'm sure it took only a few seconds, but it seemed like forever. Finally, I checked Mom for a pulse, and there wasn't one. Then I checked Dad. He didn't have one, either.

"I couldn't hold my breath anymore, so I just grabbed Mom and threw her over my shoulder and took her out front. I went back in for Dad. By then the paramedics had arrived and went to work on both of them, but it was too late. They told me there wasn't anything I could have done. They'd both been gone for hours."

Jack looked like he was on the verge of breaking down.

"I guess I've always known," John said.

"Known what?"

"That there is something wrong with her. Just a little off, you know."

"A lot more than a little."

"Obviously."

"So...," Jack asked, his voice gaining a bit of timbre. "What are you going to do?"

"Not marrying her doesn't seem enough."

"Well, I don't think we can get away with murder."

"It sounds like that would save a lot of people a lot of grief."

Jack stared into John's eyes, trying to read his intent. "You're not serious?"

"No, I'm not. But I'm not saying it doesn't feel like the right thing to do."

"I'll agree with you there."

Jack looked at his watch and again realized that it was still set to a time he would probably not ever see. Pulling on the stem, he asked, "What time is it?"

John answered, "9:42."

Jack twisted the stem, finally resetting the watch to what was now his real time. "Less than six hours to the wedding," he said meaningfully.

With a loud sign, John replied. "I know, believe me."

A look of determination set the lines of his face as he resolved, "Let's get it done."

He pulled out his phone and punched in her number. Jack settled back to listen to one side of the conversation.

"Hello. It's me."

. . . .

"Yeah. Good morning."

. . . .

"No... actually, that's what I wanted to talk to you about."

. . . .

"Not now. Not on the phone. I better see you. I don't want to...."

. . . .

"Yes. You could say something's wrong...."

. . . .

"Not on the phone, I said. I need to see you."

. . . .

"Now would be perfect."

. . . .

"I don't care. I want to see you now."

. . . .

"NO! I don't want to at least tell you what it's about. I just want to talk to you face to face."

. . . .

John sighed and rolled his eyes as he listened to her. "You *don't* have to wait. I can be there in less than fifteen minutes."

. . . .

He listened again, eventually saying, "Okay. I'll be right there." Before she could say anything else, he flipped the phone shut.

"That looked like fun."

Shaking his head, John said, "She started crying."

"Of course she did."

"She kept asking if I wanted to cancel the wedding, if I still loved her."

"Yep."

Taking a final sip from his drink, John tossed the cup into the trash can, and started to stand. "Let's go."

"I don't think I should go. That would be a little tough to explain."

John stopped and looked down at Jack. "I think we need to stick together. I really do. Just come with me. You can wait in the car or down the street from her place or whatever, but I don't think I can just leave you here."

"All right." Jack rose, and they walked to the car.

☒

John left Jack in the car, about half a block from Gail's apartment. As he approached her door, the details and images of Jack's prophecy had become more and more vivid, his anger intensifying with each picture of the slide show in his mind. Before he could raise his fist to knock, the door flew open and Gail burst out, throwing her arms around him.

"Oh, baby," she whimpered. "I've been a nervous wreck since the second you called."

John, rather than returning the hug, reached up to grasp her arms.

Squeezing him tighter, she asked, "What is it? What's wrong?"

"Let's go inside."

Reluctant to let him go, she just eased back on her embrace, turning him so they could go through the door together. As he walked beside her, he examined her with fresh eyes. Having the perspective of Jack's narrative caused John to see the indications he had either not seen or had chosen to ignore in the past. There was a hollowness and insincerity in her eyes, and he recognized a calculating and manipulative intent behind them. The flushed cheeks, the quavering voice and the tearful eyes were clearly manufactured for his benefit.

Closing the door, she turned to face John. "Before you tell me – whatever it is – please kiss me."

John turned his face away from her advance.

"Gail, we need to talk."

"We can. We will. But please kiss me first," she begged him pathetically.

At that moment, he could no more have kissed her than he could have ripped off his own arm.

"No. I want to talk to you now!"

The firmness in his voice gave her pause. For a second John saw a flicker of change on her face as she realized the current tactic was ineffectual and it was time to move on to the next.

"All right, baby," she murmured in a subdued voice, taking a step back and smoothing down her clothes. John felt her eyes on his face as her hands paused meaningfully in their passage over her chest. Not seeing the desired reaction from him, she suddenly turned, walked to the sofa and sat down at the end. Instead of sitting beside her, John went to the chair.

With a newfound calmness, she said, "Will you please tell me what this is all about?"

He decided to just blurt it out. "I want to cancel the wedding."

Her hand jumped to cover her mouth as a gasp came out.

"NO! You can't mean that. Please say you don't!"

Making his voice as firm as he could muster, he stated, "I do, Gail."

"But why?" Her voice rose and trembled.

"I finally admitted to myself this morning that I don't love you. I can't marry you." Knowing he couldn't share the secrets bestowed upon him, John added, "I'm sorry."

She broke down, dissembling into a quivering, blubbering mess. Every other time in their relationship that Gail had gotten sad or upset, he had immediately comforted her, holding her, soothing her, reassuring her until the emotions subsided. His inability to stand by and watch her cry had been a true constant in their interactions. Yet, despite the tears cascading down her cheeks…despite her racking sobs…despite the look of abject despair in her eyes…John was unmoved. It was, no doubt, the complete absence of an emotional response to her display that triggered Gail to come out of her seat and across the short distance to John in a flash. Her hands now twisted themselves into claws driving straight for his face, her expensively maintained fingernails plunging for his eyes, and an atavistic shriek springing from her mouth.

Not at all off-guard, John reacted quickly enough to grab her wrists. Although she was not a petite woman, he had no trouble as he swung her around to the side of the chair, deflecting her and landing her on the floor. She instantly began to thrash, arms and legs flailing, as she tried to break loose. He did not relax his grip.

Twisted around so that he was halfway out of the chair, John held her to the carpet as she writhed.

"YOU BASTARD!" she screamed, slamming her heels repeatedly against the floor.

John said nothing. As she looked up at his blank, emotionless face, her fury grew in intensity.

"HOW CAN YOU DO THIS?"

John still did not respond.

"LET GO OF ME – YOU SON OF A BITCH!"

Not trusting himself to speak, John shook his head.

Glaring up at him with eyes full of fury, her chest heaving with ragged breaths, she suddenly stopped screaming. For a full minute neither said a word. John observed her with a new objectivity as, one by one, Gail switched off each of the inflamed emotions. The muscles in her contorted face relaxed. The tears ceased. Her breathing gradually calmed. He felt the tension in her wrists dissipate.

Finally, after regaining total control or, perhaps more accurately, after shifting gears to implement a new strategy, she said in a calm, almost friendly voice, "You can let go now."

Unsure, he hesitated. "Are you sure?"

"Yes, I'm sure. I'm fine." Chuckling, she added, "Come on, do you blame me? You have to admit that was quite a shock. I mean, this is...was...my wedding day, you know."

Still holding her, he asked, "You're going to be calm?"

Smiling up at him, she answered, "Yes, I promise. Hey – this is starting to hurt my wrists."

"I don't know...."

"Look," she reassured him, "if you don't love me, you don't love me. I can handle that. I care for you, sure, but I don't want to be married to someone who doesn't want to be married to me. Hell, you just did both of us a favor."

Slowly, like a crocodile wrestler would release an apparently subdued opponent, he relaxed his hold. Instead of suddenly lashing out at John, she smiled at him and declared, "See, I told you."

John, flabbergasted by the lighting-fast parade of emotions he had just witnessed, twisted around in his chair and stood, reaching down to help her up. She took his offered hand and rose.

"I need to be going," he stated flatly.

"Okay. Probably a good idea. You never know, I might flip out again," she said, smiling at the end of the sentence.

John was suddenly at a loss for words. Sensing this, Gail walked to the apartment door, opened it and extended her right hand. Dazed, John followed.

He took her hand, and she shook his firmly.

Still smiling, she seemed to resign herself, "Well...have a good life."

"You, too," he replied hollowly.

Still holding his hand, she guided him out the door and turned him loose. As he stood benumbed, facing her, she added cheerily, "Be seeing you. Oh, and don't worry about all of the details. I'll cancel everything."

"Okay. Thanks."

The grin never leaving her face, she closed the door. John stood for a moment, then turned and walked away.

As he approached his car, he saw Jack standing at the front bumper. "How did it go?"

"Just peachy keen," John answered.

Neither of them noticed the partially opened curtain. Neither saw Gail looking out at them as they climbed into the car.

V

"I can't tell you how many times that kind of performance played out between us during the marriage," Jack recalled.

They were in John's apartment, sitting at the dining table, and he had just finished describing the bizarre scene with Gail.

"It was like watching a one-woman show on Broadway."

"That, kiddo, is a damn good analogy. Every time she does it, it's like she's going for the Tony Award."

"At least it's over."

"You're kidding, right?"

"What do you mean? The wedding's off. Cancelled. Ka-put."

"The ceremony may be cancelled, but after everything I told you before, do you really think it's over? *Nobody* dumps Gail. That is an unimaginable, inconceivable occurrence in her mental construct."

Feeling tension begin to knot the muscles between his shoulder blades, John asked, "So, what's next?"

"That's always the tough part with Gail, predicting her next move. If she's still of the mind set that you are to be her husband, she'll cook up something to make that happen. If, on the other hand, this... the fact that you had the audacity to do this to *her*... causes her to come to the conclusion that she no longer wants you, then she only has one option."

"What's that?"

"Revenge," Jack replied matter-of-factly.

Before John could react, the apartment door suddenly opened. They turned to see Kurt standing in the doorway.

Under his breath, Jack muttered, "I forgot. He doesn't knock."

Shaking his head, John stated, "Nope. Never has."

"Dude! I heard the news. Uncle Jack, qué pasa?"

Kurt crossed the small living room and joined them at the table.

"That was quick," John said.

"What was?" Kurt asked.

"That you heard about the change of plans."

"Oh, yeah. Gail left me a voice mail. She must've left it when I was still crashed out. So, no wedding, huh? What happened?"

"Long story. Just decided it wasn't the right thing to do."

Looking at Jack suspiciously, Kurt speculated, "Did you get talked out of it?"

Chuckling, John responded, "Yes and no. I wasn't sure, anyway. Talking to...Uncle Jack just helped me make up my mind."

A smile spread across Kurt's face. "I never liked the bitch, anyway."

"Whoa! You never told me that."

"Hey, man, I learned a long time ago that you don't get between a friend and his woman. Good way to lose the friend."

John fell back in his chair and sighed, shaking his head in surprise. "You never cease to amaze me, Kurt."

"That...," he emphasized, pointing his thumb at his chest, "is the reason they call me 'The Amazing Kurt.' Hey! What about last night, huh?"

"It was horrible." John momentarily relived the crash of the motorcycle.

"What was?"

Staring at his friend, dumbfounded, John explained, "The accident. The guy who died."

"Oh...yeah. That was definitely a crummy deal. No, I'm talking about the UFO."

"What?" Jack and John both exclaimed in unison.

Obviously glad to be able to deliver breaking news, Kurt related excitedly, "I heard it on the radio coming here. Last night about a hundred people called the police, Davis-Monthan air base, the fire department...they saw something in the sky. Lights."

Jack asked, "When?"

"After midnight, I guess, like 12:30 or so. Right about the time I was so trashed and you guys were bringing me back to the hotel."

Jack's mind flashed back to the time Cal was bearing down on him. "John, do you remember that bright light just as Cal...the motorcycle came?"

Thinking back, John recollected, "I do. I thought it was the floodlight from the police helicopter. They are downtown all the time with that thing."

Replaying the moment in his mind, Jack stated, "I didn't hear it."

"We wouldn't have, with that semi going by."

"True." To Kurt, Jack said, "Did they say on the news where the sightings were?"

Turning up one corner of his mouth in a half-smile, Kurt, relishing the opportunity to relate a delicious tidbit, answered, "Downtown, guys," his words punctuated by a lifting of his eyebrows.

The three of them paused, mulling over what Kurt had said. Finally, John asserted dismissively, "Come on, now. A flying saucer? Do you know how many times that stuff gets on the news?"

Not fully convinced, Jack shrugged. "You're probably right. It probably was the helicopter."

"I don't know," Kurt chimed in, egging them on. "Could have been the little green guys."

"Grey," Jack corrected him.

"What's grey?" asked Kurt.

"The aliens. From what I've always read, they're supposed to be grey, not green."

"I didn't know that. Cool!"

"So," Kurt changed the subject, "what's the deal with Gail? What happened?"

Obviously reluctant to delve into the subject, John minimized the details. "Just decided to pull the plug before, you know, it was too late."

"I already figured that out, man. I mean, it was the morning of your wedding day. I'm talking about the scene when you told her. Did she come at you with a kitchen knife or a frying pan?"

Unable to help himself, John laughed. "You did have a pretty good bead on her, didn't you?"

"Damn right, I did. So, come on, tell me how it went. You're sitting here, so she must not have had a gun."

Still laughing, John looked at Jack for assistance. Instead of getting his younger self off the hook, Jack simply said, "I've already heard this story, so if you'll both excuse me," rising from the chair.

John glared a silent *thanks a lot* at him and returned to his discussion with Kurt. "It wasn't horrible. Well, I guess it was. Anyway, I called her and told her we needed to talk...."

Smiling to himself, Jack left them sitting at the table and walked away. Expecting to feel some dissonance triggered by the differences between his thirty-year-old memories of this place and the reality before him, he was surprised at how accurately he recalled the details.

In the small, apartment-sized living room, he examined the oak bookcase that he vividly remembered buying from Levitz. It had been his first purchase when he moved into this place, and that particular fact had always been a revealing detail about him, a small glimpse into what was already the hierarchy of his priorities. A place to put his books came first, before a bed, before a sofa or a chair, before a dinette, and definitely preceding a television.

And it was, by far, at that point in his life, the most expensive piece of furniture he owned. Partly motivated by a desire to have a bookcase with shelves that wouldn't sag when loaded up with his library, he also knew that, underlying it all, was his reverence for his books and his need for a suitable repository.

He gently ran his finger across the spines as if trying to absorb the stories, images and emotions contained within. As he read the names of the authors, as always arranged alphabetically – Asimov, Baldacci, Bradbury, Clancy, Child...jumping forward to Koontz – he relived the experiences gifted to him by each of the books. Alphabetically resetting, there was Bacon, Burke, Cervantes, Dante, Darwin, through Plato and Plutarch, ending with Virgil.

Suddenly, the pleasurable movies and profound insights playing in the theater of his mind abruptly changed as a new image came unbidden. He saw the glossy dust jackets and burnished leather bindings browning from the edges, at once bursting into flame. Manufactured from somewhere deep within his mind, his nostrils were filled with the acrid stench of the bindings as they burned.

He could no longer tolerate the *coup d'oeil* of the eventual fate of his books and turned away. Then Jack realized that what he had just seen in his mind was no longer their inevitable destiny. He had changed it. That future blaze would never be set. Those two small, sweet children would never feel the agony as the fire first trapped them in their bedroom and then, like a marauding beast, burst through their door and consumed them.

Although not a consequence previously unconsidered, Jack realized that the change he had caused in this time would also result in neither of their births. John, Jr. would never be. Nor would Beth. They would never see the tears of joy on his face as he held them each for the first time. They would never feel the spasms of laughter as they squirmed on the floor, tickled mercilessly by Jack, or the warmth and comfort as they both crawled into his bed and cuddled against him while he indulged in an afternoon nap.

He knew their time on this Earth was to have been brief. He knew that its inevitable conclusion was horrific and inextricably tied to the fact of their births. He could imagine no scenario that would have allowed them to come to be, yet averted their horrific demise.

The fact that they were not his children, biologically, did not alter the profound sorrow as he contemplated their future absence from his, or rather John's, life.

Turning from the bookcase, Jack moved slowly to the bedroom. As he walked, he realized that the outcome of his visit to this time was more than likely the best of the possible consequences regarding the children. Whether he was now destined to live out the remainder of his life here and now, or simply return to his own time for the balance of years, the immunity granted to him by the time machine guaranteed that he would always have the clear, vivid and intense memories of the two small, helpless beings whom he had loved with all of his heart.

Jack was also comforted by the fact that he had spared John the agonies of his former time to come. He also knew that John would never know the joys of the unborn children. But never knowing that joy meant never feeling the pain of loss.

"I guess that's the best I can hope for," Jack spoke aloud as he entered the spare bedroom.

Filling the entire twelve-by-twelve space, except for a minimal walkway to the center of the room, was his...John's...Lionel train layout. Jack felt his heartbeat quicken, reminiscent of the childhood rush he felt when he found his first train set under the Christmas tree.

Although the track, scenery, buildings, engines and rolling stock which filled the table were not flesh and bones, Jack still felt a sense of euphoria, knowing his actions, his trip to this time, had also rescued this plastic, wood and metal fantasy world from the future flames.

Unconsciously, his hand reached out and turned on the power strip. His ears were instantly rewarded with the gentle hum of 110 volts converted into 18 volts for the locomotives, as well as the myriad voltages for the lighting, buildings and animations placed around the layout.

Just as he was about to send the wireless command from the handheld Legacy Cab, he heard John's voice from behind, "Don't you think you should ask before you run another man's trains?"

Jack spun around to see his counterpart smiling. Kurt stood behind, also grinning. Pushing past John to enter the room, he declared, "Playtime!"

The three spent the next couple of hours taking turns controlling the two 2-6-2 A.T.&S. steam locomotives, as the replicas of machines long-departed delivered milk, picked up loads of pipe and coal, and shuttled passengers through the miniature countryside.

During one of the times while John held the controller, Jack, standing off to the side, studied him intently. He saw himself, thirty years younger, his eyes a deeper blue, his hair much thicker and not yet traced with strands of gray, his face smooth with no hint of the latticework of lines and creases that were so soon to arrive. And yet, despite all of the apparent differences, they shared the same exuberance…the same joy of living…the same ability to surrender completely to the moment and, as a puppy patiently extracting every morsel of the marrow from a bone, both he and John educed every bit of delight, pain, ecstacy and sorrow that life had to offer.

Easing himself gently from the reverie, Jack focused on Kurt and saw that, while he was so intently watching John, Kurt was staring at him, his face showing a mixture of curiosity and something else…something Jack couldn't quite identify. Their eyes connected for a moment and Jack saw, or felt, an unspoken communication. Kurt seemed to be telling him that he understood. What it was that his erstwhile friend understood was not clear.

As their eyes remained locked upon each other, a wry grin formed on Kurt's face and he slowly, almost imperceptibly, nodded at Jack. Unconsciously, Jack returned the smile before their communion was shattered by John. "We can't just do this all day. I don't know about you guys, but I do have some things to do."

~ VI ~

The kitchen timer chimed. Pulling open the oven door with one hand, while grabbing a pot holder with the other, Gail removed the cookie sheet filled with mozzarella sticks and placed it on the counter. As she let them cool enough to eat, she got a Pepsi from the refrigerator and placed it on the table next to the cold bottle of Ragu.

Having deemed that enough time had passed, she dumped the entire batch of breaded cheese onto a plate and sat down to eat her favorite snack. She didn't bother to pour any of the sauce on the plate, preferring to dip the sticks directly into the jar.

In the background the television played loudly, tuned to a cable channel that featured the daily trials and tribulations of the current Hollywood stars. As she munched down the entire plate of starch and fat, Gail caught up on who Ben was seeing, which movie Hilary was making, and how Britney's latest comeback was going. Her countenance was neither pinched nor serene, her eyes neither darting nor tranquil.

Finishing, Gail left the evidence of her meal as it was and moved to the bedroom. Opening the closet door, she pulled out what was to have been her wedding dress and laid it out on the bed, thinking back on the seemingly countless fittings and alterations needed to make it perfect. She next reached up to the shelf above, took down the bouquet she had made herself for the occasion, and placed it next to the white and lacy gown, arranging it carefully so that the satin ribbon cascaded down the side of the bed.

From the other room, the voice of some unidentifiable young male star made its way into the bedroom, sharing with Gail his wealth of knowledge and life experiences, all gleaned by the tender age of twenty-something, as she stood motionless, staring down at the array of satin, lace and flowers.

Apparently having reached a decision, Gail skirted the bed until she arrived at the nightstand. She removed a pair of heavy-duty seamstress shears from the drawer and turned back to the gown.

- VII -

"A toast!"

Jack and John were sitting in the living room as Kurt came out of the kitchen, clutching against his chest three tumblers filled nearly to the brims with beer from his regular stash in John's refrigerator.

"Kurt," said John, "you never cease to amaze me. What are you doing?"

"We need to celebrate," he answered, pausing in front of Jack to deliver one of the glasses. Jack took the beer, and Kurt stepped over to the chair where John was sitting.

"You pulled the plug on a wedding that shouldn't have happened. And not a moment too soon. That deserves a toast."

Snorting, John took the glass from him. Kurt stood in the center of the room, raised his glass and smiled. "Here's to dodging the bullet."

Going around to each of them, Kurt ceremoniously clinked his tumbler to theirs, as Jack said, "Unfortunate choice of words considering her temper."

The men all took a long sip from their drinks. Both Jack and John, nondrinkers, grimaced at the taste. As Kurt's eyes took this in, he joked, "Good point. Maybe I should return the wedding gift I bought for you and exchange it for a Kevlar jacket."

All three of them chuckled, dissipating some of the built-up tension from the last twenty-four hours.

"Well," began Kurt, "what are your plans for the rest of the day?"

Glancing meaningfully at Jack, John answered, "Not sure. We...I mean, I have some things to figure out." He paused for a bit as the reality of Jack's dilemma returned to the fore in his mind. Shaking it off, he continued, "What about you?"

"I'm free as a bird. I was going to be the best man at a wedding today, but that got called off. Oh, beans! The tuxes."

"That's right," John agreed, "except they don't have to be back until the day after tomorrow."

Kurt shrugged. "Like I said, I've got nothing to do. I might as well take mine back today, if they're still open. Want me to take yours?"

"Sure."

Draining his glass in a long series of gulps, Kurt gathered the still nearly-full tumblers from John and Jack. He plunged his fingers into the beer and gripped the glasses from the top so that he could carry all three with one hand.

"You're cool," John teased.

"Always!"

As Kurt wandered down the short hallway to the bathroom, John looked over at Jack and they both laughed under their breath, shaking their heads. They could hear Kurt emptying their two glasses into the toilet.

"Kurt," Jack shouted, "are you pouring those out or throwing up?"

From the other room, Kurt answered, "Both!"

Softly, to avoid being heard by his friend, John asked, "Can you take me to see the...machine?"

Jack just nodded.

A minute later, Kurt returned with John's rented tux, still wrapped in clear plastic, draped over his arm.

"All right. I'm off." Looking at Jack, he inquired politely, "Did you have one? I can take yours back, too."

"No. I didn't make the cut. I wasn't in the wedding party. Thanks, anyway."

"No problem."

Kurt wrestled briefly with the door and managed to get it open. "I'll catch up with you later."

"That'd be good. Call me."

Kurt hesitated in the doorway. "Seriously, dude...you did the right thing. I'm proud of you."

Touched, John responded, "Thanks."

"It couldn't have been easy, at the last minute and all."

"No. It wasn't."

There was an awkward silence, as none of the three spoke for a moment, finally broken by Kurt. "I'm out of here. See you. Adios, Uncle Jack."

Each muttered a *good-bye* and stared for a time at the closed front door.

"Quite a noticeable drop in the energy level when he leaves, isn't there?"

A somber note to his voice, Jack said, "You have no idea."

Curious, John asked, "What do you mean?"

Jack averted his gaze, looking down, his face showing frustration.

"When we planned this...Cal and I...it was supposed to go so smoothly. In quick, out quick. No collateral impact. No catastrophes. Just stop the wedding and split. Cal hammered into my head all of the *do's* and *don'ts*.

"I could tell he wasn't altogether comfortable with the whole thing, even though it was his idea. See, the problem is that it's just so hard to predict what can happen. Impossible, actually. Let's say I come back and talk you out of the wedding. It's cancelled, I don't kill Cal, and everything's fine. I go back to my time. Even though my whole life history from this year forward, for the next thirty years, would be different, I would still have *this*," he pointed at his head, "set of memories...*this* history.

"But, from the moment I leave you, you are no longer going to be at any of the same places at any of the same times you were in that other life...the other path you didn't take."

"I know. I've been thinking about that."

"Yeah. On the other path, we know all of the horrible fiascoes which are going to...I mean, were going to happen. That path is my past, but it's no longer your future. Even with all of the misery and catastrophes, we know if you had gone that route, you'd live at least to the age of fifty. Now, today or tomorrow, you could be crossing a street you wouldn't have been on before and get hit by a bus. That's it. Dead at twenty."

John tried to imagine the scenario his older self described.

"Think about it. I've got this whole fifty-year life in my head. All of it. All the big things, all the little details. The friends, enemies, my career, my house. But *BING!* I pop back into my moment and find out that everything's different. Like I said, I could go back and find out I died years ago. Even if it's not so extreme, I could find that I live in New Jersey."

"No way!" John chimed in, trying to make the conversation a little lighter. Jack didn't respond to the attempt at humor.

"I don't think you're really getting it yet. I would be a fifty-year-old guy with fifty years of memories and knowledge in my head, but the only problem would be that everything in those last thirty years of memories wouldn't match my real history anymore."

"I hadn't really thought about it." John pondered the life, or lives, before him, visualizing that day, thirty years hence.

"What happens to me…then?"

Nodding, Jack said, "Exactly. God. Cal and I really didn't think this thing through. According to Cal, you will need to satisfy the program. You will need to get on the time machine and come back here and do all of this. The only problem is that now there isn't any Cal and there won't be any time machine."

Jack stared out the window, collecting his thoughts. "Every trip Cal made on the machine was different than this. The trips didn't really involve his younger self, or if they did, it was not of this magnitude. For instance, once he went back only a couple of weeks and told himself to do just one thing a little differently; it was a small part of an experiment he had been working on, and it went wrong. A lab assistant was badly burned. So he went back, told himself not to flip the switch, or whatever it was, and the assistant never got burned."

"Even that little trip couldn't have been that simple, could it? I mean, if Cal went back two weeks and told himself not to flip the switch and then he returned to his regular time, the result would be that the assistant never got burned and Cal had no reason to make the trip two weeks later. So when the time to go on the trip came up and he didn't leave, wouldn't there be two of him?"

"There would be. Except that when he went back, he told himself, his earlier self, three things: Number one – he told 'earlier Cal' what was going to happen and told him not to flip the switch; Number two – he told earlier Cal the exact moment to depart in two weeks, otherwise there would be two of them; and Number three – he told earlier Cal to keep a detailed diary of the next two weeks.

"The switch didn't get flipped. The assistant didn't get burned. Two weeks went by, and earlier Cal hopped in the machine, went back and satisfied the pattern. A split-second after earlier Cal tripped back, uh… 'later Cal' appeared in the machine, coming back from the trip. He read the diary, learned what changed in his life during the last two weeks, and life went on."

"Got it. And even though the guy going back two weeks this time was the earlier Cal, he still knew what to do when he got there."

"Right. The difference between that scenario and this one is that when Cal finished the trip, he only had two weeks of minor changes in his life to assimilate. If I get back, there will be thirty years of changes."

Brightening, John said, "You're wrong about one thing. Thirty years from now, when it's time for me to go back, there will be a time machine because you brought one with you. Whether you never leave or whether you go back, the machine will be there when we...I...need it."

"That's true. Even without Cal, there is still the machine."

They fell into a thoughtful silence, listening to the gentle thrum of traffic sounds from the street. Several minutes passed before John spoke. "This conversation started because you said something about Kurt."

"I know. What I was starting to explain was that telling you a lot of things about what was coming next was one of the big *don'ts*."

"Something about Kurt?"

"Yes."

"Look, this whole thing hasn't worked out the way you planned. Are you sure that telling me is really such a big deal?"

"I don't know. Cal was very emphatic that I needed to keep my influence on this time to an absolute minimum. That's really out the window now, especially if I'm going to be staying here for the rest of my life. Everything I do, everyone I meet will keep making small or big changes. As time goes by, the changes will cause other changes. It will just magnify. Who knows what will happen differently. At some point, the ripple effect could extend around the world, changing the lives of people in Pakistan. I honestly don't know."

"I don't see why you can't just go back."

"I can. Only I hate to do that just yet. If I go back without undoing Cal's death somehow, that will definitely have huge effects on the future. His impact, starting in a few years, was tremendous. Like I told you before, he went on to perfect an unbelievable number of patents. At one point, he actually broke Thomas Edison's record for patents held. All those things, which he is supposed to create, changed countless lives.

"And he was my best friend. He put it all on the line, knowing how foolish this trip probably was, just to save my life. I owe him. I've got to figure out a way to undo what I've done."

"We will. We'll think of something. Jack, you still haven't told me about Kurt."

"And I'm not going to tell you. At least right now. Let me think about it for a while?"

"I guess. Is it something bad?"

Jack gave John a look of exasperation.

"Okay, okay, I'll drop it."

"Good."

Noticing how tied up his back and neck muscles had become, John stretched and said, "Let's go see the machine."

"Okay."

"How about Casa Molina on the way?"

"That," said Jack, grinning suddenly, "sounds awesome."

⏳

The restaurant, first opened in 1947, started out as a converted ranch house. Over the years, as their business grew, several rooms were added, creating a sprawling, segmented structure of two-foot-thick walls and saguaro-ribbed ceilings. The dining tables and chairs had the heavy, roughly ornate look of handmade.

Whether by design or a fluke of the economic realities of the conversion of the original ranch house to a public restaurant, the opening into the kitchen faced the front entrance door, filling the vestibule with aromas of bubbling sauces and simmering, spiced beef and chicken.

"John!" The greeting boomed from the kitchen doorway as Jorge spotted his regular customer. Grabbing two printed placemats and sets of silverware, he smiled and said, "You brought a friend...." He stopped in mid-sentence, the waiter's eyes riveted to Jack's face.

Quickly, John introduced Jack. "Jorge, this is my Uncle Jack, from out of town."

Immediately reverting back to his usual congeniality, Jorge smiled, welcomed Jack and pivoted around them, leading the men through the first two dining rooms to John's favorite table. As they made their way to the rear dining room, the latest of all of the additions, built in the '50s or '60s, Jorge softly spoke to one of the helpers, who quickly began filling a tray with extra bowls of salsa and chips.

The back dining area was noticeably different from the other rooms. Built in the round, with an enclosed central, circular mechanical and storage area, the beam ceiling radiated outward to the curved adobe walls, accented by old bullfighting posters featuring, among others, the performances of matador

Diego O'Bolger.

Seating his guests, Jorge looked at Jack and asked, "Do you need a menu?"

"No, thank you," Jack answered, smiling.

John shot a meaningful glance at his *other* as Jorge asked, "Steak and enchilada?"

John nodded.

"I'll have the same," Jack requested, grinning with anticipation as the helper placed the warm tortilla chips and four bowls of hot salsa on the table. A second helper arrived with a glass of iced tea for John.

Jorge asked Jack, "Would you like it cooked the same?"

"Yes," replied Jack, "almost burned."

The cloud of confusion again drifted across the waiter's face as he jotted down Jack's order and walked away. The helper, a friendly, Hispanic girl, who always took a moment to chat with John during his frequent visits, asked Jack, "What would you like to drink?"

"Iced tea."

She acknowledged the order and left.

After she was out of earshot, Jack exclaimed, "God, I've missed this!"

"They're closed?"

Realizing he was probably letting too much slip once again, with a shrug Jack said, "No, not closed. Thirty years from now they'll still be going strong, but as the kids, who took over all of the locations from the original Molinas, got older... things changed."

Saddened, John wondered, "How?"

"I think the *food police* got to them. They sort of released their embrace on the authentic and went the route of that other Mexican food tradition in town and decided to go upscale."

John shuddered. "In other words, they took out all the good stuff because people aren't smart enough to decide for themselves if they want bacon grease in their frijoles. That's a travesty!"

"You're not kidding." Pulling a chip from the bowl and dipping it deeply into the bright red salsa, Jack advised, "So, enjoy it while you can."

John followed suit, savoring the intense flavors. Between munches, he said, "I've been thinking about what we were talking about earlier. The tenuousness of reality doesn't seem to fit with my... our... theory."

Crunching loudly, Jack agreed. When his mouth was empty enough, he confirmed, "You're right. At least, that's what I thought, too. But just because we're editing time…," he looked around their table to make certain no one was close enough to hear, "doesn't mean that everything we're doing didn't happen in the previous cycles."

John appeared thoughtful for a moment before responding. "I guess. It just seems like all of the liberties you and Cal have been taking with time would cause the connection between the cycles to short-circuit or something."

"Focus on it. Do you still feel the connection? If what you said were actually the case, don't you think that after what we've done in the past twenty-four hours, you would be off the tracks right now?"

Jack checked his watch and stated, "In all the previous cycles, instead of sitting here with me, eating chips and salsa, you would have already been standing next to Gail, giving your vows."

John closed his eyes momentarily, shutting out as much of the external as he could, and focused on what he was feeling at the moment. Out of respect for his younger self's attempt at meditation, Jack stopped himself from biting into another chip.

After at least two minutes passed, John's eyes opened. "You're right. At least, I think you are. I'm pretty sure I can still feel it."

After allowing the dripping chip to fulfill its fleeting destiny, Jack affirmed, "I know. I already checked."

Silence ensued as John's eyes glazed over. Since it was obvious that he was grappling with another concept, Jack did not intrude, satisfying himself with the process of sopping up every detail of his environment.

"I've been thinking," John finally said, breaking out of his meditative trance.

"No kidding."

"Maybe when you came back…and maybe all of the trips that Cal made…you weren't really going back in time."

Skeptically, Jack retorted, "What the hell do you mean?"

"Think about it." Instead of responding, John jumped up from his chair and trotted to the nearest wait station, snagging a pen. When he returned, he immediately flipped over the paper placemat and drew a straight line at the top.

"I think maybe we've had it all wrong." Placing the tip of the pen at the right-hand end of the line, he continued, "You and Cal thought that you were *here*, at the end of the timeline." He drew a small x so that the line ended at the mark.

"Yeah, so?"

"That part could be right, I'm not sure yet. Wait a minute and let me finish."

"Okay. Go for it."

"When one of you made a trip, you thought you were *there*," John pointed the pen at the x. "And you thought that you went from there" – with the pen he drew a backward arc, resembling an eyebrow, that moved from right to left above the line, and ended with an arrow – "to, let's say, here." The arc stopped, and he drew another x bisecting the timeline.

"Yes. That's how it works."

Looking up from his drawing, John smiled at Jack and said, "Actually, that's how it doesn't work."

"What…?"

Holding up one finger to silence Jack, John resumed, "That isn't what's happening." Two inches down from the first timeline, he drew a second line, immediately placing the x at the right end. "Here's what's really happening. And this is the only way that everything we've talked about makes sense."

Pointing at the x, he said, "This may be where you're starting but that's just semantics; it confuses the issue because," pointing back up at the x mid-point of the first timeline, "you are not going back in time. You are only *selecting* that particular point."

"What the difference?"

With a self-satisfied grin, John explained, "After you or Cal select the point, like moving the cursor in a word document to an exact point in a story ten chapters back, the *machine* does not send you or Cal back." Savoring the moment, John paused, dramatically. "The machine simply *copies* everything that happens from that point forward all the way to your current moment and *pastes* it…so that it starts at the second you thought you traveled back. Everything is still linear. You're not actually going back. Because the machine *copies* instead of *cuts*, everything that happened in your memory up to the point you *departed*, is still there…it's still in the past. It's just farther back now because the machine took a big block of the story, 2010 through 2040, copied it and moved it to the end, appending those chapters."

John drew a small, vertical line at the point on the timeline equal to the mid-point x on the line above and labeled that point 2010. Then he drew another vertical at the end, labeling that point 2040. He circled that 2010 to 2040 section. Next, he drew another arc, this time beginning at the circle and extending to the right, beyond the end of the line labeled 2040. As he spoke, he starting drawing a new line that began at what was the end of the timeline and stretched it approximately equal in length to the segment.

"In other words, that whole thirty years that you lived through has been plopped on the timeline in front of us. It's like taking chapters five through ten, copying them and adding them at the end of chapter ten. The only difference is that the writer of the document, the machine, has moved the cursor to the insertion point to begin rewriting the story. *You...*," again pausing for effect, John said, "are the cursor. You are now *right here*," pointing at the vertical line at the beginning of the pasted segment labeled 2010.

"Hot plate."

Neither had noticed Jorge standing at their table, using towels to hold two sizzling plates of food. As the waiter set the platter of steak and enchilada in front of Jack, John turned his placemat over just in time to get his plate. After they received the sides of refried beans, warm flour tortillas and their refilled iced teas, Jorge departed.

Cutting into the sizzling beef, Jack expressed his doubt, "I'm not sure about this. Are you saying that the machine, instead of just sending one person back in time, actually copies every detail of the lives of billions of people for thirty years and pastes it in front of you?"

John expanded on the idea. "Not just the lives of four or five billion people, but every detail of every particle in the entire universe. Everything that's happened...everywhere."

Laughing derisively, Jack blurted out, "That's ridiculous!"

Not the least bit offended, John smiled and said, "Look, you know how our theory works."

"Of course, I do."

"Everything that has happened...everything that's going to happen...has all happened before. Maybe a million times. We proved this, at least to ourselves, with the *John/Jack* thing."

"Yeah."

"Maybe the machine has access to all of those past cycles, has catalogued them like a file allocation table on a hard drive. We've always thought that when the Big Crunch happens at the end of this cycle, followed by the Big Bang starting it all again, that the details...the information from the cycle that just ended isn't actually deleted, any more completely than something you delete on a computer is really gone. It's always available with *undelete*, or at the bit level."

"True," Jack admitted begrudgingly.

"So, if it's all there, maybe what Cal invented was a machine that can access those FATs."

Some of the scorn disappearing from his face, Jack considered the theory. "It's possible."

"Amigo, it's the only way to explain everything."

"How so?"

"Think about it. You said that Cal found out he could go to a moment in time where he was already present without causing a problem, yet he couldn't go to a moment where 'traveling Cal' was. Why not? Because, if the traveler is the cursor, the cursor can only be at one point in the document at any time."

"That makes sense."

"There's more. Okay, I want you to really visualize this. 'Cursor Jack' is inserted into 2010 in the evening prior to the wedding. While he's there, he causes Cal to crash and die."

"Don't remind me."

"Sorry. Anyway, Cal is on his motorcycle and crashes, right in front of cursor Jack's eyes."

"Okay."

"Then, less than an hour after the crash, cursor Jack inserts himself into the previous day to stop Cal from dying. Now remember, in the story that we're in, something had already caused Cal to be there, on his bike, at the wrong time. It's already written. You thought that, just like Cal went back and changed his actions and saved the lab assistant from being burned, you could go back and stop Cal. But it wasn't the same thing."

"Why not?"

"Come on, man. You've already said that you've tuned in on the cycle message and you told me that it was still working. That you felt it! The only way you could be picking up the message, and feeling like you were still on course, was if all of this had happened a number of times before, creating the overlaid track that you're receiving now."

John paused to allow this to sink in.

He continued, "In who knows how many previous cycles, you came back to this time, met me, stopped the wedding and killed Cal. The fact that it took you making the extra little day trip back to provide the justification for Cal being in the wrong place at the wrong time...was irrelevant. It had to happen...it *needed* to happen; otherwise, there would be an incongruity in the story. There would have been the incident of Cal spilling the bike downtown, but no reason preceding that event which would have caused him to come downtown in the first place. You went back and ticked Cal off, causing him to get on his bike and speed away because that was *exactly* what you had done countless times before."

Jack said nothing, taking in the new concept. John resumed his attack on the plate of food, scooping up the last of the enchilada.

Both ate in silence until Jorge returned. "Sopapillas?"

"Yes!"

"No!"

The affirmative and negative responses came simultaneously from the two men. John looked at Jack questioningly. "You don't want one?"

"I have finally lost about seventy-five pounds, lowered my cholesterol close to that of a normal person, and just a few weeks ago was able to stop taking blood pressure pills. I don't need a sopapilla and neither," Jack looked at John pointedly, "do you."

Vaguely upset by this apothegmatic glimpse into his own future, John turned to Jorge, and resignedly shook his head *no*. Smiling, the waiter promised, "I'll be right back with your check."

After he was gone, Jack stated, "I don't know. I guess it makes sense."

"It's still firming up in my head. I have a feeling that I'm on the right track, but maybe there are a few details that aren't quite right."

"Assuming you are right, how does this help us?"

Jorge returned and placed the black tray with the check on the table. Both of them reached for the check, but John grabbed it first. "This one's on me. And, to answer your question, I'm not sure yet. I think I have an idea. I just want to mull it over a little more before I tell you."

"Okay," Jack declared, looking at his watch. "Let's go see the machine."

- VIII -

The alley was pockmarked with evidence of bustling commerce long departed. Jack and John approached the rear of an old produce warehouse built alongside the railroad tracks. The heirs to the original owner, in an attempt to squeeze at least a meager income from the asset, had converted the almost century-old structure, which had been abandoned decades earlier, into small, self-serve storage rooms. Fishing out a key, Jack opened the padlock and tucked both into his jeans pocket.

John cautiously followed as his *other* fumbled in the darkness for the light. The sound of the beaded pull-chain as it dragged against the ceramic base preceded the light from the single, ceiling-mounted bulb as it illuminated the storage room. Incongruous, amidst the battered brick walls and dusty floor, the time machine, sleek and shining, perched on synthetic polymer struts in the center of the small room. John was taken by the delusory nature of the setting.

He slowly circled the machine, examining the device that had been made decades from now, yet was sitting before him today. The science-fiction transport was elegantly simple. Spherical in shape, it was sheathed in a skin of glistening, seamless metal, as if it had been dipped into a vat of mercury. Were it oblong, rather than round, John found that he could easily have imagined a colossal goose who had tired of laying golden eggs and had switched to silver or platinum.

"All right, I give up. How do you get into this thing?"

Chuckling, Jack approached the device. As he neared it, the machine apparently detected his proximity and a roughly twelve-inch-square adumbration, reddish-orange in hue, was suddenly visible on the side. Although the outline appeared to be projected onto the shining surface from an unseen source behind them, John noticed that as Jack placed his hand flat on the surface inside the designated region, no portion of the outline was blocked out by his wrist or arm. John heard an almost imperceptible hum as Jack touched his flesh to the metal. A moment later a man-sized section of the hull raised outward and pivoted to create a doorway where no seams had been evident a moment before.

"Wow!" John exclaimed, impressed.

Taking his hand from the surface, Jack explained, "Biometric reader. It's been programmed to identify me and will open only for me," and with a sudden sadness in his voice, he added, "or Cal, of course."

John walked to the opening, leaning into the sphere. "Can I go in or is the entrance biometrically controlled, also?"

"No, go ahead. Just...."

"Don't touch anything," John finished for him. "I figured that out."

John slowly stepped up and into the time transport or, as he thought of it, the time editor. An interior platform was level with the threshold and fabricated out of a rigid, rubberized material. Fastened to the center of the platform was what looked like an upgraded captain's chair from an expensive recreational vehicle. He traversed the space, about two paces, to reach it and sat down, observing that the chair was also molded from the same nonmetallic material as the floor of the machine.

"The exterior skin," Jack began, "is a refined silver, the natural contaminants removed to some ridiculously extreme purity. It's basically an incredibly flawless Faraday Cage. From what Cal explained, it's what makes the traveler immune to the time changes.

"The interior is insulated and isolated. Just about everything inside is nonconductive except, obviously, the electronics. Those are all contained within another, smaller Faraday Cage." Jack, leaning inside the cabin, pointed out a sphere which was mounted with rubber grommets on the inside wall at eye level to the passenger. Studying the control sphere closely, John saw not a single penetration through the silver globe.

"I don't see any wires or fiber-optic cables coming out of it. How does it do what it does to you and the rest of the machine?"

"That's the nice thing about silver. Not only does it make a great Faraday Cage, it also makes an excellent transmitting and receiving antenna. The brains inside the ball communicate with the machine wirelessly, and vice versa."

John, impressed, said, "Wi-Fi."

"Yes...eighth or ninth generation."

"But there are still some electronics outside the little ball. There'd have to be...wouldn't there?"

"There are. They're attached to the inside of the hull skin and then embedded in the nonconductive coating."

John noticed that the interior of the main sphere was covered with the same black, rubberized material.

"How could...?"

Jack held up his hand. "Stop. I'm not Cal. I got the tour and instructions on how to drive the thing, but I'm not the one who built it and I'm sure as hell not the one who can explain it."

His curiosity throttled, John returned his attention to examining the interior.

"There really isn't much to see. Hey! Where are the controls? I don't see anything that you could use to operate this."

Jack climbed the rest of the way into the cabin, a close fit with two grown men inside, reached over John who was sitting in the only chair, and flipped open the arm console. Reaching in, he removed a handheld device, which looked like a cross between a Blackberry and a Radio Shack 100-in-1 remote controller, and handed it to John.

"All of the controls are in that. And the controller also communicates with," he pointed at the small sphere, "the brains, by Wi-Fi."

"This is too cool!"

Taking the handheld back from John, Jack turned it on. The small screen instantly came to life, displaying a menu.

"The screen looks like the GPS map display I have in my car."

"It's a lot like that. You program in the coordinates of your destination. The big difference, of course, is that you also punch in the exact *time* you want it to *be* for your arrival. The computer keeps track of your departure point for the return and, once the trip begins, it remains connected to you through the data thread.

"The machine takes you wherever you're going and then it instantly goes to the programmed pickup time, gets you and zaps back again. From the point of view of the people left behind, it all happens in less than a blink of the eye. It was really weird to be a spectator when Cal made a trip. He got inside it... not this machine. The main one... the one that sent me here... is bigger, but it looks identical. Anyway, he got in. The door closed. A few seconds later the door opened, and he came out. That was it! The first time I saw it, I thought he had changed his mind and didn't leave. Except that he had a full day's beard growth, his clothes were rumpled... you know, he looked like someone coming home from a vacation."

"Cool!"

"From the perspective of the traveler, you get in, close the door and hit the button. When you get the message on this screen," Jack pointed at the handheld controller, "that you have arrived, you open the door and you are in a different time. You step out, close the door, and the machine vanishes."

"Unbelievable! What does the trip feel like?"

"Nothing, actually. It feels like nothing occurred. If the screen didn't tell you that it was over, you wouldn't know it happened."

A thought crystallizing, John said, "I've been thinking. You told me that a traveler can't go back to a place where the same traveler currently exists. So *you* can't go back to any point in this trip, Trip A. And you can't go back to the second, brief trip you made to try to stop Cal, Trip B."

"Yes. That's right. At least, that's what Cal said. So... what's your point?"

Pausing momentarily, John blurted, "*I* can!"

Jack's eyes instantly jerked wide. "No! Absolutely not."

"Why not? It makes sense. I can go back to either time. I haven't tripped yet, so there's no danger of running into a traveling *me*."

Jack considered it for only a second before answering, "Like I've said before, I'm not Cal. I don't understand what's going on and how this all works, as well as he did. I just have a feeling that we are fiddling with a ball of string and the more we keep jumping back and forth with it, the more tangled it's going to get."

"Jack, what choices do we have? Cal's dead. The machine was never... will never be invented. Granted, we have a machine here and maybe there will be a way to undo some of the future damage, but I'm not sure how. You said earlier that Cal is destined to have a tremendous impact on the future. There is no way I can patch all that up as I, or we, go through the next thirty years. We have to do something. Sending me back to talk to him *is* that something."

John paused to let the logic of his argument sink in, hoping to bolster it by adding, "Unless you've come up with a better plan."

Jack was silent for a moment. He had to admit that what John was saying made sense. "What about the *script*? You said it yourself...what happened yesterday and the day before is now written in the script and *burned in* to the cycles. Why do you think you can change it?"

"I don't know if I can, and I don't even know if that's right to begin with," John admitted. "But if you send me back...I'm thinking a day before your Trip B...I'll figure out a way to connect with Cal...talk to him...explain what is going on and what is about to happen. Maybe I can prevent him from getting on that motorcycle last night. Maybe I can't. The difference is, I can stay longer – stay through your Trip B and even stay through your Trip A – at least until just before the time when you've sent me back. I'll just keep rewriting as I go. Trying to *burn in* the new story. Hell, I could be standing outside in the alley right now because we've already done this."

Unconsciously, both of their sets of eyes drifted to the door leading to the alley. Jack considered his alter ego's suggestion.

"The mind is not built for this maze. The more I try to visualize the jumps back and the overlapping trips, the more tenuous my grip is on the whole picture."

"I know, me too," John agreed. "Like you said earlier, at least we have some time to think about it."

"Yeah," Jack said, dispiritedly, "all the time in the world."

X̆

John led the way as they left the storage locker. Abruptly he jumped back, slamming into Jack, who was halfway through the storage room door, a startled exclamation bursting from him.

The fright-reflex slam of adrenaline hit Jack and caused him to fumble the padlock. It slipped from his fingers and bounced off his knee, skittering across the crumbled pavement toward a stranger who stood no more than two feet from them.

With the image of John's earlier comment lingering in his head, Jack expected to see a doppelganger of his younger self loitering in the alley. Instead, he saw a middle-aged, black man wearing blue jeans, a Harley-Davidson t-shirt and a denim jacket, and grinning at them as they exited the door.

Painfully aware of how guilty they must have looked, John fought to overcome his agitation. "Hey," he said with a forced casualness. "How are you doing?"

The stranger broadened his smile and nodded, not answering the greeting. Keeping his gaze on them, he reached down, retrieved the padlock and handed it to John.

"Thanks," John responded, consciously maintaining a light tone of voice and probably, he thought, sounding like a lunatic.

The man nodded once again and turned away from them. He tucked his hands into the pockets of his jacket and casually ambled away, walking deeper into the dark alley. Jack closed the storage room door, and John slipped the padlock into the hasp and clicked it shut.

"You gotta love downtown!"

Jack shook his head. "I wonder if he was listening."

"If he was, he was," John dismissed Jack's concern. "Think about it. He shows up at Channel 4 and, assuming they let him in, tells the news director that two guys have a time machine locked up in a storage room off an alley downtown."

Jack laughed. "You're right." Looking around and seeing no one else lurking, he urged, "Let's get out of here."

⧗

As they approached John's apartment, they saw Kurt sitting on the front stoop, clutching a paper shopping bag.

"Hi, guys."

John, noticing the absence of his friend's usual ebullience, asked, "What's wrong?"

Standing up, Kurt replied, "Oh, nothing. Everything's okay. I just came by to see you...*both*."

Eyeing him with curiosity, John unlocked the front door and they went in.

"All right, Kurt," John said firmly, "what's up?"

Kurt walked to the sofa and dropped down heavily. He gently placed the Trader Joe's paper bag on the coffee table.

"Like I said, nothing." Kurt waited as John and Jack were seated. "Unless, of course, you consider living through an episode of *Twilight Zone* something."

John immediately felt a tingle of apprehension. For the second time today, he took conscious control of his voice and tried to sound nonchalant. "What are you talking about?" He noticed that Jack was staring intently at Kurt, but could not read Jack's expression.

His voice level and even, brooking no argument, Kurt announced, "You don't have an Uncle Jack."

John, caught off-guard, struggled for a response, when Jack stepped in. "You're right. He doesn't."

Kurt turned to face Jack and said, "Then, supposedly, who are you?"

"Supposedly?" John snapped, expressing far more tension in his voice than he intended.

Focusing his attention back on John, Kurt explained, "Look…you don't have an Uncle Jack. I know, I asked your folks today."

"You what?"

"I asked your parents. Don't worry. They're cool. I did it in a way that wouldn't make them suspicious about anything. Anyway, that's not the point. The point is…he's not your uncle. He looks just like you, only older. He sounds just like you, or the way you're going to sound after about a million more cigarettes. He even has the same little birthmark on his temple that you have."

Unsure of what direction to take, John fell silent as Kurt stared directly at him, waiting patiently for a response.

"Of course they said that," Jack interjected. "I'm the secret of the family."

Jerking his gaze to Jack, Kurt said, "What are you saying?"

"It's simple. John's mother is my sister."

"They already told me she's not."

"They told you that because you asked them both."

"I don't understand."

"Let's just say that John's father doesn't know about me…and Kathleen, John's mom and my sister, wants to keep it that way."

"Why?"

"Because my mother is John's grandmother, but his grandfather isn't my father."

"You're…."

"Illegitimate. A bastard. My mother was less than faithful to John's grandfather. When she found out she was pregnant with me, she left town for a while and had me. She left me with her cousin, who raised me."

Kurt stared directly into Jack's eyes, a smile slowly broadening on his face. "The only truth you just told me is that you are a bastard. You're a bastard for making up a story like that about John's grandmother."

"It's true!"

"It is, huh?" Kurt reached forward and grabbed the paper bag from the coffee table. He reached in and pulled out two glasses, still covered with a whitish-gray powder.

"Then maybe you can explain why your fingerprints and John's are the same."

John spoke, "*That's* what you were doing earlier with the toast and the tux thing. You sneaked them out."

Grinning, Kurt said, "Yep. Took 'em to Wally after I left here. He said they are a dead match."

As both men were stunned into silence, Kurt said, "So, is one of you going to tell me what's really going on here?"

Jack and John looked at each other and, after a moment, reached a silent agreement. "I'm from thirty years from now," Jack explained, in a matter-of-fact tone.

John wasn't sure what reaction he expected from his longtime friend; whatever it was, it wasn't what he got.

"I knew it!"

"You *knew* it?"

"Not exactly thirty years, but I knew he came from the future." Kurt's eyes sparkled with excitement.

Still stunned, John said, "You just knew it? You saw a guy who looked and sounded like me, but was older, and just came to the conclusion that he must be a time traveler?"

"Yeah!" Kurt declared, a little defiantly. "So?"

"It *is* a bit of a leap."

"Not really," Kurt rejoined excitedly. "I mean, come on, think about it. A guy who looks just like you, sounds just like you…you know all that already…anyway, he shows up on the eve of your wedding to that witch and talks to you, and you call off the wedding. And don't forget, pal, I've known you since third grade. I know how you think. I know what you look at and what you ignore. I know how you hold your fork. Your dorky laugh. All that stuff…it's in *him*, too," he said, gesturing toward Jack. "I've seen it. I've heard it. It's all there and more. Between that and the lame uncle story…I didn't ask your parents, by the way. That was a bluff."

John started to react but was cut off by Kurt. "What other explanation could there be?"

Kurt paused, his eyes squeezing shut and his face distorting in a grimace of pain.

Concerned, John asked, "Kurt, what is it? What's wrong?"

Kurt did not answer for a minute as he struggled to regain his composure. "It's nothing." He attempted to grin and failed. "I think I had way too many vodka tonics last night."

Kurt took another deep breath and found the thread of the conversation. "I was bummed that you didn't tell me and then I figured out that it had to be one of those time paradox things, or the Butterfly Effect or something; otherwise, you would have."

John laughed. "Kurt, you're amazing!"

"Like I always say, that's why they call me The Amazing Kurt." A wide smile filled his face. Rubbing his hands together, he questioned them, "So, what's next? Jack, are you going back soon?"

Shaking his head, Jack replied, "Kurt, I think we have a little something to tell you."

⚱

"You're kidding?" Gail said, with mixture of incredulity and amusement.

"No, I would not kid about this."

Rearing back, she laughed, overcome by the ironic turn of events.

"I take it congratulations are not in order," Gail's Ob/Gyn said, looking slightly concerned.

"Oh, you are wrong about that. Congratulations are definitely in order!"

"Well," the doctor said nervously, "congratulations. Now, we need to schedule you for some follow-up visits and tests."

As the doctor waited for a reply, she noticed that Gail's eyes were focused on something far away, something clearly not within the small exam room of the twenty-four hour clinic. Finally returning from her mental voyage, Gail once again refocused on the doctor and said, "Oh, of course! I'll schedule something with your receptionist on the way out." She pointed at the manila envelope resting on the counter and asked, "May I take that?"

"Yes. Those are yours."

Sliding off the edge of the examination table onto her feet, Gail snatched up the envelope, thanked the doctor for seeing her on a Sunday evening and left.

– IX –

"Can I go next?" Kurt asked, as they walked down the now darkened alley and approached the storage room.

Jack looked at Kurt as a mother would look at her child who was asking for a ninth cookie. "Don't make me regret bringing you along."

That did not dissuade Kurt who edged closer, now acting like a young boy anxious to get on a ride at the fair. John was standing a few feet behind them, in the center of the alley, glancing around. Jack fumbled in the dark with the key to the room, trying to fit it into the tumbler slot. Suddenly, he felt the hairs on his arms begin to dance, creating an eerie, tickling sensation.

"What the…?" John cried out from behind them.

Forgetting the padlock, Jack turned in time to see that the alley was suddenly illuminated by an unseen light source, the brightest area seemingly focused on John. Jack and Kurt gaped, frozen in place, as the light coalesced into a glowing column, and tiny specks, like fireflies, swirled around John.

Plaintively, John shouted, "What's happening?" His voice sounded strangely distant and tinged with a preternatural echo.

Whether paralyzed by an external force, or simply immobilized by the spectacle, neither Kurt nor Jack were able to move to his assistance. Both watched helplessly as John's hair and the loose folds of his clothes billowed and stretched upward, as if drawn by an inaudible suction.

The beam of light, already bright enough to force them to squint their eyes, intensified. Kurt gasped as he saw the entirety of John's body levitate above the paved earth. First spanning only an inch, the distance quickly grew to nearly a foot in elevation, as John was suspended above the ground, a helpless and panicked look on his face. His lips moved desperately in speech, yet no sound reached their ears.

Mustering all of his will power, Jack consciously fought against his own immobility. With a heroic effort, he attempted to intervene, but failed to budge even an inch toward John. His arms immobilized as if they had been dipped into concrete and his legs rooted to the ground, Jack watched helplessly as John was lifted ever higher and struggled to break free within the confines of the spectral shaft.

With John ascended nearly two feet, Jack saw him cease his writhing and go limp, either afflicted by some influence of the force or surrendering to the inevitable. A frenzied mixture of rage and helpless frustration enveloped Jack.

As the soles of John's now motionless shoes reached the height of three feet, Jack felt a sudden blast of cold water strike him, instantly soaking him from head to toe. Startled and bewildered, he saw, within the imprisoning column, brilliant blue-white arcs swarming around his younger self. The deluge of water came from across the alley and was leveled at the light, and at John.

At the torrent's point of impact with the column, the sparks, if that was what they were, intensified to the level of a compact lightning storm. John seemed to be encased within a plasma ball, his body the conductive diode in the center. The jumbled stream of disconnected and swirling flickers coalesced into a single, intense bolt emanating from John's chest and, twisting and squirming like an enraged snake, extended to the boundary of the light…meeting, head-on, the violent stream of water.

The battle between the elemental forces lasted but a few seconds as the physical effect of the gushing water prevailed, the rage of the confined electrical storm spent. The light around John winked out, and he was dropped roughly to the ground, falling limply into a heap.

Jack and Kurt simultaneously found themselves free of the unseen grip that had held them, and ran to John, lifting his head off the hard pavement.

"John!" Jack pleaded, praying for a response.

"Come on, John," joined Kurt, his voice laden with worry.

As Jack's finger probed John's neck for the carotid, seeking a pulse, a voice from the darkness across the alley said, "He'll be fine."

Jack looked in the direction of the voice and saw, in the dim light from the wall-mounted incandescent above the storage room door, the same man they had seen earlier today in the alley, still wearing the Harley-Davidson t-shirt and the denim jacket. The stranger – also still wearing the identical, enigmatic half-smile as before – removed a steel wrench from the top of the still dripping fire hydrant and approached them. "Give him about twenty minutes and he'll be okay."

"Who are you?" Kurt asked, confounded by the cascade of events.

"You can call me Aloysius," the stranger answered, extending his hand.

Jack, still holding John's head up, did not reach out. Kurt, crouched on the pavement beside his friend, did, and they shook a greeting.

Finally finding his voice, Jack uttered, "What just happened?"

Aloysius tucked his hands into his jacket pockets and craned his face upward. "They wanted to stop you."

"They? Stop us? Who? From doing what?" The questions tumbled out of Jack's mouth.

Still gazing skyward, Aloysius answered in a soft voice, "The Anunnaki."

"The what?"

"The Anunnaki. They come from the twelfth planet in this system…Nibiru."

"*Twelfth* planet!" Kurt barked. "There aren't twelve planets. Only nine, eight if you don't count Pluto."

Aloysius looked down at Kurt and, in a voice reserved for small children and the terminally dense, stated, "That's just what you've been told."

Turning his eyes toward the dark sky again, he then remarked, "I best be going now," and stepped away.

"Hold on a second!" Nearly dropping John's head to the hard asphalt, Jack leapt up. "You need to explain. Stop us from doing what?"

Aloysius, several feet away and already merging into the surrounding darkness, turned back to face Jack. "Why would you ask me that?"

"Because I need to know."

With the now familiar half-grin barely discernible on his face, Aloysius said, "If you don't know what you're doing, I can't help you."

With that, he once again turned and quickly disappeared into the shadows.

☒

The three of them were back at John's apartment, having returned to towel off and change clothes. As Jack emerged, wearing a pair of John's blue jeans and a white, long-sleeved cotton shirt, he saw John, still dazed, sitting at the dining table. Kurt hovered over him, holding a bottle of alcohol and dabbing at the top of John's head with a cotton ball.

"What's wrong?"

Kurt, not noticing that Jack had come out of the bedroom, was startled and involuntarily jerked, dropping the cotton ball and spilling alcohol onto the table.

"Dude! Don't do that."

"What do you want me to do? Whistle?"

"That would be good."

"What's wrong?"

"My head got bashed," John answered. "I guess, when I hit the alley."

Curious, Jack walked over to Kurt, who was doing his best to hold John's hair away from the wound on the top of his head.

In a portentous voice, Jack said, "Oh, my God."

"What?" John asked, concerned. "Is it that bad?"

"No," answered Jack in a low monotone. "That's not it."

"What's the matter then?"

Instead of responding, Jack walked over to the seated John and squatted in front of him. Reaching up, his fingers combed away the hair on the crown of his own head, revealing an old scar.

Kurt was the first to react, "I don't...holy God! It's in the same place."

John silently stared at the top of his older head, grappling with the implications of what he saw.

When he finally spoke, his voice was subdued and touched with worry. "How did you think you got that?"

Jack stood and took the chair next to John.

"I didn't. I just found it a few minutes ago when I was drying my hair. I never knew it was there."

"I don't understand, guys," said Kurt. "That scar looks like it's been there a long time."

Jack explained to their friend, "The way it works...at least the way we thought it worked...was that the time traveler would be immune to the changes that he causes in his own past. That's why, even though I came back to *now* and convinced John to cancel the wedding, *I* still have all of the memories of the past thirty years with Gail.

"The people I left behind when I tripped back from 2040, now have a new set of memories and life circumstances, at least the ones who were affected by what I've done. Their pasts are going to be what happens for the next thirty years, not what I remember happening. What that means is that the *me* who came back here didn't have that head injury in his...my...past."

Understanding showing on his face, Kurt concluded, "So, somewhere out there," he waved his hand in the vague direction of the sky, "there's a *me* who lived through thirty years of my best friend being married to that witch and there is also another *me* who already exists in another *out there*. And that *me* already has the memories of the next thirty years as they are going to be?"

Listening to Kurt's question, John watched Jack's eyes once again cloud over as Kurt talked about having a thirty-year future. To fill the silence before it became awkward, John spoke up, "I really didn't explain this part of it to you before, Kurt, but I think I have a different way of looking at it than Cal."

"Who is Cal?" Kurt asked.

John realized that they had not previously told Kurt that part of the story. "Callen Mitchell is the person who invents the time machine."

"Man! You didn't tell me his name earlier."

"So?"

Shaking his head in wonderment, Kurt exclaimed, "This *is* a small world!"

"What do you mean?"

"Cal Mitchell. I know him."

"You do?" John blurted out, surprised.

Before Kurt could answer, Jack stated, "Yes. Cal knew Kurt. They had some classes together."

Putting together the pieces, Kurt asked, "So, Cal was the guy who died?"

John and Jack both nodded.

"You guys are a hazard!"

"No shit, Sherlock. To get back to what I was saying, Cal thought that he was actually sending Jack back in time. That time was this continuum – like a line."

"Or an arrow?"

"Yes. Maybe an arrow. Anyway, he thought he could pluck himself... or, in this case, pluck Jack up off the line and insert him in another time back on the line."

"Isn't that what happens?"

"I'm not so sure. I think it's more like a cut-and-paste, or rather a copy-and-paste."

John went on to explain his theory of how it worked, describing the conflict of the two travelers and the other oddities of the mechanism that prompted his conclusion.

When he finished, Kurt asked, "So what's the problem with the scar?"

"Think about it, Kurt. If Cal's machine copied everything from 2010 through 2040 and pasted it on the end of the line, with Jack being the cursor, then how could Jack have arrived here and now with a scar that came from this…," John pointed at the top of his head, "which just happened tonight?"

"That's right. If it worked *that* way, Jack's memories should also be changed as soon as each of his actions triggered the reaction."

Kurt turned to face Jack. "You said you still remember being married to Gail."

Recovering from his earlier maudlin episode, Jack uttered, "Every gruesome moment."

"See!" John interjected. "That's my point. How can his actions, which caused the marriage to never happen, not result in a change in his memories, but this gash on my head from tonight leaves a scar on his head? It just doesn't make sense!"

"Unless…," Kurt said ominously, "it did happen."

"Unless what happened?"

"Unless you still do marry her."

John's retort was immediate, "No way! That is not going to happen."

"No, listen," Kurt continued, "maybe it has to happen. Maybe the way this whole time thing works is such that…I don't know…there is an inertia to events. Maybe the marriage, and all of the millions, maybe even billions, of little interconnected actions and reactions that sprang from it, are so *burned in* to the timeline that they can't be changed."

"That," said Jack glumly, "is a horrible thought."

"It might make sense, though," John considered. "Remember, you went back and tried to save Cal, but instead of saving him, you actually performed the prerequisite to his accident."

"I know what you're saying, but Cal went back and changed things. He went back and saved his assistant from being injured, remember?"

"Maybe Kurt's right. Maybe it is an inertia of some sort. You park your car on a slope and get out, forgetting to set the brake. If you notice it starting to roll right away, it's easy to stop. If you don't notice it immediately and it picks up some speed, there is no way you can do it."

"Like a snowball rolling down a hill," offered Kurt.

"Exactly! Could be that time works the same way. Sure, Cal went back and prevented an injury, but that injury had happened only a few days before – in the immediate past. The car had just barely started to roll down the slope. The snowball needs time to roll for a while before it will accumulate much snow. The countless, minute reactions in the environment, from the ripple effect of his assistant's injury, had not yet gained any momentum. The snowball was still tiny.

"You said yourself that the nature of this trip was different…that Cal was worried because it was bigger in scope. Going back thirty years and talking me out of marrying Gail is…hell, it's not a car rolling down a slope anymore, it's an out-of-control freight train loaded with ore and screaming down a mountain. The snowball *has* had the time to accumulate so much that it's the size of a building. It isn't a Butterfly Effect, it's a…."

"*Godzilla Effect*," Kurt blurted.

"Exactly. The resistance to change…the inertia…may be so great that we can't divert it from the path."

"But I killed Cal," Jack objected. "He was a part of that thirty-year momentum. If what you are saying is the case, it seems like my attempt to stop him from dying would have worked…*should* have been destined to work…not the other way around."

Jack's rebuttal gave John pause. "That's true."

All three of them fell into a thoughtful silence, eventually broken by John. "I don't know. Every time we think we've put together the pieces in a way that makes sense, we get another curve ball."

Kurt got up from the table and wandered over to the desk a few feet away. As he turned on the desktop computer, which filled the small workspace, he said, "What about that guy in the alley?"

"Aloysius?" asked Jack.

"That was his name, right, Aloysius. Who is he? What was he doing there?"

"And what did he mean when he said *they* wanted to stop us?" added John.

"*That's* what your curious about?" Kurt asked, incredulous. "What about all that 'Abberknocky' and 'Neebubu' stuff?"

"The Anunnaki," Jack corrected. "They are supposedly from the planet Nibiru."

"You've heard of this garbage?" Kurt's eyebrows were raised in astonishment.

"I've *heard* of it. I'm not saying I buy it. There are lots of books about it. From what I recall, the Anunnaki came to Earth from Nibiru 450,000 years ago and colonized it. I think we are all supposed to be their descendants."

The computer had completed its boot-up sequence and Kurt clicked on Yahoo!

"Why do you use Yahoo?" John asked. "Why not Google?"

"Google is CIA," Kurt responded knowingly. "They track all your searches. Keep a file on you."

John glanced over at Jack, who was grinning and shaking his head.

Kurt typed the key words *Aloysius*, fumbling several times with the spelling of the name, and *UFO* and clicked on the search button. A moment later, the screen filled with hits, and his eyes quickly scanned the summaries.

"Look at this."

John and Jack moved behind Kurt, looking over his shoulders.

"There's an Aloysius Greyson who's written a bunch of books. Real fringe books about UFOs." Kurt paused to read more, then continued, "He says that he's been invited, not abducted, onto several spaceships. He's been given tours. Visited their home planets."

Kurt swiveled in his chair and said, "This guy's nuts!"

Reaching past Kurt, John pointed at a blurb approximately halfway down the list, "Click on this one."

Kurt moved the mouse to where John was pointing and a full article appeared. The heading read, "Greyson Member of Army Blue Brigade."

Beneath the headline, the story chronicled the life of a young Aloysius Greyson who had been assigned to a unit whose mission was to investigate UFO sightings for the government.

"Check this out!" exclaimed Kurt. "This Greyson character was involved with the Roswell investigation. That proves it. The guy in the alley was nowhere near old enough to have been in Roswell in 1947."

"True," said Jack unconvinced. "Click on 'Images.' Let's see if the Internet has any pictures of this guy."

Kurt tried it.

"Nope. Not one."

"I guess that would have been too easy."

They spent the following thirty minutes clicking on the various articles about Greyson, interspersed with the websites promoting his books, and several blogs dedicated to discussing the minutia of alien visitors and their crafts.

Having exhausted the majority of the most relevant hits, they moved from their gathering around the computer to the living room.

"Well, what do we do now?" Kurt asked.

"Go back to the machine," John replied without hesitation. "I don't see any reason to change our plans."

"What if Aloysius was right?" Jack asked. "What if whoever or whatever was in the alley was trying to stop us...you...from going back in time?"

"We don't know that. Heck, we don't know anything. That could have been random."

"Right," Jack said sarcastically. "You just *happen* to almost be the victim of a random, alien abduction just as you were about to climb into your time machine for a little joy ride."

"Good God," John groaned, obviously flustered. "In the last twenty-four hours, my life has turned into a front-page story from *The Globe*."

Chortling, Kurt said, "It's kinda cool, isn't it?"

"No!" John barked.

Under his breath, Kurt muttered, "I think it is."

John, suddenly losing his temper, slammed his fist on the coffee table and shouted, "DAMMIT! WE HAVE TO DO SOMETHING!"

Jack and Kurt, surprised by the sudden outburst, stared at him speechlessly.

"Things have gotten way too screwed up. We need to try to fix them. We can't just leave it all alone and hope it works out!"

Trying to clear from his mind the most recent events of the evening, Jack patiently turned over all of the available facts, methodically sifting through them until coming to his own conclusion. "You're right. I wasn't one hundred percent sold on the idea of you going back, but I don't see what choice we have."

Visibly relaxing, John smiled. "Let's go."

Jack looked at his watch and said, "Before you go, there's one thing I need to do."

- X -

The downtown area was quiet and desolate. Listening to the echo of their footsteps on the sidewalk, John, Jack and Kurt made their way to the old courthouse, seeing, as they rounded a corner, its tiled dome jutting into the moonlit sky.

"Why here?" John asked.

"Think about it," Jack replied, as they crossed Church Avenue and entered the grassy plaza. "When you're going to make a trip back, you are selecting not only a time, but a specific place. A *very* specific, physical location. You might think you're going back to a vacant lot; still, if you don't do your research, you could select a spot that you thought was clear but wasn't at that time. Maybe the vacant lot actually had a building on it in the past. You could materialize inside a solid wall."

"That would be bad," Kurt said gravely.

Grinning in the darkness, Jack shook his head. "Yes, it would. So, we picked the center plaza at the courthouse. We knew it was built decades before our destination time. We knew the fountain and grassy area was here."

"What about something transient?" John asked. "Maybe on the day you come back, they are doing some routine maintenance and a scaffold is set up right where you are going to pop in. Or some bum decides to sleep off his bottle of 'Mad Dog' on the nice grass that night?"

"Always a danger. But Cal has always followed a specific procedure – at least I can tell you how it relates to my trip. He sends the machine back empty first. The sphere is programmed to operate autonomously: it arrives; a porthole opens; an articulated arm comes out with sensors and an infrared camera; it does a 360 degree survey; the arm retracts; the door closes; and the sphere returns to us. We check the pictures to make sure that nothing is in the way and that no one happens to be there who would be injured, or who might see me suddenly appear.

"Then, Cal resets the controller to the exact same moment, I climb in and make the trip."

"What if…?" Kurt began, the eeriness of their purpose and locale caused him to lower his voice to a near whisper. "What if during that first scouting trip, the sphere materializes right where that bum is sleeping? Wouldn't that pretty well ruin his night?"

"You could say that. It would kill him."

Kurt's eyes widened.

"You have to remember, we are doing all of this from the future. If the machine comes back to our time, and it has evidence of something like that happening…."

"Like a leg sticking out the side of the machine?"

Jack ignored Kurt's comment and continued, "We can just rewind a few minutes back and stop ourselves from making that trip."

They reached the center fountain area and stopped.

"So, explain to me again why we are here," John said. "We already know that Cal's dead. We haven't fixed that yet. Since he's dead, the machine will never be built and he definitely isn't in the future right now, sending it back for the scheduled pickup."

"You're probably right. This is more than likely a waste of time. However, the way things are going, I'm just not sure," Jack replied. "Besides, what do we have to lose?"

Jack sat on the concrete bench in the center of the plaza as John and Kurt wandered, burning off nervous energy. His eyes swept the area, taking in the details. Although the moon was full, the plaza was in shadow, the light blocked by the courthouse dome. Jack's thoughts drifted back to a field trip to this very spot when he was in fourth grade at St. Joseph's.

"Remember Sister Mary George?"

Jack, disturbed from his reminiscence, saw that John had returned to sit beside him.

"I was just thinking about her."

Shifting uncomfortably on the hard surface, John said, "I used to love her voice."

Jack nodded in the darkness, his mind returning to the numerous choir practices when the sister would lead the children in song. No doubt accented by the seemingly mystical acoustics of the church where they practiced, Sister Mary George's beautiful voice would fill the air, as she would teach new songs to them by singing *a capella*. Jack would lean back in his pew and close his eyes, letting the worshipful lyrics and melodies wash over him.

"What a vibrato she had. I used to think that if water rippling down a stream had a voice, it would be hers."

"I know," John agreed.

"Of course you do," rejoined Jack, capturing both amusement and irony in his words.

Both of them watched Kurt as he strolled around the perimeter, appearing and disappearing as he traversed the walkway behind the stucco columns, his blond hair still luminescent in the penumbra of the archways. Softly, John asked, "What happens to him?"

After a pause, Jack seemed to come to a conclusion. In a barely audible voice, he started to speak. "He...." Before he could continue, Jack was interrupted by a high-pitched, repeating tone. Looking down at the glowing face of his watch, he pressed a button on the side, declared, "It's time," and rose from the bench.

Noticing that they had stirred, Kurt ended his nocturnal tour and crossed the grass to join them. The area remained deserted as they lined up in anticipation. John persisted, "I still think this is a waste of...." His words were cut off as, without any prelude or dramatic pyrotechnics, a silver sphere suddenly stood before them, not ten feet away.

"It came!" The surprised exclamation burst from John in a voice much louder than he intended.

Kurt, who had not yet seen the sphere in the storage locker, exclaimed, "Cool! It's like it was already there, and I just hadn't noticed it before."

Jack started to approach the vehicle as John asked, "I don't understand, how could it be here...with everything that's happened?"

Nearing the machine's side, Jack turned back and said, "I don't think it went, at the risk of sounding like Michael J. Fox, back to the future after it dropped me off. Remember, it moves through time on a preprogrammed route. To me, a day has passed since I got here. Actually, I've spent a day here, now, and a day here...uh...the day before. So to me, it's been two days since I've seen it. I think what happened is that it dropped me off and then, instead of going back to 2040, it went straight to the pickup time, now."

"So it doesn't matter to the machine that Cal is dead and that it hasn't been invented or built?"

"No," Jack answered John. "It is as immune to the effects of our actions as the traveler is supposed to be."

"That's why you wanted to come tonight, isn't it?"

"Yes. I suspected that it would show up."

"Dudes! This is all real cool and everything, but what do we do now? We can't just leave this here," Kurt said, staring at the gleaming ball resting on the grass. "Someone might notice it."

Jack acknowledged the obvious. "I know."

As they spoke, a portal on the top of the sphere opened, not visible to the three from their perspective. They all heard a quiet hum emanating for the top of the machine and took a few steps back to see what was happening.

Realization striking Jack, he shouted, "You two need to hide. NOW!"

Mobilizing immediately, John grabbed Kurt by the arm and together they dashed for the cover of one of the columns Kurt had examined earlier.

Jack's head snapped back and forth as he gauged the time needed for the two to reach the column and the time it would take for the camera array to fully deploy. He calculated that, with luck, they would make it in time. Unfortunately, luck was not to be with them tonight; he saw that out of the possible 360 degrees of orientation, the emerging cameras were aligned very nearly dead center on John and Kurt's route.

Jack lunged forward, desperately hoping the proximity sensors in the sphere would detect his presence and override the input from the cameras. But it was not to be. The reddish-orange outline did not appear on the silver surface. The cameras, fully deployed, swiftly retracted, their portal closing.

Before Jack could cover the final two feet of distance between himself and his transport, the orb vanished. Unable to halt his momentum, Jack fell forward onto the now vacated grass.

Slamming his fists into the ground he shouted, "Dammit! Dammit!"

Kurt and John, hearing Jack's outburst, emerged from behind the column and ran to him.

Rolling over onto his back, Jack lamented, "Why did I ever do this? It has been nothing but a total fiasco."

He sat up, pulled his legs to his chest and rested his face on his knees, completing a picture of dejection and despair.

John dropped down to the grass next to his *other* and put his arm on Jack's shoulder. "It'll work out," John consoled him.

Speaking into the space between his knees, Jack continued to berate himself. "How? It is all so tangled up...so messed up. And I wasn't even smart enough to realize that I needed to have you two out of sight when the machine checked the area. I knew that! And I forgot. If I can't even get that straight, how am I going to fix the rest of it?"

"We all missed it. You told us... explained it. We should have known. Don't blame yourself."

Lifting his head, he turned to face John and said, "Who in the hell am I supposed to blame? It was my own stupidity thirty years ago that got me into the marriage. It was my own inability to figure it out... to get out of it on my own before it got so out of control."

Jack stopped to take a ragged breath before plunging on. "Because of *me* every possession I've ever cared about was burned in a fire. Because of *me* Mom and Dad died. Because of *me* two small, wonderful children died. *I* was the one who couldn't handle it all and tried to kill himself. *I* was the one who sucked my best friend into my problems. And now, because all he did was care about *me* and try to help *me*, because *I* was too stupid to fix my own problems, he is dead! And who knows what other damage to the whole world *I've* caused because of that!"

John had no idea what to say. Before he could think of anything that might comfort Jack, Kurt said, "Boy, you are right, man. You have *really* screwed the pooch! What are you going to do for an encore, blow up the galaxy?"

John stared up at Kurt in astonishment. Before he could react and chastise his friend for his cruelty, he saw Jack's shoulders begin to quake. Assuming that his alter ego had completely surrendered to a sobbing hysteria, he was startled to hear laughter burst from Jack, joined instantly by Kurt. John, too, began to laugh, and all three released their pent-up tensions with raucous hoots and snorts that echoed back at them from the stucco walls of the courtyard.

In the midst of their semi-delirium, Kurt had collapsed to the ground. Wiping tears from his face, he struggled to catch his breath before asking, "So where did it go?"

After three aborted attempts to find his voice, Jack was finally able to utter, "Back, I think. Back to 2040. Back to Cal... or where Cal was supposed to be."

The joints of his jaw still sore, John said, "We may have lost the limo, but we've still got the scooter."

Jack looked at him and smiled. "That's true."

Feeling the cool dampness from the turf seeping into the seat of his jeans, John pulled out a cigarette, offering the pack to Jack who slid one out. Before he could put them away, Kurt said, "Now's as good a time as any to start that bad habit. Let me have one of those, too."

Surprised, John handed the cigarettes to Kurt, and they all shared the lighter.

Just the process of lighting his cigarette triggered racking coughs from Kurt. "How…," he said between coughs, "can you guys stand these things?"

"I can't," answered Jack. "I'm just addicted, that's all."

Chuckling, John added, "They make the voices go away."

"What?" asked Kurt.

"The voices. I read that's the reason schizophrenics chain-smoke. When they have the nicotine in them, the voices in their heads get quiet."

Concerned, Kurt examined John. "You hear voices?"

Lifting his eyebrows dramatically, John said, "Only when they're telling me what I should do to you."

Not completely certain he wasn't being teased, Kurt responded, "Cool!"

Snickering at his friend, John addressed Jack, "It's not that far from here to the storage room. Maybe the night isn't a total waste."

Jack, sitting upright with his arms resting on his knees, replied, "Sure. Let's do it. Maybe we can make it without any," he paused and looked up at the sky, "interference."

They finished their smokes and rose to leave when John's cell phone rang.

"Who would be calling me at this time of night?" He pulled out the phone and stared at the illuminated screen, not recognizing the number.

"Hello?"

A vaguely familiar, female voice said, "John! Thank God you're okay."

"Uh, yeah, I'm fine. I'm sorry, but who is this?"

"Oh! I'm sorry," her words tumbled out. "It's Kelly, your neighbor. You gave me your number a long time ago when you went out of town. I am so glad you're not home!"

A sudden chill ran down John's spine. He noticed that Jack and Kurt were staring at him with curiosity. "Is something wrong?"

"There's been a fire. It's your place. The fire department is…." She was still talking, but John was no longer focused on her words. The hand holding the phone to his ear suddenly dropped to his side as his entire arm went limp.

"What's the matter?" asked Jack, seeing John's expression in the moonlight.

"We…we need to get back to my place. There's been a fire."

⧗

As they approached the cluster of duplexes where John lived, they saw the night shattered by flashing lights from the fire trucks parked haphazardly on the street, like toys strewn about by a child who had tired of playing with them. The pulsing red lights and flickering strobes created surreal, dancing shadows on the surrounding homes.

Several of John's neighbors stood on the sidewalks in front of their houses, watching the practiced movements of the firefighters who were already in the mop-up phase of their process. Not wanting to get too close to his apartment, John parked the car a half block away, and he and Kurt got out, leaving Jack behind.

The acrid stench had not dissipated in the still night, and burned their nostrils as they neared the scene. John's neighbor Kelly saw him approaching and ran over. "John! I am so sorry. This is horrible."

John just nodded, unable to take his eyes from the sight of his home. The entire front was charred and blackened, the windows blown out. Part of the roof had collapsed and whitish-gray smoke was still billowing from the scene of destruction. Firefighters, clad in bright yellow pants and jackets and still wearing respirators, were stationed at several spots along the perimeter of the building, watching for flare-ups and applying short bursts of water from their hoses.

One of the TFD crew, seeing John and Kurt approach, broke off from the rest and walked over. It must have been obvious to the seasoned firefighter, from John's dazed demeanor and expression, that he was not just another gawker. The captain, as was printed in bold, black letters on the front of his waterproof jacket, pulled his respirator away from his mouth and asked, "Do you live here?"

"I do... did," John replied numbly.

Kurt noticed the captain's eyes as they, out of habit, glanced at John's shirt pocket. Noticing the pack of cigarettes, the captain said, "How long have you been out this evening?"

Still transfixed by the spectacle before him, John mumbled an answer the captain did not hear.

"I'm sorry, sir. I know you're upset. However, could you speak up?"

"Yes. I'm sorry. We've been gone most of the night, but we did come back here briefly... maybe a couple of hours ago... maybe a little less."

Turning to Kurt, the captain asked, "Do you live here, too?"

Shaking his head, Kurt answered, "No, sir. I'm his friend. We've been together all evening."

"Is that about right? Was it approximately two hours since you both left?" the captain questioned Kurt, seeking confirmation.

Kurt looked down at his watch. "Maybe a little less, between an hour and a half and two hours."

As they spoke, a uniformed officer from TPD arrived; the fire captain excused himself and stepped several feet away to confer with him, leaving John and Kurt standing alone. A few minutes passed before the captain left the police officer and returned to his duties. The tall and slightly-built cop then approached them and said, "I am very sorry for your loss this evening, sir."

John just nodded and said nothing.

"Would you mind getting out some identification?" the officer requested gently.

They both pulled out their wallets and handed their driver's licenses to him.

Checking the name tag on his shirt, Kurt asked, "Is there a problem, Officer Burke? Does the fireman think it's arson or something?"

Burke tucked his flashlight under his arm so that it was aimed at the licenses held in his left hand. Instead of immediately answering Kurt, he read the information and transcribed it onto his notepad. Finishing, he handed back their licenses and said, "We don't know yet. It's still too hot for the investigator to go in. I understand that you've been out all evening and night, except for a brief return one to two hours ago. Is that correct?"

John started to speak when Kurt said, "Not one or two hours ago. We've been gone at least an hour and a half, probably more."

Burke made a note and asked, "If you don't mind my asking, why did you return at that time?"

Kurt, not wanting to reply, remained silent. Realizing that it was probably best for him to field the question, John said, "We had to come back for a change of clothes."

Burke raised his eyebrows quizzically. "Change of clothes?"

"Yes, sir. We had been downtown earlier, hitting a couple of the clubs on Congress and cut through an alley. Some kids, playing a prank, turned on a fire hydrant as we walked by. We got pretty soaked."

Burke made more notes in his pad. "Could you have left any lit cigarettes when you went back out? Or perhaps dumped an ashtray just before you left?"

"No," John answered firmly. "I don't smoke inside the apartment. Never have. And I don't let anyone else, either."

More notes were entered on the pad and Burke, filling a page, flipped to a blank one. "Anything else you can think of? Did you leave on any appliances? You said you came home to change out of wet clothes. Did you put them in the dryer and leave it running?"

"I don't have a dryer. I use a laundromat. And no, I can't think of anything else we left on. Do they know where in the apartment the fire started?"

Burke stopped writing and looked at John. "Like I said, they haven't been able to go in yet." Glancing over his shoulder, he continued, "It looks like they should be able to, pretty soon. The captain said that, from the outside, it looked like the fire might have started in one of the bedrooms."

John's face tightened into an angry mask. To himself, he said, "The trains."

"Pardon me?"

Shaking his head in an attempt to clear his thoughts, John said, "I have a model train layout in one of the bedrooms. It's kind of expensive."

Following the new lead, Burke asked, "Could you have left the trains on?"

John shook his head definitively. "No. We played with them this afternoon, or maybe this morning, I'm not sure, but that was it. And I'm sure the main power strip was off when we quit."

"Yeah," added Kurt, "I remember that you turned it off."

Allowing skepticism to creep into his voice, Burke said, "That's sort of a minor detail for you both to be so sure."

"You haven't seen John's layout," Kurt replied, a touch of aggressiveness in his voice. "When the power strip is turned on, about two hundred lights come on. Turning it on and off is pretty damn obvious."

Burke stared at them both for a moment before saying, "There's nothing else I need right now. Are you two going to stick around here for a while?"

John shrugged his shoulders. "Yes. I really don't have anywhere else to go and I want to know what happened."

"Okay," Burke said. "I would appreciate it if you could stay back out of the way for a while, though."

"No problem." John turned back to the street and Kurt followed as they made their way back to the car. Jack was leaning against the fender, waiting.

As Kurt and John told him what had happened, a blend of frustration and fury distorted his face, but he kept his comments to himself until they were done.

"So, it happened anyway."

"It did," John answered. "Years earlier and, thank God, no children in the fire…but, yes, it happened."

Kurt, keeping up with their line of thought, said, "It's like these things *have* to happen, isn't it?"

Jack acknowledged the statement with an almost imperceptible incline of his head.

"So, we're screwed, aren't we?"

"It certainly looks that way," Jack answered Kurt.

Leaving Jack with the car, John and Kurt returned to the street in front of the burned apartment and sat on the curb to wait. They watched the choreographed routine of the firefighters as they doused the remaining hot spots. John recognized the captain, who had talked to them earlier, as he cautiously entered the apartment, flanked by two of his men with hoses at the ready.

Another forty-five minutes passed with an agonizing slowness. John could feel the adrenaline, which had so energized him earlier, being gradually metabolized. His eyelids began to droop as the frenetic events of the past several hours caught up with him.

Finally, the captain came out of the apartment, carrying a charred object which looked unrecognizable. As the captain walked toward them, he was joined by Officer Burke. John watched as they spoke, unable to hear them in the distance. Burke examined the object briefly, and then they approached the curb where John and Kurt sat.

Standing, John said, "What did you find?" He looked down at the blackened lump in the captain's hand.

"Well," he answered, "you can never really tell for sure with these things. It was obvious, though, that the fire started in the second bedroom where you kept your train layout. It appears to have been caused by an electrical short."

The captain held up the badly burned and distorted object and said, "I believe that this was your power supply. It was at the point of origin of the blaze."

John had no idea what to say.

Burke asked, "Are you both sure that this equipment was off when you left?"

Kurt answered firmly, "Yes. Absolutely sure. I was standing in the doorway of the room watching when John and...when John turned it off. I watched the lights go off."

The officer noticed the pause. "Was there someone else present?"

Kurt, realizing that he had put his foot in his mouth, did not answer. John spoke up. "Yes. There was another guy with us."

"Another guy?" Burke said suspiciously. "You didn't mention that earlier. What is his name?" He pulled the notepad out of his pocket.

"I don't know," John answered, instantly realizing how stupid he sounded. Before Burke could ask, he continued, "I mean, we didn't get his name, his whole name. All I know is 'Jack.' I met him earlier today and mentioned my train layout. He said he was into trains and wanted to see it, so I brought him over. That's it. He left with us, and I haven't seen him since."

"Hey," Kurt said, trying to help dig John out the hole he had put his friend into, "maybe he...this Jack guy...came back and did this!"

John shot Kurt a nasty look.

Rising to the bait, Burke asked, "Do you have any reason to think the Jack person started this fire?"

"No!" John replied quickly. "He was just a guy, someone who liked model trains."

Still trying to be helpful, Kurt added, "I'm not saying he started it. I'm saying maybe he came back and played with them some more. Maybe he left them turned on."

Trying to shut his friend up, John turned and glared at Kurt. "I don't see how he could do that, *Kurt*! We just met the guy. He didn't have a key. I really don't think he would come back here and break in, just to play with the trains."

Finally getting the message, Kurt recanted, "Yeah, you're right. That's dumb."

Burke, watching the exchange, said to the captain, "Any other explanations?"

The fire captain shrugged his shoulders. "Sure. Power strips fail. Sometimes the little rocker switch on the strip may appear to be all of the way off. The strip goes dead. The lights go off. Later, because the switch wasn't fully seated in the 'off' position, it slips back to 'on' all by itself."

John's eyes alternated between the faces of Burke and the captain, hoping this would wrap things up. Burke closed his notepad and said, "If it's good enough for you, it's good enough for me."

Turning to John, he asked, "If we need anything else, where will we be able to reach you?"

John gave the officer his cell number, as well as the phone number to his parents' house, and told him that he wasn't sure yet where he'd be staying.

Burke thanked them, and they walked away to rejoin Jack down the block.

- XI -

Exhausted, they went to Kurt's. His house, an over-priced rental tucked in the middle of the old Sam Hughes neighborhood, was adjacent to the University of Arizona. Its proximity to the campus ostensibly justified the high rent, despite the ongoing economic slump.

None of them said a word as Kurt trudged back to his bedroom, leaving John and Jack to find tolerable sleeping positions on the living room furniture.

Within minutes they were all unconscious, their minds quickly filled with a surreal kaleidoscope of images relating, in bizarre and dreamlike ways, to the events of the past several hours.

John groaned as he was awakened by a determined, narrow shaft of sunlight striking his eyelids, the light opportunistically finding its way through the branches of the tree outside and the acerate gap between the heavy curtains and the window frame.

He staggered into the kitchen, a small, galley-style utilitarian room which had been "modernized" in the 1950s. The signature motif – avocado green – was the hideous color of the refrigerator, stove and cabinet doors. No space was initially planned for the invention of the dishwasher, and none was created in the course of the remodel.

The mundane tasks of loading the paper filter with coffee, plugging in the machine and dumping a beaker full of water into the reservoir were daunting, as John fought to attain a reasonable level of functionality. The sizzling and popping sounds created by the coffee maker, a result of the cold water coming in contact with the superheated element, seemed unreasonably loud to his ears.

Gripping the edge of the fungus-colored counter for support, he made his way to the adjacent chrome and Formica dining table and dropped heavily onto the bright red, stuffed cushion of the retro vinyl and chrome chair.

The sounds of Jack's snoring from the adjacent room mingled with the rumble of the confined mini-explosions occurring at the bottom of the coffee maker, as John reexamined the details of the past day and a half. He surfaced from his reverie and noticed that there was now silence from the direction of the coffee maker. Opening the cabinet door, John grabbed the first mug he saw, noticing while he filled it that it was one of Kurt's countless Spider-Man artifacts.

He added sugar and opened the refrigerator, hoping to find half-and-half, but settling for two-percent. The brew doctored as well as possible with the available ingredients, he grabbed it and returned to the dining chair, nearly colliding with Jack who was rounding the corner into the kitchen.

Jack grunted a sound that, John supposed, approximated a greeting, and then clumsily sidled around him to fix his own cup. Rummaging, Jack asked, "Any Sweet-n-Low, Splenda, Equal?"

"Nope," John replied, "just sugar."

Jack spooned two scoops into his cup and muttered, "Forgot. Sugar was fine when I was twenty."

As Jack opened the refrigerator, John warned him, "No half-and-half, only two-percent."

"Great!" Jack grunted.

Grinning at the *who he was to become*, John watched as Jack joined him at the dinette, sloshing coffee onto the resilient surface of the table.

"We're great in the morning, aren't we?"

Clutching Kurt's Pink Floyd *Dark Side of the Moon* mug with both hands, Jack stared down into the swirling clouds of his coffee and said, "Yeah. No. Not really. Could be worse."

"Do I just pick an answer?"

Jack managed a weak chuckle.

They sipped in silence, grateful that neither was a "slurper." As the first energizing effects of the caffeine kicked in, John asked, "What's our plan for today?"

Jack took a long drink from his mug. "I guess we go ahead and make the trip, send you back to see Cal."

"For some reason, I thought we had to wait until nighttime."

"This isn't some grade-B, sci-fi movie. We can do it whenever we want. If the sphere is going to suddenly appear in a public place, late night is better just because there is a smaller chance anyone will be around to see it. But if we can figure out a good return spot for the daytime, it doesn't matter."

"I have an idea."

Both heads jerked in the direction of the kitchen entrance to see that Kurt had joined them.

Each said their *good morning* and waited while he rummaged in the cabinet.

"Hey! Where's my Spidey cup?"

John held up his mug and Kurt groaned, shaking his head.

"You can't just use a man's Spidey cup without his permission, you know."

Having awakened enough to permit only mild bemusement, both John and Jack chuckled at their friend.

"Anyway…like I said, I have an idea. Well, two, really. Idea number one," Kurt announced as he held up his index finger. "Let's go talk to the guy who rents out those storage rooms where the machine is now. We need to find out if any of the other storage rooms are empty and, more importantly…have *been* empty for a while. Then, we just pop back a couple of days, or whatever, into the other storage room. It's locked. It's empty. No one would see the arrival."

"Isn't there enough space in the room it's in, to just go back to a spot right next to it?" John asked.

"I already did that when I went back on Trip B. I don't think we should try to use it again in case you need to stay beyond my arrival time. Kurt's suggestion is not a bad idea, actually," Jack concluded. "We could even go back a week and rent one, like Cal did."

"That might be better," John added. "Because then we'd have a key."

Kurt and Jack agreed. Then Jack realized something and said, "There is one problem with that idea. Those storage rooms lock with a hasp and padlock, from the outside. If you materialize inside the room, how do you get out?"

Before John could answer, Kurt proudly stated, "I already thought of that." Grinning, he stood up, went to the kitchen cabinets and pulled open a drawer. He turned back around to face them, holding up a screwdriver.

"I haven't been inside yet, at least not all the way, but couldn't we just unscrew the hasp or the hinges from the inside?"

"That might work," John admitted.

"We'd have to check it out first," said Jack. "Kurt, you said you had two ideas. What's the other one?"

Grinning even more broadly, he suggested, "Instead of John going back, I do."

"Kurt!" Jack exclaimed. "I know you wanted to ride in the machine, but *come on*."

"No. Think about it. The reason your trip didn't work was because Cal didn't know you. How would you react if some stranger suddenly walked up to you and started telling you that he was your friend from the future and you needed to stay off your motorcycle for the night?"

Kurt paused to let them consider what he said.

"I know him. We're not friends or anything like that, but at least I'm in a couple of classes with the guy. We've talked a few times. I'm not some crazy stranger like John would be."

He examined their faces and saw that they were taking his argument seriously, so he plunged on, waving the screwdriver in the air for emphasis. "Besides, John, you don't even know what he looks like. You'd be going back and trying to find someone you've never met. As long as I go back there to a moment when the other *me* isn't present... that would be awkward... and I've already figured that out... I can walk right up to Cal and start talking to him without it being weird."

Jack concurred, "I think we've already established that my decision-making so far hasn't been the greatest in the world, but it makes sense to me."

"I'd have to agree," John said grudgingly, and added, "on both counts."

Jack shot John a look of contempt.

Kurt smiled at him, "You're just bummed because you wanted to try it, aren't you?"

Laughing, John conceded, "A little."

"Well, you can go back and rent the storage room."

Raising his hands, Jack stopped them. "Wait a minute! The machine isn't some sports car we all get to drive."

"Speaking of which," said John, "what does it run on? We're not going to run out of gas with all of these trips, are we?"

Jack shook his head. "No. We should be good for quite a while. It has a fuel cell in it. I think Cal said that it can do about a hundred trips."

"You *think*?" Kurt asked.

"No. I'm pretty sure."

"*Pretty sure?*"

"Come on. I might be off. Maybe he said a thousand. I don't remember exactly, but it was more than two or three. Lots more. I know that."

"Okay," Kurt gave up, not totally satisfied with Jack's answer.

"Okay then," John said, standing up, "let's go check out that storage room."

⧖

Kurt walked slowly around the perimeter of the silver sphere as Jack checked the inside of the door.

"This is so cool!" Kurt's voice was soft and reverent.

Jack determined that the hasp was fastened to the door with four, small carriage bolts. The smooth, rounded heads were positioned at the outside face of the hasp and covered to prevent tampering when the hasp was in the closed and locked position. The threaded ends, however, protruded through the inside face of the door and were secured with nuts and washers.

"Kurt," he said, "you can leave your screwdriver at home. All you're going to need is a small crescent wrench."

Kurt nodded. "Can I get in?"

Jack walked to the side of the transport and placed his hand flat on the silver skin inside the suddenly visible square. With a gentle hiss, the man-sized door lifted from the surface and pivoted, revealing the inside.

Kurt stared, dumbfounded. "Awesome!" He immediately climbed inside and dropped into the pilot chair, tightly gripped the arm rests and said, "Warp seven, Number One!"

Before Jack could comment, the storage room door opened and John entered, tossing a key to Jack. Catching it, Jack asked curiously, "I thought we were going to go back a few days to get this?"

"I didn't see any reason to waste the trip. When I was talking to the guy, I asked how business was and he told me that, other than the room we have now, he hasn't rented one of them in over four months. Hasn't even had any lookers for the past two weeks."

"Yeah, but what about if somebody, like the manager, just happened to be in that room recently. Depending on the timing, that could be a disaster."

John shook his head and motioned. "Come on. I'll show you."

He led Jack out into the alley and to the adjacent door. Jack unlocked the padlock and opened it, but before he could step in, John blocked the way with his arm.

"Check it out," was all John said as he leaned into the room and found the light switch.

"This one has a switch instead of the pull chain. Look, it's obvious that no one has been in here for quite a while."

John stepped aside to allow his *other* an unobstructed view of the eight-by-ten room from the threshold. With the overhead light on, Jack could see that there was a thick, even coating of dust on the floor, disturbed only by two, obviously recent footprints directly in front of him.

"Those footprints," John explained, "are from the manager when he turned on the light for me a couple of minutes ago. Other than that, you can tell this place has been left alone for a long time."

Jack seemed convinced.

They returned to find Kurt still seated in the cabin chair and punching the screen on the handheld controller.

"Stop that!" Jack barked.

"I didn't do anything," Kurt answered. "I'm just checking it out."

Stepping inside the sphere, Jack took the controller from him and put it back into the armrest console.

John, amused by his friend's antics, suggested, "Let's grab something to eat and plan this out."

The sphere secure, John slipped the padlock into the hasp and clicked it shut, double-checking it. Before they could reach his car, his cell phone chirped. Answering it, he said, "This is John."

"Mr. Augur, this is Officer Burke with the Tucson Police Department. We need to ask you a few more questions, if you don't mind."

Suddenly anxious and trying not to reveal his tension, John replied, "Sure. Where would you like to meet?"

"At your apartment. I'm here with the arson investigator right now. Could you come straight over?"

John saw that Jack and Kurt were looking at him quizzically as he answered, "Yes, sir. I can be there in about ten minutes. Is something wrong?"

"We can go over that when you get here, Mr. Augur."

"No problem. I'll be right there."

"I appreciate it."

John clicked off the phone and looked at the display to make sure the connection was broken, before saying, "That was the cop. He made a point of mentioning that there was an arson investigator with him. They want to talk to me."

A look of apprehension spread over Jack's face.

"Jack, why don't you and Kurt go ahead and eat? I'll drop you off and head over there by myself. I probably shouldn't show up again with Kurt and I definitely can't take you there."

They agreed, and John drove them to a local, family restaurant just east of downtown.

⧗

"Mr. Augur, do you have access to an older model fax machine?" The question was asked by the Tucson Fire Department arson investigator, Larry Jackson, whom Officer Burke had introduced upon John's arrival.

"What do you mean by 'an older model'?"

"One that uses thermal paper instead of bond paper."

"No. Not that I can think of. Why?"

Jackson lifted a large, clear Ziploc bag which appeared to be filled with gray dust and small, charred fragments. "We found a pile of this adjacent to and surrounding the transformer which we believe was the cause of the fire last night. From our preliminary analysis, we think it may be that type of paper."

Bewildered, John said, "I really don't understand. Why would a pile of burned paper near the transformer be... is that how the fire started? Something to do with this thermal paper?"

The investigator's expression was neutral. "It can be an effective method to deliberately start a fire."

"How?"

"Thermal-sensitive paper has a lower ignition temperature than regular paper. It also comes in a roll. A person who wants to commit arson, while making it appear to be an accidental electrical fire, can wrap several layers of the thermal paper around an electrical device that requires adequate heat dissipation, such as a large transformer. I'm sure you've noticed the metal fins on the surface of the transformers you had for the model trains."

John nodded, deciding to say nothing at this point.

"Those fins are called a *heat sink*. They are added to transformers to provide additional surface area so that the device can get rid of the heat it generates. If you take a roll of paper, wrap it tightly around the transformer, covering the sides that have the fins, and put on several layers – the heat can't escape and builds up, until it ignites the paper."

"So, you're saying someone started the fire?"

Jackson's eyes penetrated deeply into John's as he said, "Oh, there's no doubt, Mr. Augur, that this was arson. In addition to this pile of thermal-paper residue, we also found evidence that several hardbound books were piled up around the transformer. Since there was a bookcase in the living room, it's obvious that the books were placed in the train room to provide enough fuel for the fire to quickly heat up and spread."

"Why did you ask me if I had access to the paper? Am I a suspect?"

Jackson shook his head. "That's not my job. My job is to figure out whether it *was* arson and how it was done. The *who* is up to the police." As he made the last statement, he motioned toward Burke, who had been silently observing the conversation between them.

"At this point," Jackson said to Burke, "it's all yours. Thank you for your time, Mr. Augur."

Taking the plastic baggie with him, Jackson turned and walked back to the burned-out duplex. John turned to face the officer. "Now what? Is this where you arrest me?"

Burke looked down and shook his head. John thought he detected a slight smile cross his face before he answered, "Mr. Augur...."

"Please, call me John."

"Okay, John. There isn't going to be an arrest today."

"That's comforting," John said sarcastically. "But I'm still a suspect, right?"

"Everyone's a suspect at this point. You were here a couple of hours before the fire. Your friend Kurt was here. Either one of you could have dumped some books in the train room, wrapped a roll of fax paper around that transformer, turned it on and left."

"Or," John offered, "someone else could have come in after we left and done all of that."

"True, except there was only one way in and out of the duplex and that was through the front door. As you can see," Burke indicated, gesturing toward the building behind him, "the front door didn't get destroyed in the fire. When the firefighters arrived last night, the door was intact and locked. They entered through the blown-out windows and used their fire axes to create a clear access for their hoses. They never used the front door because they knew that we were going to want to check it out later.

"Whoever set the fire," Burke said, staring intently at John, "had a key."

John's mind whirled as the ramifications of what he'd just been told sank in. His avalanche of thought was interrupted by the officer.

"Who had a key to your home, Mr. Augur?"

Chewing on his lower lip, John struggled momentarily to regain his composure. "My parents," he answered. "My friend Kurt. You met him last night, or this morning. The landlord, of course. And…my fiancée, or I should say my ex-fiancée, Gail Schilling."

John watched Burke jot the names onto his notepad, writing down the phone numbers John provided. Flipping the pad closed, Burke continued, "You said 'ex-fiancée.' Do you have any reason to suspect Ms. Schilling might have done this?"

Wanting to blurt out that he had every reason in the world, considering she had done the exact same thing years into the future, John said instead, "No. Not really. I broke up with her yesterday, but I can't…." John paused, choosing his words carefully, "I can't believe she would do something like this."

He wondered if Burke was able to read the turmoil behind his eyes, hoping not.

"Yesterday, huh?"

"Yes, sir. We were supposed to get married yesterday. I called it off – at the last minute, really."

Shaking his head, Burke opined, "A lot of women, or men for that matter, wouldn't take that very well."

"No, sir."

"How did she handle it?"

John thought back to the emotional roller coaster of a conversation from the day before. "Better than I expected, actually."

Burke was quiet for a time, his gaze probing John's eyes for a clue. Finally speaking, he said, "I guess that will be all…for now. I will, or I should say, one of the detectives will be contacting you soon."

"Detectives?"

"Yes, sir. Now that this is officially a case of arson, it will be assigned an investigating officer."

John wondered how much more complicated his life could become.

"Officer," he began, "I know that I already asked you if I was a suspect. I heard your answer, that everyone is a suspect. But you don't think I did this, do you?"

Burke cocked his head to the side, the slightest smidgen of a grin curling up the corners of his mouth. "Mr. Augur, you don't have renter's insurance, do you?"

John shook his head.

"I didn't think so. It's not very often that people will burn their own things…unless they need the money and they are trying to get a big check from the insurance carrier.

"I spoke with your parents this morning...."

John felt a sudden pang of guilt, remembering that he hadn't spoken with them since before he called off the wedding. Between that and the fact that their son's apartment had been destroyed, they no doubt had been beside themselves with worry. He couldn't believe they hadn't tried to call him.

"They told me how much your train collection meant to you, especially the older pieces. They also told me how you felt about your books. From what we can tell, all of those things were still in the apartment when the fire started.

"Add to the picture the fact that several of your precious books were scattered around the ignition point...used for fuel, and no, Mr. Augur, I don't think you did this. The detective will investigate and come to his own conclusions. But, if you want my opinion, I think that someone hates you very much."

- XII -

Jack and Kurt watched John through the restaurant window as he paced the parking lot, his left hand holding the phone to his ear, his right, gesticulating in the air. Turning to Jack, Kurt remarked, "So how weird is this?"

A brief grin curving his mouth, Jack replied, "Which part?"

"All of it, I guess…but, specifically, watching your younger self talking to your parents. Don't you want to see them?"

Jack returned his gaze to Kurt, a somber expression on his face. "You have no idea. I've probably thought about it a hundred times since I got here."

"How long ago did they, you know, pass?"

Jack's eyes misted as he recalled the details. "Almost twenty-eight years," he answered softly.

"I don't think I could stand it. If somehow my parents were suddenly alive today, I couldn't stand not being able to go and see them."

Grimacing, Jack said, "I made a deal with Cal. He made me promise that I would only see John, head off the wedding and leave."

"That's already out the window. I don't think you can describe your visit here as having a minimal impact."

"No. I sure can't," Jack responded dejectedly.

They lapsed into a silence as Jack and Kurt both resumed their observation of John. By his body language, he appeared to be near the end of the call.

"Jack, can I ask you a question?"

"Sure. Go ahead."

"While you were having your breakdown in front of the courthouse last night, you rattled off a list of all of the things you'd messed up on this trip."

"Yeah?"

"Well…one of the things you said was that you came back here and killed your best friend."

"Uh-huh?"

Kurt stared at Jack's face and said, "I thought that would have been me."

Jack, unprepared for this question, stammered, "Kurt…you are…were. It was just a…just something I said."

Kurt eyed Jack suspiciously and nodded slowly.

"Then we're cool? What I mean to say is that we stay friends forever?"

Rushing to reassure him, Jack exclaimed, "Absolutely!"

Doubt and indecision obvious on Kurt's face, he nevertheless dropped this avenue of discussion.

"I'd still go see my folks, if it were me. The hell with the promise you made."

Before Jack could reply, John came into the restaurant and joined them.

"Mom and Dad told me to say *hello*."

"To me or to Jack?"

"Very funny."

"How are they?" asked Jack.

"They're okay. You know how they are."

"Yes, I do. Whatever I did was always fine with them."

Looking down at the table, John said, "Gail went to see them."

"When?"

"Last night. It's strange. The way Mom described the visit."

"How?"

"It sounded a little like the scene you described from the future. Tearful. Gushing. She told them how much she had always loved them. How sad she was that the marriage wasn't going to happen and that they would never be her in-laws."

"How did they take it?"

Raising his eyes to Jack, John smiled. "You were right. They didn't like her. They never have. So they weren't exactly moved by Gail's performance. That's what Dad called it – a performance."

Jack smiled to himself as he visualized the scene in his mind.

Addressing Kurt, John challenged, "What was up with you people? You are all supposed to care about me and nobody lifted a finger to stop me as I was diving headfirst into the rocks with this marriage."

"I can't speak for your folks, but I did try to tell you."

"No, you didn't!"

Tapping the side of his head, Kurt said, "You have a selective memory, pal. Remember the big blowup we had when you had been dating Gail for a month or two, and I told you to dump her?"

Thinking back, John did recall the argument.

"And remember what happened when you told me you were going to marry her?"

Grudgingly, John recounted, "You told me you wouldn't be my best man."

"See!" Kurt had a self-satisfied grin on his face.

"Well, it just wasn't enough."

"What did you want me to do? Hit you on the head with a two-by-four?"

Jack chimed in, "That would have been a good idea. It would have saved me from having to make this trip. And that would have saved everyone a lot of trouble."

As the three laughed, John gently touched the top of his head, his laugh interrupted by a sudden wince of pain.

Concerned, Kurt said, "Does that wound still hurt?"

John sighed. "I think it's getting worse. Maybe I needed stitches."

Tossing enough cash on the table to cover their check and a tip, Jack stood up. "Come on. I've got an idea."

⧖

"It's not *that* bad. We don't need to see Dr. Dooley," John protested as they entered the empty waiting room of his doctor's office.

Smiling mysteriously, Jack told him, "Just go check in and ask Lynn if he can see you."

"You remember her name after thirty years?"

"Oh, yeah. Go on, do it."

John approached the reception window, immediately falling into the same routine that occurred with every one of his visits to the doctor. His eyes were instantly locked on the receptionist, as if drawn by a magnet. His breath suddenly became shallow. His knees weakened.

John gripped the edge of the counter for support, mindless of the countless germs deposited on the surface by the other patients who preceded him. Lynn was perched on the front edge of her chair, the telephone pressed against her ear. As she saw John, her face lit up with a smile. While he waited for her to complete her call, John, for the thousandth time, studied the details of her face. Bewitching eyes, accented by an aqua-blue eyeshadow and a bold, dark eyeliner. Nearly jet-black hair that hung straight, just past her slender shoulders. Full, red lips. Her nose with a slight bump at the midpoint. John wondered if she disliked the insignificant protrusion and yearned for a perfectly straight bridge. He, on the other hand, found it to be perfect, as was every other aspect of her, with one glaring exception. On the third finger of her left hand was a wedding ring.

Finishing the call, Lynn greeted him and flashed a lustrous smile.

John noticed that his mouth had gone dry. He frantically circled his tongue around the inside of his mouth, trying to generate sufficient moisture to be able to speak. Lynn looked at him with a sudden expression of concern, and said, "Are you all right?"

Finally able to speak, John said, "Yes. I'm fine."

The wondrous smile returned. "Good. Because, with your tongue flying around like that, for a moment there I thought you were about to shape-shift into a lizard or something."

John couldn't help but laugh. "No," he was able to say between breaths, "I keep my shape-shifting confined to more private areas."

With a throaty chuckle, she asked, "So, if you're okay, why are you here?"

"I'm not okay. I mean, I hit my head."

"Now that explains it," she surmised, still grinning mischievously.

"No. Seriously, look." He bent forward through the window and leaned down in front of her, so she could see the top of his head.

She let out a small gasp. "That doesn't look good. What happened?"

"I was on my way to take a trip on a time machine when aliens tried to abduct me, but I was rescued by a stranger from another planet. Unfortunately, the gravitational beam they were using to lift me up to their ship wasn't short-circuited until I was up about eight or nine feet high, so when it released me, I suddenly fell back down to Earth and hit my head on the alley pavement."

"Oh," Lynn reacted as if that was a perfectly reasonable explanation. "Unfortunately, John, Doctor Dooley isn't here today. He had to go to Mars for an interplanetary medical conference."

He laughed briefly, replying, "Actually, I was serious."

Lynn leaned forward, her elbows resting on the edge of desk so that her shoulders pushed up. Riveting him with those intense, brown eyes, she deadpanned, "So am I."

They stared at each other for a moment, the spell broken by Lynn. "Come on in. I'm not the doc, but I do have some first aid training."

She stood from her chair and walked to the rear of her work area. Rather than immediately circling around to the door adjacent to the counter, John took a moment to stand and watch her retreating figure, unaware that Jack was standing at his elbow.

"Tell her you broke up with Gail," he whispered into John's ear.

"What?"

"Just tell her."

With that, Jack retreated to the waiting room, picked up an old issue of *People*, and sat in the chair next to Kurt, who was grinning like a simpleton.

John used the patient entrance and walked unsteadily down the short hallway to the only exam room with a light turned on. He had never been this alone with Lynn before and the thought of it made him feel dizzy. She was efficiently preparing to treat him, opening a bottle of disinfectant and pulling the wrapper from a bandage. John stood like a robot which had executed its final program and was awaiting input.

Finishing, she turned and patted the edge of the exam table. "Up you go."

His blank mind thankfully seized upon the new set of instructions, and he quickly climbed onto the table, clumsily kicking the nearby step stool, sending it sliding across the vinyl floor and slamming into the wall.

Lynn, watching his tortured ballet, grinned a sly smile and said, "Is it safe for me to approach now?"

Not trusting his voice, John nodded.

In his many past visits to see his doctor, some of which, he admitted only to himself, had not really been all that necessary, John's interactions with Lynn had always been restricted to the window in the reception area, with a four-foot-high wall, a counter and glass separating them. This was the first time he had experienced her this near. He found it intoxicating.

At the small work counter, Lynn saturated a gauze square with alcohol. Turning back to John, she stepped forward so that she was standing with her hips between his knees.

"Breathe," she said; her eyes, just inches from John's, sparkled.

"W...what?"

Smiling, she explained, "It's important that we *homo sapiens* continue to take in oxygen."

John had not noticed that he had stopped breathing. He obediently filled his lungs, immediately excited by the sweet, yet exotic scent of Lynn. Her proximity to him made it almost impossible to resist the urge to wrap his arms around her, pulling her body tight against him.

From only inches away, he stared as her tongue gently dampened her lips before she said, "Are you going to tilt your head forward or do I need to climb up on that stool you kicked away?"

John realized that he had completely forgotten his stated purpose for being there. He dropped his chin to his chest, and she stepped even closer to him, pressing against the front of the exam table. He could feel his senses overload as the nerves in his inner thighs tingled from the contact of her hips, his nose gorged on her fragrance, his eyes stared downward at her white uniform, so close that he almost touched it with his forehead, and his ears strained to capture every note of the symphony that was her breathing.

As her fingertips gently parted his hair around the gash, John felt currents of electricity, radiated from the top of his head, shoot through his entire body and down to his toes, obliterating any feeling of pain as she swabbed the wound.

He muttered something.

"What did you say?" she asked, her voice low and breathy.

Clearing his throat, John repeated, "What perfume is that?"

"Love."

"What?"

"It's called Love. Do you like it?"

"Uh-huh," he answered weakly.

She stepped back from him a pace and smiled. The sudden distance between them allowed him to normalize his breathing somewhat.

"In that case, I'll make a point of wearing it when I see you on the schedule."

She turned back to the counter and soaked another gauze pad. John, remembering Jack's comment, blurted out, "I cancelled my wedding yesterday."

He wasn't sure but thought that he noticed a slight tightening between her delicate shoulder blades. With her back still toward him, her voice casual, she said, "Oh? How come?"

"I guess I figured out that marrying her would be the worst mistake of my life."

He saw her shoulders rise and fall as if she were taking and expelling a deep breath. She turned back and stepped close to John again. He immediately dropped his head down to give her access to his injury. As he did, he saw that she no longer had the sterile pad in her hand.

Her hand rose and softly touched the tip of his chin, lifting his face to hers. John could not read her expression as she said, "I'm glad."

There was none of the former teasing and lightness in her voice when she said the two words, only an intensity that surprised him.

Neither moved for a time, nor did either say a word, both comfortable with the intimacy of their nearness and the connection of their gazes.

With no conscious thought, John slowly leaned forward. Lynn did not make him complete the trip alone, meeting him halfway between, and their lips touched delicately. The initial gentleness of the kiss quickly blossomed into an intense, passionate contact. John's hands moved on their own, caressing her sides and sliding around her slim waist to encircle her. Lynn wrapped her arms around his neck, pulling John even more fiercely into the kiss.

Nothing else existed. No time passed. Both of their worlds were filled with the sensations of the moment.

After their lips eventually parted, Lynn backed away a few inches, and they stared into each other's eyes. John finally said, "I can't believe this is true."

Lynn's mouth curled into a smile that simultaneously conveyed a giddy happiness and a smoldering passion.

"One moment," John said breathlessly. "One kiss. And my entire life is different...emended...wonderful."

Her smile unchanged, her eyes still engaged with his, Lynn nodded.

At last, she spoke, "I have hoped for so long...."

Still bewildered by his good fortune, John said, "You have? I never knew."

Lynn, reluctant to release John from her embrace, leaned forward and kissed him gently. Before they could surrender to a second oblivion, she backed away, unwrapping her arms from his neck. Standing a mere foot from John, she slowly smoothed out her uniform, her eyes never leaving his.

John's mind raced as the myriad of hopes, dreams, fantasies and former impossibilities collided in their rush through the process of conversion to become realities. As he watched her hands sensually stroke the surface of her dress, he again focused upon the ring on her finger.

Lynn saw the sudden shift in his expression and followed his gaze. Instinctively, her right hand reached over and covered her left, as if blocking his view of the gold band would diminish its reality.

"You *are* married, right?" A tinge of hopefulness rose in his voice as he entertained the possibility that the ring was a ruse to ward off unwanted advances.

"Unfortunately, I am," she answered, shattering the brief illusion. Before he could say anything, she added, "I have nothing but rancor for the sonofa…jerk."

John's thoughts flitted madly through his mind. Trying to seize one made him feel like one of those people who climb into the cyclonic glass cages and try to grab money as the bills whirl around them.

"We need to talk."

"Yes, we do," Lynn said, placing a hand on his knee, "but I have a feeling that it's going to be a long time before we can get around to talking when we're together."

A broad smile filling John's face, he said, "I think you're right."

Lynn cleared her throat. "Let's finish up that head wound of yours, shall we?"

– XIII –

John did not trust himself to drive, his mind still spinning from the life-altering implications of the interlude with Lynn, so Kurt was behind the wheel as they made their way back to the storage room.

"You look like a kid who just found out that his distant uncle had died and he inherited Disneyland," Kurt teased, grinning at his friend.

John stared out of the side window of the car, his eyes seeing none of the scenery that flashed by.

"I never knew. I had no idea in the world she felt that way about me."

Kurt expected Jack to explain about Lynn, but when no words were forthcoming from the back seat, he plunged in, "Jack told me some future history when we were in the waiting room. I guess that just a couple of years ago, about twenty-eight years from now, he ran into Lynn at a coffee shop, and they talked. She confessed to Jack that she had fallen in love with him back when he used to come into her office…back in 2008, but because he was dating Gail and then eventually married her, Lynn never had the nerve to say anything. I guess she never got over him…you. So she stayed in her miserable marriage. She never found anyone else she cared about, so she just stayed."

John's voice filled with amazement, as he responded to Kurt, "Unbelievable. I have thought about her, dreamt about her, fantasized about her since I first laid eyes on that face."

"I know."

"But I knew she was married."

"And you figured she was out of your league."

"That's true. Can you blame me?"

"Hell, no. *I* thought she was out of your league."

"Thanks."

"No problem. That's what friends are for."

Kurt glanced at the rearview mirror and noticed that Jack was staring out of his window, a solemn expression on his face.

"Hey!" Kurt grabbed his attention. "I thought you'd be happy about this turn of events."

Jack turned and caught Kurt's eyes in the mirror. "It isn't fair," he grimaced.

"What do you mean?" John disputed. "It's perfect."

Heaving a heavy sigh, Jack explained, "Is it? You've probably got the rest of your life to spend with Lynn. Assuming everything goes well and works out, she'll get a divorce, you two will get married and maybe have some kids. One by one, you are going to get to live through each of those fantastic days," he paused for a moment, then continued wistfully, "and unbelievable nights with her."

"Yeah. So what's wrong?"

Letting out a loud snort of disgust, Jack proceeded, "Because, assuming we are able to sort out the mess we're in, I'm going to go back to 2040 to resume my life. And, the way it looks, the life I'll be going back to assume will be a brand new one, with Lynn as my wife and possibly some kids that you and she had together."

"That sounds great," Kurt said. "What's the problem?"

Figuring it out, John answered for his older self, "When he goes back, he won't have a single memory of the thirty years with her."

Jack lowered his eyes. "As I was sitting in the waiting room back there, and you were in the exam room with her, I was going nuts wondering what was happening, hoping that it would go the way I wanted it to. You have to remember, I am accustomed to everything that you've done being one of my memories. And then it hit me... it wasn't going to be just that little block of time that you would get to experience instead of me, it was the next thirty years. All of the laughter, all of the kisses, all of the... everything."

John and Kurt sat in silence as their minds tried to wrap around the reality of Jack's situation.

Finally, Kurt spoke, "At least when you go back, you'll have her for the rest of your life, instead of what you had before."

Shaking his head, Jack elaborated, "Kurt, think about that. Is that going to be fair to her? To our children, assuming we have some? Thirty years from now *John*, the *John* she and the kids have been with for all that time, climbs into the machine – he has no choice – to make everything come out right. And a moment later *I* climb out. I'll know her… and by that I mean I'll know who she is. I won't have any recollections of the thirty years we've spent together. And the kids… they'll be strangers to me. I won't have a single memory of playing with them when they were small. Helping them with their homework. Watching their dance recitals or baseball games. Sending them off on their first dates. Dancing at their weddings. I won't even know their names! None of it. NONE!"

Clearly visualizing his destiny thirty years hence, John summarized, "It will be like Lynn is married to someone who suddenly got amnesia."

"Yes," Jack concurred, "except, instead of my slate having been wiped clean from amnesia, it'll be filled with thirty years of baggage, three decades of horrible memories."

They arrived at the alley. Kurt pulled the car to one side and shut off the engine. None of them made a move to get out.

After a silence of several minutes, Jack said, "There is an alternative."

"NO!" John shouted. "Don't even go there."

"What?" Kurt asked. "What alternative?"

Speaking slowly, his voice flat and emotionless, Jack posited, "I'm not sure about this. Cal and I never went this far when we talked about how it all works, but… I don't think that John would really need to come back when he reaches 2040. I think that what's done is done. This is now the reality and what's happened will have happened in John's past whether he comes back or not."

"You don't know that!" John argued.

"No, I don't," Jack replied softly, "but I'm fairly certain of it."

Kurt, twisted sideways on the front seat so that he faced Jack, attempted to clarify, "Then why did you say before that it was a requirement?"

"I think it's only necessary if I am going to return to my own time. It's like that short trip back that Cal took. If the non-traveling Cal didn't get into the machine at the end of the two weeks, there would be two of him from that moment forward. That's why *John* would have to travel back here and *I* would return to 2040. Otherwise, there would be two of *us*."

"What's wrong with you not going back… staying here and living the next thirty years all over again?"

"Kurt, look at the damage I've done so far. And I've only been here a day and a half. Imagine how much would get screwed up if I just stayed here."

"So what are you thinking?"

"Jack! Dammit!" John shouted.

"John, it's okay. Really. My life has been a mess. At least I had a chance to come back and make some things right. Now, you can have the life I always wished for."

Realization dawning on him, Kurt hesitated, "You're not talking about...?"

"Killing himself," John finished for him. "That's exactly what he's thinking."

"No way! Come on, Jack, there's got to be another solution...another way we can work this all out."

Jack looked at Kurt and saw the beginning of tears aggregating at the corners of his eyes. "Kurt, it isn't what I want...obviously. But if I go back, assuming we can get this whole mess back on track, I'm basically sentencing John to an oblivion thirty years from now, not to mention what a rotten thing it would be to do to Lynn and whatever children we might have, taking away their husband and father and replacing him with a damaged stranger who doesn't even know them. And if I stay here, who knows what the Godzilla Effect will do to everyone's future."

"No," Kurt groaned, desperation creeping into his voice. "If you're worried about messing up the future by staying here, you could...you could go somewhere. Go live in some cabin in the mountains, or Tibet, somewhere!"

Jack shook his head. "It's still a risk. Look, this whole trip back here was done out of selfishness. Because I had ruined *my* life. Cal sent me back even though he knew he shouldn't do it. He knew that he was jumping way outside the boundaries of all of the previous trips. I could tell he was worried at the time, but I was so wrapped up in my own self-pity that I went ahead with it, when I should have said *no*. I should have seen the concern on his face...hell, I did see it. I ignored it because I wanted to come back. I wanted to change things so *my* life would be better. *My life!* Like that's so damn important.

"So, I guess I've done a great job. My life is on the track I wanted, and Cal is dead. And God knows what else will be fouled up over the next thirty years because of that. Maybe it's time that I stopped thinking about only me."

Kurt, saddened by what he heard but unable to think of a rebuttal, fell silent.

Jack lowered his eyes once more.

"Jack," John began hopefully, "we've got time to figure this out. Before you go and make a decision like that, we still have to try and undo Cal's death. So, let's just focus on that. And who knows, once that's fixed, a solution to the other...situation, a better solution...might be obvious."

Grasping onto the small hope John offered, Kurt said, "That's right. One problem at a time."

After drawing in a long breath, Jack sighed. "You're right. We need to repair the damage first."

"Absolutely," Kurt agreed emphatically.

The three men got out of the car and, without further discussion, Jack opened the padlock, and they entered the storage room. The silver sphere still rested on its struts. Jack approached the side, and the angular outline appeared. He placed his hand flat on the surface and, with a slight hiss, the door section separated from the surface and swung outward.

"Are you going to give me a quick lesson?" Kurt asked, incipient excitement creeping into his voice.

"Yes," Jack responded, "but we need to do something first." He stepped into the machine and flipped the armrest console open. Instead of retrieving the controller, his hand came out holding a device that was about the size of a deck of cards.

"What's that?" John asked.

"GPS. If Kurt is going to make a jump to the other room, we need it to nail down the exact coordinates of that location."

The two followed Jack to the adjacent room as he walked to the center and looked down at the small screen.

"Anyone have a pen and paper?"

Kurt said, "I've got my Blackberry."

Jack read off the coordinates, and Kurt tapped them onto his screen, storing them. The task finished, they turned off the light, locked the room and returned to the sphere where Jack began the process of preparing Kurt for his trip.

The briefing took less than forty-five minutes. To get Kurt further accustomed to using the controller, Jack had him transfer the coordinates from the Blackberry into the sphere's memory.

As the two were huddled in the sphere, John's phone chirped. Looking at the display, he saw that the call came from his parents' phone.

"Hi, Mom," he answered, knowing that his father rarely made calls.

"John?" His mother's voice sounded distraught.

"What's wrong?"

"Gail was just here."

John's neck and shoulders tightened involuntarily. "What happened? Are you all right?"

Exhaling loudly, she reassured him, "We're fine, but I think you better come over here."

"Why? I mean, sure, I'll be right over. Tell me what happened."

"She left an envelope for you." Nervousness and anxiety shook her voice. "John...she's scaring me. Both of us."

"Why? What did she say?"

"It wasn't what she said so much as how she acted."

"What do you mean?"

"She's...it's like nothing's wrong. I don't know exactly. There were no tears this time. She kept smiling and chatting with us almost as if the marriage was never cancelled and this was a normal visit. But that's not it, either. Everything about her was exaggerated...her smile, her voice, her actions."

"Game Show Gail?"

"What?"

"I would tease her about it. When she was upset and didn't want people to know, she would start acting like a TV game show host."

"That's it! The very strangest thing was her final comment."

John said nothing, waiting for his mother to tell him.

"As she was leaving...after giving me the envelope...she told me to tell you that she hoped you enjoyed the barbeque."

"I'll be right over."

☒

Ed and Kathleen Augur still lived in the same house where John was born. A three-bedroom, ranch-style, brick house near the center of town, in a neighborhood which was beginning to fray around the edges. Most of the adjacent homes on the cul-de-sac were still owned by the same people who had moved in when everything was new, their children all now raised and gone. Just as their homes suffered from the decades of wear and abuse, so did their knees, hips and backs. They were no longer able to trim, weed and repaint with their former vigor.

John pulled his car into the driveway, parking behind his parents' Oldsmobile. The discarded brand from General Motors seemed to epitomize the plight of the neighborhood. Walking to the front door, as he had countless times before, John flashed back to the images of growing up here. The Augurs had not been one of the families to move onto the block when it was all brand new. They purchased the house from the contractor who built the subdivision and was moving on to Las Vegas to escape the housing slump in Tucson.

Because of this fluke of timing, John was a toddler when the children in the surrounding homes were in high school. As he got older, he was able to find friends scattered among the adjacent blocks, his friends also children of the second generation of homeowners.

As he arrived at the door, it swung open before he could ring the bell, and his mother was waiting, clutching a large, manila envelope. He hugged her, and they went in. His father was sitting in his usual chair, leaning forward and smiling, glad to see John.

After he greeted his father, they sat, John taking his normal seat on the couch as his mother nervously sat on the edge of her wing-back chair. John's mind wandered back to his adolescence, recalling how adventurous he had felt at the time when he would wait until they were not in the room and then actually sit in one of their chairs.

Kathleen had given him the envelope, but he had not yet opened it, dreading whatever the contents would convey.

"Where are you staying?" his father asked.

"Kurt's, right now."

"Your bedroom is still your bedroom, you know. You can stay here."

John studied his father's face and saw a glimpse of hopefulness.

"Thanks, Dad. I might. I haven't thought it all through yet."

"Well," Ed said gruffly, "we'd love to have you back here."

Looking at his father affectionately, John said, "I know. We'll see, okay?"

His dad nodded, disappointed.

John rotated the envelope in his hands, procrastinating. With a heavy sigh, he tore off the edge and peered inside. He had no idea what he expected to find, a slender explosive device, perhaps. Instead, he saw papers. He slid them out and noticed that they were clipped together with a smaller, sealed envelope at the top of the pile. Across the face of the small envelope, clearly in Gail's handwriting, was scrawled *Happy Father's Day*.

Confused, he slipped the envelope out from under the paper clip and revealed a blurred, black and white picture which resembled an abstract Rorschach image with extra lines, arrows and words written on the picture with a felt tip pen.

"What the heck is this?"

His mother got up from her chair and walked over to John for a better look. He handed her the print, and after examining it for only a moment, she clutched her throat and gasped, "Oh, my God!"

"Mom? What is it?"

"It…," she began, her voice faltering. "It looks like a sonogram."

"A sono…," John stopped, as a horrendous thought slammed into his mind.

His hands shaking, he tore open the envelope and found a generic greeting card with a picture of a smiling man on the front. He was holding two babies in his arms. Before John could open the card, a slip of paper fell out of it, dropping to the floor.

Retrieving it, he immediately saw that it was a printed receipt from a clinic. The receipt was a jumble of small boxes and codes, with several checkmarks next to indecipherable items. If it weren't for the handwritten note in the "Comments" box at the bottom of the page, John would have had no idea what the receipt was for.

D.&C. / Twins

His eyes stared at the scribbled, yet legible, writing within the box, his mind knowing the meaning.

"What is it?" his father asked with concern.

John, unable to find his voice, handed the sheet to his mother. As her eyes found the same box, another gasp burst from her. John's father, curiosity pushing him to lose control of his temper, leaned forward and barked, "Dammit! What the hell is going on?"

"Ed," John's mother said. "She had an abortion. She was pregnant with twins."

"Oh," was all Ed uttered, dropping back into his chair.

Kathleen sat down next to her son and put her arm around him, pulling him tightly to her side.

⛋

Gail hummed an old Chicago song as she sat in front of her computer. Patiently, she typed one search string after another, methodically reading the results from each search before continuing, occasionally jotting down a note on the yellow pad by her elbow.

After nearly an hour of this, she suddenly straightened in her chair as she found what she was looking for. Clicking on the header, she read the entire article, then read it again. A broad smile twisted her features as she turned on the attached printer and clicked on the print icon.

"There we go!" she said with satisfaction, leaning back in her chair.

☒

"She *what?*" Jack shouted at John.

"She was pregnant. With twins. And she aborted them."

Jack stared at John, dumbfounded.

"I don't understand," Kurt said. "I mean you just told her you didn't want to marry her yesterday. And that was a Sunday. How could she do all of this, the sonogram, the abortion, all of it so quickly?"

John was sitting on the floor of the storage room where he had rejoined Kurt and Jack after calming his parents down. "On my way back here, I called her Ob/Gyn. She told me that Gail had come in last week for the pregnancy test and that her office had notified Gail of the results on Friday. Yesterday, after I told Gail the wedding was off, she called the doctor's answering service and told her it was urgent that she see her. The doctor agreed to meet with her at the twenty-four-hour urgent care clinic.

"I guess Gail didn't tell her about the breakup. She told the doctor some cock-and-bull story about how I would go crazy if I found out she was pregnant, so she was thinking about an abortion. She talked the doctor into doing the sonogram right then."

"Yeah, but what about the abortion? Doesn't that take a little more time to set up?" Kurt asked.

"Normally, yes," John answered. "Gail's best friend is a nurse at Planned Parenthood and must have helped her…made it happen right away. That part I don't know for sure. I'm just guessing, but the receipt for the procedure did come from the place where her friend works."

"How do we even know it really happened?" asked Jack. "If her friend works there, couldn't she have dummied up the receipt?"

"I guess," replied John disgustedly, "but what does it matter?"

Confused, Jack asked, "What do you mean?"

"According to the doctor, Gail really is…or was…pregnant with twins. After what you told me about the future, I'm not sure they aren't better off …."

John was still clutching the papers from the envelope. Jack reached down and gently took them from him, unfolding them.

This was Jack's first glimpse at the sonogram. After a moment, he cried out,

"That bitch!"

John looked up at Jack, questioningly. Kurt said, "What is it?"

Jack handed the printout back to John. "Didn't you notice *that*?"

"Notice what? I didn't recognize it. I didn't know it was a sonogram until Mom told me."

He took the picture back from Jack and looked at it. This time he immediately recognized what he thought had been scribbles before. Someone, no doubt Gail, John thought, had drawn two lines with arrows on the picture. Each arrow pointed at one of the two small fetuses. At the other end of each line she had written *Beth* and *John, Jr.*

"I don't know if you remember from what I told you, but those were the names of our children."

"The kids who died in the fire," John said, feeling himself slip into a deep pit of despair.

"That's right."

"Oh, my God," Kurt murmured softly.

~ XIV ~

John, Kurt and Jack were, once again, at Kurt's house. Kurt paced back and forth in front of the two men. "I'm telling you it's fine," said Kurt emphatically. "I should do the trip tonight. I don't need to go to sleep right now."

"Kurt," Jack said, attempting to persuade his friend, "you've been up all day. And it's been a hell of a day so far. I really don't think it's a good idea for you to climb into the machine at ten o'clock at night when you should be going to sleep, and arrive there early last Friday morning with a whole day in front of you."

"Right," John agreed. "You're going to need to be sharp. We can't afford any more mistakes."

Heaving a sigh, Kurt dropped into a chair and resigned himself, "I guess."

They talked about Cal, Gail, Lynn, the upcoming time trip, and all of the other topics to which their tired minds wandered as the three of them unwound from the day.

"I've been meaning to ask you something," Kurt said to Jack.

"What's that?"

"Can the machine go into the future?"

"It does. That's what it would be doing when, or *if*, I go back to 2040."

"Stop that *if* crap!" John snapped.

Jack shrugged him off.

"No, I mean the real future. Like a hundred years from now."

Jack shook his head. "I don't think so. I asked Cal about that, and his answer was vague but, basically, he said that it wouldn't. I even played around with the controller in the machine, and there aren't any menu choices for a date beyond the starting time of the trip."

"Too bad," said Kurt. "That would be awesome."

"Maybe. Maybe not," John offered.

Looking at John, Kurt pressed, "Why do you say that? Wouldn't you want to see what it was like…way ahead?"

"After the last couple of days, I don't think so."

"Why?"

John answered Kurt with a question. "What if it was horrible? What if everyone was dead? Civilization wiped out? Something like that. Would you want to know?"

Kurt thought about it for a minute before answering. "Maybe I would. Maybe everything was wiped out by something that could be stopped. You know, some bio-engineered virus that you could go back and prevent from being made in the first place."

"That probably wouldn't work. Look at all of the people who are trying to stop the big companies from fiddling with the genetic material of viruses now…for exactly that reason. Nobody pays any attention to them. They're considered to be crackpots."

"Yeah, except I'd have proof."

"Kurt," John said, "what proof would you have? Something you brought back from the future? Who would believe that?"

"Well…," Kurt stopped, seeing the logic of John's argument.

"And think about this," Jack added, "what if you went to the future and found out that everything was wiped out and it was your fault?"

Kurt groaned, "Oh, man! You are on *that* again. Dude, everything is not about you, okay?"

"I'm not sure how much can be changed," John reflected thoughtfully. "We talked before about the inertia of events making it harder and harder to alter the outcome. Look, in my former future…," John grinned. "I can't get accustomed to that yet. In Jack's past, our place burned down, torched by Gail. Between the evidence the arson investigator showed me and Gail's *I hope John enjoyed the barbeque* comment, it looks like she's done it again.

"In his past, he loses two children named Beth and John, Jr. Obviously, this time around the details are different but the net result is the same."

"John, I see what you're saying, but those things weren't caused by some cosmic force of inertia…they were both caused by one crazy woman," Kurt declared. "On the other hand, there were thirty years of inertia behind Cal being alive, yet he's dead."

"Don't forget about the scar," Jack reminded them, tapping the top of his head.

"Yeah," John acknowledged, "that one has me totally confused."

"Me, too," Kurt agreed.

"I still think it's *the cycles*," Jack maintained.

"Wait a second," Kurt interrupted. "I've always been a little fuzzy on that theory of yours…this cycle thing. You've told me about it before, John, but I'm not sure I totally get it. And I don't see how it ties in with what's happening."

"I'm not sure that it does," John replied. "Let's go through it again."

"The short version!" Kurt kidded his friend. "I need to get some sleep tonight, remember."

John smirked. "Yes…the short version."

He drew a deep breath and collected his thoughts for a moment before plunging ahead. "Remember how we were taught in our Physical Science class years ago about closed systems?"

"Yeah. The elimination of outside influences. In a closed system, if all of the elements of an *action* are replicated exactly, the *reaction* will be the same."

"Right. It would have to be. Because there isn't anything – any *outside force* – changing it. The example Mr. Baldwin gave us was shooting a rifle. If you mounted a rifle to a solid pedestal and triggered it, the bullet would travel a mile or so and land on the ground. If you were able to fire a second shot, and the lead slug was *exactly* the same as the first one, and the powder charge was *exactly* the same, and the rifle bore was unchanged by the previous shot so that it was *exactly* the same, and the atmospheric conditions…etcetera, etcetera…were all *exactly* the same, then the second slug would land *exactly* on top of the first one."

Kurt nodded his understanding.

"I always thought that wasn't the best possible explanation he could have used to describe or explain a closed system. It does make the point, though. If all of the parts and pieces of the original action are present and unchanged, and there aren't any outside influences, then the outcome will be exactly the same."

"Got it."

"So…the universe is obviously a closed system."

"Now, that's where I start to have a problem. What could be more *open* than the entire universe?"

"Kurt, think about it. Supposedly, a long time after the Big Bang that creates the universe, there is, or at least according to some physicists, there will be a Big Crunch. The Big Crunch happens when gravity pulls all of the matter in the universe back into a little ball.

"Now, if *all* of the matter in the universe is inside the ball... and I mean *all* of it... then, by definition, there isn't anything left outside the ball. Right?"

"I guess not."

Smiling, John continued, "Okay, so if everything is inside the ball, there's nothing left, so there can't possibly be any outside influence. Right?"

Kurt nodded again.

"Then, at that point in time, the ball blows up... again... another Big Bang. But a Big Bang inside of a *closed* system. What that would mean is that everything... every chunk, every particle, every atom... would go to exactly the same place it went after the previous Big Bang. The action/reaction would be perfectly replicated."

John paused to wait for a comment or question from Kurt. Getting neither, he resumed, "So, let's take it a step further. Remember, we are still in a closed system. If everything in the universe goes back to where it went the last time, then every action and reaction that followed would also be the same. It would have to be.

"The dispersed matter through the universe would coalesce into the same clumps as before. The clumps would form the identical galaxies as last time. The galaxies would contain the same stars and planets as the previous time. Eventually, the first life would arise on Earth at precisely the same moment as before. And it would evolve following the exact path all over again, until there was man."

Kurt interrupted, "What about Chaos Theory? The Butterfly Effect? Wouldn't even the tiniest change from the previous Big Bang, during the creation of the galaxies or the evolution of life, cause big differences?"

"It would, but only if the change came from an outside influence, something that hadn't been present during the previous process. And how can that be when everything that was around during the first one is, by definition, present the second time around? Name something... even the smallest influence you can think of... that wouldn't have been present the first time."

Kurt thought for a moment before deciding, "I can't."

At this point in the conversation, Jack interjected, "And Chaos Theory itself doesn't dispute what John's describing; it only maintains that the outcome is impossible for man to *predict* because there are far too many variables to consider."

"Okay," Kurt understood. "Go on."

"If everything in the universe plays out the same, then the only possible scenario when mankind arrives on the scene is that each and every one of us is born at the exact same moment as before. We all live our lives, down to the smallest detail, exactly as we did before. And we all die at exactly the same moment as before. Everything that happens to us has happened before. Every word we say or hear. Even every thought. Everything."

"Wow! This blows me away whenever we talk about it. But you told me once that there's a glitch."

"There might be. I'm not sure if it really is a glitch. Anyway, I'm not there yet."

"I'm glad you're giving me the short version," Kurt chuckled.

"Believe me, I am. So, if that's what happens during this time around – an exact replica, like a movie of the last time around – and we are, again, heading for another Big Crunch...then we are obviously heading for another Big Bang, another Big Bang in this closed system we live in called the universe."

"So, it all happens again...a third time."

"Or a three-thousandth time," Jack said.

"Or a three-millionth," added John.

Kurt's eyes sparkled with understanding. "God, I love this theory. Let's get to the glitch, though."

"I'm almost there. The glitch is brain waves."

Kurt smiled with anticipation.

"Every person on Earth generates brain waves every moment of their lives. And every person's brain waves are unique, like fingerprints, or...specific frequencies, singular to each of us. And brain waves seem to be immune to the travel restrictions of the speed of sound or even the speed of light."

"I remember," Kurt said, "reading about experiments the government did where they were going to try to use telepathy to communicate with spaceships."

"Right! Once a spaceship gets too far from Earth, the time lag between an Earth-based transmission being sent and when it is received keeps getting longer and longer until it is days, weeks or even months, depending on how far away the ship is. Communication becomes almost impossible. However, it seems that brain waves would arrive at the ship instantly, even if it is out of our solar system.

"So, the moment our heads create the brain waves, the entire galaxy is filled with them. And we keep pumping them out every moment we are alive. If brain waves are immune to the space/time/gravity restrictions that everything else is subject to, I think that they are also immune to the expansion and contraction of the universe. I think they survive the Big Crunch and the Big Bang.

"And nobody knows what the brain waves are transmitting. We might be uploading every single detail of our days as we go through our lives. And each of us is transmitting this information at a different frequency. Everything we hear, smell, taste, see or feel. Everything we think. All of it!"

"Like we're probes?"

"Exactly. I think that, just like a probe we send to Mars whose job it is to record and transmit everything it sees, our job is to experience our five senses and our consciousness and transmit all of that data."

"To whom?" Kurt asked.

"Don't know. Maybe to God."

"Don't some of the philosophies and religions believe there is a record of all things somewhere?"

"The Akashic Records."

"Maybe that's what the brains waves are? Just a record floating out there, of everything."

"Could be. Now, here's the glitch. If there have been a thousand, or a million or even a billion or more cycles in the past, and in each cycle we lived out our lives exactly the same while generating a new set of identical brain waves, we would be re-broadcasting and overlaying, or amplifying those waves…those messages. All of the brain waves of everyone who ever lived …."

"Or will live in the later years of the previous cycles," Jack added.

"Right," John agreed, "or *will live*, assuming this isn't the first or last cycle of the Big Bang/Big Crunch – all those brain waves are all around us, overlaid many times and getting stronger with each repetition. Remember, each person's brain waves are unique, like a specific station on the radio. It makes sense that the only person whose brain would be tuned to the frequency of your brain waves from the previous cycles would be you.

"You would constantly be receiving those brain waves. And they would be telling you precisely what you were thinking, feeling, seeing, hearing, smelling and tasting simultaneously with your experiences as you have them."

Kurt added, "It would be like being on stage, acting in a play while listening to a recording of the same play at the same time."

"Right. Except you would be receiving everything, not just the words from you and the other actors, but all of it."

"This is so cool!"

"And if you think about it, this explains a lot of things. Like ghosts, for example. Maybe we are able to pick up similar waves, like a radio which receives a channel that's close to the frequency it is tuned to, a channel created by another person."

"Or," Jack added, "the brain waves are so intense from a particularly horrific experience that they are easier for others to pick up?"

"Right," John agreed. "You could just be picking up the brain waves of a person from the past or future and seeing what they saw… actually, not only seeing what they saw… but receiving what all five of their senses perceived, even if all of those things aren't physically in front of you."

"You'd be downloading their experience," Kurt paraphrased.

"Exactly."

"I am curious about one thing, though."

"What's that?"

"If we are tuned to the frequency of our brain waves, why does it come to us as it is happening? Why don't we get the download of our whole life all at once?"

"I think I can answer that," Jack said. "John's right. When they measure the brain waves that come out of our heads, the pattern, or frequency, is unique to each of us. When they measure the waves from a person throughout his life, the pattern changes… gradually and steadily… over the years."

"Our brain shifts its frequency slightly as we go?"

"Right. That way, we would only be able to pick up the transmission that corresponds to the current moment in our lives."

"That makes sense," said Kurt.

"And, if you think about it, the theory explains schizophrenia," Jack offered.

"Yes, it does," John continued. "Imagine what it would be like if you got this input from the first moment you're born, pouring into your head every second of your life – everything people said around you in the previous cycles, everything that you had experienced the earlier times around, everything."

"Hey, that's déjà vu!"

"Exactly. And you would get accustomed to the input, even dependent upon it. You would be comforted by it. It's even possible, since we are getting the full script downloaded into us every moment, that – right now – we are not actually bothering to physically speak clearly. Maybe I'm just mumbling these words because I've said them and you've heard them a million times before."

"That's how it feels sometimes when you're talking," Kurt grinned.

"Very funny! Then something happens to get you off your track, so to speak."

"Like déjà vu."

"Yes," Jack said. "Let's say that a man is sitting at home in the evening, watching television, and his wife is out for the evening. In all the previous cycles, she runs her car off the road and hits a tree. No one finds her for a couple of hours, and she eventually dies. In all the earlier cycles, the husband is haunted by the thought of that. He spends the rest of his life feeling miserable...torn up with guilt...because he was sitting and watching *American Idol* while his wife lay dying.

"This cycle, this time around, as he's watching *American Idol*, he suddenly has a strange feeling that something is wrong. He tries to call her, and she doesn't answer. He gets in his car and drives her route, finds her, and this time around he saves her life. It's a good ending, right?"

Kurt agreed.

"There is one problem. From the moment he gets up from the couch and leaves to find her, his life no longer matches all of those previous cycles. He's not doing the same things. He's not in the same places at the same times. Every major or minor detail of his life is different from what it had been before. Yet, he is still bombarded with those powerful brain waves, the same messages that caused him to save his wife's life. As long as the messages match what he is doing, it is comfortable, but once they don't match anymore, it would be unbelievably dissonant. To go back to your example of acting in a play, visualize trying to perform the play you are supposed to be performing, while some other, totally different play is blasting into your ears."

"No wonder you see those guys walking down the street, waving their arms and talking to no one."

"Maybe they *are* talking to someone," John suggested. "Maybe they are having the same conversations they had a million times before. This time, however, the people they were talking to in the past cycles just aren't there."

Kurt shook his head. "Weird."

"It may be weird, but if you start to really think about it, the theory not only explains schizophrenia, déjà vu and ghosts, it also explains psychics and mediums. They either have a faulty receiver in their head, or they have developed the ability to change the channel. Either way, they can receive the brain waves from people other than themselves – brain waves from the past, present...or even the future, because the future is really coming from the previous cycles, just later on in the timeline. It can also explain the experiences people have which they think prove reincarnation and a variety of other things."

"So, if we're just picking up brain waves from the other cycles," Kurt said thoughtfully, "how could you prove this theory? It seems like it would be impossible."

"That's what I…we…thought," said Jack. "Until we came up with the *John/Jack* thing."

Raising his eyebrows with curiosity, Kurt asked, "What *John/Jack* thing?"

Jack explained, "When we thought of this theory, we wanted to come up with a way to prove it, at least to ourselves. When we were, what…sixteen or seventeen?"

John nodded.

"Kurt, remember when we were that age, and John decided he wanted to be called *Jack*?"

"I do. It was a pain trying to keep it straight."

"And then he changed his mind and went back to *John*."

"For which I was very grateful."

"This was why. We thought it might be a good test. If, in all of the previous cycles, we *had* changed to *Jack*, then everyone we would meet for the rest of our life…because they would be getting the constant download from the cycles…would slip and call us *Jack*."

"That happens! I have seen it happen fifty times!" Kurt exclaimed.

"Yes, it does. And it continued after today, for the rest of my life. I don't care how clearly I say *John* when I introduce myself, or even if it's in writing, people still call me *Jack* all the time. I've even had people who have known me as *John* for years suddenly call me *Jack*."

"So, that's it," Kurt said. "But you're *Jack* now."

"Not really. I stayed with *John* until the trip back. I decided to use *Jack* when I got here."

"So, you guys think this proves the theory?"

John shrugged. "Maybe not in any scientific way, but it does for me."

"Me, too," said Jack.

"So how does this tie in to the time machine thing?"

"*That*," answered John, "is what we are trying to figure out. One possibility is…all of the things we are trying to change now weren't changed in the previous cycles, so we are fighting the download, the inertia we talked about before, of the million repetitions."

"The other possibility," Jack offered, "is that this cycle is the first cycle where Cal lived to build the time machine and that all of the previous times around, he did die, and the machine wasn't built. Maybe this is why it is so hard to undo his death."

As Kurt mulled over the possibilities, John noticed his friend's face suddenly become pale.

Concerned, John said, "Kurt. What is it?"

"God, I hope I'm wrong about this."

"What?'

Kurt held up his index finger, "Number one, your place burns down and all your books and trains go up in smoke." He lifted a second finger, "Two, the twins are aborted."

Seeing where his friend was going, John blurted, "My parents!"

They all jumped up from their chairs.

⧖

"Watch out!" Kurt yelled as they swung into the side street leading to John's parents' home. John swerved as another car was speeding out of the subdivision and they nearly collided.

"That was Gail's car!" John exclaimed, slamming down the gas pedal.

He skidded to a stop at his parents' driveway, and all three of them piled out of the car. Seeing that the house lights were all turned off, John frantically dug his key out of his pocket as Kurt said, "It's warm tonight. They probably didn't turn on the heater."

"They did," John answered. "You know how cold my mother always gets. She runs the damn thing when it's in the eighties."

Twisting the tumbler, John opened the door and dashed in, followed closely by Kurt and Jack. He crossed the living room and ran down the hallway, shouting for his parents. No answer came from the bedroom.

Kurt, gasping from the sprint, said, "I don't smell anything."

"You won't," came Jack's response. "Carbon monoxide is odorless."

They reached the bedroom, with John still in the lead, and ran in to find Ed and Kathleen in bed. John darted to the side of the bed and grabbed his mother's shoulders, shaking her firmly. "Mom! Mom! Wake up."

As John tried to rouse her, Jack opened the window above the headboard, and Kurt turned on the lights.

Neither his mother nor his father opened their eyes, and John could just make out a faint florid tinge to their skin color.

"Kurt, call 9-1-1!" he shouted, bending over to pick up his mother. Jack had gone around to his father's side of the bed and was already lifting him off of the sheets.

As John struggled to carry his mother down the hall, the effects of the carbon monoxide began to take a toll on him, and he staggered, bouncing off one of the walls and hooking his jacket pocket on the bathroom doorknob. He almost dropped his mother as his forward momentum caused him to pivot and slam into the wall for a second time. By the sheer force of his will, he maintained his grip and continued out of the hallway and into the living room. The final few steps to the open front door were almost too much for him as twice his knees buckled, and he nearly fell to the floor.

Using his free hand, John grasped the knob on the front door and pushed himself out into the fresh air. Stumbling several paces, he fell to his knees, laying his mother down on the grass more harshly than he intended.

Out of the corner of his eye, he saw Jack, supported on one side by Kurt, exit the house, still carrying his father. Wasting no time, John began to give his mother mouth-to-mouth resuscitation.

Timing, for once, was in his favor, as John felt his mother suddenly shudder and gasp for breath. He propped up her head and talked to her, beseeching his mother to open her eyes. When she did and saw her son's face, she reacted with a feeble smile which was immediately replaced with a look of confusion and concern.

Noticing that she was no longer in her own bed, she asked, "What happened?" her voice nearly a croak. "Where's your father?"

"He's right here," John answered reassuringly.

John looked over his shoulder and saw that Jack had successfully revived their father, who was already sitting up, a befuddled expression on his face as he stared at Jack. In the darkness of the front yard, John could see tears streaming down his *other's* face.

Ed Augur hacked several racking coughs as Jack held him tightly.

"Who is that?" his mother asked in a weak voice.

John turned back to Kathleen and said, "He was passing by when we arrived. He helped us."

John could tell by her expression that she wasn't buying the story, but before she could question him further, the quiet of the night was broken by the sounds of an ambulance.

John motioned for Kurt to come over to him. Kurt knelt next to Kathleen and supported her head and back, as John went to Jack and his father.

Softly, he said to Jack, "You better take off."

Jack made no move to release his embrace of his father.

John bent down and gently took Jack's arm from Ed's shoulder. "Come on. You gotta go."

Reluctantly, Jack allowed John to replace him at their father's side. With a final glance at both of his parents, he slowly turned and walked into the darkness, picking up his pace with each step.

- XV -

Even though they were both conscious and talking when the paramedics arrived, Ed and Kathleen were transported to St. Joseph's Hospital for observation and tests. John wanted to go with them, but the first police officer on the scene, Officer Kellond, asked him to stay. Within minutes, a second police car arrived, and John saw Officer Burke's tall, lanky figure emerge from the driver's side.

He approached John and Kurt, who were standing in the front yard of the Augur house, trying to stay out of the way.

"A detective is on the way, Mr. Augur," Burke advised, his voice flat and professional. If there was any curiosity or suspicion in his mind, he kept it to himself.

To explain the apparent coincidence of his presence, Burke noted, "I heard the call over the radio. When your name was mentioned, I figured I better head over here.

"While we wait for the detective, why don't you tell me what happened."

John and Kurt detailed the incident, beginning with their arrival at John's parents' house. When they finished, Burke asked, "What made you decide to come here? It's pretty late."

John's mind spun, trying to concoct a plausible reason without telling the officer about Jack or the fact that they knew this would happen because it had happened in the future. "I was worried. I saw them earlier today, and they were upset, so I thought I'd check up on them. When they didn't answer the phone,

I came over."

"Why were you worried? Had something happened earlier today?"

For a moment, John considered telling Burke that his parents were still upset about the fire, then decided against it, realizing that at some point he would interview Ed and Kathleen. He told the officer about Gail's visit to his parents, the Father's Day card, the sonogram and the receipt for the abortion. When he finished, Burke asked, "So, she wrote two names on the sonogram? Beth and John, Jr.?"

"Yes, sir. With little arrows pointing at the fetuses."

Burke shook his head in disgust and put his notepad into his shirt pocket. Looking John directly in the eye, he said, "As I said before, I think you have someone seriously pissed off at you."

John didn't respond.

Just then, Kellond walked up to them. Glancing at John and Kurt meaningfully, he asked Burke if he could speak to him alone. Burke told him to go ahead and talk in front of John.

"There was a ladder leaning against the house in the backyard. I checked out the roof and found a rag jammed into the furnace flue."

"You left it there for the lab guys?"

"Yes, sir."

"Thanks."

Kellond walked away, and Burke turned back to John. "Like I said, someone is seriously pissed off."

"Why would she leave the ladder? Isn't that a little obvious?"

"It's up to the detectives to figure it all out. My guess is that she was planning on coming back in an hour or so to take it down and put it away. It takes a while for carbon monoxide to work. I'm sure she planned on no one coming by here until morning, at the earliest. Hopefully, the lab will find fingerprints on the ladder or the flue."

John noticed that Burke was referring to the perpetrator as "she" and was comforted by his conclusion. As they spoke, an unmarked Crown Victoria pulled up to the curb and a middle-aged man, wearing a dark suit and white shirt, got out and walked to them. As he neared, John studied his face. Square jawed and resolute, the detective had an interesting combination of intelligence, compassion and determination chiseled into his features. For no apparent reason, John came to the conclusion that he was an ex-Marine.

The detective glanced at Burke and said, "Billy, why are you still on duty?"

"Nice to see you, too, Ben. I was heading in when I heard the call. This ties in to something that you and I are both working on."

The detective raised an eyebrow in curiosity.

By way of an explanation, Burke introduced the two men, "Detective Hart, this is John Augur."

A mild expression of surprise on his face, Hart turned to John and shook his hand. "Now I understand why Officer Burke specifically requested that I respond to this call. I'm the detective assigned to the arson investigation at your home, Mr. Augur."

"Good to meet you, sir."

John listened quietly as Burke brought the detective up to speed on what had transpired.

The crime scene technicians arrived; John and Kurt, feeling like they were in the way, walked to the front of a neighboring house and sat on a brick retaining wall next to the street.

"Where did Jack go?" Kurt muttered to John.

John shrugged. "He's probably hanging out somewhere around here. We'll find him when we leave."

Kurt watched the police and technicians as they methodically worked the scene. Two men, wearing dark windbreakers with "TPD Crime Unit" emblazoned on the back, carefully carried an aluminum ladder out of the backyard, using gloves to handle it. They placed the ladder inside the rear of their step-van. A third tech came from the rear of the house, carrying a plastic bag which contained a bunched-up rag.

"I know what Jack told me about the future, but I still can't believe she could do this," John spoke softly to Kurt.

"She's crazy, man! She had her whole future mapped out, and you had the audacity to mess up her plan. Arrgghh!" Kurt suddenly grabbed the sides of his head, bending forward.

Gripped instantly with concern and worry, John asked, "Are you all right?"

Kurt did not answer immediately, a low moan coming from him.

John put his arm on his best friend's shoulder, but Kurt shook it off.

"Don't," he muttered. "When these things hit, I can't stand to be touched."

John sat next to his friend in silence, feeling helpless as he watched Kurt endure the pain in his head.

After a few minutes, John tried again, "How long have you been having these?"

Sucking in a deep breath, Kurt managed to answer, "A few months." Groaning again, he leaned farther forward so that his chest was touching the top of his thighs.

"It looks like they're getting worse."

Kurt barely managed to nod his head. The anguish finally seemed to subside somewhat, and he was able to sit upright. He released his grip from the sides of his head.

"What did the doctor say about them?"

"He...," Kurt started to respond, pausing as another stab of pain lanced his brain. "He says they are probably migraines."

"You've never had migraines before."

"That's the way they come on, apparently. He said that sometimes they just start...out of the blue. In your twenties or thirties. Sometimes even later in life."

With the intensity of the episode substantially diminished, Kurt was gradually returning to his normal self.

"Has he done any tests? Does he know for sure that's what it is?"

Kurt started to shake his head and thought better of it. "He wants to do a CAT scan. I haven't gotten around to going in for it yet."

"Maybe you should."

Kurt slowly and carefully turned to face John. "Let's get this other mess straightened out first."

Detective Hart came out the front door of John's parents' house and walked over to them. "I don't see any reason for the two of you to stick around any longer. We've got quite a bit of work left to do here, and you probably want to go check on your folks."

They stood up, and John asked him, "What are you going to do next?"

"What do you mean?"

"Are you going to arrest her...Gail?"

The detective looked over his shoulder at the crime scene for a moment before he turned back to John. "We have a bit more to figure out before I can answer that."

Realizing that both Burke and Detective Hart had probably already been more forthcoming with information than was usually the case, John just said, "Okay. I think I will go to see my parents now."

"Here's my card. Call me if anything else...if anything comes up. I can reach you by phone?"

"Yes, sir. You've got my cell number." John pulled out his wallet and put the detective's card away.

Before John and Kurt could back out, they had to wait as Kellond moved his police car. Starting the engine, John said "Let's go find Jack."

They didn't have far to go. Jack was standing under a mesquite tree a few houses away, concealed from the view of the police. When he saw John's car slowly approaching, he stepped cautiously out of the shadows. John pulled to the curb, and Jack climbed in. None of them noticed the blinds slowly closing on the house behind him.

As they drove to the hospital, John and Kurt told Jack everything that had happened. When they told him about the rag stuffed into the furnace flue, Jack exploded with a string of expletives directed at Gail.

The drive to St. Joseph's was a short one, made even quicker by the lateness of the hour. As John went to the nurse's desk in the emergency room to locate his parents, Jack and Kurt found two empty seats in the waiting area.

Only a few minutes had passed before John returned. "They're asleep. I talked to the doctor, and he said they are both going to be fine. We got them out in plenty of time."

"No permanent damage?" Jack asked.

"From the preliminary exam, he didn't think so. They're going to run some tests tomorrow to make sure. Both of them are on oxygen right now."

John noticed for the first time that Kurt had fallen asleep in the molded plastic chair in the waiting room.

Smiling, he said, "Let's get him home and in bed."

"That's a good idea," Jack said. "He is going to have a big day tomorrow." He looked at his watch and corrected himself, "Or later today."

⏳

When Gail had sped away from the Augurs' house earlier, she had not recognized John's car as the vehicle she almost hit. As she returned to clean up the scene, she had not yet rounded the corner to the cul-de-sac, when she saw the flashing red and blue lights of emergency vehicles reflected off the trees and houses.

"Damn!" she exclaimed aloud, pulling over to the curb and stopping her car.

Just to be sure, she got out and carefully walked to the corner, making certain that she used the mature trees and shrubs to remain out of sight. As Gail reached a suitable vantage point, an overpowering sense of elation swept through her. The presence of the police and the crime scene technicians boldly advertised to her that she had succeeded.

She did not, for a moment, feel any fear or worry. It did not occur to her that she would be arrested for the deaths of Ed and Kathleen Augur. She did not even consider that she would be a suspect. Such was the way the mind of a narcissist with borderline personality disorder worked.

It was unfortunate, she thought, that she had not been able to return in time to put the ladder back in the carport. It was also too bad that the rag was still stuck in the flue when the cops arrived, eliminating any possibility for the success of her original plan – that the deaths appear accidental.

She wondered, idly, how the cops came to be here at this time of night, concluding that either Ed or Kathleen must have awakened and noticed something wrong. She visualized the scene, believing to the very core of her being that the sheer force of her will would make her scenario become reality. Ed, needing to use the toilet, woke up and immediately felt dizzy. Dazed and confused, he probably called 9-1-1. Then he tried to wake up Kathleen. Failing that, he attempted to carry her out of the house. It saddened Gail that it had not been practical for her to have been in there, in the living room, watching Ed Auger, loaded down with the dead-weight burden of John's mother in his arms, stagger and collapse to the floor to die. Instead, she had to settle for a more remote, and therefore a much less satisfying, feeling of revenge…revenge on them for their part in John's decision to call off the wedding.

They thought they had been so subtle, she reflected back on the last several months. They must have believed that they had pulled it off, that they had succeeded in hiding their true feelings about her – and their precious son's impending marriage to her. But she saw through them. She knew all along that they hated her…plotted against her…and wanted to stop the wedding.

Grinning to herself, Gail visualized the cops arriving, breaking down the front door and finding the Augurs in a heap on the floor, either in the living room or probably only in the hallway. After all, Ed was an old man. He couldn't have made it very far carrying his wife.

Her grin grew to a broad smile as she realized that, certainly by now, the cops must have notified John of the deaths of his parents. She was, again, disappointed that she couldn't be present to see John receive the news. To watch him break down. To gloat over his devastation.

The rag! she thought to herself. That might be a problem. She knew that the average IQ of a police officer, even a detective, was just barely above that of a frog. Still, even *they* would find the rag in the flue. And even *they* would come to the conclusion that this was a homicide and not just an accident.

She decided to worry about that later. The tingle of excitement she was feeling was too enjoyable to subdue or delay by dwelling on mundane details.

Although, Gail concluded, it wouldn't be a bad idea to be unavailable for the next few days.

Dismissing the concern from any further thought, she walked back to her car and drove into the night, humming along with a song on the radio.

⚱

John, Kurt and Jack were, once again, in the storage room. They had made it to Kurt's house before the sun rose, and managed to fall asleep, getting up well past noontime. After grabbing a quick lunch, they decided to move forward with the original plan.

Kurt occupied the pilot chair; Jack stood inside the machine next to him, completing the procedure which added Kurt to the machine's biometric library. John was seated on the threshold of the hatch. "I think that's it," Jack concluded. "Do you have any questions?"

Instead of the usual wisecrack that John and Jack both expected from their friend, Kurt answered, "No. I think I've got it."

John persisted, "Let's go over this one more time."

"Probably a good idea," Jack concurred.

"Okay." Kurt looked at Jack and recited the plans, "Your last trip started late Friday night, so I need to go back farther. I didn't have any classes on Friday and spent the day out at Gate's Pass, sketching. That works out because I know I won't run into myself all that day.

"So, I'm going to go back to Friday morning. That gives me all of Friday and most of Saturday, because you didn't catch up with Cal until late Saturday evening.

"But I shouldn't need to stay Saturday. I know where to find Cal on Friday morning. He's in a calculus class that I dropped. It starts at nine. I'll be there before the class and try to catch him then. If he gets there too late, I'll hook up with him after it. I don't think he has any other classes the rest of the day."

"What if he doesn't come to that class at all?" John asked.

"I know where he lives. I'll catch him there."

"What if he's out of town Friday? Do you have his cell number?"

"No, but I do know two of his friends. I can get it from them."

Jack thought through the plan for the hundredth time, trying to overcome any obstacles. "We haven't really talked about what you're going to say. How are you going to broach the subject in the first place?"

"Cal's pretty cool," Kurt replied. "We've had some good talks. I think I can just ease into it."

"Kurt," Jack pressed, "have you thought about *exactly* how to bring it up?"

"I haven't scripted it in my head, no. I planned on playing it by ear."

John asked, "What if he doesn't believe you?"

Kurt smiled and squirmed in the chair so he could reach the back pocket of his jeans. He pulled out a folded and rumpled sheet of newsprint and handed it to Jack. "When we had breakfast yesterday, I bought a paper."

John stood up from the hatchway and joined Jack as he unfolded Monday's edition of the *Arizona Daily Star*. Cal's accident was on the front page, with photos.

"I think that might help to convince him," Kurt said smugly.

"It should," Jack agreed. "Unless he's one of those guys who suspects that everything has been created with some photo software."

Kurt shrugged. "We'll see, I guess. Anyway, I've got the ace in the hole."

"What's that?"

"I know about you showing up at his dorm Saturday night. I know what you are going to say to him. I know that you're going to try to disable his bike. Even if I can't convince him when I talk to him, when he sees that all of the things I told him about happen exactly as I predicted, it should get his attention."

"You know," John warned him, his voice laden with doubt, "if something can go wrong, it will."

"Now *that*," Kurt criticized, "is a defeatist attitude."

"I was thinking about Jack's trip," John continued. "Kurt, what about this? If you either don't connect with Cal or fail to convince him, have you thought about catching Jack before he confronts Cal at the dorm? There'd be plenty of time while he's waiting in front. Jack, if your trip really was the catalyst for Cal speeding away to his appointment with destiny, maybe if Kurt stopped you from having the confrontation, that would be all we need."

"That's a possibility," Jack admitted, "but I'm not sure. If, for some reason Cal's accident is *burned in*, it might happen anyway. He could get into an argument with his roommate, stomp out and hop on his bike. We just don't know."

"I don't know how it could be *burned in,* as you put it. Jack, you came from a future that had Cal in it. Why wouldn't that be *burned in*? If the accident is somehow meant to be," Kurt hypothesized, "there's nothing we can do, anyway. My guess is that it's worth a try. If I flunk out completely with Cal, then, yeah, I get with Jack in front of the dorm and head him off before he talks to Cal.

"We could even hide by the parking lot. When Cal gets back to his dorm, we don't approach him. We let him go inside. While he's upstairs, we trash his bike. No bike – no bike accident."

"That might work."

"I just realized that there's one problem with this," John declared.

"What?" Kurt sighed.

"Jack, I thought you said before that the machine can't keep track of the data threads of two simultaneous travelers. Won't Kurt need to be gone before you arrive late Friday night?"

"That's right. Damn!"

"We can still basically do the same thing," Kurt suggested.

"How?" John asked.

"I can take back a letter. Jack, when you went back there, where – physically – did you go? I mean, where did the sphere materialize?"

"Like I told you before, I had it materialize right here in this room." He pointed out of the hatchway at a spot a few feet from where the sphere rested. "The room is big enough for two of the machines."

"So, when you went back," Kurt said, "the two machines were side by side?"

"Uh-huh."

"Cool! That's makes it easy. If I don't succeed with Cal, I come back to *this* room and leave a letter on the inside of the door, telling you what happened and what we've tried to do. It'll be the first thing you see as you are leaving the room. You won't be able to miss it. We tell you not to confront Cal. We tell you to go straight to the dorm Saturday night and slash the tires and rip out the wires on his bike. And then I go next door, get into my machine and split just before you arrive."

"I think that's about the best we can come up with, as far as a Plan B," said Jack.

"I guess so," agreed John. "Now, I've got another question."

"I think I've had enough of your questions," Kurt teased.

"Go ahead," Jack prompted.

"Let's assume Kurt's trip succeeds. We need to take some time to think through what happens. In just a few minutes, we'll be standing here in this room, watching Kurt climb in and close the door. *Poof!* he goes back and talks to Cal. Convinces him not to get on his bike Saturday night. Cal doesn't die. Right?"

Jack and Kurt both nodded.

"Kurt comes back to this room, a split second after he left, but *we* won't be standing here."

Understanding dawned on the faces of both men, and John continued, "Let's go back to that Saturday night. Kurt's plastered...."

"I wasn't plastered!"

"Kurt's mildly inebriated."

"That's more like it."

"And you and I are walking our mildly inebriated friend, who is incapable of standing on his own...."

Kurt snorted.

"Anyway, we cross the street, but this time no motorcycle arrives. No Cal. No crash. With me so far?"

Again, they nodded.

"The three of us cross the street without incident. What do we do after that?"

Neither Jack nor Kurt responded, so John resumed, "That's my point, we don't know what we do next. I'm sure that we take Kurt to his room and tuck him in. Then you and I go somewhere quiet and talk some more. Probably my room. You finish convincing me to not marry Gail. That's it. There would be no reason for you to stay, right?"

"True."

"So, you get back into your time machine and go back to your home time. We never tell Kurt about any of this. We wouldn't have any reason to tell him. Basically, everything that's happened since we crossed that street doesn't happen, including," John grimaced, "my little visit with Lynn.

"You're gone. The time machine is gone. We've got no way to send Kurt back to make this trip, to satisfy the requirement, as you describe it, Jack."

Jack started to speak, but John held up his hand to stop him. "So, Kurt and I live through all of Sunday. I break up with Gail, and we have that horrible scene. The fire at the apartment probably happens Sunday night, I guess. If not, then some other night. Monday night Gail plugs the flue on my folks' furnace. Tuesday afternoon rolls around and at about," John paused and looked at his watch, "two o'clock the machine appears with Kurt, *this Kurt*, here in this room. *He* knows everything that's happened the past three days because he is immune to the effect of the changes."

Addressing Kurt, John continued once more, "You probably come find me and tell me the whole story. It's too late at that point for us to save my parents. You eventually tell me about Lynn, so I can still make that happen. The only problem is that you are not only telling the story to me, you're also telling it to…."

"The other Kurt."

"Right. Because if we don't send *that* Kurt back to Friday, *this* Kurt is still going to arrive this afternoon."

Shaking his head, Kurt complained, "Man, this gets complicated."

"I don't think it's that bad," Jack reassured him.

"You can say that. You aren't the one with a sudden twin." Quickly, Kurt added, "Well, you are, but he's thirty years younger than you."

"That's not what I mean. I think we can fix all that with another message. Kurt, you would take a message back to Friday and figure out a way to get it to us. Maybe through Cal, I don't know. But all we have to do is spell everything out in detail."

"Including making sure my parents are okay."

"Yeah. Forewarned, you should be able to head that off completely. Anyway…that way, when we cross the street and no Cal comes zipping at us, we know what to do. We keep this machine here…. By the way, even if everything had gone according to my original plan with you Saturday night, I wouldn't have gone back until the machine I originally arrived in, the bigger one that appeared the night before last at the courthouse, came back to get me. Remember, this one was intended only to be the backup."

"Oh, that's right," John said.

"So," Jack explained, "we get the message from Kurt. John, you would have to make sure that Kurt gets in *this* machine at the right time, to keep everything straight. Then, I could leave, or do whatever I decide to do."

John shot Jack a look of anger, but decided to let his comment drop. "It's a weird thought. Looking at this from our current perspective, in a little while Kurt closes the door to the machine, and again assuming everything goes according to plan, a second later the door opens, I am standing here alone, and I will not have any of the memories from the last two days in my mind anymore because Kurt has changed my past. All of the memories from then will be replaced with a whole new set. And the message, the one we're going to create in a minute, will be in my hands."

"Exactly," Jack said. "Except that when Kurt climbs out of the machine, he's going to remember everything that's in his head now."

"Do-do-do-do, do-do-do-do," Kurt sang the intro theme from *Twilight Zone*.

"I don't think I could ever get accustomed to this." John vigorously rubbed his face with his hands.

"Actually, if I go back and explain all of this to Cal, when I come back here to today, instead of Jack standing here with you, it will probably be Cal."

"Enough! This is making my head hurt again."

Jack chuckled. "We better get started on the message. It's going to be a long one."

"I think I have a better idea," Kurt suggested.

"What's that?"

"Let's grab a video camera and record all three of us telling the story. Then I can take the DVD back with me. There was a DVD player in the hotel room, wasn't there?"

"Yes," John recalled.

"Good. That makes it easy. We make the disk, I leave it at the front desk for you with instructions that you are not to watch it until you get back to the room from the train station with Jack and me. Just to be safe, I take an extra copy and give it to Cal. He can come to see you both at the room after midnight."

"There's only problem with this plan," John said.

"What's that?"

"If it works, I'm going to lose the memories I have of yesterday morning with Lynn."

Kurt and Jack both rolled their eyes.

The three of them drove to a nearby office superstore and purchased a compact video camera, a cheap tripod and a box of blank disks. As they returned and began to set up the equipment, John said, "I'll get my laptop out of the car. We'll need that to make a copy of the disk."

"You'd think a fancy traveling machine like this," Kurt gestured toward the sphere, "would have a built-in DVD player/recorder."

Jack laughed. "What's the point? The trips last less than a second."

"That's true."

With everything set, John pressed the REC button and joined the others in front of the lens. It took over twenty minutes to explain everything thoroughly. John removed the mini-DVD from the camera and slid it into the side port on his laptop. They reviewed it twice, to make certain that no critical elements were left out, then burned two copies.

"An extra," John said as he handed all three of the disks to Kurt.

"Yeah," Kurt said, smiling. "There isn't any reason for you to keep one, is there?"

"Not really. If you fail, I won't need it, and if you succeed, it won't exist anymore."

"True. So true."

John packed the camera, tripod and laptop into his car and returned to the room, making certain to close the door firmly.

"I guess that's it," he supposed.

"Why do I suddenly feel nervous?" Kurt asked.

"We all do," Jack responded.

Kurt turned to Jack and surprised him by pulling him forward in a hard embrace. "If this goes well, I'm not going to see you again, am I?"

Jack hugged back as hard as he could. "Probably not. If we can get this train back on the tracks, the sooner I clear out of here the better...for everyone's sake. Besides," Jack added, pointing at John, "you've got me right there."

They separated, and Kurt told him, "Not the same thing, man. You are you and he is...whatever the hell he is."

They all burst out laughing. Kurt continued, "You know what I mean, you guys are the same...but you're two different guys. Anyway, I guess what I'm trying to say is...I'm really going to miss you." He bit his lower lip to stop it from quivering.

Jack felt the emotion welling up within him. Although he struggled to control it, the emotions won the battle and he let out a single, jagged sob. Taking a long, deep breath, he said, "I'll miss you, too."

They hugged once again. Stepping back, Kurt resolved, "I better get to this."

Jack walked his friend to the hatch. As Kurt settled into the chair, Jack instructed, "It's all programmed. All you have to do is close the door and tap the start icon."

"Got it." He looked over Jack's shoulder at John and said, "Hey dude, I'll be right back."

"They always say that in the movies just before the monster gets them," John joked, smiling.

"Thanks. That's just what I needed to hear. See you soon, you big baboon."

John smiled weakly.

"John?" Kurt began.

John noticed an odd note in his friend's voice. "Yeah?"

"Just in case," Kurt started to say, his voice less than steady. Clearing his throat, he continued, "Just in case, you know, something goes wrong...."

"Nothing is going to go wrong," insisted John.

"I know. But just in case, you know. I...."

The door to the storage room suddenly burst open.

"YOU NEED TO GET OUT OF HERE – NOW!"

"Aloysius?" John shouted, startled.

Aloysius ran into the room and grabbed him, without even a glance at the time machine. He pushed hard, and John slammed against the door jamb and fell out onto the pavement

"What the...?"

Before Jack could finish his sentence, Aloysius had turned his attention to him, took his arm with a surprisingly strong grip, and pulled him toward the alley. "We have to get out of here!"

They had progressed only a step toward the door when a sudden, overpowering blast of sound struck their ears, accompanied by what felt like an earthquake as the concrete slab beneath their feet began to shake.

They staggered through the opening into the alley when Jack suddenly jerked loose from Aloysius's grip and turned back to help Kurt. Aloysius, unable to stop Jack, began to follow him in as the roof of the storage room caved in. They were blasted with a violent cloud of dust and debris, slamming them both backwards.

Stunned from the impact, Jack saw that John was still lying on his back where he had fallen, and for a moment he thought that his younger self was injured. Then, to his relief, he noticed that John's eyes were staring straight up, a look of astonishment on his face.

Jack followed his gaze and saw that the intense, Arizona afternoon sky directly above them was several orders of magnitude brighter than usual. He was unable to discern the source of the light, his eyes barely able to remain open against it. Jack was suddenly aware of a hand on his arm and turned to see that Aloysius was holding him and talking. At least Jack thought he was talking because he could see the stranger's mouth moving, but couldn't hear him over the din.

Reading Aloysius's body language and gestures, Jack realized that he was trying to get him to help move John out of harm's way. They bent over and seized his arms, dragging him across the alley into an old alcove once used as a loading dock.

With all of them huddled in the semi-protective area, they watched as the light, impossibly, brightened. The coinciding blast and rumble of sound grew to match the light's intensity, to the point where they had to cover their ears for fear of sustaining permanent damage. The light was so blindingly brilliant, they were no longer able to see the storage building a mere thirty feet away.

As suddenly as it all began, the sound ceased and the light disappeared, leaving an opaque, brownish-gray cloud of dust in their wake. The three men covered their mouths and noses with their shirts to filter the dust and watched as the cloud dissipated.

John realized his ears must not have been damaged because he could hear sirens approaching. Jack jumped to his feet and said, "Kurt! And the machine! We can't let them see the machine."

Before Jack could reenter the disaster, Aloysius, with a note of grin finality in his voice, simply stated, "It's gone. They're both gone. They took it."

- XVI -

"THEY?" Jack screamed at Aloysius. "Who in the hell are *they*?"

"The Anunnaki."

Jack, his mouth agape, stared at Aloysius. "What are you talking about? Who are the Anunnaki, and why would they do this?"

Aloysius looked at Jack sympathetically. His voice maddeningly soothing and reasonable, he answered, "They are from Nibiru."

With his fist clenched, Jack took a step toward Aloysius, but John stepped between them.

"Aloysius," John said, trying to keep an even tone. "Maybe you could explain all of this to us. Why are they here? What do they want?"

"And how in the hell do you know all about it?" Jack shouted, pressing forward against John.

Aloysius smiled at them and stated, "All in good time."

He pointed toward the end of the alley, and both John and Jack saw the first of the fire engines pulling toward them, with its lights flashing and siren blaring.

Raising his voice to be heard over the shrill tones of the siren, Aloysius advised Jack, "I think it would be best if you were not here. That might be awkward."

The truth of Aloysius's words sank in. Jack stopped trying to push past John and turned to leave.

The firefighters, oblivious to Jack's departure, brought the ladder truck to a halt in front of John and Aloysius, scrambling out of the vehicle. The siren now turned off, the tone descended to silence, mimicking the diminishing final howl of a hound dog.

"Is everyone all right?" the firefighter asked.

"There may be someone trapped in there," John indicated the collapsed storage room.

He followed the firefighter around the truck and stared at the destruction. The roof of the building was completely pancaked down upon the slab, bringing down with it a portion of the front wall.

"Fire!" one of the firefighters shouted, pointing into the wreckage. John looked in that direction and saw bright yellow flames growing from a jumbled pile of rafters and studs.

The men, already in the process of removing their hoses and equipment from the truck, intensified their efforts as John suddenly heard a banging noise coming from the adjacent storage room, the storage room they had rented as the alternate location for the return of the sphere.

"There's someone in this one!" John shouted, a shiver of excitement filling him with certainty that it must be Kurt. He must have somehow used the sphere to travel to the adjacent room.

Two of the firefighters attacked the wooden door with their axes, making short work of it, and plunged through into the room. Smoke was already billowing from the newly-opened door, and John realized that the fire had started at the wall separating the two rooms.

His anxiety was replaced almost instantly with a flood of relief as he saw one of the yellow-jacketed firefighters dash out of the storage room with the inert figure of a man slung over his shoulder. The firefighter carried the limp body to the far side of the alley, and after two of the men quickly unloaded a cot from their equipment bin and set it up, the third firefighter gently laid the unconscious figure down.

John, rushing to the cot, abruptly stopped as he saw that the man who was lying on it, covered with soot and dust, was not Kurt, but a stranger. Speechless and unable to move, John grappled with the reality before him. Unable to conjure up a reasonable explanation, he watched as one of the firefighters, a paramedic, cleared the stranger's airway and gave him mouth-to-mouth resuscitation.

After the paramedic blew three lungsful of air into the stranger's mouth, the chest of the man on the cot suddenly heaved and spasmed as he began to cough violently. Seeing that the stranger was breathing on his own, the paramedic quickly placed a plastic mask over the victim's lower face and turned on a supply of oxygen. The racking coughs subsided, and the man on the cot deeply inhaled the pure, clean oxygen.

John stood as near to the stranger as he could, staring down at him while trying to understand what had happened. The man's eyes opened and, for a moment, wildly flitted about, vividly expressing the confusion he must have felt. Suddenly, they locked on John's eyes, and some sort of recognition was obvious on the man's face. The paramedic had stepped away for a moment, and John took the opportunity to move closer.

The stranger reached up and removed the oxygen mask from his face. He tried to speak twice, but each time was interrupted by a new bout of coughing. With a supreme effort he tried again, and this time was able to utter, "You must be John."

Baffled by the turn of events, John quietly said, "Yes, and who are you?"

The stranger forced a halfhearted grin onto his face, stuck out his hand and introduced himself, "I'm Cal. Cal Mitchell."

John, flabbergasted, also numbly extended his hand. As Cal started to sit up, the paramedic returned, placed a firm grip on his shoulder, and told him to stay down and wait for the ambulance that was en route to take him to the hospital. Cal shook him off, and insisted that he was fine and didn't need to go to the hospital. They argued briefly. Cal prevailed, and the paramedic left to assist the other firefighters who were battling what was rapidly becoming an inferno.

John and Cal were told to move farther back, away from the heat and smoke. As they did, John realized that in the confusion, he had lost track of Aloysius.

"Where's Kurt?" Cal asked as they reached the street at the mouth of the alley, a note of concern in his voice.

"What do you mean? I thought he was…. What happened? How did you get here?"

Cal looked around them to see if anyone was within hearing distance before answering, "I was on my way to class this morning… I guess it was Friday morning, actually… when Kurt caught me outside the building. He was very excited and kept carrying on about you and Jack, said that the two of you were in some kind of trouble and that he needed to get back right away."

Cal looked down the alley toward the fire engines and added, "I guess he wasn't mistaken. It took me a while to calm him down. When I finally did, he said we needed to talk someplace private. We sat on the mall, and he told me everything. Afterwards, we went to my dorm room...my roommate was in class...and he played this for me."

Cal pulled the mini-DVD out of his pocket and handed it to John.

"I'm sorry," John cut in. "This is all quite interesting, but what happened to Kurt?"

"I'm getting to that. After I saw the DVD, we talked some more, and Kurt decided that maybe it would be better if I skipped over the next few days and came here directly. That way we wouldn't have to worry about the...," Cal paused again before continuing, "the accident. We also wouldn't have to worry about saving your parents."

"That makes sense, I guess, but please tell me...."

"I'm almost there. So, the two of us came to the storage room Friday morning. He wanted me to come back first."

"Why?"

Cal shrugged. "I was a day or two away from being dead, anyway. If, when the machine re-materialized in the storage room next door, and something horrible was going on...or if something happened to me on the trip here, he would still be alive, back on Friday. Since he knew all of the details of the next two days better than I did, he thought that maybe he could do something about all of this between then and now."

"There are some problems with that plan."

"I know. We both knew that, but Kurt was frantic, and we were anxious to do something. Plus, he decided that if he did leave first, and something happened to him...to all of you...I would still be back in Friday. I guess the three of you had a lot of talks about inertia and some kind of tendency or force that keeps making things happen that are meant to happen. We didn't have much time to talk about all of that, so I really didn't understand what he was saying. He figured if he made sure I got here, at least the main part of his assignment, as he put it, would be accomplished because I would have just leapfrogged over the night of the accident."

"So where is he? If he stayed back on Friday, why isn't he walking up to us right now?"

Cal stared down at the sidewalk for a moment, his face shifting into a look of sadness. "When I materialized in the storage room and got out of the sphere, I heard a racket next door. Everything still looked okay for Kurt to follow me, so I sent the machine back, just like I told him I would if it was all clear. Then I started to use the wrench he gave me to remove the nuts on the door lock. That's when the fire burst through the wall and the place filled up with smoke.

I couldn't even see the nuts holding the lock anymore, so I started banging on the door and yelling. Then I guess I passed out."

John visualized the sequence in his mind. "If you sent the sphere back for Kurt, he would have arrived a moment after you sent it back. Did he?"

"It wouldn't have come back that quickly. When Kurt programmed it to bring me here, he set it for a couple of minutes after his departure. I'm guessing he would have done the same thing for his own trip."

"You didn't see the sphere materialize in the room before you passed out?"

Cal shook his head. "I'm not sure."

"What do you mean, you're not sure?"

"I'm sorry. I'm not. It was...it started to fill with smoke right away, maybe less than a minute after I arrived. And then it was hard to see...hard to tell...I thought...I thought that I had seen it materialize in the middle of the smoke, but I'm not sure."

John stared at the man who was to someday become his friend and saw the confusion and anguish in his eyes.

Before John could say anything else to Cal, the police arrived. John heaved a sigh of relief to see that Burke was not among the responding officers. The police questioned both of them. John explained that he just happened to be passing by the storage room when the explosion, or whatever it was, had occurred. Cal told them that he was the renter of the adjacent room and was dropping off some old things for storage when the fire started.

The police took down their names, addresses and phone numbers and told them they could leave.

"We need to find Jack," John said as they walked away from the scene.

When they turned the corner, there was Jack, sitting on a bus bench and looking around. They were walking up to join him when he spotted John and jumped up from the bench. "What...?" Jack stopped in mid-sentence when he saw Cal.

"Cal?"

Cal smiled at Jack sheepishly. "I understand that you and I are supposed to be old friends."

Jack stared at Cal with disbelief.

Looking around at the crowd, John urged, "Come on, let's walk."

Jack, shaken by the surprise of seeing Cal, walked slowly as John explained what had happened. Cal took over the narrative to tell Jack what had occurred on Friday. When they finished, Jack asked, "So where is Kurt?"

"We don't know," John stated flatly.

"He might have tried to return to the storage room and could have arrived just in time for the fire," Cal suggested, the sadness obvious in his voice.

"Jack," John said, "wouldn't the sphere check the area before it returned with Kurt, like we saw it do at the courthouse?"

Jack shook his head. "Only the big one has that gear. The smaller one, the backup machine, doesn't."

Addressing Cal, Jack asked, "Could the sphere have withstood the fire?"

"Jack, you might be asking the person who invented it, but you're asking him several years too soon. The truth is, I have no idea."

They were interrupted as a loud explosion shook the windows behind them. Panicked, they ran back to the alley, only to be stopped by the police who had cordoned off the area.

"What happened?" John questioned the officer.

"I don't know," the policeman answered. "I think the fire might have reached a gas line."

The three of them stood with the crowd of spectators, ignoring the jokes from the teenagers in the group who tried to demonstrate worldly bravado to their friends while safely behind the police line. None said anything as they observed the conflagration, hoping to catch a glimpse of something to indicate what had happened. More fire engines arrived, as did additional police who extended the cordoned area farther away from the site of the explosion.

Lingering for nearly an hour before giving up, the three men walked to John's car.

"Where do we go now?" asked Jack. "John, your place is burned down, we don't have a key to Kurt's, and I don't have a place."

"We can't really go to my dorm. I'm sure my roommate is there, and I'm supposed to be dead," Cal reasoned.

"Let's go to my parents' house. I have a key, and they're still at the hospital, as far as I know."

They drove in silence, all three filled with worry about Kurt. Arriving at the Augur home, they saw that the front door was crisscrossed with police tape.

"I need to land somewhere," said John resignedly, "someplace where there aren't any people around."

"Yeah," agreed Jack. "We have a lot to talk about."

Silence filled the car for several minutes, each of the three men lost in their own thoughts, when suddenly John slammed his fist on the steering wheel.

"I knew it!" he shouted.

Startled, Jack pressed him, "What? What's the matter?"

"Ever since Cal told us why we couldn't go to his dorm, something has been bothering me. I just now figured it out."

"Because my roommate is there?"

"No! Because you are supposed to be dead."

John paused to let them figure it out for themselves.

"He couldn't have died," Jack concluded after a moment.

"That's right. Cal couldn't have died because he left on Friday, the day before the accident."

"I don't understand," Cal said. "Isn't that what you all wanted?"

"Of course it is," answered John. "That's not what is weirding me out. You couldn't have been driving the motorcycle Saturday night when we crossed the street...because you weren't there."

"Right."

"So, it never happened."

"Uh-huh."

"Then why do we...Jack and I...still remember it?"

"Well...," Cal stopped as the implications of what John had said sank in.

"Something's wrong," Jack maintained. "If Kurt changed the past, then that *new* past is what should be in our heads."

"But I just leapfrogged over it. Wouldn't that leave everything the same?" Cal hesitated for a second before continuing. "That's stupid. Of course it would change things."

John pulled his phone out of his pocket and started to dial.

"Who are you calling?" asked Jack.

"The hospital. I need to see what else, if anything, has changed."

A moment later John got the hospital operator on the phone and requested that she put him through to his parents' room. After two rings, he heard his mother's voice say, "Hello."

"Mom! It's me. I...uh...I was checking on you and Dad." He listened as she told him they were both doing just fine and should be able to go home tomorrow. He told her that might be a problem since the house was sealed off as a crime scene.

"Oh, right. I knew that. Detective Hart mentioned it when he came by today to talk to us."

She wondered when John was going to come by, and he told her he wasn't sure right now but would call them later. After each finished their *I love you* and *good-bye*, he broke the connection and looked at Jack.

"Well. *That* still happened."

Pointing at the police tape on the house, Jack said, "I figured."

"Okay, let's look at this logically," John posited. "Kurt went back to Friday morning and talked to Cal," he glanced in the back seat and added, "to you. You departed from Friday morning and arrived here on Tuesday afternoon, which means that you were not present and available for the accident Saturday night."

"Right."

"Then, logically, there can only be two possible explanations. The first possibility is that the accident didn't happen. The problem is…if it didn't happen, why do we still have memories that it did happen?"

John paused to see if either of the two had a comment. When neither did, he continued, "The second possibility is that the accident *did* happen, which would explain the fact that our memories are intact, but would beg the question – if Cal skipped over Saturday night and is sitting here in my car, who died?"

"And, regardless of which of the possibilities ends up being the case, where is Kurt?" asked Jack.

"Right. We'll need to get to that in a minute. I think we need to solve this other issue first."

"Whether or not the accident happened should be pretty easy to resolve," Cal determined, pulling something out of his back pocket. He unfolded the newspaper that Kurt had shown John and Jack before he left.

"Kurt gave me this on Friday morning. We need to check and see if this story is still in the Monday paper. We can do that on the Internet."

John said, "I've still got my laptop. Let's go someplace with Wi-Fi and go to the newspaper's website."

Jack and Cal agreed, and John started the car. As he drove, Cal asked the question, "If this story *is* still in the paper, whose body is lying on the slab?"

"Good question," John replied. "Let's take this a step at a time."

Within minutes, they arrived at the Borders at Park Place Mall. Jack and Cal went to the counter and ordered some coffees and muffins, while John booted up his laptop and logged in to the Wi-Fi site. By the time Jack finished doctoring the coffees to his and John's liking, and returned to the table with Cal, John had his answer. As they distributed the muffins and coffees and sat down, he rotated the computer so both could see what was on the screen. It was an electronic replica of the same page that Kurt had shown to the two of them and given to Cal.

"Like you said," John addressed Cal, "this begs the question…whose body do they have?"

Jack took a huge bite out of the blueberry muffin, scattering crumbs on the table and the keyboard of John's laptop. "I know what you're thinking," he said to John. "You're trying to figure out every possible alternative before we go see the body, aren't you?"

John nodded.

"Assuming we can," Cal interjected. "Do we know whether we can get in?"

Jack smiled. "I think, considering that you don't have any siblings and your parents passed away a few years ago, we shouldn't have any problem at all."

Curious, Cal asked, "Why not?"

"Who isn't going to believe that you are the twin brother of the deceased?"

Cal chuckled and shook his head. "Now I know why you and I became friends."

Turning back to John, Jack said, "Are you going to share with me the various scenarios that you've already thought through, or do I have to do the work myself?"

John grinned. "No. I'll share. You're right, I like to think through every possible outcome before I do anything. If we get there, and it is Cal – to use the phrase from a little while ago – lying on the slab, what does that mean?"

Both Jack and Cal were silent, trying to think through the ramifications of that reality.

John continued, "The second option is that it isn't Cal."

"Wait, I saw the driver's license Saturday night," Jack objected.

"Right. You saw the driver's license. Did you see the face?"

Jack thought back to the aftermath of the accident. "No, I didn't. It was dark, and the rider had on a helmet with a visor covering the face."

"So, it could have been anyone."

"I guess. Anyone with Cal's driver's lic…."

They both looked at Cal who stared back at them for a moment before realizing the nature of the unspoken question. He reached into his back pocket to pull out his wallet. "It's gone," he said, shifting in his chair and checking the opposite rear pocket, finding it empty, also. "My wallet is gone."

"When did you have it last?" John asked.

"This…I mean, Friday morning."

"Are you sure?"

"Yeah. Well, no, not absolutely sure. I do have this routine that I follow. I never in my life have left without it."

"It's true," Jack agreed. "He does. He has routines for everything. You should see him when I'm trying to get him out of his house because we're late. He can't leave until he fulfills every step of the *leaving the house for the evening* procedure."

Cal looked at Jack with consternation and amusement. "It's going to take a little getting used to – having someone I've never met know me so well."

John grinned at the two of them and continued, "See, we're making slight progress. Jack, you saw Cal's driver's license at the scene of the accident on Saturday night, and Cal doesn't have his license. At least, two tiny little facts tie together.

"So," John proposed, biting into his muffin, "the next thing we need to do is get into the morgue and see the body."

"Can we, at least, finish eating? I'm starving," Cal retorted. "I didn't have any breakfast."

"Or lunch or dinner," added Jack.

"Whatever! I've heard of jet lag, but this is a whole new experience."

John smiled and said, "Time lag."

TUE - 3:58 P.M.

Ben Hart's cell phone vibrated. He answered it and, after listening for only a minute, disconnected and punched in a new number. When he heard an answer, he said, "Billy, Ben. Just got the results on the prints from the ladder and flue on the Augur house. They were a dead-on match to one set of the prints on the sonogram and on the Father's Day card."

"That's a big surprise. Are you ready to make an arrest?"

"I am. I'll swing over and pick up a warrant. I thought you might want in on this party."

Hart heard Burke chuckle over the phone. "I would. I'd like to meet this woman face to face."

"Your kind of gal, huh?"

"Oh, yeah. I have a *thing* for the homicidal pyromaniacs."

"I'll buzz you when I have the warrant."

☒

Forty-five minutes later Ben saw Burke sitting in his squad car around the corner from the Schilling apartment. He parked behind him, and they both got out and met at the curb.

"Before I left the station, I picked up something interesting, Ben. Thought you might want to hear it."

"What's that?"

"There was an explosion and a fire at an old warehouse downtown this afternoon."

"Anyone hurt?"

"Some smoke inhalation injuries, and one of the TFD guys got a broken arm when the gas main lit up. But guess who just happened to be in the alley in front of it when our officers arrived?"

"Don't tell me it was our girl Gail."

"Nope. John Augur."

The detective stared at Burke for a time, his mind working to fit this latest piece of the puzzle into place. Before he could respond, Burke added, "That's not all."

"You're kidding me?"

"There was someone inside one of the storage rooms when TFD arrived. They had to use their axes on the door to let him out."

"So?"

Grinning, Burke informed him, "It was locked with a hasp and padlock from the outside."

Hart again stared at his friend and said, "What the hell is going on?"

"Oh, it gets better. It was Augur who told the TFD boys that someone was in the room. That's why they busted the door down. The man inside was unconscious, and they had to resuscitate him. When our uniforms arrived on the scene, Augur and the other man were together, like friends, talking."

Burke could see the avalanche of questions tumbling through Ben's mind. Rather than letting him ask them, he continued, "Our guys talked to both of them. Got their names and stories and cut them loose. According to Augur, he just *happened* to be walking through the alley when the explosion occurred."

"He just *happened* to be walking down the alley as his friend, who was inside a storage room that was locked from the outside with a padlock, became trapped by the explosion and fire?" Ben asked rhetorically.

Burke confirmed the scenario.

With a shake of his head, Hart bemoaned the situation. "This is getting stranger by the minute."

"You haven't heard the best part."

"There's more?"

Grinning again, Burke began to deliver the breakthrough. "As soon as things got under control at the storage building, the RO, who had spoken to Augur and the friend, had time to punch the info into the mobile computer in the squad car. Naturally, when he entered Augur's name, all of the expected bells and whistles went off. He got an even bigger surprise when he typed in the other man's name."

Hart looked at Burke, who seemed to be enjoying the moment. "Are you going to tell me, or do I need to get my club and beat it out of you?"

With an ever broader grin, Burke filled him in. "It seems that the second gentleman told the responding officer that his name was Callen Mitchell."

Burke paused and waited for a reaction. Ben turned the name around inside his head for a moment before saying, "Means nothing to me. Who is he?"

"It's not *who* he is so much as *what* he is," Burke replied mysteriously.

"That's it," Hart concluded, turning back to his unmarked car. "I'm getting the club."

Before he could take another step, Burke stated, "Callen Mitchell died Saturday night in a motorcycle accident downtown."

Ben froze, then turned back to Burke, a look of disbelief on his face.

"And guess who the witness to the accident was?"

In a soft voice, the detective answered, "John Augur."

"Right."

Hart struggled to make some sense out of all of the facts. "Let me get all of this straight. Saturday night John Augur is a witness to a motorcycle accident, and Callen Mitchell dies."

"Right."

"Sunday night someone starts a fire in John Augur's house."

"Don't forget that during the day on Sunday, Augur breaks off his wedding with Gail Schilling."

"Right. Then, Monday night someone, presumably Schilling, tries to kill Augur's parents, and Augur just *happens* to show up to save them."

"Right."

"And then on Tuesday, Augur just *happens* to be walking down an alley downtown, and a storage warehouse blows up and catches fire as he's going by. Someone is inside a storage room that's locked from the outside. Augur tells the firemen that there is someone trapped in there, and they rescue the man, who just *happens* to be the same person who was killed in the motorcycle accident on Saturday night."

Burke grinned. "I think you've got it."

The detective stared into the distance for a moment before he said, "I think we need to have another little chat with John Augur."

"I had a feeling you'd say that."

Shaking his head, Hart pulled the arrest warrant out of his pocket and handed it to Burke. Then he reached into the back seat of his unmarked police car and pulled out a black Kevlar vest, strapping it on. He grabbed his shotgun, checked to make certain that it was loaded and the safety was off, and then waited while Burke followed suit.

"Ready?" Hart asked.

Burke nodded, and they walked the remaining distance to the Schilling apartment in silence. It was still during normal work hours for most people, and the apartment complex was nearly deserted. One woman, a twenty-something Hispanic, sat on her second-story balcony with a toddler and a sleepy infant she held on her lap. She watched as Hart and Burke walked across the grassy area.

They reached the door of the apartment and knocked. "Police!" Ben shouted.

As they waited for a response, the woman on the balcony yelled down to them, "She's not there. She left."

Burke stayed at the apartment door as Hart walked to the sidewalk below the stranger's balcony. "How long ago did she leave?"

"She left during the night. My Angelica has colic, and I was awake, trying to calm her down. I saw that woman leave. She was carrying a suitcase."

Glancing at the detective's vest and shotgun, she asked, "What did she do?"

"We just want to talk to her."

The woman smiled a knowing grin. "Sure you do. You always wear a bulletproof vest and bring a shotgun to talk to someone."

Ben ignored her comment and asked, "Do you have any idea where she might have gone?"

"No. I don't talk to her. She's crazy."

"What do you mean?"

"My Brianna," she said, tilting her head toward the toddler, "accidentally bounced her ball against that woman's window a few weeks ago. It didn't break the glass. It just made a loud noise. That crazy woman came running out and grabbed my little girl, screaming at her and calling her an animal. She squeezed Brianna's little arm so hard she got bruises."

Hart shook his head. "Where's the manager's office?"

"By the pool," the woman answered, pointing toward the front of the complex.

Ben turned to Burke and said, "Wait here. I'll have the manager let us in."

The detective walked away, returning ten minutes later with a woman who was in her mid-forties, with bleached blond hair and wearing a bright red business suit. Hart had already shown the woman his warrant, so she walked straight to the apartment door, a ring of keys in her hand.

"If you could show me which key it is and step away from the door, I would appreciate it," Burke instructed.

"Of course," answered the manager, thumbing through the keys until she found the one with the right apartment number. She stepped away and Burke unlocked the apartment door; he and Ben entered cautiously. The apartment looked as if it had been ransacked, the floor littered with cut-up photographs and smashed objects.

"I'm guessing these are all gifts from Augur," Burke surmised, eyeing the shattered vase and other items strewn about. He continued his inspection of the one-bedroom apartment as Hart called for the crime scene unit and an APB on Gail.

Burke spent the next hour talking to Gail's neighbors, and was returning to the apartment when he saw Ben speaking to one of the crime scene techs. As he approached, Ben explained, "It looks like we hit pay dirt. They checked Schilling's computer and, in her Internet search history, found several sites she had visited on Sunday. The last batch of them were all pertaining to carbon monoxide poisoning."

"That should help."

"Anything from the neighbors?"

"You mean, other than that they all hated her? Not really. She seems to have cut a swath through this place, ticking off everyone around her, the same way she did with the lady on the balcony."

"One wonders what Augur saw in her," Ben pondered.

Burke just chuckled. "Like we all made such brilliant decisions at that age."

"True. Very true."

Hart turned and glanced back into the wrecked apartment. "I have a feeling we better find her quickly."

☒

It had been over an hour since Gail received the *9999999* message on her cell phone. It was the code she had programmed her security system to transmit if anyone entered her apartment. "It must have been the cops," she said to herself.

As she mulled over her options, the perfect plan emerged. With a satisfied grin, she motioned for the waitress. "Check, please."

⧗

Cal had just finished his second muffin, and they were about to leave when John's phone chirped.

"Hello," John answered, feeling his back and neck muscles instantly tighten when he heard the voice on the other end.

"Mr. Augur, this is Detective Hart."

"Yes, sir," John responded, happy that his tone sounded even and normal to his own ears.

"I think we need to talk with you again."

Not wanting to get sidetracked from their planning, John asked, "Would tomorrow be all right? I have a couple of things to do today."

He heard a firmness in Hart's inflection as he answered, "No, sir. I'm afraid this can't wait. Could you come in to the station right away?" Although phrased as a question, the tone made it clear that it was not a request.

"Yes, sir. I can."

Hart continued, "You wouldn't happen to be with Callen Mitchell, would you?"

John froze. He wondered how they could be aware of Cal's...*what?*...existence. Not having prepared himself for this question and not a natural liar, John replied, "As a matter of fact, I am. We're having something to eat together right now."

"I would appreciate it if you could bring Mr. Mitchell with you when you come in."

John stared at the questioning faces of Jack and Cal, and with a grimace twisting his features, he said, "Sure. That shouldn't be a problem."

"Thank you, Mr. Augur. We'll be seeing you at the station in thirty minutes?"

"I'm going to need closer to an hour. We haven't finished eating, and we're clear across town."

"You're on the eastside?"

"Yes, sir. We're at the mall."

"Even better, let's meet at the substation on Speedway, behind Eastside City Hall. Do you know where that is?"

"I do."

"Very good. We'll see you there in thirty minutes."

John heard the connection break as Hart did not wait for a response. Slowly lowering the phone to the table, he glanced down at the screen to make certain that the connection was broken and that the detective would not be overhearing.

"What was that all about?" asked Jack.

"That was Detective Hart. He wants to see me right away."

"Why?"

"He didn't say, but he did ask that I bring Cal with me."

"Cal! How did he know...?"

"Back at the warehouse," Cal sighed, "when the cops arrived...I gave them my name."

"They must have put together the pieces," John sighed.

Jack slammed the table with his fist, causing the young girl behind the coffee counter to look over at him. "We don't need this right now. We have too much to do, too much to figure out."

"I don't see how we have much of a choice. He gave me half an hour to get there."

"How are we going to explain *me*?" Cal said.

"I don't know," answered John. "I just don't know."

⏳

From the tone of the detective's voice on the phone, John wasn't sure what to expect when he arrived. He pulled into the nearly empty parking lot, and he and Cal walked past the darkened annex building, which was closed for the evening, and found the police substation. During the short drive, he visualized himself and Cal handcuffed and kept in an interrogation room for hours as Hart and Burke took turns grilling them. However, he was pleasantly surprised when the officer at the front desk seated them in a conference room and offered them something cold to drink while they waited for Detective Hart.

They didn't have to wait long. Hart and Burke joined them within minutes.

Hart thanked them for coming so quickly. "I'm afraid recent events have prompted a lot of questions that only you and," he paused and looked at Cal, "Mr. Mitchell can clear up."

"Whatever we can do to help," John stated, and Cal nodded his agreement.

Hart removed his notepad from his pocket and, with pen poised, began, "How long have the two of you known each other?"

"We just met today," answered Cal.

"At the fire downtown?"

"Yes, sir."

"The responding officer, who interviewed both of you at the scene, had the opinion that you were friends," Hart said questioningly, although it was phrased as a statement.

"We've seen each other around, but never really met," John offered.

"It's pretty easy to start liking someone when they have saved your life," Cal added. "John was the one who heard me pounding on that door and got the firefighters to break it down."

"True," Ben agreed.

Burke decided to enter the conversation. "What has us a little confused is that you, Mr. Augur, were the witness to the incident Saturday night...."

"The motorcycle accident?"

"Yes, sir. And the victim of the accident was Callen Mitchell."

John had to admit that Cal's performance was quite good as he suddenly gasped and sputtered, "What did you say?"

"Actually," Hart said, "at the time, we believed the deceased was Mr. Mitchell, since that was what the ID on the victim said."

"Who...who was it?"

Hart looked down at his pad and said, "It apparently was Kurtis Wallace."

"KURT?" barked John, stunned.

Both Burke and Hart watched John closely as he fought to regain his composure. Cal sat silently, looking down at the table.

After a moment, Burke said, "Now you can see why we are confused, Mr. Augur – considering that Kurt Wallace was with you Sunday night when your home was burned."

John, shocked and devastated, did not reply. Hart addressed Cal, "Why would Mr. Wallace have your driver's license in his possession? And why would he be driving your motorcycle?"

John and Cal had planned on this portion of the questioning, and Cal fell into the planned answer, "My wallet was missing on Friday. I didn't know that Kurt...Mr. Wallace...had it."

"Were you and Mr. Wallace friends?"

"Not really. We were classmates and hung together a few times."

"Could you explain why he would have been riding your motorcycle Saturday night?"

"I told him he could borrow it...while I was out of town. He had...he was having a problem with his car," Cal ad-libbed.

"You were out of the city?"

"Yes, sir."

"Where did you go?"

"I went camping."

"Without a vehicle?" Ben asked, conveying a slight suspicion.

"I hiked. I cut classes on Friday and went to Catsback. There's a little valley in the pass that I like to camp in. I just got back today."

"You weren't aware that your wallet was missing?"

"I was, but I didn't notice until I set up camp Friday afternoon. At that point there wasn't much I could do, so I figured I'd deal with it when I came back."

Hart stared at Cal intensely, trying to read his face.

"John," Burke asked, his tone conciliatory, "who was with you Sunday night? It obviously wasn't Kurt."

"I don't know what to say," John answered honestly. "I have known him for most of my life, and *that* was Kurt Wallace."

John kept eye contact with Burke and could feel Detective's Hart's eyes boring into him from the side. After an uncomfortable pause, Hart said, "How do you explain the fact that Kurt Wallace is at the Office of the Medical Examiner, on a slab, dead since Saturday night?"

John turned to face Hart directly. "I can't. I only know what I know. And that is... Kurt Wallace was with me when I spoke with Officer Burke in front of my apartment on Sunday."

Both of the police officers stared intensely at John. He wasn't sure whether they were attempting to intimidate him or were simply at a loss for words. Partly to break the silence and mostly to change the subject, John asked, "Have you arrested Gail yet?"

Burke glanced at Hart, who answered, "No, sir. We did have an arrest warrant issued. But when we went to her apartment, she wasn't there. It appears that she has fled. We are looking for her now."

"Fled?"

Burke explained, "Her personal belongings were gone. A neighbor told us that she left in the middle of the night with a suitcase. And what remained in the apartment was torn up or shattered."

"I'm sure those were the things I'd given her."

"That was my guess," the officer concurred.

"As long as she is at large," Hart said, "I would recommend that you be careful."

John forced a grin that more closely resembled a grimace. "Don't worry,

I will."

The conversation continued for several more minutes as Hart and Burke questioned both of them on the details of the past two days, obviously trying to trip one of them up with slightly rephrased versions of earlier questions, and getting nowhere.

Finally, John looked at both officers and said, "Is there anything else right now? I would like to go to the hospital. I haven't seen my parents today, and I want to check on their status."

Burke again looked at Ben, who flipped closed his pad and stood. John, Cal and Burke followed his lead and rose from their seats, but none made a move toward the meeting room door.

Breaking the silence, Hart spoke, "Look Mr. Augur...John...I'm going to be candid with you."

"I would appreciate that."

"We have more questions than answers at this point. There was an accident Saturday night where, apparently, Kurt Wallace died. You were there. Sunday night, your apartment was deliberately torched. And Kurt Wallace was with you. Monday night someone – apparently Ms. Schilling – made an attempt on the lives of your parents. You coincidentally showed up at the opportune moment and rescued them. And Mr. Wallace was with you at that time, as well."

"That's right, you even met him."

"I met someone who claimed to be Kurt Wallace," Hart corrected.

John shrugged, and the detective continued, "Tuesday, there was an explosion at an old warehouse downtown that turned into a fire. And you just happened to be walking past it at the time."

John did not respond.

"You have to admit," Hart persisted, "that this all looks damned strange."

"I do," John agreed. "How do you think I feel? Look at this from my perspective. In the course of three or four days, I am nearly struck by a motorcycle, the driver is killed, and I'm later told that he is my best friend. Except my best friend is with me that night, not driving a motorcycle down the street. Not to mention the fact that he is with me the rest of the weekend.

"My apartment is destroyed, and I'm told that it was not an accident, but arson. Someone tries to kill my parents, and I'm told that the prime suspect is the woman I was going to marry. The next day I could have been killed when an explosion happens just as I'm walking down an alley."

John paused and looked at both men, "I think I'm starting to feel a little paranoid...actually, a lot paranoid."

"I think that might be warranted," said Burke, a slight grin softening his former, somber expression.

"Warranted or not," Hart maintained, "it all creates several questions in my mind."

"I understand that, sir. I really do. I guess what I want to know is... is any of what I've been involved in a *crime?*"

John watched as Ben considered his answer carefully. "Not at this time."

"If that's the case, I would like to go."

"Not a problem," replied Hart, "but I would appreciate it if you would keep in contact with us."

"Of course. I'm not going anywhere."

"Good," the detective said, moving to open the door. Thinking better of it, he stopped and turned to John. "I do have one more question, for both of you, really."

"Yes, sir?" John responded.

"Since you've been with Mr. Wallace every day for the past few days, would you mind telling me where he is now?"

"I have no idea. We grabbed a bite together earlier today, and he told me he had some things to do and took off. I haven't seen him or heard from him since."

Ben turned to Cal, who said, "I haven't seen him at all. I guess he left before my little fiasco at the storage room."

The detective considered the information carefully before he decided not to pursue it any further. "Okay, I guess that's all we need for now." He stuck out his hand to John and said, "I'm sure I'll be needing to speak with you again."

John shook Ben's hand and turned to Burke, shook his, and requested, "You'll keep me posted if anything pops up with Gail?"

Burke replied, "You bet."

Cal and John left the meeting room and walked out to the parking lot. Hart and Burke remained behind. When Burke saw that the two had exited the building, he turned and said, "Well, Ben, what do you think?"

Ben looked at his friend. "I get the feeling he's telling the truth. But I also think that I'm into something that's way over my head right now."

TUE - 9:07 P.M.

The mall parking lot was almost empty when Cal and John returned to pick up Jack at the coffee shop in Borders. As they entered, they noticed that Jack was not alone.

They neared the table, and Jack said in greeting, "Look who I found."

Aloysius turned and smiled at them as they grabbed two empty chairs from another table and pulled them over. Sitting, John turned to Jack, "How in the hell did you find him?"

"Aloysius found me, actually. I was just hanging out here, having some coffee and waiting for you when he came in."

Addressing Aloysius, John said, "Maybe now you can tell us what is going on."

"He has been," Jack intervened. "He just got started."

"Well?"

Jack looked at Aloysius. "Maybe you should start begin again."

"Well, it's really quite simple."

"That would be a relief," Cal muttered sarcastically.

Aloysius grinned again and resumed, "The Anunnaki are unhappy about the tampering with time that has been done, or will be done...depending upon your time perspective...by Callen Mitchell." He paused and acknowledged Cal. "They have come here to stop it."

John, his mouth agape, stared at Aloysius. "I thought you said it was simple?"

"It is," Aloysius answered calmly, clearly accustomed to this type of reaction to his words. In a soothing voice, he continued, "To the Anunnaki, time travel is irrelevant. They exist in all times simultaneously."

"How is that possible?" Cal wondered.

"How it is possible is not the question. All of time exists at once in the universe. That is the natural state of things. The true question, as far as the Anunnaki are concerned, is how you are able to experience time in a linear fashion, such as you do."

"I'm not sure I understand," John said, interrupting Cal before he could ask another question. "What I really want to know is: why are they interfering with our lives right now?"

"You see... because, for them, all of the future is present, they are instantly able to observe the effects of an action taken in what you call today, hundreds, or even thousands of years into what you call the future.

"The time machine that is to be invented by Mr. Mitchell, and the time traveling that is to be or, from the perspective of the Anunnaki, has been performed using the machine, although causing no reactions which are discernable in the year you call 2040, will eventually, much farther into your future, cause significant changes – changes that the Anunnaki do not want to happen."

John and Cal, who had not yet heard this, sat stunned at the extent of Aloysius's knowledge regarding their future, knowledge that they had believed only they and Jack possessed. Aloysius sat back into his chair with a self-satisfied grin, as if everything was now perfectly clear to all of them.

John and Cal took a minute to absorb what Aloysius told them, before John asked, "I'm not saying I buy any of this, Aloysius, but how do you know these things? Are you one of *them*?"

Shaking his head, Aloysius said, "One of *them*, no."

"Then who are you? How do you know all of this?"

"I am from another... group... another people. I have had access to some of the Anunnaki. They trust me. I have listened to them, and I know their plans and concerns."

John sat back in his chair, his mind whirling. His first reaction to the bizarre nature of these words was counteracted by the seemingly unexplainable coincidences of Aloysius's arrival at critical moments.

As John pondered what he had been told, Cal took over, "What other group... other people? Who are you?"

Retaining his seemingly unflappable serenity, Aloysius answered Cal, "I was born here."

"In Tucson?" Jack attempted to pin him down.

"Actually, I was born in Roswell, New Mexico. But I am a Nordic from the Rigelian system. My people were among the first to colonize the blue planet, eons ago."

"The blue planet? That would be Earth?"

"It would. We came to live here peacefully. Unfortunately, this planet is rich in resources which are coveted by others in the galaxy. The others also came here, not to simply live, but to exploit. For thousands of years, there was turmoil. They interbred with my people, while a genetic hybrid of native Earthlings were used as laborers in their mining operations and later as breeding stock for other purposes, eventually creating the race that is now *you*."

"By the Anunnaki?" John asked.

"Yes."

John became almost overwhelmed by the dissonance of the encounter, as he closely observed Aloysius who was about as nondescript and average-looking as possible. Here was a middle-aged black man, clutching a motorcycle magazine, telling them that he was part of an ancient race of interstellar travelers.

"Aloysius, I don't mean for this to sound wrong, but I have a question. You said you are a part of the Nordic race, but you're a black man?"

Aloysius once again smiled at John and said, "This is simply the appearance that I take so as to blend in."

"Blend in? What do you really look like?"

"I am fair-skinned, over nine feet tall with blue eyes and blond hair," he answered quite matter-of-factly.

Cal chuckled. "You're right. You definitely wouldn't blend in like that."

Aloysius, not responding to Cal's humor, nodded.

A jumble of questions piled up in John's mind. Not knowing where to begin, he asked, "What happened to Kurt?"

Aloysius paused for a moment and shook his head. "I do not share the Anunnaki's perspective on seeing all of time. It is the perspective of my race, the linear view of life and the logical progress of the universe, that is the source of mankind's view. We do not consider the ability of the Anunnaki as a gift, but a curse, and have struggled for centuries to breed out the residual traits of those who at times dominated us and shared their genetic make-up with us."

"So, the humans are descended from your race?"

"They are, and they aren't."

"Of course it couldn't be that simple," John commented.

Ignoring his sarcasm, Aloysius explained, "As I mentioned, the Anunnaki arrived on the blue planet, hoping to mine its riches. My people were already present. At first, the Anunnaki used their own as workers, but soon they tired of the labor and, as I described earlier, decided to create a force of workers."

"Slaves," said Cal.

"In a manner of speaking, yes. So they interbred, creating those who would become the race that you call mankind. This new breed was suited well to manual labor, and for quite some time the arrangement worked well. As is inevitable any time there is oppression, this working class revolted and nearly wiped out the Anunnaki, forcing the remainder into hiding. Humans grew to dominate this planet, living in ignorance of my race and the Anunnaki."

"What does this have to do with my question?" John interrupted. "What happened to Kurt?"

"As I explained, I cannot see the past, nor the future, as can the Anunnaki. In other words, I do not know."

The three men were less than pleased with Aloysius's response. The silence was broken by Jack. "If you can't see the future, how are you able to show up right at the times that something is happening?"

"The Anunnaki are not a monolithic people in their intent. There are those among them who do not like the actions which are occurring at this time. These are the individuals whom I have befriended. They have been able to tell me...to warn me. And I have been able to attempt to intercede."

"You don't seem to be too effective," John stated bluntly.

Not offended, Aloysius replied, "This is true. Because of the Anunnaki's ability to see the results of change in the present time as it affects the future, the only viable technique to oppose them, and their machinations, is to involve oneself in their actions at the very moment, rather than preemptively. It was this technique, painfully learned by your ancestors, that allowed your race to eventually overthrow them. Sadly, the result of this truth is that I cannot always act in time. That is why I was not able to prevent the so-called accident on Saturday night."

"So-called?"

"Yes. It was caused by them. They blinded Cal as he approached you."

"That bright light," John remembered.

"Yes. However, I was able to prevent them from seizing you in the alley."

"Why were they doing that?"

"They were concerned that if they allowed the planned trip to the past, you would succeed in undoing what they had done."

"And it was the Anunnaki who attacked as Kurt was leaving?" Cal asked.

"It was, indeed," confirmed Aloysius, "but they were too late. Your friend was obviously able to depart a moment before the attack, and he succeeded in undoing your death. Quite cleverly, in fact. I believe they expected him to simply persuade you to change your plans, and they were prepared for this. He fooled them by sending you forward and then somehow convinced them that you had died Saturday night."

Realizing that Jack did not yet know the details, John turned to him and somberly said, "It's Kurt at the morgue."

Jack was stunned. "What?"

"He had Cal's wallet and driver's license. After they found out that Cal was with me at the storage warehouse, they double-checked and figured out that it was Kurt."

"How did he...?" Jack didn't know where to go with his question, and lapsed into silence.

"We don't know," Cal answered. "Somehow, he got my wallet from me before I left Friday to come here. Then, right on schedule, he got on my bike and drove it downtown."

"To die." Jack slumped down, his voice low.

"Why would he do that?" John asked. "Why would he substitute himself for Cal? Once he had sent Cal forward in time, there was no reason for him to give up his own life."

Jack slowly looked up at John. "Maybe he knew."

"Knew what?"

Jack briefly closed his eyes and took a deep breath, allowing it to come out slowly before he said, "Kurt was dying. He had a brain tumor. That was what I was about to tell you but didn't get the chance."

John stared speechlessly at his *other*.

Jack continued, "In my past...your, well, what was to be your future, Kurt died two weeks after your wedding to Gail. The tumor was inoperable."

"I knew he had something wrong. Those incredible headaches he would get...."

Jack nodded slowly.

"I asked him about them. He told me that the doctor said they were migraines and that he hadn't gotten around to getting the CAT scan yet."

"Maybe he had. Maybe he just didn't want to tell you, because of your wedding and everything."

John could feel powerful emotions welling up within him. He didn't trust himself to speak at the moment.

Jack quietly suggested, "*If* he knew. If he knew that he only had a couple of weeks to live anyway... and he knew that his last days would be filled with horrible pain... it could be he decided to take matters into his own hands and, at the same time, do something he thought would help us."

John thought back to the last moment he saw Kurt and remembered that, just before Aloysius came crashing into the storage room, Kurt had been about to say something to him. "He could have been planning it when he left."

Aloysius, not comfortable interrupting, cleared his throat and then began, "Either way, what he did outwitted the Anunnaki. You are still alive, Mr. Mitchell. And you will, no doubt, go on to invent your machine."

Cal leaned forward, confused. "Why are you interfering with their plan? If what I do with the machine is bad for the future, why are you trying to stop them and help us?"

"I didn't say that what was to happen is bad. I only said that *they* do not want those changes to occur."

"I don't understand."

Aloysius slid to the edge of his seat and lowered his voice to a near-whisper. "My race, allied with yours, has been locked in a struggle against the Anunnaki for centuries. It is a battle for control. At times they have had the upper hand; at other times they have been driven back into hiding. Their main advantage, the reason that we have not been able to defeat them, is their ability to see the future consequences of their acts, while we cannot. Your machine substantially nullifies this advantage. This ability has a profound effect on the balance of power."

"I thought that the machine couldn't go forward in time, only backwards. How does that counteract their ability to see forward?" Jack wondered.

"Because it allows you... us... to go back and undo what they have accomplished. Every time they have a gain in the struggle, mankind can jump backwards, alter the course and cheat them out of their victory."

Jack, John and Cal took several moments to digest what Aloysius had told them. Finally, Jack broke the silence. "This is all fascinating, but we still have some problems to figure out."

Aloysius stood up. "Yes, you do. Not the least of which is what to do with *you*. Every additional moment that you are here, in this time, is dangerous. Your very presence continues to alter the course of events that lead to the future."

John noticed Jack's pained reaction, and sighed in frustration, "What can we do? The main sphere is gone. The backup sphere is either gone or was destroyed in the explosion."

"I don't know," Aloysius answered. "It is a dilemma. And it is one without a solution, as far as I can see. However, I'm afraid I must leave right now."

"Why?" Cal searched his eyes for a reason. "Why can't you stick around and help us?"

Aloysius's face showed sadness and concern. "I may be able to return. I may succeed in finding a solution to your problem. I don't know."

"How can we find you?" Jack pressed him.

"I'll find you."

The three rose, and each shook Aloysius's hand.

"Good luck," said Aloysius.

"Thanks. I think we need it," John replied with a half grin.

As Aloysius walked away, returning the motorcycle magazine to the rack, they sat down and watched him depart.

After he was out of the building and they could see him walking across the nearly deserted parking lot, Cal asked, "Do you two believe him?"

Jack shook his head. "I don't know what to believe at this point."

John cleared his throat and said, "I've had so many things, things I thought were well settled in my mind, turned upside down in the past few days that the possibility of two ancient races of space aliens living among us...using us as pawns and waging a secret war...doesn't surprise me as much as it would have last Friday."

Cal chuckled. "Maybe a little sleep would be a good idea."

"We still need to figure out a place to go," Jack reminded them.

Cal grinned and pulled a key ring out of his pocket. "I remembered Kurt giving this to me before I left. He said it had the key to the padlock on the storage room, but I'll bet it has the key to his place on it, too."

The counter clerk turned off the lights in the café, signaling that it was time to go.

⏳

As the three of them, exhausted and unaware of their surroundings, trudged up the front porch steps to Kurt's house, Gail sat, unnoticed in her car which was parked across the street, self-satisfied with her cleverness for deducing that this was the only place left for John to go. As they had emerged from his car, parked under the streetlight, she had recognized only John.

"Who are those two?" she said out loud. "And where is Kurt?"

- XIX -

None of the three used Kurt's bed. Somehow it just didn't seem right. John was the first to wake up and walked, zombie-like, into the old kitchen. The Spider-Man mug was where Kurt had placed it the day before, still resting upside down on the drainboard next to the sink.

John forced himself through the routine of coffee-making, ambivalent as to whether he should fight off the morose thoughts of his friend's early demise, or to give in to them, choosing the latter. Surrounded by the artifacts of Kurt's life, the reminders of a thousand giddy times and a thousand thoughtful talks, John slumped onto the chrome and vinyl chair.

He recalled their first meeting. It had been a hot, Tucson July day, and John had ridden his bicycle to the nearest of the small neighborhood parks that were scattered throughout the older sections of the city. The park, covered with grass and dotted with trees, was set up with playground equipment, and had been established before the residents and the city council began to consider a raw piece of desert filled with cacti, snakes and scorpions a suitable-enough environment for children to play.

The sun was brilliant and the day blazingly hot. The grass green. The shade under the mature cottonwoods and evergreens comfortable. The shiny steel of the slide, swings, teeter-totter and carousel too hot to touch.

John had built a target stand, from cinder blocks and a board, under an adjacent tree and was sitting on the ground, his elbows resting on his knees, aiming at the soda cans and zinging them off the board, one by one, with his new slingshot. As he picked up another pebble from the pile he had gathered earlier and was preparing to loose another shot, one of the cans suddenly catapulted off with a loud *thwack.*

Startled, John looked over his shoulder and saw the young boy who would become his best friend, his own slingshot at his side. Displaying on his face the lopsided grin that would become so familiar, Kurt said, "Are you, like, the only other kid in town who doesn't play video games?"

Thus began a relationship that lasted through elementary, middle and high school, and on into college. Their friendship was a pleasant procession of camping trips, long excursions on their bicycles and sleep-overs at each other's homes. As they began to drive, the geographical reach of their relationship extended outward to include frequent outings to Flagstaff, Bisbee, Phoenix and California.

The unfailing constants of their interactions were their dialogues as they explored the universe together, discussing life and death, stars, atoms and everything else that occurred to them.

It was, of course, John whom Kurt turned to when his parents were killed in a plane crash, just as he began his freshman year at the University of Arizona. John could still clearly remember the night they sat on a rock at Mount Lemmon, discussing the loss, when Kurt turned to him and said, "You're my only family now." John was at a loss as to what to say, so they sat together for nearly an hour in silence.

The two of them were mostly inseparable, never tiring of each other's company. They had become closer than brothers. And now he was gone. The reality of the last thought brought forth a burning emptiness in John. He felt his throat spasm as he involuntarily fought back the sobs, but his tears streamed freely. Giving in to the wave of sadness, he dropped his head forward onto his arms.

John felt a sudden pressure on his shoulder, and for a brief moment his heart rose as he expected to hear Kurt's voice teasing him about his childish display of emotion. Lifting his face and blinking away the shimmer of tears that obscured his vision, he saw that it was only Jack. John could tell by his expression that his *other* was sharing the same sense of overwhelming grief that he felt.

Neither spoke as Jack poured himself a cup of coffee and sat down next to him at the table.

Finally, Jack asked, "Thinking about the slingshot?"

John just nodded.

Staring out the rear window of the dining area, Jack said, his voice low and restrained, "I've had thirty years to get over it, and I still haven't. Of course, seeing him again didn't help. But I wouldn't have missed that opportunity for the world."

John stared at his older self for a time. "I'm glad you didn't tell me."

Jack raised an eyebrow questioningly.

"Knowing would have ruined the last couple of days that I had with him."

Jack agreed.

They shared a silence for a time, both lost in their own remembrances.

"You know what's weird?" John said.

Jack looked at him and waited for the answer.

"It's like he's gone without a trace."

"What do you mean?"

"Kurt lost his grandparents a long time ago...when he was in elementary school, I think. His parents are dead. Each of them was an only child, so he had no aunts or uncles. He didn't have a brother or sister. And now he's gone."

"Like his entire existence has been wiped clean from the slate."

"Yeah!"

"You...we...were all he had. We were his family."

They heard the slam of the bathroom door, and a minute later Cal staggered in.

"There's some coffee," John said.

"I hate coffee."

"He does," Jack confirmed.

Rummaging through Kurt's refrigerator, Cal found a can of Coke and opened it, the popping of the top sounding like a rifle shot in the quiet kitchen. He joined them, noisily dragged the kitchen chair out from the table, took a long drink, slammed the can down on the table top and said, "So, what the hell are we going to do today?"

Jack realized that with the news of Kurt's death, he hadn't given his own plight much thought.

"I guess I'm stranded here," he finally replied. "The main machine is gone. The backup is destroyed, thanks to Aloysius's friends, or enemies, or whatever. The only way back to 2040 for me is the old-fashioned way, one day at a time."

Jack chuckled and added, "So, by the time I get to where I left, I'll be eighty instead of fifty."

John grinned at Cal. "You could always just build another machine for him."

"Sure," Cal grumbled. "And why don't I whip up a spaceship and an interplanetary cannon while I'm at it. I should be able to do it out of some spare parts in Kurt's shed here." He leaned back and took another long drink from the can, again clanking it down on the table.

"You know," Jack said, "other than the obvious problem of what to do with me, I've got to hand it to Kurt. He really came up with a solution that put everything back on track."

"I know," agreed John. "I was thinking about that. I mean, obviously, Cal is alive again. The marriage is called off, and God knows where Gail is now. We saved my folks. It's all wrapped up with a pretty bow."

Cal lifted his soda can and somberly toasted, "To Kurt!"

Jack and John tapped their coffee mugs against the can and, in unison, repeated, "To Kurt!"

☒

Across town, Detective Ben Hart was also thinking about Kurtis Wallace. He and Burke had both personally gone to the OME and viewed the body. It was definitely the same person whom they had met in the course of the arson and homicide investigations. From what Hart had been able to turn up, Wallace had no twin. In fact, he had no other family. Apparently, John Augur was his closest friend. Although Wallace had dated throughout high school and into college, there was no girlfriend or fiancée in his life at the present time.

As Hart sat at his desk and stared at the file, Burke walked up and, noticing the piles of papers and photos pertaining to Wallace, asked, "Is this turning into an obsession with you?"

Smiling, Ben looked up and said, "It might be. Isn't it with you?"

"It's keeping me awake, that's a fact. I'm sure that it was Wallace who was with Augur Sunday night. I'm dead certain of it. Same thing at Augur's parents' house."

"I know. Me, too. So either you...or both of us...see Kurt Wallace Sunday and Monday, but he's been dead and on a slab at the OME's office since Saturday night."

"Does he have a brother? A twin?"

"Nope. I checked. He was an only child."

Burke looked at Ben and smiled. "What'd the captain have to say about all this?"

Hart slumped in his chair."The man has no imagination. I told him the whole story, and he just looked at me and said, 'So where's the crime?'"

Burke laughed. "That sounds like him."

"He's not the slightest bit curious. As far as he's concerned, if I can't cite the violated statute, I shouldn't be wasting my time on it."

"We still have to find Schilling."

"That we do. That's what I'm using to justify my time on this other thing. But, man, this is driving me crazy."

"Any progress on locating her?"

"Not yet. We've got make, model and plates out to every patrol in the state. We're watching her credit cards and bank for activity. I've got uniforms out talking to everybody that she works with or is known to be friends with."

"Anything at all?"

Ben shook his head in disgust. "I didn't think she'd be this smart. I really figured we'd have her in the bag by now."

"You're Detective Hart, aren't you?"

Ben swiveled in his chair and saw one of the technicians from the crime lab.

"I am. And you're from the lab, right?"

The tech, one of the newer members of the lab, was in his mid-twenties. He had tousled blond hair, almost unbelievably white skin that was a rarity in sunny Arizona, and had either forgotten to shave this morning, or what was on his chin and jaw was the result of a several-week-long attempt to grow a beard, depending on his hormone levels.

" Yes, I'm Wally Seavers."

"Ben Hart," the detective replied, extending his hand. "And this is Billy Burke."

The youngster shook both of their hands. Ben was expecting more of a feeble grip and was surprised by the firmness of the handshake.

"What can I do for you?"

"You're the detective handling the John Augur thing, right?"

"I am."

"I'm a friend of Kurt Wallace."

Upon hearing this, Ben instantly stood up and said, "Please, have a seat."

The lab tech sat in the only chair while Ben pushed some of the piles back, and perched on the edge of the desk.

Seavers looked nervous as he sat, and obviously attempted to prepare his thoughts. Burke encouraged him, "Just say it, kid, whatever it is."

Wally blurted out, "I hope that I don't get in trouble for this. I've only worked here six months."

Ben smiled at him reassuringly. "Nobody's gonna get fired. If you know anything about what's going on, we could sure use the help right now."

Taking a deep breath, Wally said, "I was working in the lab the other day when I got a call from Kurt. I didn't have much going on at the time, other than a PCR evolution which was in the second stage...."

"Why don't you go ahead and skip that part," Ben interrupted.

"Sorry." Seavers cleared his throat and continued, "So, anyway, Kurt called me and asked for a favor."

"What kind of favor?"

"It wasn't much really." Wally started to get flustered again, but before Hart could say something to calm him down, he seemed to get control of his breathing and resumed, "He just wanted me to check some fingerprints."

Ben's brow furrowed. "Fingerprints? Whose?"

"Well, that's what's weird. I met him at the lobby, and he gave me two glasses to check. I didn't let him into the lab."

"Of course you didn't."

"I took the glasses back and dusted them, pulled the prints and ran them through the database."

"What did you come up with?"

"Nothing! Well, other than Kurt's from his Child ID record. That's the deal. Whoever else's prints were on the glasses...that guy hadn't been in the system for any reason."

"That guy?" Ben asked. "I thought you said he brought in two glasses."

"He did, but the same prints were on both of them."

Ben tried to figure out the significance of this when Wally continued again, "I took the glasses back down to Kurt and told him what I found...or didn't find. When I told him that both of the glasses were obviously handled by the same person, he got a huge smile on his face, thanked me, grabbed the glasses and left in a big hurry."

Hart and Burke both tried to find the relevance of this incident, without success, when the technician added, "That was before the arson and attempted-murder materials made it into the lab."

Burke looked down at the young technician and said, "I don't understand."

"Well, standard procedure is to enter any fingerprint we might obtain, regardless of the reason."

"OK."

"So when I did the fingerprint work for Kurt, the fingerprints from the glasses were entered into the system with a red flag that the identity was unknown."

"Go on," Ben said, hiding his impatience.

"When the field crew brought in all of the materials from the attempted homicide, they were entered into the system, and the same prints that were on the glasses came up."

He started to ask for the name but was interrupted.

"They were John Augur's."

Ben had obviously been hoping for something more helpful.

"I'm afraid I don't see how this helps us much."

The tech nodded and stood up from the chair. "I wasn't sure that it would, but since it came up and it had to do with an active case, I thought I better tell you."

"That was a good idea. I appreciate it."

Ben stood up from the edge of the desk, to shake Seavers' hand.

"Thanks, again."

As they shook, Seavers added, "There was something odd, though."

Hesitating, Ben asked, "What's that?"

"Well, I had my supervisor look at something…an artifact, really…from those prints I lifted off the glasses, and he thought it was a little strange, too. I got a perfect right-hand, index finger print from each of the two glasses. I mean, textbook perfect. Almost as good as if the subject had come in for formal fingerprinting."

"Yes?"

"As I told you, they matched. Obviously, the same person made the two prints, but on one of the glasses the index finger print had a couple of minor flaws, you know, like damage to the skin."

"Like a scar?" Burke asked.

"Exactly, small scars. My boss said that it was normal, the kind of markings that a person accumulates over the years. We see it all the time when we compare fingerprints from a small child with those of an adult."

"I'm sorry, Wally," said Ben. "I'm just not getting your point."

"Well, the other glass…the other print from the index finger didn't have the same scars. It was like…this sounds weird."

"Go ahead," Burke prompted. "On this case, nothing is weird."

Wally swallowed hard. "My boss thinks I'm crazy, but he doesn't have a better explanation. It's almost like they were fingerprints from the same person but years apart…even decades apart."

Hart and Burke both looked at the young tech and said nothing. As the silence extended, Seavers, clearly nervous, mumbled, "That's it. I wanted to tell you about that."

Ben turned and stared out the window, his mind attempting to fit together this new piece of the puzzle. The three stood awkwardly for a moment before Burke said, "Thanks, it was Wally, right? We're glad you did."

"Yes, sir. Wally Seavers. At least you're glad, I got my ass handed to me by the boss for doing a friend a favor."

"I'm sorry about that, but I'm sure he'll get over it," Burke assured him.

"I hope so."

Seavers turned and started to walk away, saying, "He even suspended my lab access. Now I can only work Monday through Friday, when he's there. Heck, I enjoyed coming in on the weekends so I could catch up on the backlog."

Burke did not seem at all interested in the personnel issues of another department, when Ben suddenly said, "Wait a second."

The tech stopped and turned back to face them.

"Yes, sir?"

"You said he suspended your weekend access?"

"Yes, sir. I can only work weekdays now, thanks to this."

"When did you see Wallace? What day was it?"

"Oh, didn't I mention that? It was last Sunday."

Both Burke and Hart froze. The young tech, not at all sure why his comment was received like that, said, "Is something wrong?"

"I guess you haven't heard," explained Burke.

"Heard what?"

"Kurt Wallace has been dead since late Saturday night."

☒

The attendant twisted the latch and opened the door. Reaching in, he pulled out the table as Burke, Hart and Seavers stood silently. Next, he unzipped the black neoprene bag, exposing the lifeless form.

"Oh!" exclaimed Wally, turning and stepping away.

Ben walked next to him and asked, "That is Kurtis Wallace, isn't it?"

The tech swallowed twice and, finding his voice, said, "Yes. What happened?"

"Motorcycle accident," Ben answered, his voice sympathetic despite his terse response.

"I...I don't understand. He was with me Sunday, for over an hour."

"I suppose," Ben began, "that it's stupid to ask this, but are you sure it was Sunday?"

"Yes, I'm sure. And it's all logged into the system…when I entered the prints."

Seavers suddenly turned and looked at Ben. "I'm sure it would still be on the video."

Ben remembered that the police station lobby, as well as all of the corridors and rooms, were monitored by video cameras, and the videos were stored for one year.

Burke was scheduled to go out on patrol, so Seavers and Hart went to the Internal Security office and asked the supervisor to show them the digital video from Sunday.

They sat silently as the supervisor started the lobby video, beginning it at a time approximately thirty minutes prior to when Wally remembered Kurt's arrival.

"Pause it!" Wally nearly shouted as he saw the slightly grainy image of his friend enter the front door. Pointing at the screen, he said, "There he is."

Ben noted the exact time displayed on the bottom right-hand corner of the screen and then instructed the supervisor to continue forward. They observed Kurt in the lobby as Wally came out to get the paper bag, presumably containing the two drinking glasses.

After Wally left the lobby, Kurt wandered restlessly, staring at the several glass cases filled with mementos of past cases solved by the TPD. They had the supervisor fast-forward through the rest, until Wally returned. There was no sound, but they watched as he gave the bag back to Kurt and spoke with him for a few minutes, until Kurt, smiling, left with the bag and Wally reentered the security door.

Seavers turned to Ben and said, "I knew I wasn't crazy."

Ben did not respond.

"Detective Hart," Wally asked, his voice trembling slightly, "what's going on?"

Ben, still staring at the video screen, now frozen on the final scene of Kurt Wallace stepping out the front door, said, "I don't know, kid, but I am going to find *this* Wallace if it's the last thing I do."

Cal and John were getting acquainted at the dining table as Jack sat in the living room, watching the television and hungrily taking in the details of the time. Although his memories of this thirty-year-distant past were vivid in many ways, he was finding that he had forgotten so much of the minutia.

His thumb poised over the channel selector on the remote, it was rarely called into use as he discovered that he was not only fascinated with the news of the day, but even the commercials kept his interest. Occasionally, John and Cal heard him snort with amusement as certain political stories were discussed and ponderously analyzed by *contributors* to the myriad networks. The smug and serious broadcast statements were periodically punctuated by Jack with shouted expletives.

Their conversation was finally interrupted by a surprised, "Oh, my God, look at him!" from the living room. Curiosity getting the better of them, they joined Jack and looked at the television to see a young politician from a western state, being interviewed by a reporter on one of the news channels.

"Who is that?" John asked.

Jack tore his eyes away from the picture and looked at his younger self. Seeming to reach a conclusion, he said, "I guess that I don't really see the point in not telling you at least some things, since I'm going to be stuck here with you for the next thirty years.

"*That*," he said, pointing at the image on the screen, his voice drenched with ridicule, "is our future President."

John and Cal turned to stare at the face, both startled by the surreal nature of this revelation. It was obviously still early in the man's political career, and he was unsure of himself as he haltingly attempted to answer questions about the effect that illegal immigration was having on his state.

Cal chuckled, "It sounds like he is trying to take every possible position on the topic."

"And doing it very badly," John added.

"Believe me. He gets better. He's quite polished at the technique by the time he's thirty years older."

John felt a tingle of excitement at being privy to this secret knowledge, but noticed a creeping sense of apprehension at the same time.

"This is strange. I'm not sure that I like it."

Jack turned again to John and asked, "What?"

"Knowing. Having this fact handed to me. It just feels, you know, not right... knowing something like this about a stranger... about the whole country, really."

"Tell me about it," Jack agreed, switching off the television. "Just in the little bit of time I've spent here, I see things all around me which are still, I guess, in progress. They always have been, but as we go about the day-to-day aspects of our lives, we don't think in those terms. Everything seems so solid, so real... so *fixed*. But that's an illusion. The reality is that it is all in a state of flux."

Jack sighed and glanced back at the television for a moment, before continuing, "The best way to describe it is that it's like the difference between watching a movie for the first time and seeing it again. The first time, your eyes... and your mind... go where the director wants them to go. You are totally into the experience of it. You are, in a sense, living it. When you see it again, knowing how it ends, you see all of the little clues, so you don't buy into certain characters because you know what kind of person they become, all of those things.

"In other words, during the first time, you are immersed in the movie. When you watch it again, you are a detached observer. That's how I feel now. When I lived through this time, thirty years ago, it was real... it was intense. Now I feel that I'm not a part of it. It seems like I'm just a spectator. And for me, watching a movie a second time never gives me the same feelings as it did the first time. That's the same reason I never bought the things they taught us in Catholic school, about God knowing everything that was going to happen before it did. I mean, what fun would that be for Him?"

John added, "It's the same as not finding the punch line of a joke funny when you've heard it before."

"Right! If you laugh at the joke a second time, it's because you're amused by the cleverness of it, but you're not surprised. And surprise…the unknown…is what makes a joke or life, for that matter, interesting. Otherwise, everything is flat."

"Politics, too?" Cal asked.

Jack shrugged. "Politics, business, everything. Even entertainment. John, remember Dad telling us how strange it was for him to watch that old replay of *The Blob* on TV, and suddenly recognizing a young Steve McQueen?"

"I do."

"It really affected him for a day or two, but he never actually explained why."

"Maybe," John offered, "it was some kind of mortality thing, made him think about his own."

"That's what I used to believe. Now that I've come back here, I think I understand it better. When he was watching that movie, even though it was an oldie, he got deeply into it. He had never seen it before. For a little while it was real to him. Then he saw McQueen, who looked so young, and it startled him. It kind of shocked him back to his own reality. That's how I feel."

"I'm still not sure what you mean," Cal hesitated.

"Cal, I don't remember the title, but did you ever see that movie with Christopher Reeve where he falls in love with the girl in the portrait…Jane Seymore, I think…and becomes obsessed with her, so he finds a way to go back in time to be with her?"

"Yeah, *Time After Time*, I think was the name of it."

"That's it. They don't have a fancy time machine like we do…did. The strange old-timer, who advises him on how to go back to her, tells him to just sit in the room of that old hotel, wearing authentic clothes from the day, surrounding himself with only objects from that time, and to, I think, meditate or something."

"Yes."

"He goes back in time, or at least believes he does. He meets the woman from the old photograph or portrait. They fall in love. Everything is wonderful. Then he casually pulls a penny out of his pants pocket and sees the date on it. And it's the date from his regular time. *Bam!* Just seeing that coin…that date…slams him violently back to the future. There are times since I've been here when I start settling in, like Christopher Reeve does in the movie. The human mind is so amazingly adaptable, and mine has been steadily assimilating everything around me as if it were my new reality. I guess that I've been gradually acclimating back to 2010. Then, all of a sudden, I see *this* guy on the screen…my future President…and my whole other reality crashes back in on me."

John and Cal both understood.

"I am stuck here. There really isn't any doubt about that since both possible means of transportation are gone. And even if we forget about the concern that my very presence can screw up the future, and I just look at things egocentrically – I am stuck in a movie that I've seen before."

"You might be…," John began.

"I am!" Jack insisted.

"Okay, you are. That doesn't mean that you know how the rest of your life is going to turn out. You *are* here in 2010 instead of 2040, your regular time, or whatever you call it, but that doesn't mean you can't live your life here and now…get a job, find a wife, everything. Even if you do know how so many of the things around you are going to turn out, so what? Those things are only external…remote. Your life is going to be different now. You can't predict it anymore, how each day will turn out. Everything from now on for you is going to be brand new."

"Maybe even a really good life," Cal added. "After all, money shouldn't be a problem. With what you know, you should be able to buy the right stocks in the right companies…do a lot of things that you already know are going to work out. If your memory is good enough, you could buy a winning lottery ticket."

Jack looked at Cal and said, "The biggest thing that is going to *work out* in the next several years is *you*."

Cal just stared at Jack, unsure of what to say.

"You are not only destined to invent the time machine, you are going crank out about a zillion inventions – all kinds of things, things that will change the world."

John watched Cal as he attempted to assimilate what he was being told.

"Kurt mentioned a little bit about that when he came back on Friday, but I didn't realize…."

"Realize it! By the time you reach 2040, you are going to be so rich that you'll make Bill Gates look like a pauper."

"I'm not so sure Cal is going to invent the time machine," John said softly.

They both looked at John, and Jack asked, "What do you mean? Why do you say that?"

"Well, think about it. Sure, Cal is alive again. Kurt accomplished that. But,

Cal, if you were still going to invent the machine at some point in the future, why wouldn't you send it back to this living room, right now, to pick up Jack?"

They both paused to think about John's question.

Jack rolled his eyes. "You're right. Cal, you *would* send it back. You wouldn't want me to stay here, not just for my own happiness or whatever. You would not want me to remain in this time any longer than absolutely necessary, because of the effect my being here could have."

"So, are we saying that I don't invent the machine?"

"Either that," John answered, "or something still happens to you, and you don't live to build it. You can't forget that Aloysius's space aliens, or whatever they are, don't want you to do it. Just because Kurt fouled up their plan once doesn't mean that they've simply given up."

"By now they must have figured out that Kurt tricked them," Jack said. "And that you're still around."

"Exactly," agreed John.

Cal's eyes became unfocused as he contemplated this. "So, I have a huge target on my back, and I will until...."

"Until what?" asked Jack.

John answered the question for Cal. "Until he builds the damn machine."

Cal nodded and said nothing.

Jack broke the silence. "Maybe you should get started now."

Cal looked at Jack and burst out laughing. "Now? You're kidding. I have no idea where to begin."

"You haven't put together a theory?"

"I've got theories, all right. That's the problem. There are too many of them."

John, thinking back over the previous day, said, "It seems like everything that's happened would help you to narrow it down. Didn't taking a trip in the machine help? Didn't it give you any clues?"

He could see the events of the previous day play out in Cal's eyes. "It might have. I haven't had the time to really focus on it."

John acknowledged Cal's frustration.

"It went so fast. Kurt took me to the storage room. I saw the sphere only briefly. After he told me how to operate it, I got in and came forward. And that trip only took a second, so it's not like I had a lot of time during the trip to study anything. Then I got out and immediately sent it back for Kurt. I wasn't around the machine more than a total of twenty or thirty minutes."

He stopped and let out a heavy sigh. Closing his eyes to help him visualize, he continued, "It was all sealed up. The sphere, on the outside, tells me nothing."

"Other than that it's important to make a vehicle like a Faraday cage," John suggested.

"True. That tells me something. The perfection of the sphere...." He turned to Jack. "What is it made from?"

"Almost pure silver."

"Okay. Perfect sphere. Highly conductive skin. Everything inside encased in a completely nonconductive coating." They could see that he was drifting into an imaginary world, a world where he could build experiments in his mind and then try them out.

Neither wanted to interrupt his thoughts. After a few moments, Cal asked, "Energy usage?" directing his question at either of them, both of them, or no one, as he thought out loud.

"Fuel cell," Jack offered.

"Okay...fuel cell. Unless that technology proved to be drastically different in thirty years than what we understand now, that really isn't a tremendous amount of power." He paused. "That is a clue because a couple of my theories required a huge amount of energy, way more than you could get out of a fuel cell."

Getting excited now, he added, "And I did see it depart for Kurt. There was no sound...no ionization of the air around it...nothing. It just left, silently. That tells me something, only I'm not sure what it tells me yet."

"I have a question," John said.

Cal smiled. "It's a bit premature to assume I can answer it, but go ahead."

"The sphere is occupying space, right? I mean, before it leaves?"

"Sure. What's the point?"

"Well...how can it just disappear without a sound?"

Cal looked at John quizzically, his mind suddenly jumping to the point. "Thunder!" He blurted out.

"Right."

"Explain, guys," Jack implored.

Cal turned to Jack and said, "What causes thunder? When lighting strikes, it displaces the air in the column where it traveled to the earth. When it finishes, it leaves a vacuum. The atmosphere around it slams back together to fill the void and, *bang!* you've got thunder."

Understanding, Jack wondered, "So why doesn't the sphere leave a void when it departs? Why wouldn't there be a thunderclap, or at least some sound?"

"That's the question. And, as far as I can think right now, the only answer is that when it goes, it makes a connection with the point of destination and does some kind of a swap…transferring the air from the area it is about to occupy to the spot where it is leaving."

Jack considered this for a moment before saying, "Is this important?"

"I think so," Cal answered excitedly. "It's a major clue, I think."

"Why?"

Cal's mind buzzed through an array of options, considering and discarding each after a moment's consideration. His face, having started the process with a look of excitement and anticipation, gradually changed to an expression of disappointment, before he finally sighed and said, "I don't know. There must be something there, but I'm not seeing it yet."

"Let's talk it through," John suggested. "If the machine departs without leaving a void behind, there are only two possible explanations."

"Two?" Cal inquired. "I only thought of one – that the machine somehow connects to the locale of its destination and swaps the sphere for the volume of air at the other point."

"That's one," agreed John. "Logically, the only other possibility is that it didn't really exist in the first place."

Cal and Jack both stared at him blankly. Seeing their looks of disbelief, he continued, "I know that both of you think I've lost it, but listen to me for a second. Maybe the machine is an illusion whenever it reaches its *target* location…a phantom of some sort."

Cal made a point of appearing to genuinely consider what John was saying. What began as only a half-serious contemplation transformed into a real expression of excitement as a thought clicked inside his head. Turning to Jack, he said, "In all of your discussions with…me…in the future, before the trip, did I ever mention quantum mechanics?"

Jack laughed. "Oh, only constantly. Why?"

Cal ignored his question and asked another. "Specifically, did I ever talk about the theory, put forth by some physicists in the quantum mechanics field, of the parallel universes?"

Jack took a moment to think back, then said, "Yes. Actually, you did. Where is this going?"

Before Cal could answer him, John exclaimed, "Multiverses!"

Cal agreed emphatically, "That's just what I was thinking."

Jack stared at their interaction. "I feel kind of stupid at this moment. Especially since my younger self seems to have it all figured out. But could somebody please explain this to me?"

Smiling, Cal complied, "There is a theory that most of the mainstream scientists of today discount as another example of physicists, instead of religious leaders, arguing about how many angels can dance on the head of a pin. It basically contends that every time each of us faces one of the myriad of decisions in the course of a day, a whole new universe, or reality, is created, like branches on a tree."

"Okay."

"So, right now, in this universe – you are here with us, John cancelled his wedding to Gail, and everything else... that we all know as our history... has happened. However, in a parallel universe, which also exists right now – your trip failed and John went ahead with the wedding and lived out the life that you... Jack... remember. In another one, I'm still dead, and Kurt is sitting here with you. In yet another, Jack, you never came back to this time at all. It goes on endlessly... a different reality, a different universe for each of the possible decisions that could have been made."

"How does this apply to what we were talking about, the lack of thunder when the sphere disappears?"

"All of the quantum universes exist in the same physical location; they are all overlaid upon one another. The only difference is our ability to perceive the others. Maybe the sphere exists in all of them simultaneously, but we can only see it in the reality where it is supposed to exist at that moment. That way, there wouldn't be any sound when it leaves because it really isn't leaving, all it is doing is shifting to another reality."

Jack stared at Cal for a moment. "I'm sorry. Maybe I'm just tired or something, but I'm still not getting it."

"Let me try to explain," John said. "Jack, forget about quantum physics and all of that for a second, and let's just do a little mind experiment."

"Okay."

"Let's say that Cal is a stage magician and he has this marvelous new trick to show us. He stands up in the middle of this room and snaps his fingers and, from your perspective, he disappears, but I can still see him."

"Right."

"He snaps them again, and now he is visible to you but not to me."

"Okay."

"It doesn't matter for now, for the purpose of this mind experiment, how he does the trick. It could just be some optical illusion or whatever; that's not the point. The point is... each time he snaps his fingers and disappears from the sight of one of us and appears to the other, he isn't ever really, physically, going anywhere. He is just flipping a switch that determines which one of us can see him."

"Got it. So, that's how the quantum universe works?"

"We don't know," answered Cal, "but we have some clues that we can't ignore, the biggest one being the absence of the sound when the sphere apparently departs."

John added, "There is one more thing that might fit into this puzzle, Cal."

"What's that?"

"The fact that the machine can't go into the future. By that I mean the future beyond its original starting point of 2040."

Cal, immediately seeing the connection, asked, "Is that really true?"

Jack nodded. "Cal, you told me when we talked about it that it couldn't be done. I even tried to set the controller ahead, just out of curiosity, and there was no way to set it beyond that date."

"That would be because those universes hadn't been created yet," John said.

Cal took in this new fact. "It's beginning to look that way. So, this means that the sphere isn't really a time machine. It's a way to hop between one alternate universe and another."

"And that explains why the traveler keeps his memories. He is basically being removed from one parallel universe and being dropped into another. His actions aren't changing anything. He's just...."

"Changing the channel," Jack finished the thought for John.

John shifted forward to the edge of his seat and asked, "So, does this help us any?"

"I'm not sure. It might. If we knew the locale of either the main machine or the backup...and by that, I mean the location in our reality that corresponds to where it is in the other...I wouldn't have to invent the machine, I'd only have to figure out a way to make it visible to us."

"Oh, is *that* all?" Jack queried sarcastically. "Yeah, that sounds much easier."

Cal chuckled. "Believe it or not, conceptually, it might be. I don't know yet, but it just might."

"Well," John said, "while you're trying to figure out that small detail, let's think about where one of them could be. Do you think that the backup machine might still be in the storage room...or where the storage room was?"

"Even if it is, and I'm not sure it would be, that building is now blown up. And we don't even know whether the machine came into this reality just in time to get caught in the blast," answered Jack.

"True. How about the main machine? Where would it be?"

"If it stayed true to the program," Jack hypothesized, "I think it would be in Cal's lab."

"Where was that?"

"Out near Rita Ranch," Jack answered. "All of his offices, the lab, everything was at the Science and Technology Park out there."

John tried to visualize the area. "So, where his lab is going to be thirty years into the future is just nothing but empty desert now?"

"No. I don't think so. He...," Jack glanced at Cal, "you bought the whole group of buildings from the U of A."

"The former IBM complex?"

"Yes. It was another of those budget crunches that the University makes a big deal out of every few years. They were complaining about how they didn't have enough money for all of their programs, and you made them an offer on the whole campus. A very generous cash offer, as I recall. They sold it all to you, and you allowed some of the buildings to remain dedicated to advanced degree studies. You were pretty proud of yourself at the time because you not only got that huge complex, you also had a steady stream of advanced-degree students in physics, astronomy and math coming through, whom you could use to do your research, and then cherry-pick from to hire."

Cal grinned. "That's where most of my classes and labs are now."

"I know," said Jack. "I think nostalgia was another part of your motivation to buy the property. You mentioned frequently that it was in those same buildings...." Jack paused a moment before continuing excitedly, "Wait a minute! You told me that the lab I left from – thirty years from now, the room where you kept the machine – was the same room where you had your first breakthrough on the theory when you were a student!"

Cal tensed, sliding forward to the front edge of his chair. "That would have to be the physics lab! It's got to be! That's where I spend almost all of my time when I'm at school. It's where I keep my notes, experiments, everything."

"Well," John said, "my first urge is to jump in the car and drive out there, but what the hell would we do when we arrived?"

"We still need to figure out that small detail of how we can cross between the universes," Jack cautioned.

"If that's even the correct theory," added Cal.

Quiet fell over the room as the three men became lost in their own thoughts.

John eventually broke the silence, "I feel like I should be doing something!" Frustration was evident in his voice.

Jack, having slipped back into his morose mood, softly said, "Even if we're on the right track…it's going to take months, maybe years, Cal, before you can do something that'll help me."

Cal didn't respond. The expression on his face said everything.

XXI

Across town, Ben Hart felt the same type of frustration. He knew there was something he should be doing but couldn't, for the life of him, figure out what it was. His desk was littered with notes from the arson at the Augur apartment, as well as from the attempted murder of Ed and Kathleen Augur. In a neat pile in the center of his desk was a stack of sheets from a yellow legal pad, each page covered with what would initially appear to be random scribbles.

Ben was a very visual thinker, and the pages were the detritus left from his attempts to diagram the death and subsequent appearances of Kurt Wallace. As he added each date and location where Kurt had been seen, the diagrams began to resemble a sketch by Escher, where the stairways turned in on themselves.

Frustrated, he bunched up the pile and tossed it into his wastebasket. Weary from trying to follow the illogical and seemingly impossible path of facts he had accumulated on Wallace, he mentally shifted gears and forced himself to ponder the mind of Gail Schilling.

"Where would she be?" he asked himself, hoping for an answer.

"Maybe I know."

He spun around in his swivel chair and saw that Burke was standing next to him. So lost in his own thoughts, Hart hadn't noticed him approach. "Know what?"

"Where Gail Schilling might be, or at least what she's driving now."

"She rented a car?"

"She did. I guess she's smart enough to know that she shouldn't be driving her own car, with us looking for her, but not quite smart enough to know not to use a credit card. We got a 'hit' on her Visa. She used it at one of the car rental booths at the airport early this morning."

Ben started to speak, but Burke cut him off. "I've already put the make, model and plate of the rental car in the system."

"Have we found her car?"

"A unit is on its way to the airport now to check the lots."

"My guess is she dumped it in one of the long-term lots."

"I agree."

"Have the crime lab team standing by. When we find it, I want that car checked over inch by inch."

"Already done," Burke said, smiling.

Hart shook his head. "Billy, you've been doing this longer than I have. Why didn't you ever take the bump up to detective?"

Burke's grin spread farther. "I like the way I look in the uniform."

Ben chuckled. "Seriously, why not?"

Burke thought for a moment before answering, "I tried it. I don't know if you heard about it or not. It was almost fifteen years ago."

"I was still in eighth grade then," Hart kidded. "Actually, no, I didn't know that."

Burke shrugged. "No wonder. It didn't last too long." His eyes shifted to look out of the window. "I didn't feel like a real cop without the uniform."

"No kidding?"

Looking back at Hart, he explained, "Do you remember how it felt when you first came out of the academy and put on the uniform? Remember the first time that you walked into a public place wearing it? Maybe it was the same place that you'd walked into a thousand times before as a civilian. But this time, you felt different – the way the people looked at you... reacted to you."

Ben's mind returned to his early days on the force. He smiled and said, "I felt like I was ten feet tall."

"It's true. I haven't been on the force long enough to have been around during the '60s. I remember the older guys talking about those days ... when the 'hippies' spit on them and called them 'pigs.' I thank God I didn't go through that. When I was growing up, I was like most boys then. I read *Superman* and *Green Lantern*. They were my favorites. My folks bought the costumes for me. I wore them and played in the backyard, by myself. God, was I sad when I got too old to do that anymore. I gave in to the other kids teasing me and stopped. But

I think we all grow up wanting to be a super-hero."

The detective understood.

"Ben, I've never told anyone this, but when I realized that being a cop meant I got to wear the outfit, I joined the force."

Hart chuckled. "Billy, that's a part of it for all of us, I think."

"My first call as a rookie...I was partners with D'Antonio...was to a shooting at Shirley's Restaurant."

"On Pima?"

"Yeah. It was a robbery gone bad and the waitress was shot. So was one of the customers who tried to help. Thankfully, nobody died. Everyone in the place was shaken pretty badly, and there was blood everywhere. Ben, when we walked in...," Burke's eyes shifted focus to a faraway place as he relived the moment. "As we walked in and I saw how all of the people looked at me, I knew that I'd found it...that I'd found what I thought I had lost as a kid.

"Right then, for just a little while, I felt like I was Captain America. There have been plenty of times since then that it's been less than rosy, but over the years, there have been a lot of moments like that day at Shirley's, too. When I got bumped up, years ago, to detective, it didn't feel the same. Almost all the time the detectives arrive later...you're not that first one to show up on the scene when something horrible has happened. You don't get to be the one to come in when the bad guy is still inside."

"To save the day."

"I didn't like getting to a crime scene *after* it was secure. I realized that what I enjoyed was being the one who *made* it secure."

"And wearing the costume."

"Yeah! And wearing the costume. I just wish the department would hurry up and issue us a cape."

Ben burst out laughing, and Burke joined him.

When the laughter subsided, Ben turned somber and said to his friend, "Billy, what do you make of this Wallace thing? I admit it, it's driving me crazy."

Burke hitched up one of his long legs and perched on the edge of Ben's desk, a thoughtful look on his face. "I don't know, but I'll tell you that Lou thinks she's got it figured out."

Ben grinned and thought about Louise, Billy's wife. For the seven years that he'd known them, she was always talking about civilizations who lived underground, and space aliens, who disguised themselves as humans and lived among us. When she wasn't reading books on the subject, she watched movies about it. There were times, Ben had to admit, usually later in the evening when he and his wife would socialize with the Burkes, that some of what she said made sense to him. But, then again, it could be explained because by that time, he had usually consumed more than his share of scotch.

"What does she think it is?" Ben asked, almost afraid to hear her opinion.

Struggling to maintain a serious demeanor, Burke said, "She thinks that Wallace really did die Saturday night, but the Wallace that you and I and all of the others have seen since then was a *replicant*, an alien who took his form."

Ben nodded gravely, as if he were genuinely considering this option, before asking, "And what's their purpose for doing this?"

Burke, unable to stop a slow grin from creeping onto his face, answered, "She's not sure, but she is convinced that it has something to do with their plot to control us all."

"Well," Ben said, his voice even, "that's a problem. As long as it's just an arson and attempted murder, the case is mine, but if it's those world-dominating aliens again, I need to flip the case to the right department."

Smiling more broadly, Burke inquired, "Which department?"

Ben raised his finger to his lips to silence Burke. "If I told you, I'd have to kill you. They are so secret they don't even have a name. Hell, they don't even get the Crown Vics to drive like we do. Everywhere they go, they use black helicopters."

"No kidding. Even to get a doughnut?"

Ben shook his head. "That's the thing, Billy. They don't need doughnuts. They've been genetically modified so that they don't have to eat, sleep or any of those normal things. They don't even work the usual eight-hour shifts because they don't need time off. They are always on duty."

"Wow! I'll bet the folks in Human Resources love them."

Almost whispering, Ben answered, "Even *they* don't know about them. They don't have to. Because the men and women in that secret department…aren't human."

They broke into laughter again.

"I'll tell you one thing, though," Burke said seriously.

"What's that?"

"Augur was as surprised as we were when you told him that Wallace was dead."

"That's true. I don't think he knew anything about it."

"No, I don't either."

"But I do think he knows something else. There was something in the way he acted when we interviewed him. There's something else going on."

"I think you're right," Burke concurred. "I don't have any idea what it could be, but I felt the same thing when I talked to him the first night, at the arson."

Both men slipped into a thoughtful silence, finally broken by Ben, who said, "With everything else going the way it is, I'm not one hundred percent sure I want to know what he's hiding."

To occupy his mind, Burke reached across Ben's desk and picked up the manila folder that sat at the top of one of the many piles. Flipping it open, he saw it contained the canvassing reports of the uniformed officers, following up after the attempted murder of the Augurs.

Scanning each page, he noticed that the reports were typical of most neighborhoods after a crime. No one saw anything. No one heard a sound. In this particular case, due to the time of night, it was probably true that they were all asleep. Reaching the last page in the file, his interest was suddenly piqued, and he reread the officer's comments twice before speaking.

"Ben, have you gone through these neighborhood canvassing reports?"

Ben glanced over to see which file Burke had in his hand and replied, "I scanned them, why?"

"The last one, from...," his eyes went up to the top of the page and found the officer's name, "Morales, might be interesting."

"What does it say?"

"One of the neighbors a few doors down from the Augur residence woke up in the middle of the night. This was after we had responded and were on the scene. Apparently, the flashing red lights came in through their window blinds, so they got up to see what was going on."

"Did they see anything?"

"At about the time that we were done with John Augur and Kurt Wallace and cut them loose, this neighbor saw a car that matched Augur's stop in front of their house and pick up a third person...someone who had been waiting for them."

"What? Augur didn't mention that."

Looking back down at the report, Burke added, "From what the neighbor said, it looked to them like the man Augur picked up had been hiding behind a tree in their front yard. They didn't notice him until the car stopped and he stepped out of the shadows."

"I suppose it's too much to hope for a description?"

"Yep. It was too dark. They couldn't get a good look."

Ben turned his gaze to the view outside the window and added this fact to the already confusing jumble of events he was attempting to organize into a logical scenario.

He finally said, "Well, I guess that confirms our suspicion that Augur is hiding something."

"It sure does. Do you want me to call him in?"

Ben started to say *yes*, then paused. "Do we know where he is?"

"I don't think so. His place is gone. His parents' house is a crime scene. He could be at a motel."

"Or," Ben said, smiling, "he could be at Kurt Wallace's place."

He stood up and slipped into his jacket. "I think we should pay Mr. Augur a surprise visit, don't you?"

"We? You want me to tag along?"

"Sure," Ben responded. "Grab your cape, and let's go."

⋈

"I feel like we need to do something," Cal said nervously, as he stood up from the sofa.

"What?" asked Jack.

"I don't know. Let's go to the physics lab."

"And do what?"

"Check my notes…just stand in the room where the machine will be someday. Dammit, I don't know! I can't stand just sitting here and doing nothing."

"Okay," Jack agreed, and he and John rose. As they left Kurt's house and climbed into the car, none of them noticed the rented Camry parked across the street. As they drove away, they also didn't notice the other car start up and follow them. The Camry made it to the end of the block and turned the corner just as Ben Hart's unmarked police car pulled up in front of Kurt's.

"I'm hungry," Cal said.

John pulled onto Speedway, turning east, and looked at his watch, "It *is* lunchtime. I could use something, too. Jack, you're the one visiting, you pick a spot."

Jack thought for a moment before answering, "Lucky Wishbone!"

"Steak fingers!" John replied, excited. "I haven't had those for a long time."

Cal looked at them both with his mouth agape. "I can't believe you two. Deep-fried, breaded hunks of red meat. Jack, I'm surprised you're still alive thirty years from now."

Jack laughed. "Cal, you might not believe this but you, too, become a steak-finger junkie."

"Never! That stuff will kill you."

Jack talked as John maneuvered the car onto Swan Road, turning south. "Actually, no it won't."

"What do you mean? Is this one of those future things, like Woody Allen saying that scientists eventually discover that the only things that are good for you are white bread and cigarettes?"

Jack laughed again and answered, "No. In fact, it is one of your inventions that makes it okay."

Cal stared incredulously at Jack. "What are you talking about? I make something that makes the world safe from fried foods? This is a joke, right?"

Jack shook his head, still grinning. "No joke, man."

"I'm a physicist, or I will be. Not a chemist. I'm sure I didn't invent a safe fat to fry stuff in."

"You didn't, or you don't. You invented something that looks like a big microwave oven and zaps the food briefly after it's been deep-fried. It changes the molecular structure of the fats, rendering them harmless to us."

Cal flopped back into his seat, laughing.

"Don't laugh. There are a lot of people hooked on fried foods. You make millions on it. Back here in 2010, you've already seen the typical government meddling… outlawing transfats and such. Well, believe me, it gets worse in the next few years."

John pulled into the parking lot, and they climbed out, crossed the lot and entered the seating area. The restaurant, instead of providing a typical seating area for the customers, had what was essentially a lobby with a few high-school-classroom chairs with attached small tables, slightly larger than armrests.

They walked up to the counter and placed their orders, taking the plastic poker chip with their order number written in felt tip pen, and went outside to sit at the concrete benches.

A few minutes passed. It was obvious that all three of them wanted a respite from the intensity of the recent discussions, as they talked and joked about lighter issues. Jack had apparently come to the decision that it didn't matter what he told Cal about his future, and made several references to some of the patents and inventions that were to come. Cal quietly took them all in.

John left and checked to see if their food was ready, returning a minute later with three cardboard boxes. He set them on the table and went back in for the drinks. Jack and Cal lifted the lids on their boxes, immediately opened the containers of cocktail dipping sauce, and were chewing on the dripping steak fingers by the time John returned.

"You're right," Cal declared between bites, "these are great."

Jack chuckled and said, "The beginning of a lifelong obsession," taking a large bite out of the buttered garlic toast provided with the meal.

John, whose back was to the parking lot, saw Jack's expression change, and twisted around on the concrete bench just as he felt a hand on his shoulder.

"I see we have the same taste in food." John's back tingled when he heard the familiar, feminine tone. He finished turning and saw Lynn standing beside him. She was wearing a loose red top and form-hugging white pants. Her face was framed by dark, straight hair. Her full lips curved in a broad smile. Her eyes sparkled.

John's intention to greet her was foiled by the half-chewed steak finger at the top of his throat, the distraction of her nearness causing the obstruction to go unnoticed. Instead of saying something, he began choking.

Jack started laughing, joined by Cal, as John struggled to take in air, the effort audible with a loud, wheezing sound accompanying each gasp... the ordeal punctuated by sharp hacks as John's body tried to clear his airway.

"Oh, no!" Lynn exclaimed. John felt two things at once. Lynn's slender arms encircled him from behind, obviously preparing to perform the Heimlich Maneuver on him. Meanwhile, the stubborn chunk of meat suddenly dislodged from his throat during one of his frantic coughing fits, and shot out of his mouth like a projectile, landing with a *splat* on the center of the table.

With a huge, whistling gasp, John's lungs sucked in much-needed air. The laughter from Jack and Cal escalated to near hysteria, with Jack dropping his face onto his arms on the table, his shoulders convulsing with spasms.

Humiliated and red-faced, John slumped, realizing that Lynn's arms were still around him. He felt the sensuous tickle of her hair on his neck and smelled the same fragrance he had noticed when he saw her at her office. He could also feel the warmth of her breath as she moved her lips within an inch of his ear. Softly, so that only he could hear, she said, "Maybe I'm not so hungry, after all."

"I'm... I'm sorry I ruined your appetite."

She chuckled softly into his ear, and he felt her arms tighten around him as she nestled her face against the side of his head.

"Are you okay?" she asked.

Not trusting himself to speak, he merely nodded, enjoying the kinetic tension between them.

Sadly, John felt Lynn's embrace relax and her arms move away. As if drawn magnetically, he followed as she moved back, and rose from the bench.

"Can you join us? I'll buy your lunch."

He was standing in front of her, not more than six or seven inches away, and saw her look around his shoulder at the table. "Only if you get rid of that," she said, her eyes indicating the brown-gray lump that sill rested on the tabletop.

Shaking his head, John looked at Jack and Cal, who were both still laughing, and said, "Thanks, guys. You could have cleaned that up."

Between bursts of laughter, Cal managed to say, "I'm not touching that!"

John, embarrassed and disgusted with himself, grabbed one of the napkins from his meal box, snatched up the morsel and tossed it into the nearby trash can. His aim was faulty. The wad of napkin bounced off the lip of the receptacle and smacked into Cal, slipping down behind his collar and the back of his shirt.

Cal shot up from his seat and arched his back. "Gross!" he shouted, twisting an arm around behind himself and plucking his shirt away from his back. Glad to have the attention turned away from himself, John began to laugh at Cal's maneuvers.

"Oh, God! It's all the way down to my waist!"

Cal quickly jerked his shirt and t-shirt out of the top of his pants to allow the offending bite of steak finger a point of egress. The bit of beef had a mind of its own, opportunistically falling into the slight gap created by his efforts, and dropping into the back of Cal's pants.

"Aggghhh!" he shouted. "That feels horrible!"

Cal turned and ran into the lobby, intent on finding a restroom, his gait bizarre as he tried to walk rapidly while holding the rear of his pants away from his behind. John, Lynn and Jack roared with more laughter, while they watched through the plate glass as Cal immediately discovered that this old restaurant did not have a restroom in the front. He stood at the counter and tugged at the back of his jeans, explaining to the clerk that he needed to use their restroom.

They could see the counter girl hand him a long, wooden stick with a key clipped to its end, as she pointed to the side of the building. Either from something Cal had explained to her, or simply as a result of seeing what had happened out front, the young girl was also laughing.

Red with humiliation, Cal, clutching the key stick, awkwardly exited the glass door and, without acknowledging the three of them, shuffled around the corner, suffering their comments and catcalls.

Lynn and John, still giggling, dropped onto a bench side by side, joining Jack at the table. Within a minute, Cal emerged sheepishly. He stared defiantly at them and said, "Since I have to go back and face that teenage girl to return this key…Lynn, can I order something for you?"

Pursing her lips tightly to hold back another round of laughter, she managed to say, "I'll have what you're having."

That was enough to cause all of them, including Cal this time, to lose it again.

He went back in, handed the key stick to the girl, and ordered another meal. After paying and obtaining another numbered poker chip, he returned and joined them at the table.

"Here," John offered, sliding his meal box to a point between himself and Lynn. "Till yours is ready, we can share."

Lynn looked down warily at the open cocktail sauce and said, "You haven't double-dipped, have you?"

"I…uh, no. I haven't."

Seeing doubt in her eyes, John added, "Well, yeah, I did."

"Thought so," she said with a grin, "I'll wait," and pushed the box back toward him.

Feeling more dejected than this minor rebuke warranted, John reached into the box, grabbed some french fries and dipped them into the sauce. Before he could take a bite, Lynn took his wrist and steered the fries to her own mouth, guiding them in far enough for his fingertips to be pressed against her lips. During the entirety of this brief act, her eyes gazed into John's and she said nothing.

"Oh, man," murmured Cal, his eyes riveted to the play in front of him.

Jack watched them silently, a satisfied grin on his face.

Lynn slowly chewed the portion of french fries, continuing to hold John's fingers to her mouth, her lips moving gently against them. She eventually swallowed and opened her mouth slightly, wordlessly waiting. John, still clutching the other half of the fries, gently placed them between her lips.

"Guys!" Cal almost shouted. "Remember us? We're still here!"

The corners of Lynn's mouth curled upward in a smile, and she turned to Cal. "Oh, hello," she said, as if she had just noticed his presence.

She released her grip on John's wrist and turned to face the others. John cleared his throat and turned also, sliding toward Lynn as he did, so that their thighs were in contact.

"Who," she asked, "are you?"

John performed the introduction. "Lynn, this is Cal Mitchell. Cal, Lynn O'Neal."

She reached over the food boxes to shake his hand. "A pleasure to meet you."

Cal quickly grabbed a napkin and wiped off his right hand before shaking hers. His grip remained a moment longer than necessary, which John noticed immediately. He fought off the incipient anger and jealousy that was beginning to build within him. They ended the handshake before giving John an opportunity to further embarrass himself, and Lynn addressed Jack, "And you are...?"

They all noticed Lynn's eyes suddenly narrow as she apparently focused upon Jack for the first time. Attempting to nip any undue curiosity in the bud, John quickly introduced them, "Lynn, this is my Uncle Jack." Noticing that she was staring at Jack far too intensely, he lamely added, "He's from out of town."

Jack reached across, extended his hand and said, "Lynn."

She took his hand and, with a definite tinge of suspicion in her voice, asked, "Weren't you with John at my office?"

"Uh huh."

John, feeling the direction of the interaction between them going the wrong way, tried to step in. "So, Lynn, why aren't you working today?"

Rather than rising to the bait, she continued her deliberate scrutiny of Jack and answered John without turning. "Dooley is sick. He closed the office and went home. I only had to stay long enough to call the rest of his appointments to reschedule them. So, tell me, Jack, how long are you visiting?"

"Not long."

"And where are you from?"

"Dayton."

"Dayton? Where is that?"

"Ohio."

John, getting more nervous with each exchange, tried again, "That must have been a nice surprise... getting an unexpected day off?"

Lynn, refusing to be diverted, answered, "It was. Anyway, Jack, I know Dayton is in Ohio. I just don't remember what part of the state."

"Southern."

She broke into a grin, seeming to enjoy the little game they were playing. "I've heard it's pretty around that part of the country. Tell me about it."

"It's green."

"Lots of water?"

"Lots."

"What's the major industry there?"

"Tires."

Her smile broadened. "Being John's uncle, you must have some great stories to tell about him growing up. I'd like to hear some of them."

"Not really."

Her grin broke into a chuckle. "Not really? I don't understand. Didn't you know him?"

Feeling backed into a corner, Jack said, "Look...we just recently got acquainted."

"Oh, really? Why is that?"

There was a long silence. Everyone had stopped eating and was watching the mini-drama play between them. Finally, Lynn smiled a dazzling smile and reached across the concrete table, placing her hand on top of Jack's. "I'm sorry. I don't mean to sound rude. I'm just trying to get an answer from you that's longer than two or three words."

Jack stared at her for a long moment before saying, "Would you like for me to do a reading? Perhaps some...oh, I don't know...Whitman. Maybe from *Leaves of Grass*?"

Lynn tensed when she heard him say the title. Her eyes searched his deeply. She slowly took in a deep breath and said, "How did you know that?"

"Know what?" asked Jack, feigning innocence.

"That *Leaves of Grass* is my favorite?"

Jack shrugged. "Lucky guess."

Lynn still did not look away from Jack, her eyes taking in every detail of his face in the bright sunlight. "Jack is a nickname for John, right?"

"It is."

She finally turned away from him and faced John. Curiosity and suspicion were painted plainly on her face. "Are you going to tell me?"

John, invariably flustered by Lynn's direct gaze, muttered, "No."

His perturbation exacerbated by his own answer, he added, "That's not what I meant! I mean, there's nothing to tell. Jack's my uncle from Ohio."

He saw a look of disappointment cloud her face. Unable to stand being the cause of this, he turned to Jack for an okay. "Does it really matter?"

"Does what matter?" Lynn asked.

John didn't answer her immediately, waiting for some indication of consent from his *other* before he continued. Almost imperceptibly, a look of resignation on his face, Jack assented.

Next he turned to Cal, who shrugged, communicating that he didn't care one way or another.

Lynn watched this interplay, understanding that a decision was being reached, and waited.

Taking in a long, deep breath and letting it out slowly, John faced Lynn and once again felt himself falling into the mysterious abyss of her eyes. Although she tried to maintain a stern and serious expression as their eyes connected, a slight smile unconsciously turned up the corners of her mouth. She patiently continued her silent waiting, sensing that the answer was imminent.

"Lynn," John began, trying hard to formulate the best way to say what he was about to tell her. "Jack is...."

"You," she finished for him, watching his eyes for confirmation.

Startled, John asked, "How did you...?"

Her smile spread, now enveloping all of her features. "As long as we are all letting our various cats out of our personal bags, I'll give you a peek at mine." She paused for a moment before telling him, "I guess you could say I'm psychic."

Surprised, John let out a quick sound that, had it come from a golden retriever, would have been described as a *chuff*. Grinning, he asked, "You're psychic?"

Lynn nodded, her dark hair swinging along the sides of her face. "Always have been."

John, hearing Cal chuckle and say, "Well, that makes sense," turned to look at him questioningly.

"With everything else that's happened in the last few days, why not add a psychic to the mix," he explained.

John then turned to Jack, saying, "You knew, didn't you?"

Jack just smiled faintly.

Focusing again on Lynn, John grinned. "Then I guess I don't need to tell you what's going on. You must already know."

"Not quite," she answered, reaching out to put her hand on his. "It really doesn't work like that. I know now that Jack is you. I've obviously got a pretty good idea that something else is going on...something major, I guess. But I really don't have any idea what it is."

John started to fill her in on the details when a sudden realization struck him. "You're showing up here wasn't just a coincidence, was it?"

She shook her head.

He took another deep breath, glanced at Cal and Jack one more time, and said, "*Okay!*" Looking around them, he noted that the other tables were filled with the lunchtime crowd. "Just not here."

⧖

Across the street, the rented Camry was parked under the shade of a tree in the bank parking lot. Gail watched as John and Lynn sat close together on the bench, holding each other's hands and talking. Her own hands gripped the steering wheel so tightly that her knuckles had turned white.

- XXII -

After having knocked on the door to Kurt's house and getting no response, Hart and Burke had checked the perimeter, not looking for anything in particular. The next step was to talk to the surrounding neighbors, but most were not at home at that time of day. They did get a stroke of luck at the residence directly across the street from the house.

The occupant, a student, had no classes scheduled that day, and was sitting at her front window, working on a paper, when she saw three men leave Kurt's house. She told Hart and Burke that she only recognized one of the three. By her description, the young man she recognized was, apparently, John Augur, whom she had seen at Kurt's many times before. The other two were unknown to her. From her recollection, it appeared that Hart and Burke had only missed them by a few minutes.

Back in his unmarked police car, Ben said, "I guess that Augur and Mitchell have really bonded since the fire and explosion."

"They seem to be inseparable," agreed Burke.

"At least we now have a decent description of the older man."

"Do you think this is the same person Augur and Wallace picked up on the street after the attempted murder?"

"That'd be my guess."

"Mine, too. But who is he?"

"That," Ben said too loudly for the confined space, "is the big mystery, but it's one I'm going to figure out."

"What's the point?"

Ben turned to Burke and asked, "What do you mean?"

"At the risk of sounding like the captain, what does the identity of the third man have to do with either the arson or the attempted murder?"

"I don't know yet. Something is telling me that if we figure it out, the answer will have everything to do with it."

Burke looked out the front windshield, staring at the mature trees lining the street, lost in his own thoughts for a moment. "Okay. Then let's do this the old fashioned way. Let's backtrack."

"Backtrack to where?"

"Why don't you stay here? Stake out the house. I'll go back to the beginning, the Hotel Congress, and nose around. Maybe we'll pick something up."

Ben nodded his agreement, and Burke snatched the radio microphone from the dashboard to call dispatch. Since he had ridden with Ben, he needed a vehicle.

⌛

Burke approached the lobby desk at the Hotel Congress, noticing the slightly uneasy expression on the face of the clerk who was watching him closely. *This is always the way it is*, Burke thought to himself, *whenever we come in without having been called by someone who's in trouble.* After all of his years on the force, he had grown accustomed to that look, understanding that most people harbored an unconscious fear of the police. Burke had long ago chalked this off to the public having seen too many movies where an innocent person is arrested and goes to jail for a crime he didn't commit. His mother always told him that people just had guilty consciences.

"Can... can I help you?" the young clerk asked, doing a poor job of masking his nervousness.

"Is your manager available?" Burke inquired brusquely.

"Actually... no, sir, she isn't. We're having a large party at the hotel tonight, so she's coming in this evening."

"What about an assistant manager?"

Not looking very enthusiastic about providing the information, the clerk said, "That's me."

Burke pulled out his notepad and pen. "Your name, sir?"

"Gil. Gilbert Sanchez."

Burke noted the name and continued, "Were you working last Saturday night…the night of the fatal motorcycle accident that occurred out front?"

"No, sir. I work days."

"Were you working the desk during the day on Sunday?"

"Sunday? Yes, I was."

"You don't happen to specifically recall John Augur, one of your guests from Saturday night, do you?"

Sanchez brightened as he ascertained the direction of the questions and realized he might be of some help. "I do. I worked Saturday and checked him in. There was a bachelor party for him that night, and when he checked in, some of his friends were in the lobby and he took a lot of teasing from them."

"What do you remember about the time he checked out on Sunday? Was anyone with him?"

The clerk thought back for a moment and said, "Yeah. He did have someone with him."

"Did you know the other person?"

"He looked familiar, but no. I didn't know him."

Burke asked the clerk to describe the other man and received the same general description of the mysterious older stranger, matching what he had heard earlier from the neighbor across from Wallace's house.

After noting the details provided by Sanchez, Burke asked, "Is there anyone else on staff who might know more about this other man?"

Sanchez shrugged. "Maybe. I don't know. He might have eaten in the restaurant…had a drink in the bar. I don't know."

Burke knew that most people want to be helpful to a police officer, so he deliberately put a look of frustration and disappointment on his face and waited. It didn't take long.

"Wait. I just remembered something."

"What's that?" Burke asked, self-satisfied with his tactic.

Sanchez turned around so that he faced the wall behind the desk, and pointed up at the wall. Burke immediately saw the small, concealed video camera mounted inconspicuously.

"How long are the tapes kept?" Burke knew that frequently the recordings were on a twenty-four loop.

"Tapes!" the clerk exclaimed derisively, as if Burke had asked him where he could send a telegram.

"It's digital. MPEG. We've got a huge hard drive to store them all. We can go back weeks!" Sanchez looked quite proud of this fact.

Smiling, Burke said, "Well...may I take a look at the recording for Sunday?"

"Of course. The computer is right over here, in the manager's office." Sanchez started to walk to the end of the desk when he suddenly stopped. "I just remembered something."

"What's that?"

"Just a second." The clerk rummaged through a stack of papers on the back credenza until he found a single envelope.

"Here it is." He handed the envelope to Burke, who took it and immediately saw the name *John Augur*, hand-written on the face.

"What is this?"

"The maids found it in the room after Augur checked out." Sanchez looked a little sheepish before he continued, "It wasn't sealed, so I read it. I just looked at it to find out if it was...."

"It's okay. Don't worry about it," Burke said as he removed the hotel stationery pages from the envelope.

"I'd better warn you," advised Sanchez, adopting the tone of a person describing a strange movie, "it's pretty weird stuff."

☓

"So, this is where it happens, huh?" John asked, looking around at the large physics lab as Cal led them in.

"This is definitely the room I left from...thirty years from now."

The four of them crossed to a small table used for meetings, informal discussions, and mostly hurried lunches by the students too wrapped up in their projects to leave for a meal.

As they sat, Lynn remarked, "Thirty years from now, huh? I think I've been patient long enough, waiting for that explanation."

John, in the chair closest to her, reluctantly began, "All right, here goes." He swallowed first and hedged, "Maybe a drink of...."

"Now!" she reiterated firmly.

"Okay...okay," he gave in, holding his hands up defensively.

John leaned toward Lynn and grabbed her hands where they rested on her knees. Looking her directly in the eyes, he said, "I guess it all started Saturday night about midnight. I was at my bachelor party and went outside for a smoke. Jack started talking to me. He told me that he was *me*...from the future, from 2040."

He expected a look of incredulity or disbelief or, at the very least, skepticism. Instead, Lynn calmly returned his gaze, looking no more surprised than if he had told her that he stopped at the store and bought a loaf of bread.

He continued, "Anyway... he told me that marrying Gail would be a horrible disaster."

"*I* could have told you that," Lynn interjected, a smile crossing her face.

"Yeah, well, apparently everyone could have. It looks like I'm the only one who didn't know. I had a tough time believing him at first, but he convinced me fairly quickly. We walked for a while, talking, and Kurt found us at the train station."

"Kurt?"

"Oh, that's right. You've never met him. Kurt is... was... my best friend. He's the one who threw the party for me."

"Was?"

"I'll... I'll get to that," John sighed, a stab of sadness piercing his heart momentarily. "So... Kurt found us, and we were walking back to the hotel. As we crossed the street, Cal came around a curve on his motorcycle, swerved to miss us, and spilled the bike. He crashed into a parked car and died."

John had managed to reach her threshold as that look of incredulity finally arrived on her face. "Cal? You mean *this* Cal?" she asked, pointing across the table.

"Yes," John said, "this Cal."

"So, you're dead?" she asked, her voice colored with a bit of sarcasm.

"Nope. Greatly exaggerated." Cal answered simply.

Lynn turned back to John. "You better go on."

John attempted another swallow, his throat dry. He looked up beseechingly at Cal, who said, "I'll get some water. Anyone else want one?"

As it turned out, everyone was thirsty from the salty lunch. As Cal left them, John continued, "What's really bad about what happened... about Cal dying... other than the obvious... is that Cal is the person who eventually invents the time machine Jack uses to come back here."

"Oh!" exclaimed Lynn, her mind readily accepting the outrageous turns of events. "The two of you... or, I should say, the three of you... counting this Kurt fellow... killed the guy who...?" Her voice trailed off, and John simply nodded.

"But I don't understand. The way I thought time travel worked, or would work if it existed, was that if you changed something in the past, it would alter the future. If you three killed Cal, and Cal is the one who invents the machine that brought you here, wouldn't that undo the future? I guess what I'm asking is, wouldn't you just disappear at that instant because you couldn't have been sent back in time?"

She had directed her question at Jack, who answered, "Other than that obviously *not* being the case, no…the way it works, from what I understand, is that the person in the machine is immune to any changes that are made. Also, I am now in the *past*. Whatever the results of Cal's death will be…or would have been…those results haven't happened yet."

Lynn thought for a moment as Cal returned to the table with four bottles of water. John took advantage of her pause to unscrew the lid on one of them and take a large drink.

Marshaling her thoughts, Lynn stated, "So, to use the old paradox…if you were the person who goes back in time and kills his own grandfather, you would continue to exist, even though the lineage is broken?"

"Exactly," answered Jack.

As her brow furrowed in concentration, John said, "Hey, so far, this is the easy part. It gets worse."

Her eyes turned back to him. "Worse?"

"Oh, yeah."

"Well, you better keep going then."

John resumed, "After all *that* happened and we realized Cal was dead, Jack got back in the time machine and went back in time to Friday night."

"So he could undo Cal's death?"

John was taking another swig from his water and couldn't immediately respond to her, so Cal said, "That's right. Except it was a bust. All he did, supposedly, was confront me in front of the dorm and get me mad, so mad I jumped on my bike and raced downtown to die."

"What?" Jack nearly shouted. "That isn't what happened."

Cal just grinned as Jack continued, "I spent all day Saturday waiting for you, but you never showed up. It was getting close to the arrival time of my first trip…Saturday night…so I just gave up and came back."

Instead of saying any more, Cal stood and walked to one of the many desktop computers in the room, picking the one with the largest flat screen monitor and turned it on.

"That's only what you remember now," Cal said.

"Your memory of that day is different?"

"No," Cal answered. "John, do you still have the DVD that I gave you?"

John checked his pocket and pulled out the mini-disk, handing it to Cal.

"I don't have any of those memories either, since I left on Friday morning and skipped forward to Tuesday. However, when I saw Kurt back on Friday, he showed me this," he explained, holding up the mini-disk for a moment before inserting it into the CD-ROM drive of the computer.

"Wait a minute!" Lynn exclaimed. "Jack, you're saying that, as far as you remember, you took the time machine and went back to Saturday morning…."

"Actually, late Friday night."

"Okay, late Friday night… and you spent all of Saturday looking for Cal, but you never found him."

"Right," Jack answered.

"Cal, you're saying that he did see you Saturday evening, and you two had an argument?"

"Actually, I'm not saying that… Kurt told me that's what happened."

The computer finished its boot-up sequence, and Cal clicked the mouse. All of them moved to a cluster around the monitor and sat down. A moment later the video resolved on the screen, showing Jack and Kurt, joined a moment later by John.

"That's Kurt," John pointed out to Lynn.

"Oh."

Cal adjusted the volume, and all of them listened silently to the message that had been originally intended to brief John and Jack had the motorcycle accident never occurred.

When it finished, John was the first to speak, "This is so weird."

Lynn shook her head, "That's the understatement of the year."

"It does make sense, though," Jack noted.

"It does?"

"Yeah. If the sequence of events happened like we described… where I went back and had an argument with Cal Saturday night, and he got on his bike and drove downtown and died… and then Kurt went back to Friday morning… the day before all of that happened… and he talked Cal into getting into the time machine and going forward to Tuesday… that means that the argument never happened. I wouldn't have been able to find Cal all day because he wasn't there. He didn't exist Saturday because he had skipped over Saturday, Sunday and Monday."

"This makes sense to you?" Lynn asked dubiously.

"It does." Jack answered, grinning at her. "Maybe I've just gotten used to it."

"Well," she said, "okay, I guess. I can see how Kurt's trip would change your memories because he went back to a day before your trip back. But if Cal didn't exist, as you put it, on Saturday, how could he have died in the crash?"

"He didn't," Jack explained, "Kurt did."

"What?"

John shook his head to clear it and took over the story, "From what we can figure out, Kurt swiped Cal's wallet with his ID, put on Cal's helmet so we wouldn't recognize him, and took his motorcycle. At the right moment, when Kurt knew it was supposed to happen, he came barreling downtown and crashed."

"He did it on purpose?" Lynn asked, now incredulous.

John nodded.

"He killed himself?"

"That's the way we have it figured out," Jack answered.

"Why would he do that?"

"Because he cared about me," John said. "Actually, *us*," gesturing at Jack.

"I really don't understand."

John took a deep breath. "You have to remember, Cal is the person who eventually invents the time machine."

Lynn's eyes widened with the beginning of understanding.

"Jack came back here to talk me out of marrying Gail."

Lynn turned to Jack, smiled at him and said, "Thank you."

"The pleasure was all mine, believe me."

John continued his explanation, "That was it. He was supposed to come back, talk me out of the wedding, get back in the machine and go back to his own time. Unfortunately, things spun out of control."

"You can say that again," Jack commented.

"While we were still discussing the whole wedding thing, Cal came zipping around the corner and died."

"Which," Lynn said, "other than the fact that you seem like a nice guy, Cal, was bad because you would no longer invent the time machine."

"Right," John agreed, "and a lot of other major inventions which substantially affect the future."

"Okay. I understand that. But your friend Kurt killing himself? He had already talked Cal into skipping forward to Tuesday. Cal was safe at that point. Why did he have to get on that bike Saturday night and die?"

John bowed his head. "I've really been dreading this part of the explanation."

Raising her eyebrows, Lynn shuddered. "It gets worse?"

"You could say that." Heaving a sigh, John softly began, "Kurt killed himself for two reasons. The first one was that he had a brain tumor and was going to die within a couple of weeks."

"Oh, my God," Lynn gasped, jerking her hand to her mouth.

"And the other reason is that he wanted to make sure everything else, other than Cal's death, still happened between Saturday night and Tuesday afternoon."

"Everything else? What?"

"It's been a busy few days," Jack said.

"What's happened?"

"Between Saturday night and Tuesday afternoon," John summarized, "someone, presumably Gail, torched my apartment, burning it down. She also stuffed a rag into the flue at my parents' house. They almost died from carbon monoxide poisoning. And I came and saw you... and told you that I wasn't going to marry Gail."

A brief smile flickered across her face in response to John's last comment before she went on, "Now I really don't understand. Those things sound horrible... except for the latter. Why would Kurt deliberately kill himself to make sure those things all happened?"

"You have to remember, we didn't know he was going to do it, so we never talked to him about his motives. Kurt knew that whether he killed himself or not, those things were going to happen. He wanted to make sure they happened the way they did."

"Why?"

"Because I wasn't home when my apartment burned down. If things had gone differently, I might have been in there when it happened. Also, I showed up in time to save my folks. Again, if anything had drastically changed, I might not have been in time."

Understanding showed on her face. "I guess that makes sense. Now, tell me the other part."

"What other part?" John asked with mock sincerity.

"You know," she said.

John smirked. "I keep forgetting about this psychic thing." He glanced at Jack, who tilted his head as if to say *what the hell*.

John returned his gaze to Lynn. "You're right, of course. There is one other little detail."

"I'm waiting."

"It seems that there are some space aliens who are trying to stop Cal from building the time machine."

"*Space aliens?*"

"Well... we think so. At least, that's what we've been told by Aloysius."

"Who's Aloysius?"

"Aloysius? Oh, he's a nine-foot-tall Nordic from the Rigelian system, who has assumed the appearance of a middle-aged black man so that he can mix in with us Earthlings."

"And hide from the Anunnaki," added Jack, grinning.

"Aloysius Greyson?" Lynn squealed, "I've read all of his books!"

Lynn's mouth hung open as she stared at John. "Why didn't you tell me earlier that the Anunnaki were involved?"

It was John's turn to be surprised. "What?"

"Those reptilian bastards have been tampering with us for eons!" she exclaimed.

"You...you know about the Anunnaki?"

"Know about them? My God, don't you read David Icke, Zecharia Sitchin? There's a controversy over the reptilian angle, but the Anunnaki have been riding roughshod over mankind for centuries...even longer than that."

John had no idea what to say to this woman of his dreams. He just looked at her, wide-eyed and speechless.

Reining in her excitement at this latest development, Lynn turned to Jack and said, "We'll get back to that in a minute. So, tell me...how did informing me about the cancelled wedding plans become incorporated into your trip itinerary?"

Jack couldn't help but laugh at the nimble way that she was assimilating all of the facts and shifting from one topic to another. "Not too long before I came back here, you and I ran into each other, quite by chance. We had a long talk, and you told me that you had loved me ever since we first met in 2008. Because you were married, and then I got married, you never said anything to me. I guess you and I both had pretty miserable lives with our respective spouses. And you said you had never stopped thinking about me and how different things might have been."

Lynn's expression became melancholy as she visualized the grim future Jack described.

He continued, "I confessed to you that I had always been in love with you but never had the nerve to tell you, either."

Her eyes traveled between the faces of Jack and John, a soft tenderness showed in her eyes as she said, "So, you saved my life," her voice soft and fragile.

Jack shrugged, "I hope so. What's happens, from now on, remains to be seen."

This time, she stared deeply into Jack's eyes. "This is very strange."

"What's that?"

"I'm looking at the man I'll be married to thirty years from now."

Although John was well aware of the connection that had been made between them, to hear her speak those words electrified him.

Jack cleared his throat and said, "God, I hope so."

WED - 4:02 P.M.

Hart punched the button on the remote to pause the DVD, his eyes staring at the screen, as Burke sat silently in the swivel chair next to him. Frozen in time, John Augur and an apparently thirty-years-older John Augur stood at the lobby desk of the Hotel Congress. Clutched in Ben's hand was the letter that Burke had brought back from the clerk.

Breaking the silence, Burke said, "I made a copy of the letter and gave it to the handwriting tech, along with a sample of Augur's writing that I picked up from his parents' house on my way back here."

Ben said nothing, his mind trying to wrap itself around the chain of events described in the letter.

"After I read the letter," Burke continued, "I had the assistant manager check the guest register for Friday night. A *Jack Wells* checked in, paying cash."

"Wells," Hart said. "Cute!"

"Yeah! Real cute. We checked the video from Friday night and found this."

He handed Ben another disk. Hart tapped the button on the player, and the tray slid out. Removing the first disk, he dropped in the second one and closed the tray. A moment later, the same view from the fixed camera appeared on the screen. Since the lobby desk was situated close to the entrance, the absence of outside sunlight on this recording was obvious, but the lighting was more than bright enough to allow them to make out the features of the man checking in. It was clearly the same person who had stood with John Augur during checkout on the first video.

"He uses *Jack* instead of *John*?"

"Yes," Burke answered.

"I guess to cut down on the confusion when they're together."

Chuckling, Burke said, "Well, it's sure helpful for me to keep it straight in my mind."

Ben shook his head, bewildered.

"Billy, what do you think? Is this real?"

"How can it be? Come on, time travel…a fifty-year-old other version of the same twenty-year-old man?"

Hart looked down at the floor, not wanting his friend to see his eyes as he said, "I think I believe it."

"You do?"

"It sure explains a lot."

"I don't know. How does it explain Kurtis Wallace dead on Saturday night, yet walking around and talking to people for days afterwards?"

"If they have some kind of a time machine…and I'm saying *if*…then sometime after all of this happened," Ben waved the letter he still held in his fist at the screen showing Jack Augur, "Wallace could have gone back in time and died Saturday night."

"That's one hell of a big *if.*"

Ben looked up at his friend. "I know that. And I'm not saying I'm ready to buy it all. But we've been wracking our brains trying to reconcile some seemingly indisputable facts. Fact one: Kurt Wallace died Saturday night on a motorcycle he apparently borrowed from Cal Mitchell. Fact two: Wallace was seen after Saturday by several people…including you and me…walking around, healthy as can be, and talking, leaving his fingerprints and his image on video cameras."

"Plus," Burke added, "the two drinking glasses Wally told us about, with the fingerprints of the same person; yet, one of the sets of prints had all of the markings and wear and tear of a much older man."

"And Augur just *happened* to show up in the middle of the night to save the lives of his parents."

"Almost as if he knew it was going to happen," Burke agreed.

Ben dropped his copy of the letter on the desk and snatched up the phone. He dialed and only had to wait through two rings before he got an answer.

"This is Detective Hart. Have you had a chance to take a look at the handwriting samples Officer Burke gave you earlier?"

Ben listened for a minute, his face showing no change of expression.

He thanked the person on the other end, hung up the phone and said, "Preliminary analysis says they match."

"Yet another fact to add to the pile."

"Yep!"

Ben surveyed the top of his desk, looking at all of the notes, photos and reports he had compiled so far on the Augur cases. His eyes moved to his trash can, which nearly overflowed with the various diagrams he had attempted to use to bring some semblance of logic and order to the known facts. After a long pause, he looked at Burke and asked, "Can you think of any other explanation? Anything at all?"

Burke loudly let out a breath. "You know, Ben, for all of the years I've been married, I've been telling Lou that she's full of beans about this kind of stuff."

Ben silently watched his friend work through the question in his mind.

After a long hesitation, Burke said, "You gotta promise me that you'll never tell her I said this, but, no... I can't. I cannot think of another explanation that even comes close to fitting the facts."

Ben grinned. "Hey, pal, I've got news for you. I can't wait to tell her."

⏃

"Okay!" Lynn shifted gears, rubbing her hands together vigorously. "Let's get back to the Anunnaki. How are they involved?"

John told her about the blinding light the night of the accident, along with Aloysius's explanation that the light was from the Anunnaki and was intended to cause Cal's death. He went on to describe the first incident in the alley, where he was being levitated, presumably up to the mother ship, when Aloysius intervened.

"So when you came to my office with your head wound, you were *serious*?" Lynn was beaming with excitement at the direction the narrative was taking.

John smiled broadly and told her that he had been dead serious. Continuing with the saga, he described the attack on them all as Kurt departed, resulting in the fire and explosion. As he spoke, he was, again, amazed at how equaniminously she accepted the outrageous story.

"So," she again addressed Jack, "you've lost your ride home?"

Jack corrected her. "That was just one of them."

"One of them?"

"The time machine in the storage room was only intended to be the backup."

"Oh, so you can get back."

"No, I can't." Before she could ask, he explained, telling her about the incident at the courthouse lawn.

When he finished, she said in a matter-of-fact voice, "So, you screwed up and sent your main machine away?"

Stung, Jack replied quietly, "Uh, I guess I did."

"What are you going to do to get back?"

"You mean, other than the same way you're going to get there, a day at a time? That's what we're trying to figure out."

"What do you mean? Without either machine, what's there to figure out?"

John answered for Jack, "We don't have the machine, but at least we have the man who is going to invent it."

She turned and looked at John, then glanced at Cal and, with a skeptical expression on her face, remarked, "That might be true, but how close is that to happening?"

"Not very," Cal answered truthfully.

"That's horrible," she said emphatically, a sympathetic look on her face. "So, you're stranded here?"

"I'm not at all sure it's that horrible," Jack stated in a low voice.

"What? Why?"

Before Jack could respond, John began, "Remember what we told you about the machine making the whoever or whatever is inside of it immune to changes?"

"Yes," she answered. "That's why the disk Cal brought from Kurt still has the other version of reality on it."

"Exactly," John agreed. "The same thing happens to the traveler himself...and that includes his memories."

She concentrated on what John was saying for a moment before she said, "But Jack's a traveler. Why was his memory changed as a result of Kurt's trip?"

"The machine only provides the immunity to the person inside it," Jack explained. "Once I get out of it and someone else makes a trip, I am as subject to the influence of his changes as anyone else."

"I understand, but I still don't see why that would mean you wouldn't want to go back to your own time."

John spoke up to explain. "Okay, just for a minute, forget about all the details and facts that we've already told you and view things from the linear perspective of Jack."

"Okay."

"He lives through every day...every minute...of thirty years of hell being married to Gail. They have two children together, or at least for most of his life,

Jack thinks they are his kids, but she actually has them as a result of a long-term affair. Anyway, she kills them."

"Oh, my God!"

"Oh, that's not all. She kills his parents because she suspects that they are trying to turn him against her."

Lynn's eyes widened. "Didn't you say she tried to kill them now... I mean this time around?"

"Yes. I'm sure she thinks they had something to do with my cancelling the wedding."

Lynn shook her head in wonderment and disgust.

John continued, "Things get so bad for Jack, after he finds all of this out, that he tries to kill himself."

"How?" Lynn asked.

John couldn't remember whether Jack had ever told him that detail, so he turned to his *other*. Jack said, "Pills. The psychiatrist who told me all of those things... the one who also had been seeing Gail and decided to break the confidentiality rule and tell me everything... was worried that I was too upset to be able to sleep, so she gave me a prescription."

Lynn, a quizzical look on her face, started to speak but John resumed his narrative. "In 2040, Cal and Jack are close friends and Cal is devastated by his friend's attempted suicide, so he makes an exception to his normal rules on the time machine and allows Jack to come back here to stop the wedding. With me so far?"

"I am."

"Okay, so Jack comes back, and we've already told you what a mess things turn into, but forget about all of that for a minute."

Lynn rolled her eyes and said, "I'll try."

"Just think about the basic linear aspect of Jack's progression. He's in his fifties; he's had a horrible life. He tries to kill himself, and his best friend sends him back to 2010 to get me, John Augur, on a different path. He succeeds at that, and the wedding is called off. Now, let's say that somehow he is able to hop back in the time machine and return to 2040."

Lynn stared at John with intense concentration, following the scenario like a movie in her mind.

"Now remember," John cautioned, "and this is important... everything inside the machine is immune to any changes which have happened."

"Right."

"Including his memories."

"Got it."

"So when Jack gets back to 2040, after having succeeded at putting his younger self on a different path...."

"He'll still remember everything that happened," Lynn finished for John, jumping to the conclusion, "all of the horrible things that made him do it."

"Right!" John said. "He'll get back there, all right... but his whole past, *his original past*, will still be there in his mind *and his mind only*!"

"That stinks!"

"Tell me about it," Jack groaned.

"And that's not all," John added.

"What else could there be?"

"He's not only going to have that whole lifetime of crummy memories, he's *not* going to have any memories of the new and improved thirty years between 2010 and 2040 – the years that were altered because of the changes he made when he went back. He won't have any memories of those three decades because when he travels back to his own time, he skips right over them, just like Cal skipped over last weekend." John stopped to let that sink in, knowing she would quickly come to the obvious conclusion. It took less than twenty seconds.

"He won't remember his whole life with me!"

"How could he? He... this Jack... doesn't get to live through any of those years."

Lynn's mind spun as she assimilated this. "So, the most recent memory of me he'll have is going to be... like... this discussion today." The import of her realization caused her voice to become subdued and somber.

Before John could answer, Jack added, "And if we have children together, I won't even know them."

As Lynn visualized this future scenario, her shoulders slumped as if suddenly burdened with a heavy weight. Her voice becoming a whisper, she said, "Good God, that's horrible! As far as you are concerned, Jack, you haven't really fixed anything. It's almost as if you helped a stranger get his life together, instead of your own."

Jack lowered his head, acknowledging the enormity of what she described.

"Didn't the two of you... you and 'future Cal'... realize this before he sent you back?"

Jack shook his head. "No. He had never made a trip back that affected him personally which was longer than a few days at the most. And... both of us were pretty upset at that point." Jack stopped for moment, thinking back on the time prior to his departure. "If he thought of it, he sure didn't mention it to me."

It only took another moment for the next revelation to occur to her. "Wait a minute! I guess I'm just trying to visualize this whole thing, so give me a second. If you, Jack, somehow figure out a way to go back to your own time, does that mean that in 2040 you are going to just suddenly pop into our lives? Mine and John's? Will there be two of you?"

"There can't be," answered John.

"Why? What happens?"

He leaned forward, moving closer to her, and said, "From what Cal said to Jack…not this Cal, but future Cal…if I don't climb into the time machine thirty years from now and come back here to do all of these things, it would mean that they wouldn't have happened. Everything…I mean everything…would be undone."

"You mean us?"

"Yes. Us. The way future Cal explained it to Jack was that at the moment the machine appears in his lab with Jack returning, if I hadn't gotten into it a minute earlier to come back here…then the same thing would happen to all of us…everybody ….like what happened to our memories of Jack's little trip back to stop Cal." John's expression conveyed a profound sadness as he finished. "All of those memories…and all of the physical manifestations of the changes…would suddenly not be in our heads…or in the reality anymore."

Her voice even deeper than before, Lynn asked, "I'd still be in the same marriage I am now?"

"Everything!" Jack emphasized. "It would be as if I had never made the trip."

"In other words, Jack would return," John added, "and if I hadn't left, it would be like a big, red reset button had been pushed…returning everything back to the old reality, resetting his life, and yours, to the way it was before he made the trip."

Her eyes wide, she said, "We can't let that happen."

"I know," agreed John.

Lynn turned and stared silently out of the window, as the sun neared the horizon, and watched as the lengthening shadows dappled the campus with bizarre forms. The three men allowed her some quiet, giving her time to run through the life-altering ramifications in her mind. Finally, she turned back to John and said, "Either way it's a rotten deal."

John nodded.

"If, thirty years from now, you climb into that machine to come back here, I'll be losing the man I have spent thirty years with, in exchange for someone I just met today... no offense, Jack."

Jack managed a faint grin. "None taken, believe me."

"But if you don't leave in thirty years... in the blink of an eye, I will suddenly be back in that same miserable relationship that I was in when you ran into me in the future and we talked."

"That's right," Jack said softly.

As another thought came to her, Lynn exclaimed, "Oh, my God!"

"What?" John asked, concerned. "What is it?"

"I just now realized the third possibility. Jack, if you never figure out a way to get back... if you just stay here and live out the rest of your life from today forward, that means that thirty years from now, I'll still lose my husband... because, John, you would still have to make the trip to insure that you don't marry Gail and that you and I get together."

"That's true," John acknowledged.

"But I won't even get Jack at that point, because he... you... will have already lived out the rest of your life. I'd be alone."

Everyone around the table knew that she was right... that her summation of the options was as complete as could be. None of them had anything to add.

After another long and thoughtful pause, Lynn took a deep breath, forced it out of her lungs, expressively slapped her thighs with the palms of her hands and, in a brisk voice, said, "Well, Jack, I guess you're better than nothing."

Jack smiled weakly. "Thanks."

She turned to John, saying, "And I believe with all of my heart that the next thirty years with you... even if we both know during the whole time, it has to end on that certain day in the future... will be worth it."

John, overwhelmed by his feelings for her, simply smiled and said, "Me, too."

Lynn smiled back. "*You* think *you're* worth it, too, huh?"

John laughed and wrapped his arms around her. She leaned into him, and they held each other tightly.

It was Cal and Jack's turn to look out the window in an attempt to afford the other two some privacy. When the embrace ended, Lynn said, "There is another thing. I do have one more really important question for you, Jack."

Jack swiveled to face her. "What's that?"

"This Lynn character that you met with, thirty years in the future...."

"Yes?"

"How did she... how did I hold up?"

A broad smile spread across Jack's face as he stared into her eyes. "You looked beautiful…just beautiful."

She returned his grin and, in a stronger voice, said, "All right! Let's get this show on the road. Cal, build that damn machine or something, will you?"

– XXIV –

Backing away from the door, Gail vigorously rubbed her ear, attempting to restore the circulation lost after pressing it against the hard surface for so long.

"Thirty years of hell, huh?" Gail muttered to herself. Her mind jumped from one scenario to another as she assimilated the outrageous story she had just heard through the lab door.

Strangely, the revelations she overheard about Jack traveling back in time did not give her pause. She took them in stride, as if hopping from one decade to another was routine. Her focus was on nothing but the details she had gleaned about her own future life.

She smiled as she visualized the lifetime with John – her long-term affair right under his nose, which resulted in two children he would raise, thinking they were his own.

Her smile was erased as the reality of her current situation sank in to her. She would no longer have that version of her future, thanks to the intervention of others. The others, whom she now viewed as her enemies, comprised a list that was lengthening by the minute.

There was, of course, Jack... this thirty-year-older version of John. He was the one who started it all by coming back in time and talking to John last Saturday night, persuading him to cancel the wedding. Cal was next on the list. And frankly, she didn't care that this Cal, sitting in the lab on the other side of the door, was not yet the Cal who did the deed, who sent Jack back. He was still ultimately responsible.

She was startled to learn that Ed and Kathleen Augur remained alive, and determined that must be remedied, also. Gail's eyes flashed as her mind focused next on Lynn... relishing the revenge she would take on that bitch when the time came.

She turned away from the door, satisfied that she had heard enough, and backtracked down the hallway to the exit near where she had parked. Pushing the door open and emerging back out into the night, she said aloud, "Well, at least Kurt is already dead."

⏳

Hart and Burke waited silently, nervously shifting their respective weights from one foot to another. Ben was clutching a large manila envelope as his eyes darted around the darkened campus.

Soon a Jeep Cherokee pulled into the lot, parking in a space reserved for faculty, and a lone man got out. Seeing the two of them, the man walked across the grass toward the building entrance where they waited.

"Dr. Mueller?" Ben asked.

The gentleman extended his hand and said, "You must be Detective Hart."

They shook hands, and Ben introduced Burke. The formalities complete, the professor unlocked the door, waved his RFID card in front of the reader, turning the LED from red to green, and they went in. The three walked without speaking, the sounds of their footsteps echoing loudly from the terrazzo floor. As Ben followed the professor, his eyes captured the countless details of academic life. It seemed that every available square inch of space on the walls was covered with notes, posters, bulletins and various announcements of upcoming events.

They reached the end of the long hallway, and Mueller unlocked another door, this one leading into his campus office. As they entered behind him, Ben realized that he was expecting the room to look like some movie version of a professor's office, with books and papers stacked haphazardly on every horizontal surface. Instead, he saw that the lone desk in the room was bare, except for a computer, monitor, keyboard and a telephone. The credenza behind the desk was also neat and tidy, holding only several three-ring binders, arranged vertically, with handwritten labels tucked into the clear plastic holders.

As they entered the office, Hart realized that they must have traversed the depth of the entire building in their walk. The left wall was filled with windows which, at this time of the evening, offered a view of the campus mall, bathed in the sickly yellow glow of low-pressure sodium lighting. The wall to his right was covered with a built-in, floor-to-ceiling and wall-to-wall bookcase, completely loaded with books, the titles of which Ben knew, without looking, that he wouldn't recognize.

Mueller, rather than sitting behind his desk, took a seat in one of the three straight-back chairs, gesturing for Burke and Hart to take the others.

"Your phone call was fairly mysterious, Detective. I must admit you have definitely piqued my interest."

"Thank you for meeting us at this hour, Professor," Ben said. "I normally don't have a need for an expert in physics to assist in one of my cases, but I'm afraid I'm feeling a little bewildered."

"No worries about the time of day, Detective. I frequently return to my office in the evening after dinner, to read or catch up on my work. And please, call me Richard. Hearing myself addressed as Professor from anyone other than a student always makes me uncomfortable."

Ben grinned. "I understand. I prefer being called Ben by anyone who isn't spread-eagle on the ground, wearing handcuffs."

Mueller chuckled and said, "I hope I am helpful enough to you to insure it doesn't come to that."

After Burke asked the professor to call him Billy, Mueller inquired, "So what do you have for me?"

Although Ben had organized his facts numerous times before the meeting, he still paused to collect his thoughts before plunging in.

"Do you know a student named Callen Mitchell?"

"Cal! Of course. Horrible, what happened. I still can't believe it."

"How well do you…uh, did you…know him?"

"Well," Mueller said, glancing at the ceiling for a moment, "Cal was one of my students. Gifted, truly brilliant. He already had his master's and was working on his doctorate in theoretical physics. I relied quite heavily upon him in this department, used him whenever possible as a TA."

"TA?" Burke asked.

"Teaching assistant. I'll only confess this to the two of you, but I was much more comfortable with Cal teaching some of the classes here, than several of the tenured faculty in this department."

"Why is that?" Ben wondered.

"Like I said, Cal was brilliant. Not only was he smart as a whip, but he was able to…to use a tired phrase…think outside of the box. So many of the other professors on staff are far too rigid for my taste. They have a tendency to stifle an original thought from a young student, instead of nurturing it. Cal wasn't like that. Whatever new ideas popped into the heads of these youngsters, raised on *Star Trek* and fantasy games, Cal encouraged them, helped them explore their ideas, until something either fruited or the students figured out for themselves that they were headed down a blind alley. That's science, the way it should work."

Ben nodded, adding these latest facts to his mental picture of Callen Mitchell.

"If you don't mind my asking," said Mueller, "why the questions about Cal?"

Ben glanced at Burke for a moment. Seeing no indication from his friend that he should hold back any longer, he replied, "Callen Mitchell is alive."

"Alive! That's wonderful. But I thought…I heard that he died Saturday night in a motorcycle accident. I can't tell you how many times I told him to stop riding that death trap."

"We thought he was dead, also," explained Hart. "As it turned out, it was a case of mistaken identity. The actual rider was not Cal; he was only carrying Mr. Mitchell's identification."

The professor sat back in his chair for a moment, absorbing the news, before asking, "Then, if it wasn't Cal, who was it?"

"Kurtis Wallace," Burke said.

"Wallace?" Mueller looked slightly quizzical. "I think I know him." He turned around to face his desk and switched on his computer, waited for it to boot-up, and then began a series of mouse-clicks and typed commands, until he reached the screen he was searching for.

"Yes. Here it is. Kurtis Wallace is enrolled as a student in my department. I haven't had him in any of my classes." Mueller turned away from the monitor and asked, "How on earth did this happen? Why would Wallace be carrying Cal's ID?"

Before Ben or Burke could answer, Mueller continued, "That was a ridiculous question. How would you know that? That's probably one of the reasons you're here talking to me, isn't it?"

Ben enjoyed watching the professor's mind work and attempted a reassuring grin as he said, "Actually, no, sir. We think we know the *why*. We've come here to talk to you about something very different."

"Oh?"

Ben hesitated for only a second before deciding to plunge forward. "We're here tonight because we have uncovered some facts which are, frankly, impossible for us to reconcile."

A quick smile spread across Mueller's face. "Lovely. I never have had an opportunity to assist the police." Rubbing his hands together in anticipation, he said, "What are they?"

Hart stared at the professor. The man was in his early forties, his dark brown hair lightly dappled with gray, his posture erect as he perched on the front edge of the chair. Hart noted his gray eyes, and how they were almost sparkling at the moment. *This is someone*, Ben thought to himself, *I would have enjoyed having as a professor*. Even though Ben was not a physicist, he knew that what he was about to tell this person would violently wrench out a few well-placed cornerstones in the man's intellectual foundation.

"Well, sir. It appears, from what we've been able to put together so far, that Callen Mitchell actually did die Saturday night."

Mueller's brow immediately furrowed, and he began to speak. Ben held up his hand to stop him and said, "Maybe you should just let me get all the way through this before you ask me anything."

Mueller stopped and sank back into his chair. His hands gently gripped the armrests, almost as if he were preparing himself for a carnival ride. Hart thought that was more appropriate than was probably expected.

"Apparently, Mitchell did get on his motorcycle that night and he did crash. It was he who died in the accident. But, from what we can tell...." Ben stopped again, not for dramatic effect, but only to focus, not wanting to mis-speak. "Kurt Wallace, who was present as a witness at that accident, sometime on Tuesday went back in time to a moment well before the accident and took Cal's place."

Ben was not sure what he expected from Mueller upon telling him this, but certainly did not anticipate the reaction he received.

The professor leaned forward calmly and looked Hart directly in the eye. "Back in time, you say?"

Ben himself felt like a student who was being confronted by a skeptical teacher. "As I said, sir, that's what it looks like from the facts we've been able to put together."

Mueller's voice was even and steady as he said, "Maybe you should share those facts with me. Perhaps you've overlooked something."

"Certainly." Ben went on to recount to Mueller the incidents where either he or Burke had personally talked to Wallace in the days following the accident. He described Kurt's visit to the tech at the police lab, telling Mueller about the issue with the Augur fingerprints, but not explaining their significance. He then slipped the DVD from the envelope and handed it to Mueller. Together, they all watched the video from the police station, clearly showing Kurtis Wallace in the lobby. Then Ben pulled out a morgue photo, showing Wallace on the stainless steel table.

A strong look of distaste contorted Mueller's features, disappearing almost as quickly as it came, while he looked at the face of the dead Kurt Wallace. Ben could tell that Mueller very much wanted to jump in with questions, but was obviously struggling to restrain himself in his attempt to comply with the request to wait until all of the information was shared.

After Hart replaced the photo in the envelope, he pulled out the handwritten note Burke had obtained from the hotel clerk. "It wasn't until Officer Burke found this note that we had any explanation of what had occurred. Before you read it, I'll tell you that the note was found by the maid at the Hotel Congress on Sunday morning. It had been left behind in a room which had been occupied by a John Augur."

"John Augur?" Mueller asked. "That is the man whose fingerprints were at issue?"

"Yes, sir."

Mueller shifted his jaw thoughtfully to the side and stared intently at Ben. "Well, let me have a look at it."

Ben handed over the pages, and Mueller sank back in his chair and quickly read them. As he read, he slid each completed page beneath the bottom of the stack, his expression changing from neutral to slightly amused, and then to a look of surprise. Reaching the last page, the professor immediately began again, at the beginning, this time reading much slower.

When he finished the second reading, he handed the pages back to Ben. "So what you are saying is that, based upon this letter and the other evidence, you have concluded that both this Jack Augur and Kurt Wallace have traveled through time?"

Ben chuckled and said, "I haven't concluded a damn thing. This is way out of my league. That's why we are here."

The professor crossed one leg over his knee. "I must confess, as you began to tell me all of this, my first reaction was to think that one of my colleagues put you up to it, that it was nothing but a gag.

"I was surreptitiously surveying my office for the subtle indication of a tiny camera and microphone, certain that the result of this meeting would be an evening of raucous hoots and laughter at my expense some point in the future."

"I can understand you feeling that way."

"However, there is something about you and your partner here... something about your eyes and your voices...," Mueller looked around the room and said loudly, "If this is a joke, if this is nothing but an elaborate hoax, then I admit that you've got me. You may go ahead now... let the laughter begin."

Mueller turned back to Ben. "You realize, of course, if this is all true, how profound it is?"

Ben said, "I do."

"I must also ask, at the risk of insulting your competence and intelligence, if the two of you have already exhausted all of the obvious explanations, such as a twin or doppelganger?"

"As far as we can tell, sir, according to public record, Kurt Wallace had no siblings. It is, of course, possible that he could have a doppelganger, but we pulled the prints from his Child ID, his house and the glasses that he brought in to the lab, and they all match the prints on the corpse. I also had the lab check him against dental records and they, too, are a match."

"So, in other words," Mueller said, "if this is a contrivance of some sort, then it was executed by a group as sophisticated as the folks from *Mission Impossible*."

Ben nodded.

"This has nothing to do with the matter at hand, but I am curious, what do your superiors think?"

Burke chuckled as Ben answered the question, "Richard, we haven't shared our theory with anyone in the department yet."

Mueller also chuckled. "I can see why. It was visualizing that conversation in my own mind which prompted me to inquire."

Accurately reading the expression on Hart's face, he added, "When the time comes for you to tell your supervisor about all of this, I will be more than happy to add my voice to the chorus, for whatever it might be worth."

Ben grinned and said, "That will be most appreciated."

"Back to this evening's dilemma...what, if I may ask, is it you would like from me?"

"I...," Hart hesitated, "I honestly don't know. Confirmation, I guess. Billy and I put all of this together, and it seems to be leading us to this one explanation, but we aren't qualified and certainly don't feel comfortable coming to that conclusion without some expert input."

"And I am qualified?" Mueller laughed. "Coming here tonight and talking to me about a time machine is like...you might as well be handing a cell phone to a caveman and asking him if the technology makes sense."

"I hadn't really thought about it that way," Ben said. "I was hoping you would, at least, have an opinion on the facts. Because, if you're that cave man, I'm the ape you descended from."

The professor laughed again. "I've been in this field far too long to succumb to flattery."

Mueller tilted back his head and stared at the high ceiling as both Hart and Burke sat quietly. After a few minutes of thought, he explained, "There have been several theories over the years on time travel. Some of them are utter hogwash; others, though promising theoretically, require such huge quantities of energy that they are rendered moot."

"I have a question," Burke said.

"And I'll do my best to answer."

"Was Callen Mitchell working on anything related to the subject?"

Abruptly sitting up straight in his chair, Mueller exclaimed, "See! That's why you are the police and I'm not. Now that you've asked the question, I can't believe I didn't think of it. Just a moment."

He got up from his chair and circled the desk to the credenza. Running his finger along the row of spines, he pulled out one of the binders and brought it back to his chair.

"I am Cal's advisor. This," he indicated, holding up the binder, "is the prospectus for his dissertation."

He handed the binder to Ben, who flipped open the rigid cover and looked at the first page.

"*The Manipulation of Time – Utilizing Elemental Flux-Polarity at the Quantum Level*," Ben read aloud.

Mueller nodded excitedly. "As you can see, that is exactly what he was…is…working on. It looks as if he might have succeeded."

⏳

Gail sat in the convenience store parking lot, across the street from her uncle's store on Pima Street and carefully looked around. She knew the police were watching her place, and assumed they were probably keeping an eye on the homes of her family members, hoping she would be stupid enough to simply waltz into their arms.

But she was fairly certain that even capturing *her* wasn't a high enough priority to warrant staking out every possible place she might go. Still, she took a few more minutes before getting out of the car, staring at the shadows around the shop, looking for any telltale sign that one of the idiots from TPD was present.

Satisfied that she was alone, she opened the door and got out, walking briskly across the street. When she reached the front door, Gail pulled out the key that her Uncle Morris had given her long ago when she had worked for him part-time, and was glad to see that it still worked. With a final look around, she stepped into the store and closed and locked the door, immediately hearing the piercing *beep... beep... beep* of the alarm. This, she knew, was the next crucial step.

Gail punched the four-digit code into the keypad, hoping that Morris hadn't changed it recently. She was relieved to hear the repeating tone come to a stop as the final button was pushed, and saw the red LED change to green.

There was no need to turn on any lights, which might alert someone who was passing by, as her uncle kept two of the overhead fluorescent lights turned on as night-lights. Not wanting to press her luck, she grabbed a long gunny sack, quickly went about the task of gathering what she needed and, within minutes, had everything.

The sack slung over her shoulder, she carefully rekeyed the code into the alarm panel, arming it. A quick twist of the thumb lock, and the door was open. She, again, took a moment to survey the parking lot and street, seeing that all was clear. Stepping out, she pulled the door closed, locked it, and with a conscious effort, maintained a casual pace as she crossed the street back to her waiting rental car. The entire shopping trip had lasted no more than ten minutes.

⧗

Hart and Burke were pulling out of the U of A campus onto University Boulevard when the police dispatcher's voice came over the radio, "Unit 47."

Ben grabbed the microphone. "This is Unit 47."

The anonymous female dispatcher gave Ben the name and number of a citizen who wanted to speak with him, which Burke jotted down since Ben was driving.

His curiosity aroused by the caller's name, Ben quickly backed the car into one of the diagonal spaces along the street and slipped his cell phone off its belt clip, put the phone on speaker mode and keyed in the number repeated to him by Burke.

The call was answered on the first ring. "Hello."

"Mr. Schilling?"

"Yes, this is Morris Schilling."

"This is Detective Hart with the Tucson Police Department."

"Detective, thank you for calling. I am on my way to my shop right now. I received a message from my security-monitoring company, telling me that someone had entered my store this evening. Considering what's going on right now with my niece Gail, I thought you folks would like to know about it."

"You think she might have broken in to your store, Mr. Schilling?"

"No. She has a key and the code to the alarm. When I heard about her…troubles…I intended to have them both changed tomorrow. The security company told me that someone with the code just went in a little while ago. I immediately started heading toward the store, but I had only made it a couple of blocks when they called me back and told me that the alarm had been re-armed. Whoever it was only stayed for eight minutes. That's when I thought I should call you."

Ben paused for a moment, thinking, then said, "We'll meet you there, sir. I would suggest that you remain outside until we arrive."

"Okay. I'll do that."

"Where is your store, sir?"

"It's on Pima, between Swan and Columbus. You should know it."

"Why is that, sir?"

"Because you gentlemen come in to my store all the time. I own the Viper Police Supply."

A sudden shiver ran up Ben's spine. He finished the call quickly, handed the phone to Burke and pulled out onto the street.

"Call the Crime Scene Unit," he told Burke. "Have them meet us there."

Burke was already dialing the phone as Ben switched on the flashing red lights concealed behind the front grill.

⧗

The group of four, despite being filled with an urgent need to do something to help Jack get back to his own time, reluctantly realized that there was nothing they could do at the physics lab, so they departed and drove to Kurt's house.

"Not that I'm not enjoying your company," John said to Lynn, as they settled into the living room, "but don't you need to get home? I mean, isn't your husband wondering where you are?"

"No. He's back in Kansas, visiting his family for a week."

"You didn't go with him?" John asked rhetorically.

Lynn smirked and said, "Oh, good God, no! I hate it there. It gives me the creeps."

Jack returned from the kitchen with bags of snacks and cans of soda, passing them out.

"You know," said Cal, "I've been thinking."

"I hope so!" Lynn responded. "You are our only hope out of this mess."

Cal looked at her, his brow furrowed and his eyes expressing a profound sadness and worry. "I know."

She immediately felt rotten for her comment and was about to say something apologetic when Jack said, "What? What have you been thinking?"

Cal jammed a handful of Fritos in his mouth and chewed loudly as the three waited. Washing them down with a long drink from the soda, he replied, "I've just been going over the whole routine you told me about...you know, the way the main machine is programmed."

"Yes. What about it?" Jack asked.

"It doesn't make any sense."

"Which part?"

"The *going back to Cal* part...the 2040 Cal, that is...after it detected you, John and Kurt at the courthouse plaza."

The three of them were all silent, waiting to hear where he was going with this.

"I keep playing it through in my mind, and I'm certain that isn't the way I would set it up."

"What do you mean?" Lynn asked, getting impatient with his long pauses between each statement.

"I wouldn't have any good reason to bring the machine back to 2040, and after all we talked about in terms of the damage that his presence here can do, I definitely wouldn't leave Jack stranded."

He paused again, and Lynn began to prompt him when he continued, "I'm sure that I would have just programmed the machine to keep trying."

Jack got instantly excited. "Of course! That makes sense!"

John, feeling his adrenaline rising rapidly, said, "But where? When?"

Cal looked at John and, for the first time since he began talking, he smiled. "The courthouse, naturally. I'll bet that it will appear there every night at the same time until Jack gets in it to go home."

They all moved at once. John looked at his watch and saw that, if Cal's guess was correct, they had less than an hour to get there. Leaving on the lights and forgetting the bags of chips and sodas, all four of them dashed through the front door and piled back into John's car.

They sped away, completely unaware of the unmarked police car across the street.

XXV

The hour late, downtown was again deserted. As always, the last of the government offices closed for the day at five o'clock, and the various law firms and related businesses, who existed to serve the bureaucratic beast, followed suit. The restaurants and bars, catering to those folks, remained open only until seven or eight that evening. Quickly shuttering and barring their doors and windows, employees scurried from the section of Tucson targeted for a revitalization that was never to occur.

John, Jack, Cal and Lynn skirted the north end of the pink building and circled around to the front of the courthouse.

Looking across the street toward the east, across the open, grassy area around the main library, Lynn asked, "Are you sure this is the place, not over there?"

Everyone paused to look in the direction she was pointing and saw, accented with site lighting, the bright red, metal monstrosity which passed for art in front of the library entrance.

Jack chuckled and said, "Yeah, maybe you're right. Time travel machines and attacks from vicious aliens all do seem to fit in better around that *thing*."

He turned back toward the courthouse, and they followed him in. "Now remember, *this time*, all of you need to stay out of sight," Jack reminded them. He checked his watch as they entered the plaza and saw that they had less than fifteen minutes. He added, "Only until I open the hatch. After that, we're okay."

They reached the breezeway at the west end of the plaza and stopped. Jack turned and surveyed the area. "This should be good. There isn't a direct line of sight between here and where the machine will appear...or should appear."

He hesitated for a moment, looking into the eyes of each of the members of the group in the dim light. "Everyone...I just wanted to...," he stopped again, his throat obviously constricting with emotion.

"Go!" John said abruptly. "Get out there so when that thing arrives, it'll see you. We can talk after you get the hatch open."

Jack swallowed, his eyes conveying gratitude for the momentary reprieve. He left the three of them standing in the shadows and turned to walk around the column to the center of the plaza.

As he departed, John stared at his *other's* retreating back and said, "I was getting used to having that guy around."

Neither Cal nor Lynn could think of anything to say to him, so they remained silent.

"Cal?" Lynn asked, her voice restrained in the silence of the alcove where they waited.

"Yeah?"

"I've been thinking...about how I acted back at the lab."

Cal stared at her face in the murky light, and saw a vulnerability and tentativeness which had not been present earlier. "What about it?"

"I've...I've been a little harsh since I got involved in all of this." A short laugh burst from her and she added, "A little harsh...actually, I was acting like a bitch."

"No, that's not true," interjected John quickly.

She smiled at him and said, "Yes, I have. I just wanted you and Cal to know...that isn't really the way I am."

Cal grinned and shrugged. "Don't worry about it. We've all had a little more time to get used to this than you have. You were pretty much thrown into this whole situation suddenly."

He looked at his watch. "Six more minutes."

John sighed. "Cal, I hope you're right about the machine returning tonight."

Lynn took a step closer to him, and he put his arm around her.

"Me, too," she said quietly.

It had been prearranged during the drive downtown that they would wait out of sight and only Jack would stand alone in the middle of the plaza. When the machine arrived...if it did...Jack would open the hatch and retrieve the handheld controller. At that point, when he was certain that it would be safe for the others to come out without triggering the departure program, he would return to the alcove for them.

Even though they all knew the machine would make its arrival in silence, they anxiously strained their ears, listening.

"What's that?" Cal whispered, alerted by something he heard. Holding their respective breaths, Lynn and John heard it, too. Coming from the direction of the west end of the breezeway, the end that opened to a set of steps which descended down to El Presidio Park, they heard the scuffing of shoes getting progressively louder, obviously approaching them.

"Someone's coming," Lynn also whispered. John quickly looked around them for a place where they could conceal themselves. There was none.

Cal, stepping nearer to them as they clustered against the wall, asked in a soft voice, "Security?"

"God, I hope not," John answered.

"We're stuck here. We can't go out the other way – the machine is supposed to arrive any second," Cal reiterated, still speaking softly.

The footsteps sounded closer; silhouetted by the subdued light coming through the west-facing archway, two figures were now discernible, walking up the steps toward them.

At that moment, one of the two approaching men switched on his flashlight, the intense halogen beam momentarily blinding all three of them. The second man illuminated his, also.

John reflexively brought up his arm to shield his eyes from the lights, shouting, "Hey! Turn those off!"

The two walked nearer and directed the beams downward. "Mr. Augur, would you mind telling me what the hell you are doing here?"

John simultaneously recognized the face and the voice of Detective Hart. Dropping his arm down to his side, he saw that Hart was accompanied once again by Officer Burke.

Trying his best to sound calm and slightly indignant, John said, "I could ask you the same thing."

Ben stared John in the eye. "You were followed here by one of my men. He called us as soon as he figured out where you were going."

"Followed me? Why would you have me followed?"

Ignoring John's question, Ben turned to Lynn and inquired, "And ma'am, who might you be?"

Lynn, still tucked snugly under John's arm, responded, "Lynn O'Neal," a touch of defiance in her voice, quickly shaken by Hart's next comment.

"Oh…you're *the* Lynn."

Burke started to take a step toward the plaza as he said, "Ben, I'm going to take a look around."

Before Hart could answer him, John shouted, "NO!" He immediately added in a more normal tone, "Please don't."

The urgency in John's voice caused Burke to hesitate and look back at Ben for guidance.

Hart, still standing directly in front of John and Lynn, asked, "Why is that, Mr. Augur? Is there something you wouldn't like us to see?"

Ben grinned as he watched the panorama on John's face. The parade of possible stories he thought of and rejected animated his features at a rapid-fire pace. Deciding to let him off the hook, Ben said, "Or maybe it's *someone* you wouldn't like us to see. Like, maybe, the thirty-year-older version of yourself you've been hiding from us for the past few days."

John was suddenly speechless. The very last thing he had expected was for the police to figure things out, and he had no idea what to say in response. As John continued to look at the detective, dumbfounded, Ben turned to Burke and motioned for him to go ahead.

Cal, who had been silent to this point, spoke up, his voice steady and ominous, "I really wouldn't do that, if I were you."

There was something convincing enough in his delivery to cause Burke again to stop in his tracks.

Ben took a half-step back from John and Lynn, and turned to Cal. "Mr. Mitchell…."

"Please, call me Cal."

"Mr. Mitchell, you've got thirty seconds to tell me why we shouldn't go out there before I pull my radio off my belt and flood this entire area with officers, backed up by the police helicopter."

Cal returned the detective's intimidating glare, his eyes unwavering. With a slight grin, he answered, "I sincerely doubt you'll do that, Detective."

Hart's eyebrows raised slightly in surprise. "And why is that?"

"It's really quite simple," Cal said, his voice patronizing, as if addressing a classroom full of elementary students. "You obviously found something. I have no idea what that might have been, but it was something that explained all of this to you."

Cal paused for a second, then added, "Actually, it couldn't have explained all of it, but obviously the good parts."

"The letter!" John exclaimed. "I must have left Jack's letter in the hotel room."

John could tell by Hart's expression that he had nailed it on the head.

Cal continued, "As I was saying, you and your partner here have done a pretty good job of putting together the pieces and, frankly, I'm a little surprised that you have."

Ben took a partial step closer, but Cal did not back off. "However, I find it incredibly hard to believe that either one of you have built up the courage to share this story with your supervisor or, for that matter, anyone else in the police department."

Even in the dim night lighting of the breezeway, John could see that the detective was unaccustomed to having his authority challenged. As Ben tensed and was beginning to lift his right hand, Burke snorted and said, "Ben, chill out, man. He got you."

For a moment, Burke's comment didn't register on Hart's face. Then he visibly relaxed and took a step away from Cal. Letting a smile slowly creep across his features, Ben replied, "You're right, you know."

Cal just shrugged, returning the smile.

From over Ben's shoulder, Burke said to Cal, "Mr. Mitchell…I'm sorry, Cal…let's try this a different way. Would you mind sharing with us what the hell is going on?"

Still grinning, Cal said, "No. Not at all. As you obviously already know, John Augur came back to 2010 from the future…from 2040."

"To stop a wedding?" Ben asked, a hint of disbelief in his tone.

"Believe it or not, yes. To stop a wedding between himself and Gail Schilling."

"From what we've seen of her," Burke chuckled, "I can understand that. And also to make sure that he would get together with Ms. O'Neal here?"

Cal nodded.

"Like my partner said," Ben interjected, "from what we've seen of Ms. Schilling, it would appear that being married to her would be pretty unpleasant. But isn't coming back in time to undo a marriage a little drastic? And where is the older Mr. Augur…I believe you are calling him *Jack*…now?"

"It wasn't a little drastic, as you put it," answered John. "From what's been described to me, my marriage to her resulted in the deaths of my parents and two small children, plus a lot of other misery – as well as an attempted suicide by me, thirty years from now."

Ben took this all in and said nothing.

Cal explained, "Maybe it would make more sense if you knew that John and

I went on to be the closest of friends. From what Jack told us, he was so despondent, due to all of the horrible things Gail had done, that after he tried to kill himself, he confessed to me he was going to do it again. And if that didn't work, he'd keep trying until he succeeded. I offered him a chance to change things."

Trying to sound as nonchalant as possible, Cal added, "To answer your other question, Jack is out in the plaza right now, waiting for the arrival of the time machine to take him back."

Ben chuckled and shook his head. "Of course. But why are all of you waiting here? Why wouldn't you be standing with him when it arrives…to send him off?"

"I built it, or will build it, with all types of sensors so that if it suddenly appears in the past and anyone is around other than the person waiting to be picked up, it disappears."

"I can see why that would be a good idea," Burke said.

"So that's why I asked you to stop," explained John. "If you had gone around that corner, Officer Burke, just as the machine appeared, we would have lost it again."

"Again?"

"Yeah. We tried this two nights ago, and Jack had completely forgotten about the sensors. Except that time Kurt Wallace was with Jack and me. We learned it the hard way. Kurt and I were not out of the sensors' line of sight, and the machine closed up and disappeared before Jack could get in it."

During the conversation, a morbid curiosity caused John to watch Detective Hart closely as he took in the bizarre details of the past few days. He certainly showed more equanimity than John expected as he received each new tidbit in what, to most, would be an outrageous story.

"While we're on the topic," Ben asked, "what exactly happened with Mr. Wallace?"

"The original victim of the motorcycle accident was Cal," John explained.

"We've already figured that part out," Burke interrupted.

"Then you know from the letter," John continued, "that Kurt Wallace, Jack and I were crossing the street downtown, and Cal came around the curve on his bike. He was going too fast, and when he swerved to miss us, his tires hit a patch of sand on the street. He lost control and crashed."

"At that point," Ben asked, in order to clarify the facts in his mind, "it actually was Callen Mitchell on the bike?"

"It was. When we realized that, we were in something of a panic, and Jack made an aborted attempt to undo the accident almost immediately."

244 -- John David Krygelski

"That's when he wrote the letter to you?" Burke asked.

"Exactly. But the trip didn't work. After a couple of days, Kurt went back, and that's when he substituted himself for Cal."

The profound sense of loss again swept over John as he continued, "Kurt gave up his own life. He knew that Cal needed to live...that he needed to invent the time machine in the future...so he went back to before the accident, took Cal's ID, put Cal in the machine and sent him forward in time."

"To the storage room?" Burke asked.

"Right. Well, actually Cal returned to the second storage room next door to where the auxiliary time machine was stored. It was from the first storage room that Kurt departed. After sending Cal to us, he got on Cal's bike at about midnight Saturday night, drove downtown and crashed. Jack and I had just sent Kurt off on his trip when all hell broke loose."

John, sensing that Ben was about to ask another question, saw two things happen at once. Coming from the same end of the vestibule where Hart and Burke had arrived, John saw a bright flash of light. At the same time, Hart jerked violently as if pulled by an invisible rope, and spun around, falling heavily to the tiled floor.

Instinctively, John grabbed Lynn and pulled her down and against the nearby wall. Burke reacted instantly, whirled to face the direction of the flash while simultaneously unsnapping the leather thong on his service revolver, and pulled his weapon.

John hunched next to Lynn and was only able to make out a silhouette framed at the west entrance. Even in the gloom, he could tell that it was Gail. Although her gun was silenced, Burke's was not, and the *boom* from his Glock sounded like an explosion in the tiled and masonry alcove.

Unfortunately, Burke had fired a split second too early, and his shot missed Gail, ricocheting off the arch next to her with a flash of sparks and a vaporized chunk of stucco. Burke was not as lucky as Gail. Firmly planted in a shooter's stance, and with the minimal lighting still favorable to her position, she let loose with a series of three rapid shots. The first two struck Billy Burke – one in the left arm, the second hitting him right-of-center in the chest. The impact of the two shots slammed him against the wall, where he reeled, tumbled down, and lay motionless.

John saw that Cal had also dropped to the floor next to them. As their ears adjusted to the silence after Burke's lone shot, he heard a throaty laugh come from the end of the breezeway and saw that Gail was walking slowly toward them.

As she neared, John covered as much of Lynn's body as he could, knowing how little protection his flesh and blood would offer to her. Gail reached the overhead night-light, and John could see that her face was contorted into a maniacal sneer, the yellow light making her face resemble more a zombie than a human.

Just as she reached them, Jack suddenly burst in from the plaza. "What the hell…?" His voice trailed off when he saw Gail holding a pistol and standing over the five supine forms.

She pointed her pistol at Jack and stared at his face. "I'll be damned. It really *is* you," she said, her voice laden with hatred and contempt.

Jack stood immobile. His eyes darted from the two strangers who were lying still on the floor, to John and Lynn, huddled against the wall, to Cal, tucked into an almost fetal position on the floor. He slowly raised his hands above his head, assuming a submissive pose. He was betrayed by an unbidden look of absolute hatred directed at Gail.

She crossed the two paces to Jack and, with the barrel of her pistol, smacked him violently across the side of his face. "This is all your fault!" she screamed, spittle flying from her lips and splattering onto his face. "You are the bastard who ruined my plans."

Jack, ignoring the pain from his jaw and cheek, kept his hands up and said, "*Your plans?*" He raised his voice in anger. "You're the bitch who ruined the lives of everyone you met."

Gail's eyes flashed with a demonic furor, and for a moment Jack was certain she was about to pull the trigger. He cringed in anticipation of the horrific pain of the bullet ripping through him…but no bullet came. He watched as, with a visible effort, she regained her control and, in a steady voice, said, "Actually, I want to thank you."

"Thank me?" The contempt in his voice was undisguised.

Gail laughed again. The sound of it, an echo from his painful future/past, sent shivers down Jack's spine.

"Yes, thank you for bringing me a present."

She said this with an exaggerated snugness so familiar to him that it made him want to retch.

"Let's go see this machine I've just heard so much about."

Before Jack could respond to her, she took a step back, turned, pointed her pistol in the direction of Cal, John and Lynn and said, "Get up! Come on. We're all going out there. NOW!"

"What about these two?" John asked, looking at Hart and Burke as they both lay motionless on the floor. "They need help."

"Screw them! They are going to come out of this a lot better than the four of you!" she barked. "Come on, get up!" With that, she waved the gun threateningly, and they all rose. John positioned himself between the gun and Lynn, a feeble act of gallantry which Gail noticed immediately. Feeling furor once again bubble up within her, she took two quick steps and grabbed Lynn by the hair, jerking her away from him and shoving the gun roughly into her ribs. Lynn let out a single, small whimper of pain.

"And this witch is the first to go if anyone doesn't cooperate. Now move!"

John stared helplessly at Lynn, who, not wanting to further aggravate Gail, averted her eyes from his. He was growing more enraged by the moment, which was exacerbated by the reality that he could do nothing to help Lynn and that *he* was, in fact, the reason her life was in danger.

On the verge of doing something rash, John felt a sudden contact on his shoulder and abruptly turned to see that Cal had come up behind him. "Come on, let's go."

John searched Cal's eyes, looking for some sign that he had a plan, but was not able to find anything reassuring in the return glance.

They all trudged slowly out to the plaza where the sphere was waiting, its hatch open, the interior light spilling out onto the grass. John heard Lynn's surprised gasp and realized that this was the first time she had actually seen the machine.

They crossed the tenebrous courtyard and stopped at the side of the gleaming sphere, which seemed to capture and then reflect more light than was ambient. Gail still held Lynn by the hair and was pulling it downward, causing Lynn's head to be cocked at an extreme angle. She kept the tip of the silencer, still screwed onto the end of the pistol barrel, jammed painfully into Lynn's side, and said almost conversationally, "You know, when I was hiding by the entrance and heard the whole thing, I didn't believe it. But, I'll be damned, here it is – my ticket out of here."

"WHAT?" Jack barked at her with alarm.

Gail turned to face him and with utter contempt, snarled, "After what you've done to me, you've got to be kidding, right? I've got the cops after me. My life here is trash. I've been wondering what I was going to do next, after I took care of lover-boy here… and his little girlfriend. But now," she glanced at the interior of the machine, "now I won't need to move to Mexico and learn Spanish."

She grinned a mirthless smile and said, "Starting over in 2040 sounds pretty good to me."

Ⴘ

Ben couldn't believe the pain. Most of the right side of his body felt as if it had been injected with hot grease from a deep fryer. Checking further, he saw that he was bleeding from his hip. Remaining down, he twisted his neck until Burke came into his line of sight, not more than six feet away. His first thought was that his friend was lying too still to be alive. When he reached Burke, he was relieved to find that he was still breathing.

Grabbing Burke's face, he shook it and softly said, "Billy, wake up, man."

Burke's eyelids fluttered briefly before fully opening. When he saw Ben's face, he grinned. "Let go of my face. I hate that."

Ben smiled, releasing his grip.

"Bet you're glad I suggested the vests before we walked in here?" Burke said.

Speaking softly, Ben replied, "That's so typical of you, Billy, always thinking of yourself. I seem to have taken a shot in the hip. But, man, I didn't realize I was going to be up against a cannon. What the hell did I get hit with . . . and who shot me?"

Burke shrugged, immediately grimacing from the pain the movement caused. "I'm thinking it was the .50 caliber missing from the gun shop. And the *who* was Schilling."

Ben started to say something but noticed the pool of blood around Burke's arm. "Whoa! You're hit, too."

"No shit, man. Think I've lost about a gallon of blood so far. Didn't think to wear Kevlar jammies."

"The ones with the feet in them?" Ben said. "Yeah, that would have been good."

Burke added, "And the long sleeves."

Ben slowly turned around to check the alcove, the movement agonizing, and asked, "Where are our friends?"

Burke shook his head. "I was busy playing dead, but I think Schilling is planning on taking the time machine for a joy ride."

Burke witnessed Ben's mind quickly figure out the ramifications of this and added, "I better call for some backup."

"And while you're at it, how about having one of the guys bring me a Band-Aid for this hip?"

"Band-Aid? Wus! You like the ones with the Smurfs on them, right?"

"Wonder-Woman."

Burke unclipped the radio from his belt and keyed the mike.

⧗

"Okay, tell me how to drive this thing," Gail ordered Jack.

"No way," Jack refused, stepping forward. Before he could get close, Gail painfully rammed the muzzle of the silencer even deeper into Lynn's side. Lynn let out an involuntary gasp of pain and bit down on her bottom lip.

"Don't take another step or *little Miss Priss* here gets splattered all over this shiny machine."

Jack abruptly stopped, and Cal said, "It won't work, anyway."

Gail, her eyes lingering on Jack for another moment to make sure he wasn't planning anything, turned to Cal and demanded, "And why not, Mister Brain? And you better tell me the damn truth."

Cal, his tone steady, explained, "There are actually two reasons. The first one is that the machine is only programmed for a specific person. It won't go anywhere with anyone other than Jack."

"I don't believe a word you're saying. I heard back there that you, Kurt and just about everyone else have taken a ride in this. I am curious, though, so let's hear the second reason this won't work."

Cal put an ironic grin on his face before continuing, "The second reason is that you're planning on killing all of us, right?"

Gail smiled at Cal and said, "You *are* pretty smart, aren't you?"

"It doesn't take a genius to figure that out. However, the problem with your plan is the time paradox."

"The what?"

"The time paradox... you know, the one we've heard about in every science fiction book we've ever read, where the time traveler goes back in time and kills his own grandfather. At that point, the time traveler ceases to exist. Same deal here. I'm the one who builds this machine at some point in the future. If you kill me, I never build the machine... so, *poof!*... no machine for you."

Cal watched Gail's face as she thought through what he had said. Rather than the look of disappointment he hoped for, instead she laughed at him. "You really think I'm stupid, don't you?"

Cal shrugged but didn't reply.

"You've already been dead once. I know, I just heard about it. The machine didn't go *poof!*"

"That was different," Cal answered. "They were able to undo my death before the time came for me to invent it. If you kill me and leave in the machine, no one is going to undo that."

The macabre smile still twisting her features, Gail said, "Look, I don't believe you. I think this little silver ball is here right now, and it is going to continue to be here after I put a big hole in your forehead."

Her eyes suddenly brightening with a new realization, she added, "And...I just figured out something else."

"What's that?" Cal asked, dreading the answer.

"If I don't kill you all, then you will be waiting for me thirty years from now when I open that door, with about ten cops standing in front of you."

Cal had nothing else to try. Gail bellowed, "Enough of this drivel. Jack, start the driving lesson or somebody dies right now, and it'll be a lot more painful that way than if you cooperate."

Jack hesitated, and Gail pulled the gun muzzle from where it was and pointed it downward at Lynn's leg. "I'm going to shoot her right there...right in the leg. Then you can all listen to her scream and watch her bleed to death. It's up to you, *Jack*." She said his name with utter contempt.

"All right, I'll show you."

"Much better."

Jack pulled the controller from his shirt pocket and ran through the same steps he had explained to John just a few days ago. As he talked, John's mind raced, trying to think of something he could do and came up with nothing.

Wed - 11:17 p.m.

Burke attempted to get to his feet so he could walk to the end of the alcove, but the resulting dizziness from the loss of blood caused him to tumble back to the floor. He fell to his left and landed jarringly on his wounded arm, the intense blast of pain nearly resulting in him losing consciousness. Gulping in several deep breaths as he struggled to remain alert, he decided to crawl to the pillar, clutching his 9mm pistol as he went. Carefully, he peered around the corner and saw the five people clustered near the mysterious shiny sphere with its hatch open. In the quiet of the night he could hear Gail threaten them with shooting Lynn in the leg, and heard Jack begin to explain how to operate the machine.

"Oh, damn," he muttered aloud. "She's really going to get away."

Burke mentally calculated the time it would take the S.W.A.T. team to respond and regretted having called in a *hostage situation* instead of a simple *officer down* call. He knew that in a hostage situation, where the S.W.A.T. team was deployed, precious minutes would be traded for the additional mobilization and staging that occurred with the carefully coordinated response. On the other hand, the dispatcher receiving the straightforward call that an officer was down would result in every uniformed and plainclothes officer within a five-mile radius screaming toward the scene with lights and sirens blaring. And since the old courthouse was less than a mile from the station, that response would have been within a mere couple of minutes at the most.

Burke listened as Jack finished briefing Gail, bitterly noting that the entire explanation lasted less than a minute.

"I can't let her kill them all. I can't let her get away," he repeated to himself, shaking his head to keep it clear and edging farther forward, hoping for a fortuitous shot.

⧗

Jack hoped that the loud gunshot from the police officer, whom he assumed was Burke, had been heard and reported by someone, unlikely as that would be at this time of night in the middle of downtown. Even so, he tried to drag out the explanation for as long as he could in an attempt to buy more time. Unfortunately, Cal had made the process too simple, and he finished in no more than a minute or two. His mind raced as he tried to think of something more to say, but nothing came.

"So, that's it?" Gail said, surprised. "That's easier than my DVR."

She looked around at the four people and, in a mock playful voice, taunted them, "Time's up, kids. Any volunteers? Who wants to go first?"

John took a step forward. "At least turn Lynn loose for a minute."

Gail stared at John, her hatred for him obvious on her face. "Why? Why should I do that? So the two of you can have one more loving embrace?"

For only a moment she showed indecision; then suddenly, her face twisting into a mask of rage, Gail jerked harshly at Lynn's hair, which she was still holding in a tight grip, and yanked her downward. Lynn, unprepared for the sudden force, tumbled to her knees in front of Gail, her eyes locked on John's, a look of despair etched across her face, mixed with a determination not to give Gail the satisfaction of making her beg for her life.

As Gail swung the gun around to bear on Lynn, they heard a shouted command from the alcove at the edge of the plaza, "DROP YOUR WEAPON!"

Gail, a startled expression on her face, released Lynn's hair, spun around to face the source of the shout, and saw Burke leaning out from the side of the column. She swung the heavy pistol around to aim it at him, but before she could complete the move, Lynn, suddenly free from the vise-like grip, lashed out from her awkward position. Striking the nearest available target, she punched Gail directly in the stomach as hard as she could muster.

Seeing a sudden opportunity as Gail doubled over momentarily, John lunged forward and grabbed Lynn, pulling her away. While John pulled Lynn away from Gail, Jack sprang into action, intent on tackling Gail. Before he could cover the steps to reach her, she recovered from the punch, pointed the gun at Jack and shrieked, "That's it, asshole."

Jack jerked to a halt, wavering on his feet from the rapid stop, and stumbled to the ground. He rose slowly. Despite his submissive compliance, it was obvious that she was going to kill him. Burke finally saw his chance. Glad to see that Augur had gotten Lynn out of the way and afforded him a clear shot at Gail, he saw that she was about to kill the stranger Burke assumed must be Jack. Simultaneously, he shouted and fired. The pain he was enduring and the distance to Gail conspired against him, and his shot went slightly wide, the bullet glancing off the side of the sphere and ricocheting harmlessly away. Gail, reacting to his primal scream and the boom of Burke's pistol, instantly fell to the ground to reduce the size of the target she offered, dropped the controller for the machine and returned his fire. Gail's inexperience, coupled with the surging of adrenaline through her body, took its toll. Her shot also missed its target, taking a large chunk of granite out of the column next to his face. However, the violently dislodged granite projectile slammed into the top of his head, knocking Burke unconscious.

While she was distracted by the brief firefight with Burke, Jack made another move toward Gail, in a desperate attempt to seize her gun. Anticipating more than seeing his advance, she quickly rolled over on the grass and, lying flat on her back, pointed her gun directly at his chest. Jack froze once again, knowing that the slug which would rip him to pieces was inevitable.

Having seized back control of the situation from the chaotic blur of events, Gail slowly stood up. Her breathing ragged, her clothes damp from the grass, she took a menacing step toward Jack, a guttural sound coming from deep down her throat, all through the process never letting her aim waiver from dead-center on his chest.

"This has gone on long enough," she said, the sentence fragmented as she panted for air, breathless from the sudden brief firefight.

Gail slowly elevated the barrel of the gun so that it was pointed squarely at Jack's head, and with a wicked grin twisting her face, she snarled, "Good-bye, you rotten son of a bitch."

The clarity of the moment astounded Jack. He saw Gail's pupils dilate with anticipation. He noticed the muscles of her finger tighten as she began to pull the trigger. In a flash, the entirety of his disastrous life tumbled past his mind's eye, ending with the script of the past few days and his pathetic attempt to makes things right.

Jack had what he knew was to be his final thought, as he decided that this horrible ending to his life was somehow appropriate and deserved. Not fearing for his own demise, he was filled with regret for having dragged so many other people into the shambles which was his life. Although he wanted to close his eyes, he found that he could not, and stared calmly down the shaft of the silencer.

In one horrific instant he was blinded, certain the bullet from Gail's gun had slammed into his brain, killing him so quickly and efficiently that he did not even have time to process the muffled sound from the gun, and plunging him directly into the often described after-death experience. As his brain processed those thoughts at lightning speed, he was distracted by the myriad of sensations coming from his body. Confused, he found that he could still feel the ground beneath his shoes, still hear all of the vague sounds of the evening, still smell the grass in the plaza, and even sense the hairs on his head and arms as they danced, fluttered and stood straight up.

His eyes adjusting to the light, he could now barely make out Gail's form, just two feet in front of him, still pointing the gun at his head, her face a mixture of determination and confusion, her mouth locked in the open gape of a soundless scream.

Jack was able to see her arm flex with effort as she frantically attempted to get her trigger finger to respond to the command from her brain to fire the gun. Coming from the direction of his left side, Jack clearly heard Lynn's voice gasp, "Oh, my God!"

He turned his head to look at her and saw that she was staring skyward with the expression of a child witnessing a visitation from an angel. Shifting his glance slightly, he could see that John, who still held Lynn in a protective embrace, was also looking straight up, an expression of bewilderment and disbelief on his face. He then turned his eyes to Cal, only to see that he, too, was transfixed in an upward gaze, his features displaying an expression of wonder.

Jack returned his attention to Gail and saw that she was still rendered motionless, like a statue destined to aim at an unseen target forever…unchanged, save for one detail. She was now several inches higher in the air than she had been a moment before. The previous look of fierce determination was now replaced with unadulterated terror.

Unable to tear his eyes away from the drama, Jack watched as she slowly continued to rise upward, her arm still extended forward in what now looked like a parody of the shooter's stance, the gun aimed well above Jack's head. He attempted to watch her progress, but the intensity of the light source made it nearly impossible to see details as she was inexorably pulled upward.

No longer able to perceive her shape amidst the brightness, he looked downward and moved next to John, Lynn and Cal. They all watched as an aperture, like the pupil of an eye, encircled and closed around the light from all sides, steadily reducing the size of the opening. As it closed, the diameter of the intense beam gradually diminished from a girth of feet to an area of inches, growing ever smaller until it was nothing but a pencil-thin shaft of whiteness, just before blinking out completely and leaving the sky dark, as it had been a few moments before.

During it all, they had heard no sound from above. No roar of rocket engines. No whirring of motors. Nothing. All they could perceive was an inky blackness immediately above them, so dark that it blotted out even the stars. The boundary, where the vista of the stars ended and the blackness began, decreased, creating the impression that the large round shape, which had been blocking their view of the sky, was either rising or shrinking in size, becoming smaller and smaller until it was completely gone and the vista of the nighttime stars was once again unobstructed.

As if released from a trance after the last traces of the mysterious visitor were gone, Jack, still staring at the dark sky, murmured, "Oh, my God."

John was about to make a similar comment when he was interrupted by Lynn. "Burke!" she shouted, dashing to his recumbent form. The officer lay awkwardly against the side of the column, his head wound having bled enough to form a pool around his upper body.

"I need a bandage!" she yelled. "Hurry!" She knelt beside him and gently lifted his head, resting it upon her legs, oblivious to the blood that began to soak her slacks.

John quickly pulled off his shirt and tore it into three pieces as he ran to her. He handed her the strips of cloth, and she immediately used one of them to wipe the blood from Burke's head and face. Finding the gash, she swabbed it once and then wrapped the material around his head to cover it and slow the bleeding.

Jack, who had joined them, alerted her, "His arm is bleeding, too."

Lynn looked down at Burke's left arm and saw the second source of the blood. Wordlessly, she took another strip of cloth and bandaged his arm, gratefully noticing that her efforts were rewarded with an obvious reduction of the stream of blood.

"I'll go check on Hart," Cal said, running into the alcove, followed by Jack. They found Ben sitting on the cold tile floor, half-leaning against the wall where

Burke had left him, in the middle of a large circle of blood. They saw that he had used his own shirt to apply a compression bandage to the wound and were happy to see that no new blood appeared to be flowing.

"Are you okay?" Cal asked, crouching in front of Ben.

Hart's eyes were only half-open, but he was still conscious. "I've had better days," he answered weakly. "I heard shots. She didn't get away, did she? Did Billy stop her?"

Cal grinned and said, "If it wasn't for Burke, I think we'd all be dead. At least Jack would be."

Ben nodded feebly. "She's dead?"

Glancing over his shoulder at Jack, who shrugged as if to say that it probably didn't matter, Cal then answered, "I'm not sure *dead* is the way I'd describe it...she is no longer a problem, that's for sure."

Ben could tell that there was something he wasn't being told, but he was too weak to care at the moment. "What about Billy? Is he all right?"

"He's in about the same shape you are."

"We called in for backup. They should be here any second."

Jack immediately visualized the impact that the sphere would have on all of the responders and said, "Detective Hart, that might be a problem."

Ben looked up at him questioningly, and Jack continued. "The time machine is still parked out front. I really don't think all of those people seeing it...and crawling all over it...is a good idea."

Jack and Cal could tell that focusing on the problem was taking a monumental effort from Hart. After a few moments, a slight grin played across the detective's face. Groaning from the pain, he tried to unhook the radio which was still clipped to his belt. Unable to reach it, he uttered, "I think I have an idea. If one of you could just hand me the damn radio."

X̆

In the thirty minutes that had passed since Gail's abduction by the strange ship, the entire courthouse area had been transformed. Church Avenue was jammed with emergency vehicles, each with its strobe lights flashing. The grounds were now packed with police officers, paramedics and S.W.A.T. team members, all milling around in ordered chaos. Metal stands with intense halogen lights had been hastily positioned at several spots around the courtyard.

In the midst of it all, brightly illuminated by the floodlights, stood a black, neoprene-draped structure, approximately sixteen feet square and twelve feet tall.

Although the various first responders seemed to criscross every inch of the plaza, alcoves and walkways around the courthouse, almost like a colony of ants covering a large morsel of food, none of them entered the enclosed structure or even paused to peer into it through the unsecured flap. If they had, they would have seen John, Jack, Cal and Lynn clustered near the entrance to a strange silver-coated sphere.

"I think they'll both be okay," Lynn said, referring to Hart and Burke, who had been re-bandaged, stabilized and taken to St. Mary's Hospital.

"The paramedics seemed to think so," John concurred.

Jack let out a heavy sigh, "Thank God." Looking around himself at the temporary structure they were within, he remarked, "I can't believe Detective Hart pulled this off."

"How, exactly, did he do it?" Lynn asked.

Cal chuckled and explained, "He told the dispatcher that he and Burke had stumbled into an ongoing Homeland Security issue and that the device in the courthouse plaza...," Cal placed his hand on the side of the machine, "this baby, was Ultra Top Secret and that no one was cleared to see it. The brass held everyone off the scene for a few more minutes until they could send in that first team of three men, who put up the framework and neoprene. Then they let everyone else come in."

"Yes," Lynn said, "but how did he explain that there were no bad guys when they got here?"

"That was easy," Jack replied. "I overheard him explaining it before they took him to the hospital. Hart told his captain that they had assisted a team from Homeland Security and had stopped a group of terrorists from seizing our new secret weapon. He said the Homeland Security team took the terrorists into custody before our boys arrived."

Jack laughed and added, "He said that the bad guys were probably already at Gitmo by now."

"He has quite an imagination," John noted with respect.

"He'd have to," Cal agreed. "Otherwise, he would never have caught on to our scenario."

"That's true," Jack smiled. "It is quite a stretch for anyone to buy into a time traveler from thirty years in the future."

"Tell me about it," John said, and they all laughed.

When they stopped, Jack began in a subdued voice, "Speaking of which, I guess I better be going."

Everyone was instantly silent. Although they all knew that his departure was inevitable, no one wanted it to happen quite yet.

Jack picked up the controller from the grass where it had dropped earlier and stared at it as his mind fumbled for something to say, but nothing would come.

Cal stepped forward and broke the silence, sadness clouding his features. "You know, I've gotten to like you in the past day and a half."

Jack looked at him and forced a weak smile. "Same here."

An idea suddenly blossoming in his mind, Cal said, "Jack, when you step out of that thing, thirty years from now, we'll have a present for you. The next thirty years of my life... and theirs," gesturing toward John and Lynn, "are going to be the most documented lives ever. We will video everything we possibly can so that you won't feel like you missed anything... after we have had the chance to... brief you."

John added, "Not just events, I'll keep a journal. All of the things I think about... big and small... everything. It'll all be waiting for you."

Jack felt his eyes beginning to dampen. Trying to look casual, he reached up and wiped them, turning to John. "I can't tell you how sorry I am."

John, surprised, said, "*Sorry*? For what, man? You saved my life."

Visualizing the future events from both perspectives, his, which would only span the next few minutes, and John's, which would be spread over thirty years, Jack felt a profound mixture of happiness for the new life John would have and an intense sorrow for what was certain to be a painful and agonizing departure for his *other* thirty years in the future.

"I don't know... it just seems cruel as hell... what you're going to have to do thirty years from now."

John's grin looked sincere to Jack as he responded, "That's ridiculous. Instead of thirty years of misery, you've given me the gift of three decades, the chance of a much better life. I'd call that a good deal."

Jack looked into his younger eyes, trying to see if there was anything other than what John's words conveyed, and found no conflict, no ambivalence at all.

Finally, he allowed himself the reprieve of accepting John's sentiment. Taking a long, deep breath, he exhaled heavily through his nose and remarked, "This is too strange for me."

"What do you mean?" John asked.

"When I step out of this thing... which, for me, will be in a couple of minutes, I guess... I'm going to see Cal," Jack smiled and looked in Lynn's direction, "and Lynn. At least, I hope you haven't done something to get her mad and leave us by then."

Lynn smiled back at Jack and did not speak, a single tear on her cheek glistening in the bright halogen lights. He saw a slight shake of her head, conveying the message that his fear would not be realized.

Jack turned back to John and continued, "But *you* won't be there." His words fell out into the night like rocks dropped one at a time into a pond.

They were standing less than a foot apart and Jack could clearly see John's happier expression melt away, replaced by a profound sorrow. He watched as John's lower lip tightened in an attempt to stop it from quivering. He saw the tears begin to well up in John's eyes and his body suddenly seem to sag.

Wordlessly, Jack and John both took a small step forward and wrapped their arms around each other, the contact enough to break down any residual resistance, both succumbing to the overpowering pathos of the moment, and sobbing. Cal and Lynn looked discreetly away, giving the two as much privacy as the small, black tent would allow. After a minute passed, they separated, still saying nothing.

Jack, wobbly on his feet, turned to Lynn. "You take good care of him, okay?"

Overcome, with tears now streaming down her face and her jaw trembling, she ran forward into his arms, their embrace intense. When they finally parted, Jack took a half-step back, still holding her by the shoulders, and whispered, "I'll see you soon."

Lynn fought against the urge to dissemble once again and, with a deep breath, found herself able to say, "This is something for you to take with you," and leaned forward, kissing him.

Jack felt a wave of emotions break over him as he received a glimpse of the future he would be denied, clouded by the awkwardness of kissing the woman who was to be John's, not his. At least, not his in this time.

The kiss ended. Jack backed away and looked into Lynn's eyes, seeing an indefinable jumble of emotions. She forced a smile and, with her voice wavering, said, "You better get in that thing. I'm waiting."

Jack nodded, not able to find his voice to speak.

He released his grip on her shoulders and turned to the others. Cal smiled bravely, waved and said, "Be seeing you."

John, suddenly looking years younger than he was, sighed, "Take care."

Jack crossed the short distance to the hatch of the sphere, stepped inside and turned around to face John. "You think you can handle the rest of your life without screwing it up?"

An involuntary single laugh burst from John. "I'll try."

"You better," Jack said, "I'm not coming back to bail you out again."

John smiled at Jack and did not respond.

There was obviously nothing more to say, so Jack gripped the interior handle of the hatch and slowly pulled it closed, taking in one last glimpse of each of them as it swung shut.

Lynn, Cal and John all moved together into a cluster, and stared at the shining orb silently. Within seconds where there had been the sphere, there was now nothing but air.

◧ XXVIII ◨

Sᴜɴ - 1:52 ᴘ.ᴍ. (2040)

"…less than two weeks away. And when he or she arrives, you'll be a grandfather. By the way, I've been insisting it's going to be a girl. It still amazes me that Jackie couldn't have timed this better. Just kidding. Oh, and don't forget, the crib I made for the new baby needs one more coat of lacquer. Use the right stuff. I've marked it 'baby crib.'"

John hesitated, "I…I can't believe I'm not going to be here when it happens. No! I take that back. I'm sorry, that wasn't fair of me to lay that on you."

Taking a deep breath, he said, "Okay…that's it, I guess. We're almost to your departure time that you made me promise to remember. This is the last recording I'm making for you. Lynn is…well…she's looking forward to your arrival. We're all at Cal's lab…you know the place…waiting for you. I locked myself in Cal's office to make this final recording."

John paused and took another long, deep breath. Slowly releasing it, he said, "I've missed you, Jack. The last thirty years have been unbelievable. Lynn has been the most wonderful wife a man could ask for…she's been my soul mate. Our kids, Kurtis and Jackie…not kids anymore, as you'll see…have grown up and turned into my best friends."

He felt tears beginning to well up in his eyes and quickly dragged the sleeve of his shirt across them before he continued. "I can't begin to thank you enough for what you did. I have been the happiest man on Earth.

"You know what's weird, though? Several times over the past three decades, late at night, after Lynn has fallen asleep and I'm lying in bed still awake, I've had these flashes of the other life…the one with Gail…the life that didn't happen, thank God. I've dreamed about it, too. Dreams, hell…more like nightmares. But it's made me believe that there *are* parallel universes – that somewhere, just one slight adjustment of the frequency away, the other life is still going on right now. God help the *me* in that one.

"Either that or we are right about *the cycles*. Maybe in every other cycle before this one, for millions of times, you didn't go back to 2010, and the other life is what has happened over and over again. So now, I would be picking up the brain waves from the *me*…the *us*…who lived through all of that misery."

John sighed. "Anyway, it didn't happen this time. We got it right. You did it, partner."

He stared into the tiny, round glass lens of the camera, wishing he could look directly into Jack's eyes instead. "I hope when you get here you are able to put away all of those demons you had from living through it…all of the baggage…and just be happy.

"Ever since you left from that plaza at the courthouse, I've been living my life as if it's been mine. This day, for so long, always seemed so far off. I knew it was coming. So did Lynn. We were never able to completely forget that it was, but for a lot of years it seemed more abstract than real. Then, all of a sudden, it arrived. Here it is. And now I feel like the advance man for you. I've gotten everything ready as well as I could, and now it's time for you to take over."

The tears began to flow once again, and this time John made no effort to wipe them away. "You did your part…now it's time for me to do mine. Jack…as hard as this is for me to do, the thought of not getting into the machine and leaving…taking the chance that if I don't do it, everything will instantly revert back to the other horror of a life…is unbearable. I couldn't do that to Lynn, Kurtis, Jackie, my new grandchild, or any of the others who have been along on this ride."

John paused and stared down at the floor, collecting his thoughts. Finally, he continued, "So the rest is up to you. Everyone…Lynn, Kurtis, Jackie, Cal…all of them are ready to help you get up to speed on your life the way it is now. Cal kept his promise. He's got journals and videos and audio…piles of images, data…you name it. I think my last three decades have been the most documented of any life on Earth. It kind of feels like…remember those so-called reality shows back in 2010…that's what my life has been like.

"I really don't believe that any of them are going to feel even the slightest bit of resentment toward you because I had to leave. They all know how much they gained because of what you did…and what I have to do.

"So, take care. And, one more time, thank you, Jack."

John reached out and tapped the button on the console, stopping the recording. Taking a minute to compose himself before walking out of the room, he entered the lab…the same room that he, Cal and Jack had come to thirty years ago to tell their bizarre tale to Lynn…and saw his wife standing next to their son, Kurtis, and their very pregnant daughter, Jackie. The three were engaged in a hushed conversation, and John thought back to a comment made by his *other* so many years ago.

Walking across the room, he joined them and said to Lynn, "You know what, baby, Jack was right."

She turned to look at him and smiled. The years *had* been more than kind to her he thought, as his eyes took in the lines, contours and textures of her face.

"Right about what?" she asked.

"He told you thirty years ago that you were going to be beautiful. And you are beautiful."

Lynn reached up and gently placed her hand against the side of his face, staring at him intently. "So are you, my darling."

She looked him up and down, double-checking, "We're sure you're wearing the same outfit Jack had on?"

John glanced over at Cal and shared a grin.

With a sigh, he said, "For the umpteenth time, yes, I am."

They looked at each other silently. Knowing this day was coming had allowed them plenty of time to say all that was to be said to each other. He put his arms around his wife and pulled her close, wanting to extract as much of the comfort and absorb as much of her essence as he could. Both Kurtis and Jackie moved toward them and joined the embrace, with Jackie being the first to begin to sob, triggering the same reaction from her brother, and then her mother and father.

Cal entered quickly from the hallway and skidded to a stop on the polished floor, embarrassed. He did not want to move or make a sound, knowing they deserved this time as it was. John, noticing him, eased his embrace and, over Lynn's shoulder, asked, "It's time?"

"It is."

Lynn, reacting to this, squeezed her husband harder, believing that if she held on tightly enough, this moment could linger forever.

Turning back, John whispered into her ear, "I have to go."

She sobbed harder, her shoulders heaving, and said nothing.

Another minute passed like this, with none of them wanting to be the first to let go, until John reached up and gripped Lynn's arms, gently steering her back away from him.

"We're almost out of time, baby. You know what could happen if...," his voice ebbed off.

Her mascara ruined, dark blotches of it trailing down her cheeks, she fought to stifle the sobs, still saying nothing.

Kurtis and Jackie relinquished their grips as well, and backed up only a few inches, not wanting to put too much distance between themselves and their father.

John unsteadily walked to the waiting open hatch of the time machine and turned to face them. Lynn, who had followed right behind, rushed again into his arms and kissed him passionately.

Reluctantly John ended the kiss, and turned to his son. "Be good to Jack," he said, fighting back another onslaught of tears.

Kurtis nodded and hugged his father tightly, crying.

John then turned to face his daughter. He looked down at her swollen abdomen and smiled, saying, "Make sure you tell her that I love her, will you? And I love you, too."

Jackie burst into tears and hugged him. "I love you, Daddy," she murmured in his ear.

"John...," Cal began nervously.

John backed away from Jackie and looked at Cal, saying in a resigned voice, "I know."

He turned back to Lynn one last time and quietly said, "I love you with all of my heart...I always have."

Lynn, no longer trying to hold back her emotions, wept as she managed to say, "I love you, John. I love you very much."

They kissed once more, knowing that they were tempting the fate of time. John stepped into the machine, glanced at Cal and said, "So long, pal."

Cal, unable to resist the contagiousness of the emotions in the room, also had tears on his face as he forced a smile, managing to say, "Have a good trip."

John pulled the door closed, and they all heard the locking mechanism snap into place as the seam around the hatch disappeared into the surrounding silver surface.

The four of them drifted together into a group and stared silently at the orb. Within no more than thirty seconds, the sphere was gone, as if it had never been there.

The room was filled with silence, except for the humming of the lab equipment. No one spoke as they watched the empty space and waited – the quiet broken only by an occasional, muted whimper from Lynn as she grappled with the torrent of emotions coursing through her.

As she stood and stared, her mind traveled with her husband back in time. She visualized the hatch opening on that dark night, thirty years ago. She tried to imagine how he felt as he stepped out onto the grass in the courthouse plaza. He would take a few paces forward and turn around to watch the sphere disappear as it proceeded on its preprogrammed journey. Then, with a final look around, he would turn and begin the five- or six-block walk toward the Hotel Congress to keep his appointment with a young man who was soon to step outside for a breath of fresh air.

Her mind created the movie which played before her eyes, as she tried to remember exactly what she would have been doing at that instant thirty years ago, just like she had tried so many times before. Yet again, the specifics did not come.

As she played out the scenario, a shiver of fear ran through her. She and John and Cal had talked about this countless times over the years. They had obsessed endlessly about the chance that this trip back, although needed to fulfill the process or whatever it was, could somehow change things. They had spent at least hundreds of hours talking about the possibility that John going back, with a whole new set of memories in his head, could somehow, accidentally, create a different outcome.

The single most terrifying aspect of this possibility, which Cal, motivated by compassion, kept trying to reassure Lynn would not happen, was that they would never even know. If their worst fear came true, then in the blink of an eye, they would all suddenly find themselves somewhere else, doing something else, blithely going about the mundane details of some alternate life with absolutely no recollections of any of the past thirty years. There would be no moment of transition for them to experience as they were thrust violently into their new reality. No Hollywood-movie, kaleidoscopic light show, flashing around them with overpowering sound effects as accompaniment. Nothing!

Lynn could not imagine a more frightening event. Both John and Cal had promised her this would not occur... *could not occur*... but she still did not understand why it couldn't. And so, here she stood, desperately trying to keep a vise-like grip on the billions and trillions of stored sensations within the synapses of her mind, which had made up the majority of her life; and believing that if she concentrated hard enough, grasped them strongly enough, she could somehow hold on to them with the sheer might of her will, no matter how powerful the force would be that came to rip them away.

She closed her eyes and said a silent prayer that in a few moments the sphere would suddenly appear before her... that she and Kurtis and Jackie would still be standing here waiting... and that Jack would open the hatch and step out. Although losing the *John* who just left was the most difficult thing she had ever done in her life, the thought of losing her own reality, as it now was, was unimaginable to her.

At least if the sphere appeared and the hatch opened and Jack came out and she was still here to witness it, then it would mean that all of the rest, everything else which had brought her to this point, had survived intact.

She finished her prayer but before she could open her eyes, she heard a small gasp come from Jackie. Blinking them open, she saw the sphere resting in front of her.

S_{UN} - 2:01 P.M.

"Look!" Cal exclaimed, pointing at the side of the silver orb.

"What?" Lynn said, nearly shouting. "What is it? Is something wrong?" She felt a flash of panic triggered by the urgency in his voice.

"The side of the sphere...it's the gash...where Burke's bullet hit it."

All of the details of that night came flooding back to her as she recognized the linear crease in the otherwise perfect silver skin, caused so many years ago by Burke's desperate attempt to save Jack's life.

Lynn heard a nearly inaudible, "Oh, no," from Cal and jerked her eyes away from the sphere to look at him.

"What's wrong?" she asked, a shiver of fear slicing through her, fear picked up by Jackie and Kurtis.

"Uncle Cal," Jackie said, her voice quivering, "is something wrong?"

Cal, unable to tear his eyes away from the orb, answered them in a low, controlled tone, "The integrity of the sphere...the perfection of it...is essential...," his voice trailed off.

"What do you...what does it mean?" Lynn asked anxiously.

Before Cal could respond to Lynn, her son said, "Mom, look!"

Her gaze followed the direction he pointed, and she saw the transformation occurring in the side of the sphere. Although Cal had explained that it was only nanotechnology and the utilization of a special silver matrix which caused the seam around the hatch to appear and disappear, it still looked like magic to Lynn as she saw its outline materialize on the surface.

Anxiousness and fear caused her to tremble as she stared silently at the outline of the hatchway, afraid to utter a word. Seconds passed with nothing happening, the brief passage of time feeling unendurable to the four people watching in dread. None of them noticed that they were all holding their breath in anticipation of the opening of the sphere.

"I can't stand this!" Cal barked impatiently and took a step forward, intending to place his own hand on the recognition area, knowing that the on-board computer would accept his biometrics so he could activate the mechanism himself and open the hatch.

As he raised his hand to place it on the skin of the sphere, there was a slight hiss triggered by the sudden equalization of differing atmospheric pressures, and he saw the hatch begin to rise and swing away.

Cal stepped back hastily and almost tripped and fell. He heard Lynn and Jackie gasp in unison as the door swung clear.

In the hatchway, looking just as he had when Lynn bid him a tearful good-bye three decades earlier, stood Jack – an expression of joy, diluted with something that resembled confusion, etched upon his face; his clothes stained with large blotches of brown and green, from the confrontation with Gail on the grass of the courthouse plaza.

Jack stepped down from the portal and opened his mouth to speak. Before he could utter a single word, Lynn ran up to him and threw her arms around his neck, holding him tightly. Unable to hold them back any longer, she allowed herself the release of her powerful pent-up emotions. He wrapped his arms around his wife, passionately returning the embrace.

"John! I mean, Jack," Cal said anxiously. "Are you all right?"

Jack looked at Cal from over Lynn's shoulder and simply nodded, not wanting to say or do anything that might shatter his moment with Lynn.

His eyes then traveled to Kurtis and Jackie. They had been standing back nervously, not knowing what to expect or how Jack would react to them, as it had been explained so many times before. Jackie was nervously twisting the bottom hem of her maternity blouse like it was an old dishrag, wrinkling it hopelessly. Kurtis stood erect, his face tightly controlled, except for his bottom lip which he was chewing unconsciously. Although the man standing in front of them was their father – the man with whom they clearly remembered spending all of the millions of moments of their lives – they knew that he had never laid his eyes upon them before this instant.

They had both tried, with the help of their parents, to prepare themselves for this day throughout all of their adult lives. Even so, both of them were shaken and stunned by the reality of the moment…or, actually, the unreality of it. Jackie wanted, with all of her being, to run forward and join her mother in the embrace with Jack, but found that she could not budge because she was unsure what reaction she would receive.

Kurtis, feeling tears begin to run down his face as he watched Lynn hug this man who was indisputably his father, frantically searched his mind for something to say and found nothing that at all came close.

"You're here!" Lynn gasped, her face buried in Jack's neck. "Thank God."

Jack held her ever more tightly. As the incapacitating wave of emotion ebbed slightly, he focused on the frightened and concerned faces of Kurtis and Jackie. He could see that both of them were staring at him, searching desperately for a glimmer of recognition from their father.

Tilting his head back slightly away from Lynn so that he could speak, Jack said, "Jackie…Kurtis…aren't you going to say *hello* to your dad?"

The profound implications of those few words struck all of them like a lightning bolt. Kurtis reacted first, shouting, "Dad!" He dashed forward, throwing his arms around Jack and his mother. The spell broke for Jackie a moment later, and she also ran forward, adding herself to the familial embrace as all of them wept with joy.

Cal stood awkwardly to the side, feeling like a voyeur during this intensely private and emotional moment. His mind whirled with the ramifications of the revelation…Jack's recognition of his children.

"It must be the gash in the skin," Cal muttered to himself.

Jack, hearing the comment, angled his head so he could see his old friend and said, "I remember everything…all of it."

Lynn finally backed away so that she was only a few inches from her husband, happy just to be gazing up at his face. Jack looked down at her, dabbed at one of her cheeks with his thumb and teased, "Your eye make-up was running down your face the last time I saw you…in the courthouse plaza. Is this getting to be a new look for you?" Her emotions already rubbed raw, Lynn couldn't help herself as a laugh burst from her lips. She hugged him again.

When the powerful release of dammed-up emotions began to ease, Kurtis and Jackie detached from the group hug but remained standing next to their father. Lynn also partially relinquished her embrace and turned to face Cal, her right arm still wrapped tightly around Jack's waist, determined never to let him leave her again.

"Cal," she uttered, finally finding her voice, "how could this happen?" She then quickly added, "Not that I'm not grateful."

Cal had a quizzical look on his face and paused to think for a moment before he answered her, "Lynn, I'm not sure. The skin...the silver coating that overlays the structural sphere itself...has to be flawless...polished to a nearly impossible tolerance. Otherwise, the time traveler wouldn't be immune to the changes he makes as he travels."

"The gash!" Kurtis exclaimed.

"Exactly. Somehow, by some bizarre fluke of physics, the ding in the skin caused by Burke's bullet must have changed things...created some sort of unintended effect."

"Why do you call it a bizarre fluke?" Kurtis asked. "If the skin is what protects the occupant from the effects of the changes, wouldn't it make sense that damaging it would allow this to happen? Allow Dad to come back with memories?"

"No. You see, the protection of the skin is a lot more complex than that. You're right, without the protective skin, the traveler would come forward in time and gain memories of all of the changes he had caused. However, there would also be a very bad side effect...he would...should have...also aged those thirty years."

"Oh," Lynn hesitated, involuntarily turning back to Jack and closely examining his face.

Cal also stared carefully at Jack's face, looking for the telltale signs of aging.

Finding none, he walked over to the sphere and studied the slight dimple created by Burke's ricochet, noting, more to himself than to the others, "The silver is still intact...there's just a dent."

Everyone waited for Cal's mind to process the information and come up with some sort of a conclusion. He finally turned back to them and admitted, "I'm clueless. I guess it comes back to it being a fluke."

Then, he suddenly asked, "Jack, I'm curious. Do you have *both* sets of memories? Your life with Lynn and the kids *and* your life with," he shuddered, "Gail?"

Jack's eyes became unfocused for a moment as he scrutinized and inventoried the contents of his own head before he concluded, "I do. It's kind of weird because my life with Lynn, right up to the moment I got in the machine to go back to 2010, is the most...it's hard to find the right word...prominent, I guess. Then," he paused again to concentrate before continuing, "I vividly remember the duration of the trip back to 2010...like I just went through it...I did, I guess. But it doesn't feel like *I* was really the one who did all of those things. It seems like I was a spectator. God, this is hard to describe."

"What do you mean?" Lynn asked. "Are you saying that you didn't actually live through those five days back there?"

Jack turned to face her and shook his head. "Yes... I mean, no!" He took a deep breath and tried to explain. "You know how the three of us have been talking for a long time about how critical it was that all of the things that happened, as we recalled them, had to happen exactly the same way when I went back?"

"Of course I do," she said. "We must have spent a thousand hours talking about it."

"Well, the way it feels... at least, the way my mind is remembering it... is that we never had anything to worry about. I couldn't have changed a thing. I left all of you here, got in the machine and punched the button to go back. Now this is where it gets strange because I don't actually think that I went through all of those days back there. I remember them... clearly... in my mind; they are now the most recent memories that I have. But it just doesn't feel like I did it." Jack looked helplessly at Cal and asked, "Does that make any sense?"

"Copy and paste?" offered Cal.

"Right!" said Jack excitedly. "Like I explained to Jack, or like John explained to me... whatever... that day at Casa Molina."

"Copy and paste?" Jackie asked, confused.

"It was something John came up with," Jack explained to his daughter, "while we were eating lunch. He didn't think Cal had actually built a machine that traveled through time, didn't think I was time traveling. What he thought was that we were actually copying sections of time and pasting them at a different point along the timeline."

"Wow!" Jackie said. "That is really an intense concept!"

Jack paused for a moment, then speculated, "Maybe he was right. Maybe this thing, this machine, *is* just a time editor. As we think we are traveling around making all kinds of changes, the machine, just like a word processor, is copying, cutting and pasting to create the new version of reality. I don't know."

Kurtis suddenly proposed, "Maybe this explains the mystery of the scar that you had on your head right after... uh... John was dropped in the alley."

Cal slowly mulled over that possibility. "It might. Jack, you have both sets of memories, you had the scar. Maybe the *Jack* who was with us during the trip we all remember was you... *this you*... from this trip."

Lynn, her voice dubious, questioned him, "Are you trying to tell me that the *Jack* we all spent those five days with was the person we just sent back, the man who has been married to me for all these years?"

"That," Jack reflected, "is a weird thought. I'm not sure I understand how it all happened."

"I don't either," Cal said. "And I'm not sure we ever will."

His expression suddenly changed to one of excitement as he added, "What has happened does tell me something... something important. All I have to do is analyze it... test it... until I understand and can manipulate the phenomenon. Then I can incorporate dimples, gashes, striations, whatever... right into the skin. The silver coating and the structural underlayment is already dynamic because of the nanotechnology. So once I understand what happened, I can program the machine to allow manipulation of the surface. I could control exactly how the traveler is affected by the process."

Lynn shook her head, and with derision in her voice, chastised him, "Cal, haven't you learned your lesson from all of this?"

Cal stopped abruptly, like a person who had just been slapped across the face. Taking a minute to collect himself, he shook his head to clear it and sheepishly looked at Lynn. Now gone was the flush of excitement at the possibility of a new breakthrough. In its place was an expression of sincere repentance. With a subtle nod, he conceded, "You're right, Lynn. This whole adventure was a close call. Way too close. It could have been a total disaster."

Jack looked back and forth between them for a second before he said, "Cal, either way, it's done. You're alive, the machine is intact... well, relatively intact, and we are all on the right track."

"And you're home," Lynn sighed, her gratitude for this fact obvious.

"Right. But, Cal, I do agree with Lynn. I think we need to learn from this. We came so close to really messing things up, in ways we can't even begin to imagine."

Cal turned to look at the sphere. They all knew him well enough to know that his mind was spinning through all of the possible alternatives, frantically trying to come up with a way to do what he wanted while safeguarding against the kind of cataclysmic results they all feared. Cal couldn't help himself. He did this because that was who he was. For the past three decades it had been this very determination, this urge to charge forward, which had led him to the nearly countless breakthroughs and successes he had achieved.

After no more than a minute or two, he turned back to face them and assented, "I guess you're right, both of you."

Before Cal could continue, he was interrupted.

"By the way, now that this ordeal is over, can we please drop the whole *Jack* thing? I've been *John* my entire life, actually both of my lives. I might have been some guy named *Jack* for thirty years in everybody's memory, but I really only used that name for five days."

Cal chuckled as Lynn kissed her husband on the cheek and said, "Thank God. I never liked that name, anyway."

"Hey!" Jackie exclaimed.

"Neither did I," their son Kurtis chimed in, his eyes twinkling as he saw an opportunity to tease his sister.

Jackie pouted, her bottom lip jutting forward as John assured her, "Honey, I love the name."

Jackie smiled at him, and he added, "But only for you, sweetheart, not me."

Cal cleared his throat and announced, "I think you have some people waiting for you outside."

Remembering, John said, "That's right! We probably shouldn't keep them waiting."

Leading the way out of the lab, Cal opened the door to the hallway. John, following him, saw a completely gray-haired Ben Hart, leaning heavily on a cane and standing next to Billy Burke.

As they saw John emerge, they both stood straighter and waited with anticipation for an indication of the outcome of the trip, not yet knowing the status of his memories.

Deciding to have a some fun with them, John deliberately glanced at them both casually and turned to walk away as if he had not recognized either of the two men. From the corner of his eye, he could see the look of sadness and disappointment on the faces of these two men who had become his close friends in the ensuing years since the night in the plaza.

He only made it a few steps before he heard Burke shout, "Freeze, dirtbag!"

John stopped in mid-pace and turned back to look at Burke, forcing an innocent and befuddled expression. Keeping his voice neutral, he said, "Excuse me, do I know you?"

Burke walked to John, stopping when he was only inches away. Although John stood slightly over six feet tall, Burke looked down at him, and a slow grin spread across his face. "I didn't survive a total of thirty-nine years on the force without learning to read a man's eyes. Welcome back, John."

John grabbed Burke in a bear hug as Ben hobbled over to them and complained in a good-natured way, "That was a rotten thing to do."

Stepping back from Burke, John smiled at them both and defended himself, "I couldn't help it. This was the first chance in a long time that I was able to get to the two of you, and I couldn't pass it up." He greeted Ben with an equally exuberant hug.

"I thought," Burke mused, his head tilted inquisitively, "that you weren't going to remember any of this."

John shrugged. "None of us can explain it, but I do. I remember everything. And apparently, Billy, we can all thank you."

"Me?"

"From what we can figure out, your bullet that hit the sphere somehow changed it...changed the way the skin works...allowing me to come back here with all of the memories."

Burke's face lit up with a huge smile. He turned to Ben and gloated, "See, all of the abuse I've taken from you for the last thirty years about my crummy marksmanship, and it was *my* shot that made everything come out all right."

Ben grunted. "I still say you can't hit the side of a barn from twenty yards." A slight look of confusion appeared on his face as he asked, "You said you remember everything? Including the...you know...other life?"

"Both of them."

"Fascinating!" The voice came from behind John and he turned to look at Richard Mueller, who was in his early seventies and sat in a mechanized wheelchair, specially designed and modified by Cal to fit his needs.

The next few minutes passed, with John once again describing his trip to his three lifelong friends – and the inexplicable overlaying of memories which had occurred.

As he talked, Lynn never left his side, her arm wrapped tightly around him, her face bearing an expression of happiness which looked as if it would never diminish. As he neared the end of his narrative, John's voice took on a somber note, the altering of his mood reflected in his face. Lynn, noticing the change, wondered, "What's wrong, honey?"

He turned to look at his wife and sadly said, "I was just thinking...none of us would be standing here right now...together, like this, if it wasn't for Kurt and what he did back then."

"I know. I have thanked him every night in my prayers."

Almost to himself, John murmured, "God, I miss him."

Cal, vividly recalling the fateful Friday so many years ago, remarked, "I have replayed that day over and over again in my mind. Things had gotten so messed up. That he was able to do what he did...and fix it all...was absolutely amazing!"

Suddenly, coming from the doorway he had just exited, John heard a voice say, "That's why they call me The Amazing Kurt!"

At the sound of the familiar voice, John whirled around, bewildered, and saw Kurt Wallace – like a ghost, yet real – standing in the lab doorway, looking exactly as he did when John last saw him a few days, or thirty years ago in the storage room, with the so-familiar lopsided grin on his face.

"My God!," Lynn gasped. Kurtis and Jackie both stared at the stranger they had heard so much about for their entire lives, with a myriad of fleeting expressions, dominated by confusion and astonishment.

Cal, standing closest to the doorway, was the first to find his voice. "Kurt! You're here!"

The sly grin still on his face, Kurt teased, "What's the big deal? I said I'd be right back."

Broken from his trance, John covered the distance between them in a flash and grabbed Kurt by the shoulders, an almost impossibly wide smile filling his face. "You came *here*!"

Kurt gripped John's arms tightly. "Well…yeah! You had made a pretty good mess of things back there, so I figured it was time to change venues."

Cal stepped to them and put his arm around Kurt's shoulders. "Why didn't you tell me what you were going to do?"

"It's really simple, man. I knew you would try to talk me out of it. I also thought that one of the three of you just might be dumb enough to try to make another trip back to stop me. I didn't want that. Things were already fouled up enough. The way I had it planned, I would die in the crash *and* Jack wouldn't have the machine, so there would be no way you could come back to mess up my plan."

John shook his head in amazement. "You just left and took the machine with you! How did you know I would be able to return here?"

"I didn't, for sure. I assumed that the main machine was programmed to come back over and over again until you could return... and that even *you* would figure it out eventually. Besides, it looked like all hell was breaking loose at the storage room as I was leaving. I didn't want to risk following Cal back there. So I took his fancy, hand-tooled leather belt, pickpocketed his wallet and sent Cal on his way. And anyway... if the main machine wasn't coming back, I just planned on getting here, and then this Cal and I would send the backup for you."

"My belt?" Cal exclaimed. "That's right. I forgot about that."

"What's this about the belt?" asked Jackie.

Kurt turned to her and explained, "John told me that the night of the crash Jack had recognized Cal's belt. I knew I'd need it if I was going to pull off my little switch."

"How did you get Cal to give up his belt?"

Kurt just grinned at Jackie. Cal, chagrined, admitted, "He told me that the metal from the belt buckle would interfere with the machine."

Lynn, who had been listening attentively, questioned him, "How can you be here right now? You died."

Kurt, still grinning happily, said to John, "I saw this beautiful lady once in the doctor's office, but I don't think I've been formally introduced." He turned to her, extending his hand. "Hello, Lynn... I'm Kurt."

She side-stepped the outstretched hand and kissed Kurt on the cheek, giving him an emotional hug, "I finally get a chance to thank you."

Kurt, looking awkwardly uncomfortable to be on the receiving end of Lynn's display of emotion, shrugged from inside her embrace and replied, "No worries, ma'am. It was purely selfish, anyway."

Lynn stepped back and persisted, "But you didn't answer my question... I thought... we all thought you were dead."

"I was. Well, at least one of me was."

"That's right!" John exclaimed. "When you went back to that Friday, there were two of you."

Kurt chuckled and said, "*Mister Smart Guy*, you've had thirty years to think about this," then turned to Cal and added, "and the genius here... and neither one of you figured it out? I can't believe it."

"I don't understand," Jackie reacted, moving closer.

"It's simple. When I went back to Friday, I was going back to a day I had previously lived through. I knew I was out at Gate's Pass that day, doing some sketching, so after I sent Cal forward in time, I went out to see me."

Kurt laughed as he relived the moment, "You should have seen the look on my face. Man, it was something. I...he...was sitting at a picnic table, staring peacefully at the desert, when I just walked up to him, bigger than life, and said, 'Hey, dude!' I thought he was going to pass out! You've got to remember...that was Friday...so it was before *he* had learned all of this stuff about time traveling."

Kurt paused in his narrative and looked at Jackie and then at Kurtis. "I'll bet that you two are the offspring from this lovely lady here."

"I'm sorry," John apologized, "Kurt...this is our daughter, Jackie."

"Jackie? A tad sentimental, are we? Naming your daughter after Jack."

"We thought," Lynn explained, "that since we wouldn't be together if it wasn't for Jack coming back, it would only be right."

Kurt shook Jackie's hand. "A pleasure to meet you." Glancing down at her swollen mid-section, he added, "And it looks like you're about to turn these two into grandparents."

"I am." She smiled sweetly at Kurt.

Kurt then shifted his attention to Lynn's son and said, "And you are... ?"

"Kurtis," he answered proudly.

Wallace was suddenly speechless. After a moment, he recovered sufficiently to shake the hand of his namesake.

Kurtis prompted, "Please finish telling us what happened. How did you talk the other *you* into killing himself?"

"It's not as big a deal as it sounds. We both knew that we only had a few weeks to live, anyway. And we were already having horrendous pains from the tumor. We had been thinking about taking matters into our own hands...just to avoid going through the final days. So it made perfect sense. I guess we must have talked it over for hours. After I told him what was happening...or going to happen...after the bachelor party, he agreed with me that it was a good idea."

"Please don't take this the wrong way," Jackie said, "but why him...why not you?"

Kurt looked at her and smirked, "Thanks a lot. I thought you liked me."

Jackie started to respond defensively, when Kurt held up his hands and resumed. "Just teasing. Actually, I told him that I would do it. That was my plan all along. Going to find him and talking him into killing himself just didn't appeal to me. I didn't think it was right, you know? But he vetoed the idea. He figured that since I was the one who had gone through those four days, I was the only one who could go through them again and get all of the details right...and I was the one who had operated the machine before. He made up his mind I should be the one to go to 2040, not him."

Kurt hesitated at this point in the story, the grin slipping from his face. "It was kind of weird, really."

Taking a moment, he continued, "Even though it made sense...I still wanted to be the one to...you know."

Kurt stared into the distance for several seconds before he forced a smile back on his face as he recalled the next scene in his mind. His voice light, as if he were describing a routine event, he said, "So we flipped a coin."

"Flipped a coin!" Jackie cried out.

Kurt looked her in the eyes and nodded. "Yeah, he won the belt."

Everyone was quiet for a moment, then Kurt began, "So...old whiz-bang Cal...after all of this trouble I went through, I sure hope that in the past thirty years you figured out those nano-bots, the ones Jack described to me – the ones you can put in me and get rid of this monster growing in my skull."

"Jack told you about what I was going to do?" Cal asked with surprise. "When?"

"When he and I were cooling our heels in the waiting room while John and Lynn were smooching in one of the exams."

Jackie giggled at his comment and Kurt, suddenly embarrassed, backtracked, "I mean, getting acquainted."

Cal shook his head in disgust as John grinned sheepishly. "So even though I told you not to, you blabbed just about everything while you back there, didn't you?"

John shrugged and said, "Have you ever thought about that, Cal? I mean *really* thought about it?"

"What do you mean?"

"Come on, how many of the things that you invented after the visit would have just naturally occurred to you if I hadn't told you about them all that day?"

Cal did not answer, his mind contemplating the implications of John's question.

"Hell, maybe it's possible that you wouldn't even have invented the time machine itself if I hadn't come back and you hadn't seen it with your own eyes."

Cal shook his head, "That's not possible. It can't be."

John gazed at his friend intently, asking, "How can you know that for sure?"

There was a long silence, as Cal tried to find a flaw in John's hypothesis. Finally, he admitted, "I can't."

Turning to Kurt, he said, "To answer your question…yes, Kurt, I did invent the nano-bots about two years ago."

"Whew! It sounds like I cut it pretty close. So they work?" Kurt asked, intense interest plain on his face.

"Yes, they work like a charm."

"Cool!" he responded, his relief palpable.

Kurt then turned to Burke and Hart, who had been standing discreetly off to the side during the reunion. "Let me see, now…Detective Hart and Officer Burke, right?"

They both came forward, Ben wobbling on his cane, and Burke responded, "We've both been retired for a while. Now it's just Billy and Ben."

As they each shook Kurt's hand, Ben addressed Burke and boasted, "I told you I would eventually find him."

Burke laughed. "In reality, I think he was the one who found you…but, okay, partner…you can call the case closed now."

Kurt noticed the old man sitting patiently in the wheelchair. It took several seconds before he recognized him, but Kurt's eyes widened as he exclaimed, "Professor Mueller!"

They exchanged greetings as the rest of the group looked on, with Mueller filling Kurt in on the details of his involvement since it had all happened after his departure.

When they had finished, Cal asked Kurt, "As you were going through those four days all over again, did you feel like you wanted to change anything?"

"I couldn't. I don't really mean I couldn't, but there was, like, this strong feeling that I can't explain. I felt as if I was more of a…."

"Spectator?" John suggested.

"Exactly! Either way, I didn't want to change anything. I was determined to make sure it came out the same."

"I think you made the right choice," John assured him.

"You obviously did," Cal agreed.

"Well, I did manage to make one little change," Kurt confessed, a trace of guilt in his tone.

Cal's eyebrows jerked up in concern. "What? What did you do?"

Kurt glanced at the group and answered defensively, "Look around, dude. We're all here. Everything's cool. So it obviously didn't affect anything."

"Kurt, what was it?" Cal asked firmly.

"I'll be right back," Kurt excused himself and turned to go back into the lab. The rest of the group followed him and saw the backup sphere now resting on its base next to the main machine. The hatch of the backup was still wide open and Kurt reached inside, grabbing a small pouch. He turned to John and handed it to him.

"Here you go. A little present from the past. Hey, I like that! Present... past, get it?"

John rolled his eyes in exasperation and took the pouch from his friend, first noticing the heft of the object inside.

"What is it?"

"Take a look," was all Kurt would say, his trademark grin returning.

John untied the leather thong on the pouch and reached in, immediately recognizing the object by touch.

"You didn't!" he exclaimed with undisguised happiness.

Kurt just nodded and smiled as John pulled out his old Lionel Sante Fe steam engine.

"I rescued it before the fire."

John looked down at the beautifully detailed engine in disbelief.

"I didn't see how bringing that with me could affect anything since it was going to be melted into a lump in the fire, so I snagged it after we finished playing with the trains."

John looked at Cal questioningly. Cal thought for a moment, then shrugged. "The world seems to have survived intact with all of the other things you did while you were back there, so I don't see how this could make a difference."

Gratefully, John cautiously tucked the engine back into the pouch as Kurt grumbled, "As much fun as this reunion is... I'm famished."

John laughed. "You think *you're* hungry? When I left to come back here, it was around midnight. I haven't had a meal in...."

"Thirty years," Lynn said, finishing his sentence.

They all broke into laughter, due as much to the humor of her comment as the release of tension from the events of the day.

"Let's go," Cal prompted, leading the way out.

The group followed behind, deliberately walking slowly to accommodate

Ben's hobbled gait, until they reached the building exit.

Stepping out, they were all briefly blinded by the bright afternoon sun after coming from the artificially-lit interior of the lab building. As all of their eyes adjusted, John was the first to notice someone leaning against a tree twenty yards from them, taking advantage of the shade. Before John could recognize him, Cal suddenly exclaimed, "Oh, my God...Aloysius!"

Sᴜɴ - 3:09ᴘ.ᴍ.

They gathered around Aloysius under the tree, taking advantage of a concrete table and benches positioned in the shade. After they were all seated and introductions were made to those who had never met Aloysius, Kurt remarked, "It looks like I'm not the only one who hasn't aged."

Aloysius looked the same as he had when John and Cal had last seen him thirty years ago, down to the denim jacket and Harley-Davidson t-shirt. He smiled and greeted them, "It's good to see all of you," his kind, brown eyes lingering first on one face and then the next, around the table.

Burke, who had heard all of the stories about Aloysius, worried, "So what's going to happen now?"

"What do you mean?" Aloysius asked.

"Well, from what I was told, just about the only time you made an appearance was when all hell was breaking loose. Are we about to get attacked by some aliens?"

Jackie involuntarily glanced skyward, seeing nothing but the dense foliage of the acacia tree above her head.

Aloysius grinned and answered Burke, "No, I assure you there won't be any attack. This is purely a social visit."

"Does this mean…," Cal began, struggling to find the words, "are you going to… dammit, what the hell really happened back then?"

His grin breaking into a broad smile, Aloysius responded, "I gave you answers. I explained everything."

"You might have told us what you wanted us to believe," Cal retorted, "but we all know that it was a load of...."

Before Cal could finish, John interjected, "Aloysius, look...that whole thing about the Anunnaki just didn't make sense."

"It didn't?" Aloysius asked, an expression of innocence on his face.

"No. It didn't."

"Why do you say that?"

"Well...for one thing, you told us the Anunnaki didn't want Cal to build the time machine. You said that was why they attempted to abduct me in the alley before I could go back and undo his accident."

"Yes. That's true."

"And you told us that Kurt outsmarted them when he went back and substituted himself for Cal, outsmarted a race who, according to you, could supposedly see into the future."

Aloysius started to respond, but John cut him off. "And then, that last night in front of the courthouse, when Gail was about to kill all of us, including Cal, they stopped her. All they had to do was sit back and do nothing and they could have accomplished their goal, but they sucked *her* up into their ship, allowing Cal to live and build the machine. I'm sorry. That just doesn't fit."

"You're right. I misled you. With what all of you have gone through...everything you've all done...we've decided that you deserve to know the truth."

"We?" Cal pressed him. "Who? And don't start with that Anunnaki and Nordic stuff again."

Aloysius took a deep breath, exhaling slowly. When he finished, he said, "It *did* start with the Anunnaki...."

"Dammit, Aloysius!"

Aloysius held up his hand for Cal to stop, which he did, and Aloysius continued, "The Earth *was* visited and, indeed, populated by many groups in its history, including the Anunnaki. So when I told you that the visitors were the Anunnaki, I was telling the truth...technically. Because all of you...*all of us*...are, to some degree, from the Anunnaki."

"Descendants?" John asked.

"Right."

"I knew it," Lynn reflected with satisfaction.

"So whoever was in the spaceship that night, whoever abducted Gail, was...an Earthling? Good grief, I feel silly saying that out loud!" Burke groaned, shaking his head.

"See, Billy," Ben chuckled, "Louise was right all along."

"For thirty years, ever since I told her about what happened in front of the courthouse, I haven't heard the end of it."

Amused by the friendly banter he had heard for so many years, John returned his attention to Aloysius and asked, "Just to be clear, Aloysius, you're saying that we weren't visited by space aliens?"

"That is correct. I think, before I go much farther, some perspective is needed."

"*That* would be a great idea," Cal snorted.

"As I mentioned, this planet was populated eons ago by many races from several other planets. Their motives varied from simple colonization to overt exploitation of resources. As time went on, with the help of some deliberate genetic modifications, the races melded together to form what we now consider to be the human race.

"As the original resources were depleted to the point where easy and practical extraction was no longer viable... or as other sources, less troublesome and expensive to obtain, were found elsewhere in the galaxy... the visits to this planet diminished.

"At that point in time, the new hybrid race, the *humans*, were spreading out all around the planet, becoming increasingly more territorial as they went. You see, by a fluke of genetics, the Anunnaki had unknowingly created a breed of workers who were not as docile as those created on other planets that they had exploited in the past. They found themselves being challenged and defied at an increasing rate by the humans."

"So, we've always had a kick-ass attitude," Kurt interjected proudly.

"Because of all of these factors, the visits simply stopped completely. The planet Earth was no longer a stop on any of their itineraries. The people here were left to progress and continue to mingle and merge, which they have for countless thousands of years."

"They were abandoned?" asked Kurtis.

"Abandoned implies something that was not the case. As I said before, some of those who arrived here came specifically with the intent to colonize. They wanted to be here and felt no more abandoned than the Americans felt abandoned when the British withdrew after the Revolutionary War. They were happy to be left alone, happy to be rid of the oppressive presence of the interlopers."

"You said that some of those left behind were the Anunnaki," Lynn reminded him. "Why didn't they take their own offspring when they left?"

"The true Anunnaki, those who came here to exploit, felt no kinship with those left behind because they were not pureblood descendants; they were the result of genetic engineering and both planned and unplanned interbreeding with the others. From the biased perspective of the Anunnaki, the people they left here were no more kin to them than livestock is to a farmer.

"As the population on Earth grew, and as the technological proficiency of those who were here…and therefore the ability to defend and attack…progressed, the Earth was considered throughout the galaxy as a place never to visit or, in fact, a place to avoid at all costs, much like mariners of old would mark islands on their maps as being too inhospitable to visit."

"So, are you saying," Lynn quizzed him, leaning forward with interest, "that the visits we've heard and read about our whole lives, like Roswell, never happened?"

"No, I'm not saying that at all. What I am telling you is that those visits throughout our recorded history were not the Anunnaki or, for that matter, any being from any other planet."

"Then who made them?" John asked.

"We did."

"We did? You mean humans, from Earth?"

Aloysius nodded and said nothing.

"That's not possible. We don't have the technology to do all of the things we've seen…or do we?" John asked.

"Is there a secret base, like Area 51, where we really do have flying saucers?" Jackie added to her father's question.

"No," Aloysius answered, looking at John. Then he turned to Jackie and repeated, "No."

Feeling the beginnings of frustration with Aloysius's coyness, John, with an edge to his voice, pushed the subject, "Aloysius, if it hasn't been space aliens in those ships, and *we* don't have the capability to do the things which have been seen, who in the hell is it?"

Aloysius, his unflappable composure intact, grinned at John and said, "Frankly, John…and all of you…I'm surprised you would ask that question. I would have thought that you, of all people, would understand."

"The future!" Cal exclaimed. "Of course! The trips were made by us, all right, but they were human beings coming back from the future!"

Aloysius leaned back, a self-satisfied expression on his face.

"They have been time traveling," John concluded, full comprehension dawning upon him.

"Are you saying that all of the UFO sightings in the past were actually humans coming back from the future?" Lynn pondered, incredulous.

Aloysius explained, "We have made visits to points in the past, visits which spanned centuries."

"The spaceships in the background of paintings from the Renaissance...?" asked Lynn.

"Yes," Aloysius affirmed. "Those were attempts by the painters of the day to record something seen by many."

"What about the ancient cave paintings or stone carvings by the Egyptians? Those also have images that look like flying saucers."

Aloysius shook his head and answered Lynn, "The stone carvings found in Egypt and the cave paintings in France, as well as other places, were images made by the original workers of the Anunnaki. They were an attempt to record our history...to make certain that we, as a race, would never forget our roots and would always be ready to oppose the Anunnaki, should they ever return."

"So, it wasn't the Egyptians who made the carvings?"

"No. Nor was it the Egyptians who built the monuments we call the pyramids. Those structures, along with the Sphinx and others were built thousands of years earlier by the Anunnaki, using their sophisticated technology and the original work force they had created."

"If the Anunnaki built the pyramids," Jackie realized, "that would mean they weren't built as tombs for the Pharaohs, wouldn't it?"

"That's correct. The pyramids were later co-opted by the Egyptians, designating that purpose. It was the intent of the original people left behind by the Anunnaki that the pyramids remain standing forever, as they were useful in keeping away explorers from other planets. Utilizing them as sacred tombs accomplished that goal."

"Then what were they?" Jackie inquired.

"Claim markers."

"Claim markers?" Lynn repeated, fascinated.

"That was the accepted protocol for the travelers. If you came to a planet to either colonize or exploit the resources, it was the practice among the various explorers to create a marking that was distinctive enough to be visible from space, telling others who might arrive later that the planet was taken. The configuration of the pyramids, as viewed from space, was intended to be a representation of their constellation of origin, as it appeared from Earth, thereby identifying the claimants of this planet."

"And the Sphinx?"

Aloysius shrugged. "The Sphinx is nothing but an edifice, designed to intimidate those who were brought into it."

"Brought in? Edifice? What do you mean?" Jackie asked, puzzled.

"In the 20th century, all of the immigrants to America were deliberately brought in to one specific location, Ellis Island. The Statue of Liberty towered over that small island and was used by America as a powerful symbol to those who came to this country from across the sea. That symbol was meant to instill within the newcomers a sense of benevolence, but also to convey the might of their new country.

"Between the paws of the Sphinx was an entrance, an entrance to the laboratories which were built under the monument. That was where all of the genetic modifications were done to the workers. The massive Sphinx loomed above them as they were brought in, to instill fear and, therefore, obedience in the laborers. When the humans finally escaped from under the tyranny of the Anunnaki, one of their first acts was to chisel a new face on the Sphinx, the face you see today. And then they sealed off the entrance to the lab."

"I've read that the face was redone in the distant past," Lynn recalled. "What face was originally on it?"

"Of course it was the distinct features of the Anunnaki," explained Aloysius. "The face that all of the workers were to obey and fear."

"And the lab?" Cal inquired. "Is it still there?"

"It is."

"I know the Egyptians won't allow anyone to explore beneath the Sphinx," Cal asserted. "Do they know what's there?"

Aloysius shook his head. "No, they don't. The specifics of what is buried beneath have long ago faded from the memory of all humans. But the first members of the newly-free humans, after altering the face of the Sphinx, left behind a small band to settle along the Nile. They were charged with the sacred undertaking of barring any from entrance. Those who were given this task were specifically not told what was buried, so as to insure that no one in the future would be tempted to use the technology for their own gain."

"How do you know all of this?" asked Kurtis. "Have you been back there?"

Aloysius grinned. "No, I haven't. All that I have told you is what I have learned. It is taught to children in the future, just as you received a history lesson when you were small."

"Then they must have gone back to that time," Kurtis persisted.

"Of course they did. Just as it is the current standard in the quest for knowledge to send out teams of archaeologists to tediously dig through damaged and incomplete ruins in the hope of discerning partial details of a past civilization, the future humans have systematically visited and observed every era of the past, to obtain the *true* history of our world and people."

"That's why the flying saucer appears in artwork going back for centuries," said Lynn. "Those were all reconnaissance missions."

"Scientific expeditions," Aloysius clarified. "Like Carter's trip to Egypt, except much less invasive."

"What about Roswell?" Kurt asked. "It was pretty invasive. Did that really happen?"

"It did." Aloysius paused for a long moment before adding, "I was there, I know."

John, intrigued, reasoned, "You're obviously one of them... from the future. Of course you were at Roswell. You were a part of the scientific team, or crew, or whatever you call yourselves, right?"

Aloysius shook his head. "No, I am not from the future. When the Roswell incident occurred, I was a local boy of five years old. I was a witness to the crash."

"The crash!" Kurt exclaimed excitedly. "So, there was a crash."

"Yes."

"And a cover up?" Lynn asked.

"Yes."

Burke spoke up, "Wait... if you were five years old in 1947, that would make you ninety-eight years old now. You don't look a day over forty. Have the folks from the future shared some rejuvenation drug with you, or what?"

Aloysius shook his head again and said, "In the distant future, from the point in time where the travelers originate, they have a great many medical technologies, including regimens that allow them to live substantially longer than our race does today, and that allow longevity without the deterioration of the body which is so inevitable with us. However, I have not been the beneficiary of the technology. No, I appear to be this age... forty-three, to be precise... because that is how long I have actually lived."

"You've time traveled," Cal concluded.

"I have."

"You have basically skipped over a total of fifty-five years."

"I have."

"But how... why... if you are one of us?" Lynn wondered. "Why did the travelers from the future allow you to do this?"

Resting his elbows on the table, Aloysius leaned forward and explained,

"After I witnessed the Roswell crash and the subsequent cover up, and as I grew older, I became obsessed with the subject. Despite what I had been told by the so-called authorities, I knew what I had seen. Or, at least, I thought I knew. As far as I was concerned, it was space aliens who had come to Earth.

"When I reached adulthood, I made it my life's mission to investigate UFOs. I eventually met with success and discovered incontrovertible proof of their existence. That is... proof I interpreted to validate the existence of flying saucers and space aliens."

"I'll bet that you were paid a visit before you could release your proof," said Lynn, knowingly.

"Exactly. The evening prior to the day when I was going to tell the world what I found, I was lifted."

"Lifted?" John started to correct him. "You mean abducted... like what happened to Gail?"

"Abduction is our term," Aloysius clarified. "They call it lifting."

"Did they threaten you if you talked?" Jackie asked conspiratorially.

Aloysius laughed. "No. They didn't threaten me. They didn't stick any needles into me. Nor did they perform any medical procedures."

"Then what *did* they do to stop you from telling everyone the truth?" Lynn persisted.

"You must understand," Aloysius continued patiently, "as long as I believed we were being invaded by aliens, I thought that it was important for the world to know. Once I found out that the visitors were from Earth... from our own future... that they meant us no harm and, in fact, were only coming back to our time for benign purposes, I saw no reason to tell anyone. After I spoke with them, I understood that telling the world about them would cause problems for both their time and for ours."

Kurt chuckled at his own revelation, "So, they recruited you to become their local PR guy, didn't they?"

Aloysius smiled at Kurt. "Yes. It was actually my idea. I was already fairly well known among the UFO community and had accumulated a substantial amount of credibility, so it seemed natural for me to run interference for them whenever their forays into our time received too much attention."

"Did you get a round trip to their time out of the deal?" Kurt asked with a smirk.

"I did. They gave me a glimpse of their world."

"So, whenever someone saw their ship," Kurt surmised, "you, as a prominent ufologist, would arrive on the scene and make sure that the focus remained on space aliens visiting Earth, instead of anyone coming to the correct conclusion."

"Precisely."

"Just like you did with us back then."

"That is correct."

"Aloysius, I have a question," said Mueller.

"Yes, Professor."

"Of all of the countless UFO sightings and reported abductions, a recurring theme among eyewitnesses has been the appearance…the look…of the aliens themselves. The short stature, the grey complexion, the large eyes have been remarkably common descriptions among almost all of the disparate reports. If the visitors are from our future, and the reports are accurate, how could this be? The amazingly consistent descriptions…the numerous sketches I've seen…don't resemble humans, to my eye."

Aloysius paused for moment before answering. "We haven't yet discussed the era from which they come."

"I was intending to ask," said Cal. "From how far in the future do they come?"

"They come," Aloysius commenced, "from a time distant enough for all of the various races on Earth to have become…homogenized."

He did not continue for a minute and no one spoke, waiting anxiously for the revelation which was obviously to come next.

"They are from the year 9859."

The implications of what Aloysius said struck all of them, bringing a long silence to the table.

Mueller was the first to speak. "So what you are saying is that the various artist renderings of the so-called aliens are accurate?"

"They are accurate."

Mueller continued, "And those beings are what the human race will evolve into 7,800 years from now?"

"Yes," Aloysius responded solemnly. "By that time, there will be no distinct races. All of mankind will have interbred, changed, mingled and evolved, reacting also, by the way, to our changing environment, to create the race that we, in this time, call the *Greys*."

Mueller, profoundly affected by this glimpse into a future he had long ago reconciled himself to never even being able to imagine, was impressed. "So, we make it that long? Unbelievable!"

Lynn cleared her throat, also clearly touched by this disclosure, and proceeded, "The Roswell aliens from the crash? That alleged autopsy video of the Grey...the video which circulated for a while on the Internet back at the beginning of the century...did that really happen and was it...*them?*"

"It was."

"I've never understood why the government would keep it a secret," John said. "Did they really cover it up because they had acquired some sophisticated technology from the crash that gave us a big advantage during the cold war?"

"No. They kept it a secret out of sheer embarrassment. The Greys simply made another trip after the autopsies and removed the bodies, as well as all of the other physical evidence, except for the few items which had been secured by the rancher and some others who were the first on the scene and had secreted scraps as souvenirs."

"So, all of their evidence disappeared. They either had to claim the incident wasn't real to begin with or explain how they could lose everything."

"Right. And all humans, even the military, despise admitting something like that. They chose the path of least resistance."

"I guess that was really a close call for them...the Greys, I mean. I understand what you told us about them sending expeditions back in time to learn our history," Kurtis said, "but aren't they playing Russian Roulette with their own reality on every trip they make?"

"They are. And that is why they only make trips now for very good reasons."

"Like what?" asked Lynn.

Before Aloysius could answer, John blurted, "Like making sure that Cal doesn't get diverted from building the time machine! It's his machine that is the basis for what eventually becomes their airborne craft...the so-called flying saucer, isn't it?"

"That is true, it is," Aloysius admitted. He hesitated for a moment, apparently gathering his thoughts, before he said, "But that wasn't the reason the Greys intervened."

John was stunned. "I...I don't understand. It seems like that would be pivotal to them."

Aloysius shrugged. "You have to keep in mind the number of years between now and their time. A brief delay in the invention of the time machine was irrelevant to them."

"A brief delay?" asked Cal.

Aloysius turned to face Cal and told him, "In that far distant future of 9859, you no longer have the fame that you enjoy today."

"Shucks!" Cal joked.

"However, your life and times were of great interest to historical scholars, particularly your memoirs, which you wrote...are to write...in the latter years of your life."

The lightheartedness showing in Cal's face disappeared as he visualized his life from the perspective of a scholar 7,800 years in the future.

"In those memoirs," Aloysius continued, his voice subdued, "you tell of John's suicide and share, in your notes and recollections from the time, your frustration at having not yet perfected the machine. Your failure to do so...your inability to offer John the opportunity to go back to 2010 and change his past...resulted in his death."

John and Lynn silently looked at each other, the image of this other life, thankfully averted, disturbing them.

Cal, feeling his own emotions as they were churned by this image of an alternate reality, murmured a soft, "My God!"

"All of my memories now," he related, "are comprised of the details of a life that includes the visit from *Jack* in 2010. I know what supposedly happened in that alternate version of his life, because he told me about it back then, but I don't *remember* it because it never happened *to me*. Now you're telling me that there was actually a third version...a version that was the original story. The version which survived intact until the time of the Greys?"

"There was that version."

"I do remember both...or I should say...two of the scenarios," John said. "I remember this one, where we are all here...now. I also remember the other, including trying to kill myself, and Cal sending me back to 2010.

"Aloysius, you mentioned my successful suicide, but you didn't say anything about the first attempt, which prompted Cal to send me back."

A slight curl of a half-grin showed on the corner of Aloysius's mouth as he informed John, "In the history of the Greys, there was no failed attempt."

Upon hearing this, John's mind began to spin, struggling to absorb the importance of this fact. After a moment, he quietly said, "No attempt?"

"That's correct."

"So that means...I'll be damned!"

"What?" asked Lynn, racing to catch up with John's thoughts.

John looked at Aloysius and, with confidence, stated, "The interventions from the Greys didn't begin back in 2010, did they?"

Aloysius shook his head, indicating that John was on the right track.

"They began now! Just a couple of months ago. At the time of my suicide?"

Aloysius nodded, his half-grin spreading to completeness. "Somewhat before that, but, yes."

"You're losing me, guys!" Kurt leaned forward.

Shaking his head in wonderment, John continued, "Aloysius, correct me if I get it wrong, but I think the Greys intervened, somehow, at the point when I took my life, changing it from a suicide to an attempted suicide."

"They did."

"How did they do that?" Burke asked.

Aloysius was about to answer when John interrupted him, excitedly exclaiming, "It must have been the psychiatrist!"

"Exactly," Aloysius confirmed.

"What psychiatrist?" Jackie asked.

John turned from Aloysius to face the rest of the group as he explained, "In that previous life, the one with Gail, I received a call out of the blue from a woman who claimed she was Gail's psychiatrist. She was the one who told me all of the horrible details she had learned in her sessions with Gail... all of the things I told you about before... all of the things which pushed me to the point of suicide."

John glanced at Aloysius for confirmation and could tell by the expression on his face that he was on point, so he continued. "Coincidentally, after telling me all of these atrocious things, she then told me that she was concerned I wouldn't be able to sleep and gave me some sleeping pills."

"Unbelievable," Ben commented. "You've told me this before, John, because Jack had related it to you. Now, from this perspective, it all seems fishy as hell. No psychiatrist would break the patient's confidence to the patient's husband. If she had reason to believe that Gail was planning to commit a crime, she would go to the police, not you."

"Right," John agreed.

"And any psychiatrist worth her salt wouldn't lay all of those upsetting revelations on you, then hand you a full bottle of sleeping pills, and tell you to go home and get some rest."

"No kidding," Lynn added. "Under those circumstances, they are required to limit sleeping aids to less-than-lethal quantities... only enough to last the patient two or three days... for exactly that reason."

John turned to Aloysius. "She wasn't Gail's psychiatrist, was she?"

"No. She had never met her."

John stared at Aloysius in amazement. "This was all planned out by the Greys."

"Aloysius," Burke requested, "maybe you can walk us all through it, step by step."

"It was really fairly simple. *I* am not the only current-day...."

"Agent?" offered John.

Aloysius smiled and said, "That's a bit melodramatic, but I suppose it applies. I am not the only one in this time who works with the Greys. The woman who talked to you, John...in the previous version of your reality...she was another. Her task was to approach you, before you discovered the facts through other means, and disclose to you all of the things Gail had done. In the original version, which was the history of the Greys according to Cal's memoirs, you had a confrontation with Gail and she told you everything. In a blind rage, you left and drove your car off of a cliff on Mount Lemmon. It was a fatal crash."

Lynn unconsciously put her hand on John's, gripping it tightly.

"The Greys decided to rewrite their history. They enlisted the aid of the woman who then called you several days before the confrontation with Gail. She told you everything and gave you the pills which you believed would be sufficient to use for suicide. They were actually a medication created by the Greys to simulate an overdose of sleeping pills, but insure that you would not die."

"But you said that Cal had not invented the time machine by that point in time – in their history." John pointed out.

"That was true. Our tampering actually extended several months prior to your staged suicide. It was a simple matter to have one of Cal's assistants provide him with the right suggestions that would lead him to the breakthrough which, as I said before, was to inevitably occur within a short time, anyway."

"Aubrey?" Cal suspected.

Aloysius affirmed.

"Who's Aubrey?" Lynn asked.

"Aubrey was the assistant who was injured by one of my mistakes, the injury that caused me to make the brief trip back to undo the mistake and prevent her injury. And I remember, she did come to me one day with a whole list of avenues she thought we needed to pursue. The breakthrough was one of them."

"And I'll bet," surmised John, "that Aubrey was the same person who also played the psychiatrist, wasn't she?"

"She was," Aloysius acknowledged.

Kurt, who had been quietly assimilating the story, broke his silence, "I don't understand one thing."

"Only one thing?" said Jackie, showing exasperation. "You're doing better than I am."

"What's that?" Aloysius asked Kurt.

"If Cal had invented the time machine, in both versions of the Greys' history, at that point – then why was the trip back to 2010 needed? I mean, that seems like a fairly major tampering with the past for something that was going to occur anyway. Was it to save John's life? And if so, why?"

Aloysius, his elbows resting on the table, leaned forward toward Kurt and said, "You're right. It was a major tampering... a substantial risk for their future. However, it wasn't done to facilitate the time machine. Nor was it done, as you just suggested, to save John's life." Aloysius smiled and added, "Although, from a personal perspective, that was certainly a positive."

"Then what was it?"

Aloysius stared directly into Kurt's eyes. "It was to save *your* life."

Sᴜɴ - 4:77ᴘ.ɴ.

Stunned, Kurt was unable to speak for a moment, his mind wrestling with the implications of Aloysius's answer.

"Why me?" he was finally able to ask, dumbfounded. "How could I possibly be so important to the Greys for them to risk what they risked?"

"To answer that," Aloysius began, "some additional historical perspective is needed. As I told you, this planet was populated by various races from different planets. Through Darwinian selection, interbreeding and deliberate genetic engineering by the Anunnaki, a single life form eventually emerged – the human race.

"As you know, the human race was...is, at this time...comprised of several sub-races, the remaining distinctions a holdover from the prototypal immigrants to Earth. These distinctions offered a genetic variability which has provided and continues to provide a beneficial resistance to attack by organisms, such as viruses and bacteria.

"As evolution continues to march forward in the numerous millennia ahead, these genetic distinctions fade and eventually disappear. And with the disappearance of variability, humans, as a group, also lose the ability to survive the myriad of mutations which are yet in store for them and their tenacious microscopic foes.

"What results, at some point in the distant future, is a vulnerability that endangers the continuation of mankind on Earth. At first, the Greys fought this battle by simply returning to a time when there were living humans who carried the specific resistance that they themselves lacked. By lifting several subjects and testing them for this resistance or immunity, they were able to process it into an inoculation for their population."

"All of the abduction stories by people who swore they were taken up and experimented upon were true!" Lynn concluded, a tone of vindication in her voice.

"They were," Aloysius agreed. "They were used as breeders for the antibodies the Greys so desperately needed. Because of the proliferation of stories of these abductions, the Greys changed their methodology and began to utilize *locals*, or agents, as you called us a moment ago. The locals infiltrated medical establishments and provided what the Greys needed, either blood or tissue samples, which eliminated the need for the trauma and ordeal of abductions."

"If that was working for them," Cal began, "then why did they need Kurt to live?"

Aloysius shook his head in dismay as he recalled the descriptions he received from his friends in the distant future. "The war between organisms never ceases. It escalates. As each new technique is brought to bear, pushing the enemy back, the enemy regroups, alters its approach, and attacks again. Thus, the errant organism of 9859 – no longer a bacteria, as we would know it, and no longer a virus either, but rather a whole new life form – mutated to the point where it became so effective, so deadly, so efficient that it was wiping out the entire race, and doing it so rapidly that simple inoculations produced from cultivated blood samples of the past were not effective."

As the group around the table listened to Aloysius's solemn words, they fell completely silent, each visualizing the demise of an entire race of people.

When they were finally able to speak, John was the first to voice a question, "What happened to them?"

"They all died…the entire race," Aloysius answered in a muted voice.

"Then who intervened? Who saved my life and came up with this plan?"

"A lone, surviving expedition. The time machine built by Cal can only accommodate one passenger…one traveler…at a time. One of the improvements in the design over the years was to make it a massive craft, capable of carrying an entire contingent of scientists. The other modification, obviously, was to enable the machine to fly. When the first outbreak of this deadly new disease initially appeared, a team was hastily assembled and sent off to the past…to our time…to find a person who carried resistance to the disease. It was a long and frustrating journey. There were many times when they believed that they would not find a suitable donor, that they would fail.

"After months of searching, the quest spanning nearly a millennium of different stops on the route, they finally found what they needed, obtained by a local in Tucson from the year 2010. Their excitement, as it was described to me, was boundless as they took the small quantity of tissue and cultured it in their on-board lab. The culture grew and they were able to produce millions of doses."

"They could make millions of doses while on their ship?" Cal found that hard to believe.

"Yes. The craft itself is quite large and the process, with 7,800 years of technology behind it, is automated to a level that is astounding by our standards.

"Unfortunately, when they returned to their time to provide the inoculations, they found that everyone was already dead."

"Everyone?" Lynn asked, astounded.

"Yes. So virulent was this disease that every person on Earth was dead. Fortunately, they had followed the standard protocols for a return and had remained on the craft while their sensors determined this horrible fact. Since they did not open the hatch, they were not infected and survived. They quickly departed, traveling only a short time back, to moments after their original departure.

"Everyone was still alive at that point, and the team delivered the doses. Someone on board was paranoid enough to maintain the integrity of the seal on the craft, basically instituting a reverse quarantine for themselves as they waited to see if the treatment would work."

Aloysius paused and stared into the distance, his eyes unfocused, his expression blank. After a time, he resumed his narrative, "The inoculations slowed the disease. In fact, a few survived, demonstrating to the Greys that they were on the right track with the donor they had found. But less than ten percent of the population lived through the ravages of the infection.

"The scientific contingent, still on board the craft and with the dosages depleted, contemplated their next move. The plan that emerged came about in a most serendipitous fashion. One of the junior scientists on the ship was an ancient history buff... one could even say a fanatic. That ancient history, by the way, was our time and he was obsessed with this era, especially any facts about you, Cal. Since you were the inventor of the first time machine, you were something of a hero to this young man.

"He happened to recall something that would normally be a worthless piece of trivia. He remembered that the subject who was finally found... the one person on Earth, at least as far as they could determine, who carried the resistance…had been an acquaintance of yours, and the former best friend of your best friend. He also knew that their donor was to die from a fatal tumor without ever producing offspring."

"Kurt was the subject, the person with the resistance?" Cal asked.

"Yes, it was Kurt. When the young scientist shared this with the team, they couldn't help but notice the synchronicity…the irony…of these two facts. The one carrier of the genetic hope for their race was closely associated with the one man who could not only transport him forward in time but would also be the person who would develop the cure for his tumor, allowing him to live and procreate."

"Couldn't they have just gone back to 2010 and lifted him, as you put it, to some future date where the procedure to cure his tumor already existed?"

"Could they have, Cal? Certainly. They had the means to do so, but there were two factors at play. First of all, from the very first day of their training to become time travelers, they all had drummed into them that it was absolutely essential to minimize their impact on the past. Secondly, these Greys are a kind and a gentle people. They understand how traumatic an event it is to be lifted. From past experiences they know that this one event has had a profoundly negative effect on the people who have gone through it, ruining their lives and stigmatizing them within society.

"They eventually decided, after nearly endless discussions, that if they were to preemptively go back to 2010 and snatch up Kurt, plopping him into some future time far enough forward to benefit from the medical advances needed to cure him, but not so far forward as to make him an outsider…an oddity…there was a better than even chance he would not assimilate into that future society. And if he didn't assimilate, he would not find a wife. He would not have offspring. He would not send forward, into the future, his gift to mankind…his genetic code…which was so desperately needed."

"So they decided," John concluded, understanding their dilemma, "that if they were going to be able to pull off this trick…the series of changes we have all just lived through…Kurt would feel comfortable. He would not only fit in and not be traumatized, but the trip itself would have been his idea."

"And," Aloysius added, "he would have all of you as a support group. He wouldn't be *a stranger in a strange land*."

"Absolutely amazing," John responded, awestruck at the complexity of what Aloysius described.

"Hey," Kurt said, "they don't call me…."

"I know! I know," interrupted John before Kurt could finish his famous line. "This time, my friend, I would say that is well deserved. You really are The Amazing Kurt!"

Feigning hurt, Kurt asked, "You mean I haven't deserved it in the past?"

John chuckled, followed by the others around the table.

The banter was enough to release some of the tension which had developed during Aloysius's explanation. Several conversations started at once, splintering the group into pairs. The common thread of all of the chatter was the revelation about the distant future.

Finally, the obvious question was spoken by Lynn, "Did it work, Aloysius? Do you know whether this change has affected the future as they hoped it would?"

Aloysius looked chagrined as he answered her, "I don't know yet. They haven't come back here yet to tell me."

"Why not? It seems like they would know by now. The moment that Kurt arrived here safely, wouldn't they have gone back to their own time and checked?"

"It's not that simple. You see, their past – the history that led their race to extinction – was, for lack of a better term, the *established* past."

"*Burned in,*" offered Cal.

"Essentially, yes. You also have to remember that we are talking about an incredibly lengthy span of time. Even the smallest change to this established past during our era is magnified a million-fold."

"There's that Butterfly Effect again," John sighed.

"So what *are* they doing right now? Well, right now being 7,800 years in the future," Lynn persisted.

Aloysius took a deep breath and began, "This is a little hard to describe. And, remember, I've never experienced it myself. I've only had it explained to me. Imagine sitting in that time-traveling craft in the year 9859, floating in the sky above the Earth and just watching."

"Watching what?"

"Watching to see what happens. As long as the team remains on the craft, they are impervious to the effects of the past. They are, essentially, in a bubble, watching everything around them.

"Now, imagine that there is something happening in the past – something they have planned, scripted and engineered – that is different from the established past."

"The past where their whole race eventually wound up dead?" Lynn tried to keep it straight in her mind.

"Right. So the team went back in time and implemented the plan – a plan deliberately intended to cause a change to your present time, an overt act which would normally be avoided at all costs."

"I've got that," Lynn said. "Wouldn't the change have had its effect by the time they got back to their own time?"

"Maybe, or maybe not," answered Aloysius cryptically. Seeing the slight frustration beginning to show on her face, he quickly resumed, "You see, everything that has happened since Kurt stepped out of the machine could also, somehow, affect *their* outcome. This is a simplistic example, but he could have tripped as he stepped out of the hatch and hit his head, giving him a concussion and causing his death. Then he would never get married or have children, and they would have gained nothing."

"But he made it…safely…he's here now, and talking with us," Lynn maintained.

"Yes," John added, beginning to understand Aloysius's point, "but he still hasn't found that wife and had those kids yet. Anything might happen which could prevent that from occurring, right?"

Aloysius nodded.

"I do understand that," Lynn said. "But until something actually happens to change things, isn't there always a future…some future?"

Aloysius smiled. "You're right, of course. Kurt didn't trip and fall as he exited the machine. He's made it out here to this table and we are talking. But everything we've discussed in the past several minutes hadn't yet been said, and thereby plugged into their future, until just this moment. And everything we will say…everything we will do from this moment forward… will cause subtle changes because it didn't happen in their established history. The result of that truth is bewildering from their perspective because, as they sit in the craft above the Earth and watch, the long-term effects of every move we make and every word we choose will have a ripple effect, or Butterfly Effect, if you prefer. So they are perched within their impervious platform, and they are watching an ever-changing cascade of new realities flash before them down below."

"That's how it works?" Cal was astonished. "That's the result of all of their efforts? To watch some kaleidoscopic light show of realities flash by? Why would they do what they did? What would be the point, if their reality has become that tenuous for them?"

Aloysius smiled again and said, "Because it is better than what they left behind, which was a near total destruction of their race. And," he added before anyone could interrupt, "it *will* settle down. As all of you, especially Kurt, become more entrenched into this reality, the cascade of possibilities they witness will become lessened until it stabilizes into a new stasis."

"It would be like watching the three windows on a slot machine, waiting for the jackpot to appear," suggested John.

"Yes," Aloysius stated, "an excellent comparison."

"Then they will be able to get off the ship?" Jackie asked.

"Yes...but cautiously. They will keep a contingent of staff on board at all times, just in case. It will be the responsibility of those who remain on the ship to monitor what, for them, has become a reality in flux."

"That sounds horrible!" gasped Jackie, obviously shaken by this vision of the Greys' future.

Aloysius attempted to calm her. "I've described a worst case scenario. As we talk, as each detail and level of understanding falls into place with regard to Kurt, the array of possibilities for them may diminish."

"What do you mean?" Kurt asked.

"Kurt, you now know everything I have told you thus far. Unless you are a completely selfish and heartless person, you will not consider a life without a wife and children."

"That's true."

"Which would make one of the 'cherries' stop in the first window," John said.

Aloysius continued, "You will also take extra care to make certain that the wife you pick is...."

"Good breeding stock," Kurt joked.

"Crudely put, but yes. You will make sure that you don't marry a woman who cannot have children. And if some mishap were to befall your future wife that would render her incapable of childbirth, you would...."

"Dump her and find another," Kurt again supplied, grinning.

"KURT!" Jackie snapped

"I'm just joking!" he responded defensively.

"Additionally, you will not be tempted to limit your offspring to only one or two children."

"Nope. I'll have a real brood. Heck, since the whole future is counting on me, I might even try polygamy."

Jackie poked Kurt in the ribs, glaring at him.

"I doubt that would be necessary," said Aloysius, amused by the display across the table.

"But it couldn't hurt, right?" Kurt prodded, egging Jackie on.

Aloysius's grin broadened as he watched Jackie turn a brighter shade of red.

"And, also, you will do your best to make sure that all of your children do not choose a life of celibacy. So, as I said, with every moment that passes, we can substantially reduce the possible outcomes for our friends in the future."

"The second cherry!" John exclaimed.

"Hey, I just thought of something!" Kurt smiled.

"I can't wait to hear this," Jackie interjected sarcastically.

Kurt winked at her and continued, "Since their entire existence depends on me, I bet they are going to be watching over me for the rest of my life like…guardian angels. Even though they have returned to 9859 to observe the parade of realities, that doesn't mean they aren't going to come back here to, you know, tweak things once in a while…make sure I'm okay."

"You're right," Aloysius agreed. "You could say they have a vested interest in your well-being."

"Only until you've served your…purpose," Jackie pointed out with more than a little glee, "and then they'll dump you like an old leftover."

Kurt turned and looked at her with an expression of mock injury.

"Seriously, for a second please," John interrupted, "wouldn't it be a good idea for Kurt to become a sperm donor?"

Before his daughter or anyone else could say anything, John raised his hand and went on, "Really, think about it. Sure, he can get married and have a load of kids, but wouldn't it be better, for the dissemination of his genetics, to cast those seeds a little broader?"

Aloysius shrugged. "Yes, that would obviously help, but you all need to remember one thing. None of what we've discussed can be discussed with anyone else, with the possible exception of Kurt's future wife."

"Why is that?" Burke probed. "Wouldn't it make a lot of sense to kind of make a public project out of saving the Greys? I mean, Kurt could donate a bunch of his…'stuff.' There could be a PR campaign, giving everyone a chance to save the future and asking for volunteers. That could really multiply the chances of success."

John, expecting another humorous comment from his old friend, waited before responding. But he noticed that Kurt was listening intently, so he said, "I don't think that would be a good idea. Remember, their future…the future the Greys want to recapture prior to the disease…was built upon everyone doing what they normally did before. The only exception can be the introduction of Kurt. And that probably needs to be kept as low-profile as possible because he wasn't around the last time. Ideally, Kurt, you should probably find that wife and

304 -- JOHN DAVID KRYGELSKI

then go live like a hermit, interacting with no one from the outside and cranking out as many kids as you and she can."

John was still watching Kurt as he spoke. Instead of the expected reaction, Kurt, his voice absent of the normal boisterousness, stated, "I already thought about that. The truth is…I wasn't here, in anyone's life, before. I just now realized that every time I go out in public, I'm risking changing things…even if they appear to be small things.

"If I happen to be cruising down the street…. You still have streets and cars in 2040, don't you?"

Cal nodded.

"I happen to be driving down the street and just by being there, I cause someone to catch a red light instead of a green. And then, ten blocks later, after I'm long gone, he gets creamed by another driver – and would have missed that accident if I hadn't existed. Then, because of me, that man won't go on to have the life he would have had. Maybe he's a young man who would have gone on to have three kids. And those three kids would have had more, and so on. So, by the time the world gets all the way to 9859, I'd actually be responsible for about a million people not being there."

The assemblage again fell silent, dwelling on the picture Kurt had painted for them.

At last Aloysius spoke, "You are, unfortunately, correct. Our efforts may have saved your life, but your new life cannot be a conspicuous one. The long-term ramifications are far too great."

Kurt reflected on this, his eyes focusing on the distant Rincon Mountains. No one cared to intrude on his solitude.

Finally, taking a deep breath and letting it out through pursed lips, he concluded, "That's a fair deal to me."

He turned to Aloysius and said, "And, let's be honest – if the Greys were a more pragmatic bunch, they would have whisked me off somewhere, kept me to themselves, away from the world completely, while turning me into a sperm factory. Then they could go back to their old ways and lift unsuspecting females every night, impregnating them with good old Kurt's 'stuff,' as Burke here put it. So, asking me to keep my head down, and give up my dreams of becoming a movie star, is all right with me."

John watched Kurt throughout his comments, unable to think of anything to say. Looking down, he stared at the texture of the concrete bench for a time. Quickly bored with that, he refocused his eyes to examine his own fingers, noticing that he still had the soil under his nails from the episode with Gail in the courthouse plaza, and was briefly struck with the surreal nature of dirt from thirty years ago still jammed there. His gaze then moved to the surface of his arms, which rested upon the table, studying the pigment spots and imperfections, when he suddenly noticed the hairs dancing and swirling, before standing erect.

It took a moment for the familiarity of this to sink in. He muttered to himself, "The third cherry...*jackpot*!"

As he said this, Jackie gasped loudly, quickly reaching over to seize his hand.

He turned to Aloysius, who was staring skyward with a look of elation on his face, and said, "It's them, isn't it?"

Aloysius, without looking away, answered, "Yes. It is."

Sun - 5:11p.m.

John stood up from the bench, with Lynn following and clutching his arm tightly. The others also rose and moved from under the umbrella of the branches that obstructed their view, Cal almost breaking into a run to get a better look.

Ben, who had not witnessed the phenomenon many years before, breathed out, "Well, I'll be...."

Jackie and Kurtis stood in a tight cluster around Kurt, who was looking skyward with a broad smile on his face. Mueller, recklessly maneuvering his wheelchair, was the last to move into the open area, a look of childlike excitement on his face as he realized what was happening. John noticed that Aloysius had separated from the group and stood several yards away, waiting patiently.

John remembered that he had never gotten a good look at the saucer that day in the alley behind the storage room, when he had almost been lifted. The exterior of the craft was metallic. To him it appeared to be very similar to the silver coating on Cal's machine, but even more highly polished and reflective, rendering it mirror-like. As it hovered above them, he noticed that it was circular and much larger than a football field, as had been hinted at that night in the plaza.

The convex bottom of the machine reflected and distorted the grounds and landscaping around them. John was able to locate the compressed image of his group on its surface.

As he stared, he saw a pinpoint of light suddenly originate from the bottom of the craft, off-center and directly above where Aloysius stood. The diameter of the shaft of light grew, again as if an aperture was slowly opening, until the beam was at least ten feet in diameter. Squinting from the brightness, which far overpowered the intensity of the afternoon sunlight, John was barely able to distinguish a descending figure seemingly captured within the column of light. He followed the form's progress downward, until it came to rest at a point next to where Aloysius stood.

The light abruptly winked out, and there stood a diminutive figure, wearing a bright yellow cloak, its specific features too distant to discern.

John stood rooted to his spot, as did all of the others. Making a conscious attempt to move, he found that he could not and began to feel a vague sense of anxiety. Before the feeling was able to escalate into panic, he noticed the figure from the craft make a small hand gesture, and instantly felt himself released from his immobility.

Without hesitation, John took a step forward to join Aloysius and the stranger. His movement signaled the others and they all slowly began to walk, their pace quickening with each step. By the time they reached Aloysius, they were nearly at a trot, except for Mueller who scooted forward in his wheelchair, and Ben, hobbled by his cane.

As John approached the stranger, he immediately recognized the face and shape of the head from the countless artist's renderings of the Greys...the skull broad at the top, tapering toward the bottom to form an almost petite jaw line, the large brown eyes, which John found to be far more expressive than any picture had ever captured.

What first struck him was the essence of the being. Throughout his life, as he looked at the sketches of the Greys, there was, either implied by the artist or inferred by John, always a sense of menace in their countenance. Now, as he stood face to face with this being, he saw nothing but kindness and a benign ambiance that, it seemed, could be construed as affection or even gratitude for him, his friends and his family.

As he stared into the mystifying eyes of the Grey, John heard Aloysius say, "This is my friend John. John...this is Allen."

John wasn't sure what he expected, but the utter normalcy of the introduction caused him to automatically extend his right hand. The Grey, Allen, did the same, and John felt the hand of the stranger grip his in greeting. Allen's hand was slight in size, compared to John's, yet the fingers were substantially longer, probably one-third greater in length. The grip was firm and the hand was warm; the texture of the grey skin was familiar.

Allen ended the handshake and Aloysius next introduced him to Lynn, who was still at John's side and still clutching his arm. She hesitated only for a moment before she released her grip on John's arm and took Allen's hand, gracing the visitor with a sincere smile. Aloysius continued around the circle, introducing Allen to each of the party, and John watched, fascinated by the reaction of each person to this phenomenal event. John observed that the visitor hesitated as he shook Cal's hand.

Lynn turned so that her lips were close to John's ear and whispered, "What a cool vibe!"

"That's for sure," John agreed, noticing that Allen's head turned at her anachronistic comment, his mouth forming a smile.

After the introductions were complete, the group gathered on the grass around Aloysius and his guest. Allen turned to look at all of them once more, his gaze lingering on each person's eyes. Then he began to speak. John realized, no doubt stoked by the numerous movie depictions he had seen, that he had expected the visitor's voice to be higher pitched. Instead, it was a full baritone, soothing and melodious. "Thank you all for greeting me so graciously. Our reception in the past has not always been so pleasant."

Another of John's preconceived notions was wiped away as he listened to Allen speak in flawless English with no trace of any accent or affectation.

"Is English you natural language?" Mueller inquired, a respectful tone to his voice. "You speak it beautifully."

"Thank you," Allen responded, his expressive eyes displaying pleasure at receiving the compliment. "No, as time passes, not only is there an inevitable mingling of genetics, there also occurs a blurring of the distinctions between languages. Our native tongue is an amalgam of all of the variations on your present day speech. My proficiency in English, and many of the other indigenous languages of this day, was part of my training to be on this team of travelers."

"I assume from your presence," Kurt speculated, "that things have...uh...settled down 7,800 years from now."

Allen turned to face Kurt directly. "They have, indeed. And we, as a race, have a debt of gratitude to you."

Kurt broke into a broad smile, followed by a sudden mischievous expression. "Hey, I just focused on something. You know my whole life, don't you...the woman I'll marry, how many kids I'll have, everything?"

Allen nodded and said nothing.

"Aren't you going to tell me? That sure would make things easier."

Smiling, Allen explained, "I am guided by what is now my new past. Because of the profound effect of your contributions to our very existence, your life is well chronicled, down to the smallest details. Those details include this meeting and what I do, or do not, say to you. I have studied the minutia of this meeting for quite some time before coming here."

"Like an actor studying his lines," John assumed.

"Precisely," Allen answered, glancing at John.

Intrigued, Cal asked, "I'm curious. In your history of this meeting, did John make the 'actor' comment at that point in the conversation?"

Allen gracefully inclined his head and said, "As did you ask that question."

John studied Cal's face as he assimilated this.

"Absolutely fascinating!" Cal remarked.

"What about telling me my future?" Kurt interrupted. "Can you?"

Allen shook his head. "No. I'm afraid not. It was not in my past to do so."

"It just seems like it would make it so much simpler if you did," Kurt persisted. "That would save me all the trouble of figuring it out on my own."

"It is not up to us to decide. We have found a past that most closely restores our race and our present time as it was before the disease. And this discussion, down to the smallest detail, is a part of that past. I am here... to use the actor analogy... to play my part."

All of the group fell silent for a moment, their minds grappling with the concept Allen conveyed.

"It's almost like we don't have free will," John said, "if we are all playing out these parts, down to every word that we say."

The comforting smile returned to Allen's face as he responded. "I understand how distressing that concept is for you. It is for us, as well. You see, human nature changes very little in the next 7,800 years. However, you must remember, what I have told you has nothing to do with free will. Everything that you have done up until this moment, in this *iteration*, has been a result of your free will. It only appears that all is written, because of my presence and the perspective I provide. Once that perspective is removed, the illusion will depart with me."

The gathering fell silent once more, as they struggled to grasp the import of Allen's words.

Burke, who had been quiet since the arrival of the visitor, changed the subject by asking, "What happened to Gail Schilling?"

"That is a good question." Ben said. "What did you do with her? Is she in jail?"

Moving his gaze to the two former policemen, Allen stated, "We have no jails."

Seeing the quizzical look on their faces, he quickly explained. "If the two of you were to visit my time, you would not find any agencies similar to your police department or Federal Bureau of Investigation. Our race has accomplished wonders in terms of eradicating the criminal urge from the human spirit. Therefore, we have no institutional means of incarceration.

"As a result, Ms. Schilling became something of an oddity to be studied for historical purposes. The behavioral scientists are fascinated with this first-hand glimpse at the unrelenting manipulation and the seemingly boundless desire to do evil…a personality not seen in countless generations. Despite her obvious shortcomings, some of my people have actually befriended her."

"So, she's like a rat in a lab," Burke said with some glee, still vividly recalling his shoot-out with her.

Allen smiled sympathetically. "In a sense, yes."

"That works for me," Ben grinned, as his mind created a satisfying vision of her plight.

"I have a question," Mueller said.

Allen turned and acknowledged him.

"Undoubtedly, 7,800 years is a long time for most things. But considering how little mankind has changed…evolved…over the previous similar span of years, it is hard to believe that we could become the beings who resemble you by then. Evolution and genetics have never worked that rapidly."

"An excellent question, Professor. The variable which was not present for the preceding eras was mankind's ability to manipulate the very structure of our genetic make up."

"We tinker with what we are?" Mueller asked, amazement in his voice.

"Of course you do," replied Allen, his tone verging on the dismissive. "As you know, it has already begun, albeit on a small scale. Motivated by a desire to extend life, avoid diseases, enhance intelligence, or…," Allen paused for a moment and John was certain that he detected a trace of distaste for what he was about to say next, "respond to political or social pressures, the scientists who make genetics their field will not be able to resist the urge to *improve* our race."

"It doesn't sound like you think all of the changes are improvements," John suspected.

Allen only shrugged and said nothing. Ever since the revelation that the visitor was acting out his lines, John had begun to study him closely, watching for subtle signs. During this pause, he was not disappointed as he saw Allen's eyes turn to look at Lynn, obviously expecting what was to be the next comment or question.

Before John could follow his gaze, Lynn said, "When you were talking about free will a moment ago, you mentioned 'in this iteration.' Are you saying that we, all of us in this group, have been through some variation of the past thirty years more than one time?"

Allen's hesitation was for only a moment, before he began, "When we, the crew of my ship, first saw the laying to waste which had befallen our people, our first reaction was that of devastation. I cannot begin to describe the impact it had on us. Then we realized that the restoration of our civilization rested solely upon our own shoulders.

"After much debate on how we could accomplish our goal, with many ideas proposed and rejected, it was decided that my suggestion to *rescue* Mr. Wallace was our best option."

"It was you who thought of it?" Cal asked.

"It was. Regrettably, the plan created a schism within our ranks. It was felt by some to be so invasive…to have such a profound impact upon your time…that we were playing God. That if we were to implement it, we would be willfully affecting the lives of untold numbers of people in the years between now and our time, only so we could selfishly restore our own race. Those same people believed that perhaps it was our destiny…the fate of our civilization…to die out. The demise of our race, after all, was the result of our own past mistakes and not something which should be undone, especially if the undoing required such a cavalier tampering with your time."

"Obviously, your side won the argument," Lynn concluded.

"For which I am grateful," Kurt added.

Allen smiled at Kurt and continued, "Yes, after many intense discussions, our side prevailed. It was then that the plan was written and implemented. Unfortunately, due to the almost infinite variables at every step, it did not succeed and the world's future followed a much different path. We returned to the first step and began again, also without success.

"In one version, John was not lifted in the alley and he was allowed to travel back in time to talk to Cal. In another, we did not set fire to the storage room just as Kurt departed. There were other renditions, as well, each achieving an unsatisfactory result.

"It is difficult to describe the experience, watching variation after variation of our future unfold before us – many of the versions wildly different than the one before, even though the changes we had made in the past were minor. This pattern continued until the past that you all recall was effectuated. The pieces appear to have fallen into place in such a way that, when we returned to our own time, our people…our civilization…was remarkably restored, without, of course, the presence of the fatal disease."

John, sensing a weariness in the visitor's voice, asked the question, "In what has been *real time* for your team on the ship, how long have you been working on this? How much time has passed for you since the discovery of the disease?"

Allen turned to face John; the perceived weariness was now evident, as Allen answered, "Three years."

"What?" Cal cried out. "How could that be? In the craft, you can bounce around time like a ping-pong ball, jumping between 2010 and 2040 and then to 9859 at will, to check the results. How could you possibly have spent three years doing this?"

"Because each time we failed, it was necessary to devise a new scenario. Each time, this took much discussion and planning. Each time, the new plan was dissected and edited by many, prior to its implementation."

"So, even as advanced as you are," said Kurt, "you still have to deal with bureaucratic red tape?"

"I'm afraid," replied Allen with more than a little chagrin, "that mentality is fundamental to human nature."

"The obvious question is," Lynn began, trying to get back to her point, "how many times have we all been through this until we finally got it right?"

The visitor did not answer her immediately. He took a moment to make eye contact with everyone in the circle. When he spoke, his voice was subdued. "Forty-seven."

"What?" The almost-shouted question came from Ben. "We have lived out the past thirty years a total of forty-seven times until you got your future exactly the way you wanted it?" His outrage at the concept was palpable.

Allen gazed at Ben sympathetically. "I'm afraid so."

"I know I can't remember any of those other attempts, but that just doesn't seem right!"

"Your sentiments," Allen replied to Ben, "are shared by those who originally opposed the concept of tampering with your time. And they have found an ally in those whom we restored."

"What do you mean?" Cal asked.

"When we viewed the success of this iteration and found that our people had been restored, so to speak, we were quite happy to reconnect with them. Once they discovered what we had done…the tampering, the numerous iterations, the drastic rewriting of history…they agreed with the minority of our expedition. They forbade us from any more tampering with the past, even if it meant the extinction of our race. We are only here today to fulfill our role in our history."

His sentiment of disapproval apparent in his voice, Allen continued, "They have gone so far as not to allow us to keep a contingent on the craft when we return from this trip. There will be no fail-safe, no team who will remain impervious to any changes that may yet occur – changes that could result in the abrupt disappearance of our entire species."

Before anyone could respond, Allen resumed, "If it is any consolation, Detective Hart, in the original version, without the benefit of your injury at the courthouse to force the police department to assign you to a desk, you were fatally injured in a shoot-out in 2010."

He turned to Lynn, "And Mrs Augur, you already know what your life was to be like without the changes. As do you, Mr. Augur."

John and Lynn glanced at each other and then looked back at Allen.

"And your children would not be standing with us today."

Kurtis started to fidget slightly, clearly uncomfortable with the thought of how capricious his very existence suddenly felt to him.

Allen's eyes then swept over the group. "With the obvious exception of Mr. Wallace, who, without our intervention, passed away in 2010, none of the rest of your original futures have changed as dramatically. I can tell you that all of you are, at least, as well-off in this outcome, if not better."

"I understand that, I really do. And, believe me, I am very happy with my life as it is today, but what about the others?" Lynn wondered.

"The others?" Allen asked.

"Yes, the millions or even billions of people on Earth who have been affected by this. Haven't there been other changes that touched all of their lives?"

"We do not have the ability to know the details of every person's life on Earth and how it has been altered. I can say that time and/or life, as you surely noticed back in 2010, has a certain inertia to it…a resistance to change. Once we were able to manipulate the microcosm of events, as they related to all of you, to provide our desired outcome, it was remarkable how so much of the rest of the world's progress reverted into its former…original…pattern. That should not have surprised us. How else could the eventual result, 7,800 years thence, be so similar to the world we knew, without all of those details falling so neatly back into place?"

No one spoke, their minds filled with visions of a multitude of lives that they could not recall.

The visitor turned to Aloysius. "It is time for us to go."

Aloysius nodded, and John said to him, "You're leaving? Why can't you stay here?"

Aloysius grinned at John, his kindly eyes conveying much more than a casual connection. "I need to return to my time. I need to go back to 2010. That is where *I* belong."

John started to respond. His desire to persuade this stranger – who had, in some way, become a friend to them all – to remain was choked off by his understanding. "I know. I guess I've gotten used to you popping up during times when all hell is breaking loose."

Aloysius chuckled. "It has been my pleasure shepherding all of you through this."

A startling thought flashed into John's mind and he asked, "Aloysius, did you live through all of the iterations... all forty-seven of them?"

Aloysius smiled. "Yes, I was the liaison. It was my job to go through them all with you, until we finally got it right."

John stared at Aloysius, trying to imagine what it must have been like, when Aloysius added, "That is why I feel such a strong friendship with all of you. Because, although you have only known me for several days, I have known you for three years. I have seen many trials and failures befall all of you before we reached this point. I can tell you that whatever happened, in each of the attempts, every one of you acted with dignity and nobility. It has been a pleasure to know you all."

No words came to mind, so John stepped forward and shook Aloysius's hand. One by one, the others did the same, and then they all took several paces back.

Allen, standing next to Aloysius, looked at the group and said, "Because we are now under a new and clear edict from our superiors, we will not be visiting again... no matter how dire the need may be. Please know, all of you, how much my people appreciate what you have been through and have done for us."

The visitor's hand made a slight gesture and the pinpoint of light once again appeared from the ship above their heads. They all watched as the light spread and grew in intensity, until it enveloped the two. John felt the now familiar immobility that affected witnesses to the lifting process.

He was barely able to see within the shaft of light and noticed, as the friend from the past and the acquaintance from the distant future began to rise, that Aloysius smiled at him and raised his hand in a farewell wave.

They all stared skyward and watched as the craft rose straight up, its convex, reflective bottom surface quickly capturing the vista of the sky, rendering the machine essentially invisible.

"Wow!" Kurt said, being the first to find his voice.

John, his eyes still trained on the spot in the sky where he last saw the craft, concluded, "Well, I guess we're finally on our own."

"Thank God," replied Lynn. "Even though I can't remember any of the other lives we had, it gives me a really creepy feeling to know about them...like I was a guinea pig or something."

Pulling his gaze down from the sky to look at his wife, John shrugged and said, "Hey, all's well that ends well."

There was a murmur of agreement from the rest. Kurt, turning to Jackie, asked, "How come your husband wasn't here for this little show?"

Jackie, looking slightly embarrassed, her hands gently massaging the sides of her swollen abdomen, answered, "I don't have a husband."

Kurt, glancing down at her obviously pregnant mid-section, said, "You don't?"

"Well," she replied, "I did. At least I did until this little tyke announced his or her presence. I guess he didn't want to be a father."

A slow grin curled up at the corners of Kurt's mouth. "Too bad. Really! That's a shame. Can I buy you dinner?"

Jackie burst out laughing, joined by most of the others in the group.

"Kurt!" John admonished, a stern note in his voice.

Before John could say any more, Kurt said, "Hey, it's just dinner," winking at Jackie.

John shook his head and sighed loudly.

"Besides," added Kurt slyly, "I am supposed to make sure that I only hang out with fertile females."

This was too much for Lynn who started to respond, suddenly stopping herself. Instead, she turned to John and said, "I doubt that he has any money or credit cards that will work in this decade. If he's going to buy our daughter dinner, maybe you should...."

John reached into his pocket, glanced at Cal and grinned. "It looks like I spent my allowance thirty years ago. Cal, can you...?"

Making a show of mock exasperation, Cal pulled out a wad of bills and handed it to Kurt.

Kurt took the money. "Wow, this is hundreds. For a meal? How bad has inflation been the last thirty years?"

Laughing, the group turned and walked back into Cal's lab, their voices trailing away as the door closed behind them.

$$\underset{\Delta}{\overset{\Upsilon}{}}$$

None of them were aware that they had been watched throughout the entire visits from Aloysius and Allen. None of them saw the lone figure hunched behind the corner of the nearby maintenance building, her body trembling with unbridled rage. Slowly, Gail turned and walked away.

If you enjoyed reading *Time Cursor* by John David Krygelski, you will be truly captivated by his first novel - *The Harvest*.

The following is a synopsis of his first work...

Doctor Reese Johnson, a professor of psychology and anthropology, who specializes in theology and religion, is brought in to interview a stranger who claims to be God. Unsure what to expect, Reese is immediately surprised by the profound and insightful answers that the stranger provides him. He also witnesses something that might be a miracle. It is at this time Johnson discovers that the stranger prefers to be called *Elohim*. Being a religious scholar, Reese already knows that this name, in Hebrew, is the word for God. But he also knows that in some ancient cultures, it was used to describe the cadre of angels from whom Lucifer descended. In some, it was even used as the term for a group of aliens from another planet who came to colonize the Earth. Reese is now faced with the choice that the stranger is either God, the devil, or an alien from another planet. Other experts are brought in to talk to Elohim and, as a result, word leaks out to the press, who announce prematurely that God is on Earth. People and governments react strongly to the news, and it is during this turmoil that Elohim reveals what he has come to do. It is a plan that will affect all of humanity, and the timetable is only five days. Reese is now in a race against the clock as he attempts to determine whether Elohim's plan will be a wonderful event for mankind, or something truly horrifying. Events and characters lead to a surprising and monumental climax that will answer all of your questions and leave you breathless.

You can buy a copy of *The Harvest* in either a softcover or hardcover edition by going to *www.readtheharvest.com*.

Other fine books by *Starsys Publishing Company*

The Ghosts of the Copper Queen Hotel

Bisbee's historic Copper Queen Hotel was finished in the year 1902. Originally built to accommodate investors for the copper mine, the Copper Queen's luxurious rooms and its proximity to the entrance of the infamous Brewery Gulch, a rowdy and raucous street, jam-packed with saloons and houses of ill repute, attracted many of this area's denizens of the night.

Throughout its over 100-year history, the Copper Queen has had countless guests check in ... but a few have never checked out.

This book is an eerie collection of hundreds of real-life experiences at the Copper Queen Hotel – written by the guests ... in their own words!

Final Option - Leighton Rockafellow

An out-of-control surgeon, an embezzling hospital administrator, and a client who wants to kill the doctor who ruined his life are the least of Larry Ross's problems. After narrowly escaping justice in a desperate dash to Mexico in Leighton Rockafellow's previous novel - *Immaculate Deception* - Lindy Roller is back in this latest installment of the pulse-pounding series, featuring the Tucson attorney and his partner, Bill Wilson.

And this time Lindy is the hired killer for drug lord Juan Pacheco.

As Ross struggles to put a stop to the mayhem caused by the reckless surgeon, keep his severely injured client in check, and chase the trail of money as it hemorrhages out of the hospital's coffers, Lindy becomes the wild card, plunging into the midst of it all, with a contract to kill and vengeance on her mind. And just when Ross doesn't think it could get any worse, he finds himself in the middle of a lawsuit – where he is the defendant!

The Bread & Butter Chronicles - Starr Cochran

Described as *Rich Dad, Poor Dad* meets *Sex and the City*, *The Bread & Butter Chronicles* is a financial novel about four women, Rita, Marla, Jade and Lori, who decide to transform their weekly lunches into mini money workshops after Rita's husband dies unexpectedly and she discovers that their financial situation is not what it appeared. When Marla voices some interest in knowing about their family's finances, her husband gets defensive and she gets concerned. Jade, a single architect, spends what she makes and her money habits are making her feel trapped in her current position. Lori, a financial planner, is married to a shopaholic, who's driving them into the poorhouse. If she can't get him on the same financial page soon, their family's financial future may be in jeopardy.

There are two ways to read this book. You can enjoy the story as you would any novel. Discover how these women solve their financial dilemmas and enrich their lives at the same time. You can also choose to explore *your* personal financial situations interactively through the book's Appendix. At the end of many chapters, there are prompts to guide you to articles and financial forms.

Learning about money is a necessity, but it doesn't have to be a chore. I hope you enjoy the story of Rita, Marla, Jade and Lori as they tackle their financial challenges and learn as much about themselves as they do about money.

And coming soon – *Theft of Innocence* by C. Vance Cast

To read more about any of these books, or to order a copy, go to
www.starsyspublishing.com.